# Meet My Wife
### Book 2 of the Loverly Cave series

### Daisy Thorn

All rights reserved.

The characters and events portrayed in this book are fictitious. Any similarity to real persons, living or dead, is coincidental and not intended by the author.

No part of this book may be reproduced, or stored in a retrieval system, or transmitted in any form or by any means, electronic, mechanical, photocopying, recording, or otherwise, without express written permission of the publisher.

Printed in United States.

Cover: Marina Gilkey

Proofread: Caroline Palmier

Copyright © 2023 by Daisy Thorn

# Contents

| | |
|---|---|
| Dedication | VI |
| Playlist | VII |
| Heads Up | VIII |
| | IX |
| Prologue | 1 |
| 1. Joy | 11 |
| 2. Joy | 27 |
| 3. Joy | 46 |
| 4. Jacob | 63 |
| 5. Joy | 71 |
| 6. Joy | 82 |
| 7. Hope | 97 |
| 8. Grace | 98 |
| 9. Joy | 99 |

| | | |
|---|---|---|
| 10. | Joy | 108 |
| 11. | Jacob | 115 |
| 12. | Joy | 125 |
| 13. | 50 Reasons | 134 |
| 14. | Jacob | 135 |
| 15. | Joy | 142 |
| 16. | 50 Reasons | 156 |
| 17. | Joy | 157 |
| 18. | Joy | 174 |
| 19. | 50 Reasons | 189 |
| 20. | Jacob | 190 |
| 21. | Joy | 207 |
| 22. | 50 Reasons | 216 |
| 23. | Jacob | 217 |
| 24. | Joy | 220 |
| 25. | 50 Reasons | 228 |
| 26. | Jacob | 229 |
| 27. | Joy | 239 |
| 28. | 50 Reasons | 251 |
| 29. | Jacob | 252 |

| 30. Joy | 266 |
| 31. 50 Reasons | 279 |
| 32. Jacob | 280 |
| 33. Joy | 285 |
| 34. 50 Reasons | 299 |
| 35. Joy | 300 |
| 36. Joy | 308 |
| 37. Jacob | 316 |
| 38. 50 Reasons | 326 |
| 39. Joy | 327 |
| 40. Epilogue | 340 |
| 41. Bonus Scene | 346 |
| Afterword | 348 |
| The Romance is Dead | 350 |
| Also By | 357 |
| About the Author | 359 |

*I honestly have no idea why am I dedicating this book to you since you were the one putting your cooties all over my bed and candies, on purpose, I may add, but the world needs more people like you, my little Brother...*

# Playlist

Justin Timberlake – Can't stop the feeling
Max Oazo – Airplane
Justin Timberlake, Timberland – SexyBack
Dua Lipa – Love again
Miley Cyrus – Flowers
Ellie Goulding, Diplo, Swae Lee – Close to me
David Guetta, Birdie, James Young – I'll keep loving you
Ed Sheeran – 2Step
Post Tense – Tell it to my heart
Alok, James Arthur – Work with my love
Lana Del Rey, The Weekend – Lust for life
Taylor, Swift, Zayn – I don't want to live forever
Pharrell Williams – Happy
Labrinth, Emeli Sande – Beneath your beautiful
Rita Ora – Don't think twice
Bebe Rexha – I'm not high I'm in love

### ***FIND THE REST ON MY SPOTIFY
https://open.spotify.com/playlist/6BMcFBx4hG9HnYaD-sTB6Du?si=51c2d271a9364bfa

# Heads Up

Welcome to Loverly Cave Town, where we are expected to go through a long series which will be interconnected but could be read as standalones.
Please note that I cannot promise you won't encounter spoilers if you read the books out of order.
Meet My Wife is book TWO of the series and drops hints here and there of what to expect before/next.

P.S. The book features explicit sexual content and is meant for mature audiences only.
I hope you will enjoy reading it as much as I did writing it.

# Prologue

*"Women cannot complain about men anymore until they start getting better taste in them."* — Bill Maher.

## Joy

"Zoe, has my dress been delivered yet?" I call out to my assistant across the lab.

Tonight, we have our annual awards ceremony and dinner at KePah University. It's an event that takes place on the same date every year for as long as the institution stands and is meant to honor the hard work of our faculty members throughout the year.

Each year the board selects a few of the most accomplished professors, deans, and so on to present them with special awards. And if you think it's just some silly little thing to humor the employees, think again.

KePah is considered number one in the national ranking of universities in the United States. Number two in the world rank right after Oxford. If your GPA is not at least four-point-oh, or you haven't been in AP classes and doing copious amounts of volunteering, don't bother applying to our school. Because this is one of those old-stay-in-the-family-type-places. KePah is only run by the Hunt family and if you'd like to work at KePah University, you better be a genius or have the necessary connections in the necessary circles.

Good thing for me; I am a genius. Since coming from nowhere, Ohio–better known as the small town of Flitzburg–does not provide me with the necessary connections.

I am a thirty-one-year-old leading pathologist in the field with my own lab, assistants, and students. My name is well-known in the industry, and my opinion is valued everywhere. If there is a problem with your body—dead or alive—I'll find the answer.

No questions asked.

And tonight is my night to shine. Mine and his.

Tonight, both Justin and I are being presented with awards for valuable contributions to the school in the research department for our findings on intravascular lithotripsy. In short, it's a technique to break apart garbage clogging your arteries. And it's huge. So, Justin and I are like proud parents, protecting our medical baby.

Who is Justin, you ask?

Oh, he is another fellow genius cardiologist slash professor at our university. Devilishly handsome with his perfectly kept short blonde hair and clean-shaven face with that strong jawline. He is the heir to the KePah dynasty, the one groomed to take over in a year or so, and he also happens to be my boyfriend.

That's right, after years of misery in reliving one of the worst days of my life ten years ago, I finally found my own happiness. My Justin.

I am not one to be sentimental, but the connection we share is special. I know it. He knows it. The universe knows it and has proved it to us by nominating both of us at the same time for these awards.

How special is that?

Meant to be...

"Yes, the dress is here, Doctor," Zoe responds to my earlier question, and I hurry out of my office to go change out of scrubs.

Would I like to have my family present while I'm moving onto yet another huge step in my life? Yes, yes, I would.

Is it possible? No, it is not.

My family fell apart on that same horrible day ten years ago, and we have yet to put it back together. I'm fine with my parents—well, fine-ish—but my sisters? Yeah, no. No, thank you.

It was enough to watch my younger one get in the car with my boyfriend of five years and drive away with him. And it was definitely enough to find out the youngest sister knew all about it and never said a word to anyone, therefore aiding in Hope's quest to steal my life from me.

Newsflash: She had succeeded.

I haven't spoken to either one of my sisters in ten years, but I've seen Brian's name—my ex—splashed all over the news, so I know they made it big. Brian always wanted to be a famous musician, and he got there...without me.

But those are old and very much healed wounds at this point. Whatever doesn't kill you makes you stronger, and all that? And that is exactly what happened to me. Truth be told, I no longer care about it. Like at all...

I am only grateful for the push it provided for me to be where I am today.

I channeled my anger into my school, and today, I am reaping the fruits of that effort. One of the youngest females to get into KePah University, one of the youngest to finish it with a pristine GPA, and not to mention finishing medical school a year before normal graduation. I never took a break. I studied all the time and interned with the best of the best.

I volunteered any chance I got and worked my ass off to be where I am today. I never dated, hung out, or got drunk at parties. Hell, I never went to those parties in the first place.

I didn't have any friends, only colleagues, so as not to be distracted, and clearly, it paid off.

I was hired by KePah right away, and a few years later, Justin got transferred into our university from England, and the rest is history. We clicked right away, and he became my best friend, my family, my mentor, and my lover.

So, it sucks that Mom and Dad aren't here, but I have him.

Smoothing out my black silky floor-length gown, I fix my makeup and change out my simple pearl earrings to diamond ones. The ones Justin got me for our first anniversary.

It seems like it was just yesterday, when in reality, we have been together for almost three years now.

"Dr. Levine, I just sent you the report for body number fifty-seven. Is there anything else I can do for you?" Zoe's voice carries through the bathroom door, and by the tone of it, I can basically see the anxious expression she has on her face. I can hear that bottom lip getting chewed up and her index fingers tapping on her thighs. Those are her "I'm nervous" tells. The my-boss-is-a-tyrant ones.

Zoe is terrified I'll pile another project on her when she was really hoping to go to the awards ceremony herself. Normally I would give her a shit ton of work to do, but I'm feeling extra nice today.

"It's fine, Zoe, you can go," I tell her, still talking to her through the door. I swear I hear her mutter, "Oh, thank God," but then she says, "Thank you, Dr. Levine."

Short and professional. Just how I like it.

Is Zoe justified in her fear of me?

Absolutely.

I am a tyrant, but only because I know what it takes to be the best, and Zoe has the potential to be the best of the best. So, yes, I'll work her hard, and she will thank me later since I don't really care about being liked at the moment.

With a last few touches, I grab my clutch, pull on my winter coat—we are in Chicago, after all, warmth tramps fashion for me—and head out of my domain, my lab.

The ceremony is being held in the university theatre, which is only a few minutes of walking from my lab on campus. But even being far away, I can already spot all the glitz and glam the university has put up for this night.

KePah is one of the oldest universities in the country, and therefore, it has that grand old-school feel about it wherever you go. The theater being one of the fanciest places on campus, with its gothic architecture and castle vibes.

The night is magical, with the white snow covering every surface and the lights reflecting off it, shining bright and far into the sky, illuminating the dark night. The red carpet—royal blue in our case—has been rolled out, and the journalists and photographers are lined up on both sides, clicking away at their cameras with each new body who walks it. The dark stone walls are covered in blue and gold banners—the colors of our school—on each side of the grand entrance.

I step foot onto the carpeted walkway, and immediately, the cameras get busy working, capturing my every angle. I hear my name getting called out, asking for my attention and a smile for their shot, but all they get is a slight nod and hard-set face.

I don't do the warm and fuzzy. I am no cuddle bear, and smiling is a waste of time. I don't do fake, and most smiles in this world are just that. Especially the ones we give to the press. Plus, it gives you wrinkles. So, I see absolutely no benefit in doing it.

"Doctor Levine," I keep hearing, and another, "Doctor Levine, it's a big night for you! Congratulations!"

I give them a few more nods as I finally reach the end of this masquerade.

Not one of them actually cares about my personal success. Sure, they care about the work I do, but not me as a person.

There is only one person who does, and I am trying to find him in the crowd. Where is Justin?

Would it be nice to finally attend any of these functions together as a couple? Yes, yes, it would be. But he is being groomed to become the next headmaster, and the timing isn't right. Or at least that's what he keeps telling me.

Three years and we are still hiding our relationship. Sure, I am a bit younger than him—eleven years, to be exact—and it might be frowned upon, but I think he could do a lot worse than me. That fact is slowly eating me away, nudging me to put my foot down and make our love public, but then he comes to my bed at night saying how much he loves me and how much he needs me, and all my nudging goes right out the door.

However, it quickly returns as he leaves the said bed a few hours later.

There is always some kind of surgery, meeting, call, or consultation he needs to tend to, and I know what it means to be a doctor, so I don't get mad at him for leaving. It is just how things are.

My eyes scan the room once again, but I don't see him. Hmm, maybe he hasn't arrived yet? I move toward the entrance, trying to peek outside and see if I can catch his handsome self anywhere out there, when I hear the cameras go crazy once again.

Someone important must've shown up.

Justin.

And now my lips twitch into a small, tiny smile on my face as I think about him, walking in here in his perfectly tailored tuxedo. The one I helped him pick out, the one that has matching black silk lining his lapels. I only sort of smile for him. No one else.

No one else deserves my smile—fine, lip twitches, but that's basically laughing in my terms.

I grab a champagne from the passing tray and wait for him. It is well-known that Justin and I are friendly, so it's never weird when he comes up to talk to me. I take a sip, letting the cool, bubbly liquid warm up my tense body.

You know when you have that gut feeling that something is about to go wrong? That is me right now. Anticipation coursing through my blood, and then the sweet champagne turns acidic and gets stuck on its way down, causing me to choke and go off in a fit of strangled coughing.

*What. The. Hell. Am. I. Seeing?*
*What are my brown eyes looking at?*
*What the fuck is this?*

I catch his blue ones, and I watch as he swallows hard, then quickly diverts his gaze from mine to focus on the man greeting him and extending his arm out for a handshake. The same man then gestures to the person standing next to Justin and smiles a warm smile at her.

Yes. Her.

As in a woman. As in, she has her hand wrapped around his arm as she clings to him the same way her red gown clings to her fake boobs. As in, he came here with someone else. As in, his hand is wrapped around her waist, holding her tight to his perfectly tailored tuxedo.

Watching this woman, I note how we literally could not be any more different. Where I have an hourglass figure in a firm medium dress size and full-to-the-brim C-cups on my chest, she is an extra-small with a dash of underweight and the same C-cups popping out, but they are of the fake kind.

There is absolutely nothing wrong with skin and bones; my little sister Grace wears that look proudly—or she did ten years ago, at least—but I simply don't understand how he picked me *and* her.

Did he want variety? Is that it?

My coughing fit finally seizes as I take a few more sips of my champagne, this time not so much for pleasure but patience, and stare at the pair in front of me. I am so confused. I have so many questions, and I can't exactly pull him aside to ask those now, can I?

No, I can't. Because doing so would cause a scene, and my name and reputation in this society are very important to me. Now more than ever, it seems. So, I turn around and pretend to be very interested in human liver repair with the use of lab-grown cells, and normally, I would be all over this topic but not now. Not tonight when my eyes can't stop from following the elephant in the room.

Justin and his escort move from their spot, going from person to person and making small talk. Working the room as a future headmaster. And everyone wants to kiss his ass, so there will be absolutely no talking to him tonight.

Is there even anything to talk about?

How could he possibly explain this? She's just a friend? She is his long-lost sister? The questions swirl around, and then they stop with one glance at her hand. And his.

The left ones.

They are not bare.

They carry precious metals on them. Rings. Wedding rings. Hers being a ginormous oval monstrosity, and I have to blink a few times to make sure I am not dreaming but also to kickstart my brain.

Married.

*They are married.*

I feel nauseous. I feel sick to my bones, and I need to get myself under control.

For how long, when, and why are all the questions I'll probably never get answered because with this kick-start, I also drop down a black-out curtain. The one that cuts off anything associated with the name Justin from my life.

I'm good at that. I'm good at shutting off my emotions right on the spot to put up a perfect picture for the world.

What happens on the inside? Well, that is a whole other discussion that we won't get into until the sham of an evening is over and done with.

Throughout the ceremony and the dinner, I leave the curtain drawn—slowly solidifying it as a new, permanent wall—and keep my emotions purposefully blank. Empty.

Not exactly difficult, because seeing him with his *wife* did put a dent in me. A deep, enormous, heavy dent. The one that is just shy from creating a massive hole, the kind that sucks you in and makes you disappear from this life. People are talking to me, asking me questions, and I respond on autopilot, silently thanking myself for the years of self-control I practiced before tonight. Because, words? Words are difficult right now.

I know he's watching me. I can feel his eyes on my body, roaming it like he always does. And if before tonight, it would make me feel incredibly desirable and sexy, now, it makes my skin crawl.

Oh, the irony...I blamed my little sister for being the other woman in my teenage relationship, only to become one myself in my early thirties...

I would laugh if it wouldn't hurt so much.

Why does it hurt so fucking much? And does it hurt because I have loved the man or because I was lied to again?

*Have I been here for an appropriate amount of time?* I glance at my phone, noting it's eleven PM and decide it's been more than enough.

I'm not sure I could keep the curtain down much longer. I'm strong, but I'm not indestructible.

I never wanted to be it. But I guess I don't have much choice now, do I?

Time to go...

In more ways than one.

I won't sink; I'm too strong for that. Instead, I will drift mindlessly through the hectic river called life.

# 1

## *Joy*

*"Remember, beneath every cynic there lies a romantic, and probably an injured one." — Benjamin Franklin*

Hi, my name is Joy, and I live in a joyless world. Surrounded by lying, backstabbing idiots.

Twenty-four ceramics, four glasses, four flutes, and a serving bowl later, the hole in my chest is still there, but the anger is slightly dulled thanks to the physical exhaustion I've put myself through.

That's my outlet for anger. Not tears. Those are as pointless as smiles. They do absolutely nothing to make you feel better—only make you stuffy and swollen and dehydrated. But the smashing of my entire set of plates and glasses? Yeah, that one really helps.

Especially when I pull up his name on Google and dive into who my Justin really is. And let me tell you, he doesn't exist because, with every line I read, I realize every day, every hour, and minute of the last three years were made up. Every single moment he lied to me.

Please don't ask why I only now typed his name in to research him. The answer would be that I was an idiot who believed when he said the internet makes up way too many lies about him, and he doesn't want me to get upset reading it.

Me being a person who generally doesn't give a damn about social media, didn't argue and never searched him.

But now, Pandora's box has been opened.

He has been married for twenty years. Twenty. Years. And they just celebrated their wedding anniversary last fall. The fall when he told me he'd be in Europe, attending Starlight conferences all month long, and I believed it like the gullible idiot I tried hard not to be.

Newsflash: it turns out I'm exactly that.

I should have known something was wrong. I should have felt all the off times, put together the weird phone calls, and the fact that we were so secretive about our relationship.

Hell, he never stayed the full night with me, and I was simply fine with it. Was I that desperate for attention and dick that I just picked up the first person who smiled at me?

Two hours later, my insides are turning heavily, and I contemplate running to the bathroom to throw up when I hear the doorbell ring and come face-to-face with the liar of the year, flesh and blood, on my doorstep.

"Can I come in?" he asks, and I'm fighting the manic laughter bubbling in the pit of my stomach.

I'm totally unhinged at this point, but my need to keep myself guarded away from the rest of the world keeps me intact.

Can he come in? Can he fucking come in?

"I don't know, can you?" I say in a cold, detached voice, folding my arms in front of me. "What does your wife think?

You know, the one you've been married to all this time? The one I never knew about."

He exhales loudly as if I'm the one who is exhausting him. As if I'm the unreasonable one. As if I'm the one who hurt him and lied to him, and pretended to be in a committed relationship for the last three stupid years.

Seriously?

*Breathe in, breathe out, Joy.*

"Just let me come inside. It's freezing out here." He sighs in that same frustrated manner.

"I never told you to come over in the first place, so I don't see how your being cold is my problem now?"

"And that right there is why I wouldn't have ever married you," the asshole dares to snap back and point his dirty finger at me. "You are a cold ass bitch. Fucking Antarctica."

"Was that supposed to hurt me? Or make me cry? Because I hate to break it to you, it didn't, and it won't."

*Lies.*

"Yes, I'm a cold ass bitch, but at least I'm an honest cold ass bitch, and I never lied to you. Now," I make a move to shut my front door closed, "Get out of my face."

Justin stops the door from closing with his foot wedged in between it and the frame, and his hands are clutching to the sides of it nervously. His eyes are frantic and terrified, all that cocky bullshit wiped right off his face.

"Come on, Joy, can we just move past this? Go back to the way things were? We were so good together! I had to bring her tonight; I didn't have a choice."

My eyebrows shoot up, and that's the most emotion I've shown tonight. Thank God he *had to* bring her tonight, or else how much longer would I be in this mess? For the rest of my life? But he has got to be out of his asshole mind if he thinks we can just go back to the way we were!

"Did you have too much to drink, or is your wife's silicone seeping into your brain when she kisses you?"

"Joy!"

"Get the fuck out of my face before I slam this door on that pretty nose of yours that you are so obsessed with."

He swallows hard. Yep, vain to the bones. Vain, lying son of a bitch whom I was in love with.

What does that make me?

An idiot.

Something I haven't thought of myself in ten long years. Not since the last boyfriend who dumped me for my sister.

"Fine. You weren't that great piece of an ass anyway, and your weight? It started getting out of hand. But can we at least keep this civil, or do I have to let you go from your job?" the bastard asks, and I swear my internal jaw hits the freezing cold concrete. Internal because on the outside, I'm Miss Cool and Calm, even when his words slash through me like a thousand surgical scalpels. Those sharpest blades. The ones meant to slay you open in one swoosh.

"So?" he prompts me, getting more and more fidgety by a second.

Oh, I quite enjoy making him sweat because we both know what I could do to his precious career in KePah. I could squash it in zero point one second, but I won't.

I don't care about him enough to drag myself through that shit. He can rot in it himself because one thing is clear, Justin will sink. Maybe not today or in the next year. But he will. Liars like him can't stay clean forever. With a deep breath, I push all the hurt away and look into his blue eyes one last time.

"As long as you stay out of my way, you are nothing more than a colleague. Never was and never will be."

"Good." The relief on his face is immediate, and I catch myself wondering if his "I love yous" ever meant anything.

No, they did not. Not a single one.

*Did mine?*

Pathetic. I am freaking pathetic. So desperate to be loved, I ignored common sense, and every red flag waved right in front of my face.

Justin pulls himself up, turns around, and leaves without another word.

Great. Amazing. That's what I wanted.

But even I can't deny much longer that the hole Justin opened up most likely will never heal, and I definitely won't allow it to do so. No, I need to keep my thoracic cavity empty, dark, and cold. I need to make sure that stupid organ inside it never gets any ideas of skipping a beat for someone else again.

I need to channel my sister Hope for once in my life, learning her photographic memory trick, and never forget about the pain every man in my life leaves behind himself. Even if it's been only two idiots. More would surely follow, and I am not interested in being anyone else's side piece anymore.

I am Joy fucking Levine. The best pathologist in the country and lead researcher in the field.

Men, who???

Why is it so cold today? Was it always this cold in Chicago, or was the dark hole inside my chest robbing me of the internal heat I used to have?

*Let's be rational, Joy.* Hard, cold facts and no other bullshit.

It's early March outside, and temperatures are still below freezing; therefore, you are cold.

And no, it has absolutely nothing to do with you not getting any sleep last night and your internal system shutting down on you. Nothing at all.

It's the weekend, and everyone is either off campus or still in bed, but I can't sit at home any longer. The whole night on my own with all those self-destructive thoughts was torture enough.

I am not an insecure woman. Not at all, but after yet another blow to my ego, I can't help but wonder what exactly is wrong with me that I can never be enough for the men I am with. Actually, I've spent the whole long and very miserable night pondering this. At dawn, I came to the conclusion that it was simply *me*.

I am not enough for them. Or maybe I am too much for them. Too intense, too cold, too hard, too everything.

Thoughts were running rampant inside my head. Should I change? Should I try to be softer, warmer, easier to love? But in the end, with the rise of the cold early spring sun shining over the mounts of snow and a cup of hot coffee in my hands, I decided it won't be happening.

I like who I am. I am comfortable in my own skin, and if these small-dicked men can't handle me...well, then alone for life it is.

Alone and in my lab, where I am happy. Important. Needed. That is why I'm walking across the parking lot over to the research building and spending my Saturday with the cold metal, dead bodies, and clicking sounds of my computer keyboard.

The normal routine keeps me grounded, and wards away the toxic memories of Justin and his fake love, of Brian and his betrayal, of my sisters and their alienation—granted, I'm no better, but the point stands. I haven't spoken to either one of them in ten years, and on days like this, I wonder if my life would be the way it is if we hadn't broken each other back then.

I am busy and grounded, but I'm lonely. So damn lonely. Joy is living her life without joy...oh, if someone could hear this right now. How pathetic and hilarious I sound.

*Suck it up, Joy.* There is no time for sulking or, God forbid, tears. Only work.

It's a little past noon when I hear another voice in my lab. Huh, that's strange. I get up from my desk and head over to the front, where I see Zoe pulling on her lab coat.

"Zoe?" I ask with furrowed brows, and evidently, my voice startles her because she jumps up and lets out a high-pitched squeaky sound, clutching her fisted hand to her chest.

"Oh my God, Dr. Levine." She is breathing heavy, and I'm torn between laughing at her reaction and apologizing. In the end, a weird, once-in-a-lifetime smile tugs on my lips, and her eyes grow even wider.

"Sorry to spook you," I tell her. "What are you doing here?" I ask her, and only then do I take in her bloodshot eyes, her slumped shoulders, and her defeated face.

"Um, I-I'm always here on Saturdays. Catching up on work."

"You are?" I ask; the surprise is clear in my voice since it's the first time I've heard of this.

"Y-yes," she stutters again. "Um, there is a lot to do, and I can't quite do it all during normal hours." Zoe looks to the ground when she says that, and I realize how big of a tyrant I really am.

Sure, I chose this loner lifestyle, but this beautiful young girl should be out with friends, not stuck here.

Look at me, having all these revelations about myself today.

I told you I was a genius.

Okay, maybe not based on recent events, but I am smart.

"Zoe, go home, I'll take care of it today."

"Um, what?" she asks, stunned. Yeah, I'm way too strict with my perfect assistant.

"Go home; I got this today."

"But you are never here on Saturdays."

No, I never was before, because Saturdays were for Justin...

"Well, that's no longer true, and I'll be here all the time from now on. So go, live your life. Don't be stuck like I am."

Oh my God, what's wrong with me? Why am I spilling my heart out to my poor, overworked assistant? *Get it together, Joy.*

Zoe looks down once again. "Um, if you don't mind, could I stay?"

Something tugs on my now empty heart at the sight of her, and that stupid tug propels me to say the next words.

"What's wrong, Zoe? What happened?"

"N-nothing." Her voice is small. Is she crying?

"Zoe." I am using my authoritative doctor's voice, and she turns ramrod straight.

"Please, let me stay here. I can't go home today. Please," she pleads with me right before bursting out in ugly, messy sobs.

Jesus, what do I do now? I'm not equipped to deal with crying. I haven't been around crying girls for ten years. Do I hug her? Is that what I used to do with my sisters?

Crap, she is crying even harder now. Wailing.

"Damn it," I curse under my breath and step forward, putting my hand around her moving shoulders and patting her back awkwardly. "Zoe, how about you calm down and tell me what happened so I can help you, okay? I don't have solutions for tears; I need real words." But she just keeps crying, so I used *the voice* again. "Zoe!"

She hiccups once but stops crying, looking up at me with those big brown eyes. So similar to mine. In fact, Zoe always reminded me a bit of myself when I was that little lost eighteen-year-old girl. She is older than I was back then, but still.

"I saw him with his wife," she mumbles under her breath quietly because she doesn't want to be saying this, but she can't deny my command, and with her words, every hair on my body stands for attention.

Every. Single. Hair.

"You saw who?" My heart is racing, my palms are sweating, and my throat clogs up with anticipation.

Zoe swallows hard. "My boyfriend. My stupid, stupid boyfriend. The one who kept lying to me for the past year. He is fucking married, and he showed up with his wife at the ceremony yesterday."

My face drains every ounce of blood. No, that can't be. No.

He can't be that much of an asshole, right? But I need to know. I need to hear this.

"Zoe, are you talking about Justin?"

Her eyes snapped up to mine too fast, and it's was all the answer I need. I take a sharp breath and a short step back.

Fuck. Me.

"H-how did you know?" she asks in that same small voice, but now it's laced with confusion.

This can't be happening right now. It simply can't, yet it is. Zoe watches me with questions swirling in her eyes, and then something so out of the norm happens; it startles her.

I laugh. I start laughing so hard, my stomach hurts, tears stream down my face from it and I can't stop. I laugh and laugh and keep laughing.

"Doctor Levine? Are you okay?" This girl, this poor, young girl who hasn't lived through stinky shit before, is getting thrust into it face first.

So fucking brilliant to have a girl waiting for you, no matter what. If one is away, you have a backup. If the other is on her period, you have a backup. If you get into a fight, you have a backup.

Genius.

The only thing I can't figure out is how *I* got sucked into being a backup.

"Oh, Zoe, I think we need to move on to first name basis after this," I say, still wiping the moisture underneath my eyes, but the fit is slowly passing. I take a good, hard look at my assistant. Silky blonde hair, dark eyes, and a slightly smaller figure than mine but overall, she could have passed for my sister better than Grace ever did.

"I guess he has a type. Shame his wife doesn't really fit the bill, huh?" I continue, and Zoe only furrows her brows further into confusion.

"What are you talking about, Doctor Levine?"

"Joy," I correct her. "Women whom I have shared a boyfriend with get to call me Joy."

"Joy, honey," my mom's voice booms out of my phone.

"Hey, Mom." Unlike my sisters, I still keep somewhat in touch with our parents. We call each other once every few months, and she always messages me, letting me know about their new life in the new town they have moved to.

Not that I ever respond, but it doesn't deter her from keeping on doing it, and part of me secretly loves it. They seem so happy in Loverly Cave, which is just two hours away from Santa Cruz, California, and I'm happy for them. From what I know, it is super tiny and super hippy. But hey, I am not the one living there.

But now her voice doesn't sound happy. No, it's the one that has all the hairs on my body raise up as if she's singing the national anthem, and it's a knee-jerk reaction to stand up. "Mom, what's wrong?"

"Um, do you think you could come to visit us?" My eyebrows draw together. She asked me this before, but it was always more of a playful type of question along the lines of "You never visit us" and "What have we done to be all alone in this big world."

Yes, my parents—mostly mom—have a knack for dramatics.

But this time, her voice is small and unsure. It's almost terrified.

"Mom, please tell me what's wrong?" The desperation is seeping through me at this point, and I just need her to spit it out finally.

"Um, well, Daddy has been having some issues, and I think it would be a good time to come visit us now before it's too late."

A bomb. A bomb went off as she spoke those last words. *Before it's too late...*

"Mom, I swear if you don't tell me exactly what happened, I will lose my ever-loving mind right now."

I am usually the calm and collected sister of the bunch and deal with crises like a pro—just remember last week, I was amazing—but now I'm pacing my room like a nervous wreck. I can't lose my parents. They are all I have left.

"It looks like Dad has cancer." Her words might as well have been like a bucket of ice cold, stinging water with ice cubes added for extra sensation.

I stop pacing immediately, and thankfully, the couch is right next to me because my legs give way, and I fall down to it. Slumping into it like a deflated blow-up doll.

"Cancer?" My voice is a tone above a whisper.

"Um, yes."

"What kind of cancer? How long? How progressed is it? Why haven't you called earlier? Mom, I'm a freaking doctor!" My deflation quickly morphs into fear and slash anger.

How come I wasn't made aware of this? How come she tells me about it over the phone like it's not the worst fucking thing in the world?

While my sisters were always super close with our mother, I was daddy's girl through and through. I guess not having the same genes for the dramatics drew us closer together. And I know this must be hard for Mom since they have been together forever now, but it's equally as hard for me.

I'm tough, but I'm afraid this just might be my final blow.

How much more can my armor take before the dents become permanent holes? How much more can I take in one shitty week?

No, I can't get all soapy here now. My dad needs me, and I need a plan to pull him through this mess. Screw my broken heart; I can live with that, but not without my father.

"It's too much medical talk for me, honey, do you think you could come and just check it out yourself?"

"Mom, you have to give me something! At least, what organs are we talking about? And how bad is it?" I pinch the bridge of my nose, praying it's not too late and already going through all the doctors we have here who like me or owe me favors.

And I am definitely banking more on the latter one. I am respected here, not liked. I don't gossip or go out to drinks, but I help when I am asked.

And now they owe me favors, more than I care for, but I'll cash them all in now.

"It's very bad. Very very bad. In fact, if you could move to Loverly for the time being, it probably would be best. I know how much your father misses you, and he'd be thrilled to spend this time with you."

Move? Move? Freaking move? "Mom, I can't—" I start to tell her I can't move and leave my important job and boyfriend when I catch myself.

A. There is no boyfriend, and apparently never was.

B. My job will always be here when I come back. And if Mom says it's really that bad, I might be back sooner rather than later.

"I'm coming, Mom. Just send me the name of a local hotel or something, please," I tell her and start pacing again, but this time to pull out my bag and stuff it with clothes.

"Oh, poopsies," she says, and that warrants me to stop dead.

Poopsies. Of course... it's my mother we are talking about, after all.

"What's wrong, Mom?" I ask with a loaded exhale and a creeping suspicion I won't like her next words.

"Well, you see, we don't have a hotel here, only a B&B place, and it's all booked up."

"Great." My tone is flat.

"You can stay with us, honey; we have a spare bedroom."

Yeah, that's not happening.

"Any other options?" I ask, biting my lips from saying something else. Something close to many colorful curse words my mom won't appreciate.

"Well, you can call up Nina Colson; she is the realtor in LC, I think she mentioned having a small cottage up for sale the other day."

Sale. Of course. I close my eyes, taking a deep breath. "Send me her number."

"Will do. Oh, and maybe don't call Daddy before you get here. I want it to be a surprise for him. That man could use some good news, you know?"

"Sure, Mom. Sounds good."

Not one to waste time on stupid antics or useless chitchat, I hang up and dial Dr. Zinger, the leading oncology researcher at KePah. Given I have no idea what type of cancer Dad has, I need to cover all my bases.

After thirty minutes on my phone, I have three oncologists, five surgeons, and at least one doctor from each department on standby, waiting for me to transfer the patient file over to them.

Next up, living arrangements prove to be rather easy to deal with. It so happens that Nina does, in fact, have one small, outdated cottage up for sale, and now I am the lucky owner of the prime estate. When she mentioned the price, I triple-checked if it was correct, seeing as it was only eighty-thousand dollars, but yes, it was. And without wasting a second, I started packing.

I don't have any student loans, and the mortgage on my house in Chicago isn't too bad since I didn't go crazy and didn't buy a fucking mansion even though Justin was insisting I do just that. Prick.

For what reason? I have no fucking idea since he never planned on living with me in it. Screw him; he doesn't get any more room in my mind or heart. The eviction notice was sent out, and the tenant is almost all moved out.

The last call I make is to my assistant, who now also doubles as my best friend and fellow idiot who leads with her vagina instead of her head. "Zoe, can you please book me a plane ticket to Santa Cruz, California?"

One week, two days, eight hours, and God knows how many minutes have passed since Zoe and I were acquainted on a whole other level. And if there is one thing I'll be grateful for coming out of this mess, it's her. How come I never noticed my selfless, kind, smart student is beyond me, but we changed that real quick this past week. After our revelation on Saturday, we spent the rest of the weekend at my place, drinking. And sharing notes.

Lots and lots of notes.

The idiot didn't even bother to send different text messages to us. He simply copied and pasted them, so I'm starting to feel a little bad for his wife. At least we had an option of dating him in secret and not being tied down by rumors like she is.

Poor, silicone-out, underweight woman.

"Okay," she drags out. "When would you like to fly out, and what is the return date?"

"No return date for now; fly out as soon as possible."

"What?" she yells out into the phone, and I have to pull it away from my ear so as not to rupture my eardrum.

"Jesus, Zo."

"What do you mean no return date? You are leaving me here all alone? Alone with him walking around like the king of the fucking castle?"

"What is it with women in my life and dramatics?" I ask no one in particular, sighing and dragging a hand through my face.

"No, no, you cannot leave me!" Zoe demands.

"Zo, I just found out my father has cancer, and the only thing my mother told me was that it's very, very bad, and we don't have much time left."

"Oh." Understanding floods her tone. "Shit, I'm sorry, Joy. That sucks. Can we do anything for him here?" Bless her soul.

"I sure hope so, but I'll have to go see him for myself first, so I'll be staying in Loverly Cave for an unknown amount of time. And let me tell you, I am not looking forward to it."

"I understand, even if I hate it. And done, your flight is booked."

"Thank you. Please carry on with the study of bodies number fifty-eight and seventy-two. I'd like the reports sent to me at the end of each day, and I'll be calling you daily. Also, since I'm leaving, you must finish the pathology report for Dr. Asshole for me."

"Fuck, Joy. Can't we assign it to someone else?"

"No, we cannot because we don't walk away with our noses down. Never. He might've delivered one fucked up blow to both of us, but hell if that will kill us. So, yes, finish the report and hand deliver it to him with your head held high. You hear me?"

"Easy for you to say; you're leaving," she mutters under her breath.

"I heard that, and good thing I'm still your boss, so what I say goes."

"And here I thought being friends with the boss would have some perks."

"It does."

"Like?"

"Becoming a fellow genius. You're welcome."

# 2

# *Joy*

*"It's like at that moment the whole universe existed just to bring us together." —Serendipity.*

In hindsight, I should've known I was going to have a shitty month after the ceremony, but for some reason, my brilliant brain refused to believe I was rapidly falling down the drain.

Well, thankfully to the gentleman in seat 12A, I am finally catching up. He and his stupid, half-rotten, boiled eggs.

Please, can anyone explain to me who the hell allows eggs to be part of a snack pack on a fucking plane? What kind of blubbering idiots decided sulfur-smelling things are completely fine in confined spaces with no fresh air coming in.

Can I call nine-one-one on a plane? Is that a thing? Because someone needs to charge this man with attempted murder of me. I am so disgusted; I have to think of my dead bodies to not throw up. Yes, that's how bad it is, and I bet this guy will load up the bathroom near our seats in the next hour or so.

Amazing.

First, the airline randomly changed my flight to tonight, making me scramble to get all my belongings together like a lunatic and rush to the airport as if the world was on fire. I can't reach my parents to let them know I am arriving sooner. *Then* my business class reservation somehow got canceled, and now this...rotten eggs right next to my face.

"Would you like some?" The guy picks up his egg and thrusts it in my face, and God, please have mercy.

I narrow my eyes at him, holding my breath. "Do I look like I want some?" I grid out, and he just shrugs, popping the whole thing into his mouth.

Hallelujah. The egg torture has been completed.

What's next, universe?

The plane will crash? My rental car won't be available? All the hotels around Santa Cruz will be booked, and I will be forced to either sleep in the car or on the street? My sisters will magically show up at my parents' house after not contacting them for ten years? What? What should I prepare myself for?

Well, the plane didn't crash. Thank you for small miracles, but other than that, the good news is done. Finished. Concluded. Because the car I requested wasn't available until tomorrow—my original booking date—and I spent two hours trying to find a replacement. To top it off, absolutely all hotels in Santa freaking Cruz are booked for the night—how that is possible, I have no idea—but here we are, and now I am driving down the serpentine road in complete darkness to the town I've never been to, only to sleep in my car outside my parents' place.

Because, of course, my flight was rescheduled to the late evening, and by the time I arrived in Santa Cruz, it was nine PM, add in two hours of pointless arguing with idiots at the car rental and two more for the drive to Loverly, and here we are. One AM.

My parents have been in bed for at least four hours, so there's no crashing their place. There are no hotels here, and I might as well add murdered by a hippy weirdo to my own eulogy.

*Dumped by her boyfriend for her younger sister at nineteen.*
*Used as a mistress for three years in her late twenties.*
*Murdered by a hippy weirdo after suffering sulfur poisoning from rotten eggs on a plane at the ripe age of thirty-one.*

Wow, Joy, your list of achievements in this life is absolutely staggering. I mean, who can trump being murdered by a hippy weirdo? See? I knew I was special.

*Breathe in, breathe out, Joy.* If everything you've been through hasn't killed you yet, chances are the hippy weirdo won't either.

Pep talk done, I wind down the curvy roads and wish it was light out so I could catch a glimpse of the town I'm about to call home. But all I see are a few lights shining through from here and there, and the shadow of a huge imposing Loverly Cave itself looming over the town. Standing guard to protect its residents through the dark night.

From what I can tell, though, the town is sort of nestled in a valley, surrounded by vast mountains and an open, wild ocean up ahead.

What a weird place...

With a few last turns, I finally descend from the crazy road and find myself in front of a large sign.

**Welcome to Loverly Cave Town, where love is the answer to any question.**
**Population three thousand one hundred and two.**

Well, this should be quite an adjustment. My university alone has over six times more people in attendance than this whole town put together. But I can't say whether it's a good or a bad thing.

Chicago has been my home for the last ten years, and I enjoy everything about it. I don't mind the crazy, snowy winters or the freezing winds blowing from Lake Michigan. I don't mind that we only have about three warm months or that we are one of the largest cities in the US.

Maybe it's simply because I spend at least twelve hours a day in my lab, and the rest was at home with Justin or my book, since we never went out anywhere.

Jesus, could I be any more blind? For three years, we haven't been out once!

It didn't seem to bother me at the time. I am not a social person myself, and I don't go out much, so there I was, thinking I found a kindred soul.

Soul, my ass.

More like a kindred snake.

Nope, I'm not going there. Justin and his persona are no longer part of my thought process. I wiped it clean a week ago, and that was that.

As I pass the sign, the small and very much lived-in streets greet me. It's dark, but the old-school lanterns light up the path, and I look around the dark windows of the shops on Love Street. Yep, it's their version of Main Street, I guess.

This town doesn't look real in the dead of night with its tall trees everywhere, European architecture, and colorful buildings covered in ivy, so I can only imagine how it looks in the daytime. Probably like the fairytales I've read as a child.

Too bad I haven't dropped those books as soon as I started them. Maybe if I had, I wouldn't be still clinging to the idea of it and realize it was a bunch of bullshit.

I am about to take a right and turn into my parents' street when the lights and noise from the local bar catches my attention.

Wow, they are open at one AM. I didn't expect that in this small town. I was under the impression this is a retirement land, and everyone is off to bed by nine PM. Guess not. And a good thing that is, because I could use a beer or two or ten after the week I've had.

I park my rented Lexus SUV on the side of the road and look over at the sign, Love and Peace Bar. "Of course it is," I say to myself, rolling my eyes at their "creative" names around here.

I'm pretty sure I've passed Bagels and Love, Sip of Love, and Serendipity Goods on the way here as well.

Tell me you're surrounded by weirdos without telling me...

Let's hope I don't kill myself in this town before I can leave. With another sigh, I cross the street and pull the front door open. Stepping inside, I'm greeted by soft Beatles music playing quietly and just a few patrons sitting around the place.

It's not too bad in here. Clean and good smelling. The long bar is on the left side with a big chalkboard up on top of it, and quite a large collection of my best friend—aka alcohol—lines the wall case. The walls around are covered in hippie art with sayings like "Make love not war" and so on.

On the right side, the now-empty stage with karaoke set up is taking up the whole space. The middle is occupied by funky high-top tables with mismatched chairs, and I see some comfy booths in bright colors lining the back and sides, but I ignore those in favor of direct access to booze and slide into one of the bar stools, dropping my head into my hands.

When was the last time I've been to an actual bar? Never mind one as weird as this one? Although it looks very much put together. Everything belongs.

Years... It's been years...

"Tough day?" A warm female voice greets me, breaking my thought process, and with a sharp inhale, I lift up my head to face her. The lady in front of me must be somewhere in her fifties, yet she doesn't look a day over forty. She is petite and curvy with a jolly attitude bouncing off her like a rubber ball.

She is wearing at least twenty different eclectic-looking necklaces, and her slightly gray hair is in two braids.

"You can say that," I respond, and I feel her eyes drilling through me, willing me to share more. Yeah, that won't be happening. "Can I get a beer, please?"

The lady doesn't bat an eye at my brush off; she nods and takes out a bottle from the fridge below the counter.

"I'm Willow," she tells me, placing it in front of me.

"Nice to meet you, Willow," I take a sip and look away. "Thank you."

"You're most welcome..." she trails off, waiting for me to fill in my name part.

"Joy."

"Oh, what a wonderful name." She claps her hands together. "Are you visiting Loverly?"

"You can say that," I repeat again.

"Fine, fine, I won't bother you." She smiles a soft motherly smile at me and walks away, but not before saying, "Welcome to LC. I think you will find peace and love here."

Peace and love...right...

I breathe out, grateful for her not soliciting my ears with any more unnecessary chatter when a body flops down onto the stool next to me.

A large, solid, smelly body.

A good kind of smelly. The manly kind of smelly.

My back instantly snaps up, the hairs on every inch of my skin rise to attention, and all my senses sharpen themselves as if sensing a fellow predator. Or mate.

We humans are primal like that. It's hunt or breed.

I shouldn't even look his way. I should get up and walk away really fast before my whole murder-by-a-weirdo scenario plays out like one of those Netflix documentaries, but I can't. My feet won't move, and my body feels like a dead weight, tethered to the chair by his presence.

I don't even know how he looks because I refuse to turn my head his way, but his scent is enough of a lure for me to stay seated and sniff him up.

When was the last time I noted a male scent like this? When was the last time the smell of damp mountain ground and fresh ocean breeze penetrated my nostrils and filled my lungs with enough air to keep breathing the rest of my life...?

Never...

I've never been ambushed by a scent before. I've never felt compelled to drag my nose through someone's neck to taste all the hidden tones of the aroma branded in their skin and then drop my panties and spread my legs for a total stranger just because he smells like my wet dream. Hell, I didn't even know my wet dreams consisted of soggy ground and salty waters, but I guess they do now.

*Don't look, don't look at him, Joy. If his scent is doing weird things to you, what will happen when you look at his face?* And based on the size of his presence, I'd say there would be plenty to look at. Finish your beer and get the hell out.

Do you think I listen to my useless brain?

Of-fucking-course, not. I'm doing a piss-poor job lately.

I look.

I turn my damn head, and only years of training my features to resemble an impassive mask save me from gasping and dropping my jaw to the ground at the sight in front of me.

I must admit, it was easier to fake calmness when I witnessed my boyfriend with his wife than it is to do the same now.

This is not a man. No, he's a perfect predator. The one Edward Cullen was describing in Twilight—yeah, yeah, I've seen the movie, get over it.

The perfect specimen created to lure you in by his scent, looks, and presence is seated right next to me.

This guy—whoever he is—has long, dirty blonde hair wrapped in a low messy bun. The side profile view of him shows me his short beard, but not the color of his eyes. His strong shoulders are covered in a plain white T-shirt but aren't doing much to hide the tattoos beneath it. He is penetrating my personal bubble because this guy is large. Too large to sit this close to a woman he doesn't know or want. And the strong, blond, hairy thighs are practically all exposed to my eyes since his shorts are painfully short.

Are those rubber duckies on his shorts? And is he wearing shark slides on his feet?

Since when do I find all of *this* sexy? Since when is perfectly combed hair and a three-piece suit no longer necessary to get my attention?

Apparently, about the same time as I decided the soggy ground was a wet dream. Meaning now. Meaning since I experienced *his* presence.

And then his head slowly turns my way, and this time, there is absolutely no way I can prevent the reaction I have. I stuck in a sharp, quick breath because the eyes and the smile greeting me are lethal.

The greenest of green eyes bore right into my soul, dissecting it into tiny pieces and shelving them accordingly. And that smile? That slow, sexy, loop-sided smile has my legs moving apart on their own without my permission. It's as if his smile was the secret passcode I kept intact, only to be stolen right this second and used to unlock me.

He is a real-life Viking, I decide.

*Breathe in, breathe out, Joy.* It's just a guy.

*Yes, he's the hottest guy you've ever seen. The guy that you would never classify as your type, yet you feel compelled to present yourself as a gift to, but just a guy. Drink your beer and go home.* Well...car.

Only, the unexpectedly perfect stranger opens his mouth, and I immediately find out his eyes and smile were only codes to the first door.

Because that voice? That voice holds the key to my vagina.

And God forbid... my heart.

"Well, hello there." That smooth, husky, and disgustingly happy melody floods into my ears right down to the now-unlocked lady bits.

"Hello," my answer is short and clipped as I take a sip of my beer.

I swear, this could only happen to me. Only I could meet the hottest guy on the planet after I just got out of whatever it was Justin and I had, in the unlikeliest place on earth, at one AM.

Can luck ever be on my side?

"I'm Jacob."

"Good for you," I reply, deciding to be as short with him as possible. I sip my beer and look up ahead, reading all the funky cocktail names on the board. Why does he have to have a sexy name, too?

Out of the corner of my eye, I spot a little tempting smile pull up on his plush, beard-covered lips, and the craving I get to feel that rough mouth on mine is short-circuiting my genius brain.

I'm just tired. That is why I'm having this abnormal reaction to this Viking. That or those rotten eggs did, in fact, poison me, and now I'm hallucinating.

"That's okay, I'll ask. And you are?"

"No one you need to concern yourself with."

"I happen to disagree." Of course, he does.

"I happen to not care what you happen to do."

"Hmm, a little wild thing. I like it."

"Did you come here to drink or ruin my peace?"

"No, apparently, I came in here to meet you."

I finally turned my head to face him again and realized my mistake instantly.

Stupid, sexy stranger. Stupid, sexy stranger whom my body wants very, very much.

Those stupid moss-green eyes and Viking hair. And tattoos. I haven't met a woman who didn't get weak between her legs at the sight of sexy tattoos before. Apart from me. I never knew I liked tattoos on a man so much before.

What the fuck is wrong with my tastes tonight?

"There you are. I thought you'd never turn again, and I wouldn't be able to see the eyes of my future wife." And there I go, choking on my drink.

"Oh, goodie, you are drunk!" I cough out, but the weird, sexy stranger only smiles wider at me.

"Nope, not drunk. At least, not yet."

"Well, I don't think I'll sit around waiting for you to get there. Who knows what you are capable of once your intoxication level rises."

"Damn it, your smart talk turns me on, Wildflower."

I shoot him a menacing glare which usually has all my students shit their pants but it does nothing to ward him off.

Jacob orders something from the same lady I did, and sits watching me with his hands clasped in front.

And no, I will not discuss what hearing him say he's turned on by me did to me. I will not mention how hot my skin feels, how fast my heart is beating out of my chest, and how tingly I feel in between my thighs.

Nope.

Ignorance is bliss. Look at my past relationships...

"So how did the most beautiful girl I've ever seen ended up in our little paradise on the beach?" he asks with a smile.

"Do you pick up all the girls with those lame lines?" I ask, half annoyed with his nonchalance, the other half with how hot he is. I don't like to lose control, and this guy is making me lose my whole head.

"Nope," is all he says, still looking at me like I'm the most fascinating thing ever.

"Are you going to keep staring at me?"

"Yep." And then when I narrow my eyes at him, he adds, "What? When angels come down to earth, you can't pass up the opportunity to be near them." Jacob then brings his hand to his hair and runs it through his blonde locks. Slowly. Seductively. And he knows it's doing it for me based on the stupid smirk he got going on.

"Ah, I see, this is the line you use for pick-ups."

"Is it working?" He wiggles his eyebrows.

"Does it look like it's working?" I ask him with a stone-cold face when, in reality, it might be working a bit too well.

"Nope, it does not." He picks up his drink and downs half of it in one go.

Is there such a thing as drinking porn? Because my eyes can't look away, and they are rapidly sending SOS signals to my vagina as I watch those beard-covered lips close around the brim of the cold glass. I watch as he swallows his sip, but it's me who feels it run down my throat. I'm fighting a losing battle here when my own mouth props open, and a silent sigh leaves my lips.

Fuck, when did I become this desperate girl? And for a guy like this, nonetheless.

Jacob makes a moaning sound as his glass hits the bar top. "Ah, this one always hits the spot. Wanna try?" He tilts the glass my way, and all I can do is bite the inside of my cheek and shake my head, tipping my beer into my mouth instead of placing my lips right over his on that glass he is holding.

"Okay then, story time," he announces happily. "Come on, let's hear it."

"Hear what?"

"What got you in such a pissy mood? This is Loverly town. No one is allowed to be sad here."

"Good thing I'm not staying then. Wouldn't want to tank your ratings and all."

"A tourist. Great, so what's the harm in laying it on me? Chances are we will never see each other again, and I will take your secrets to the ground."

"Good one, but my life is perfect. Nothing is wrong. I'm perfectly happy," I tell him with fake cheer.

"You don't smile."

"Your shorts are ridiculous."

"What?"

"Oh, sorry, I thought we were stating the obvious."

"Come on, what happened?" He is like that one annoying mosquito at night, zooming past your ear, interrupting your peace and quiet until you kill it. "Look, I don't even know your name. I am the perfect person to unload to. Lay it on me." He pats his chest.

"Your mouth is still moving. Why is it still moving?"

"Trust me, you want it to move."

"No. I don't. I want to enjoy my beer and go."

"Go where?"

"Away from you."

"Where are you staying?"

"Like I'm going to tell you so you can come murder me at night. Don't think so, buddy."

"Would you rather I do something else?" The sexy smirk is back. I am so out of my element here. I have no experience with guys like him. I have no experience, period.

"Yes, you, walking away."

"I already told you. Can't do that." He places his elbow on the bar top, laying his hand on his propped-up arm facing me. His green eyes shine with mischief.

"I think you really are drunk." My voice is breathless. Freaking breathless. I blame the beer, sulfur poisoning, and his eyes.

*Pull yourself together, Joy.*

"Do these pick-up lines work on every girl?" I need to go back to my walls. I need to build them back up and hide where my heart is safe.

"I wouldn't know." He shrugs. "I've never felt compelled to try them on anyone as much as now."

I don't buy that for a second, but my stupid natural curiosity gets the best of me, and I shift in my chair, fully facing him as I say, "Okay, let's hear it then." I motion for him to go on, and his mouth slowly stretches into a blinding grin.

"How about we make this more interesting?" I lift an eyebrow in question, and he continues. "If I make you smile five times with my lines, you will owe me a kiss."

"That absolutely does not sound more interesting to me."

"I happen to disagree."

"I happen to not care what you happen to do."

"You already said that tonight."

"You needed a reminder."

"Ahhh, I see, you are afraid you are going to lose." I threw him a glare because, damn it, he's got me.

Not about losing. I won't lose. But he just challenged me. You can't challenge me. I didn't get to be where I am in my career by not being competitive. So, I inhale a large breath through my nose, making my nostrils flare and say, "Fine. And if I win, you leave me alone."

"It's cute, you think I will lose." Jacob winks at me.

Cute. I scoff internally. Did he just call me cute? I don't do cute. Not even remotely.

"What's your name?"

"Still not telling you."

"That's okay, because I'll just call you mine."

My brain is fighting me between an eye roll and a twitch that resembles a smile. *Stop it, Joy. Do better.*

"Pass," I tell him and add, "Next."

"Do you believe in love at first sight?"

"A total no."

"Okay, let me walk by again." He literally gets up, walks away, and comes back a second later, and I have this strange, warm sensation spreading in my chest.

This guy is something else. Something I've never come across before, and I'm not sure how to feel about it.

"Can you pull up a map on your phone?"

"Why?"

"Because I just got lost in your eyes." I bite the inside of my cheek to keep myself in check.

"Ah, ah," he sing-songs. "That right there is cheating. Release that cheek right now, and I'm counting this as your first smile."

"No such thing."

"Yes. Now it's time to step it up." I roll my eyes at him, as he's clapping and rubbing his hands together like a little excited child.

The next thirty minutes, he hits me with every possible pick-up line he can, and I'm almost certain all of those came from Google. But nevertheless, I gave up two more smiles to some.

"They say nothing lasts forever, so will you be my nothing?"

"You should have your license suspended for driving me crazy."

"Know what's on the menu today? Me 'n u."

"Are you a loan? Because you've got my interest."

"Are you from Tennessee? Because you're the only ten I see." Yeah, that one got me. And it wasn't even one of my little twitches. This was a full-on laugh-out-loud moment.

From there on, it was like a dam burst open. I could not contain myself. My belly hurt from the new sensation I've never felt before. My mascara was smudged from all the laughing tears, and I have long lost a bet.

The first one in my life.

"Stop, drop, and roll!!! Because baby, you're on fire!!!" He shouted this one for the whole town to hear, and I had to slap my hand to his mouth to shut him up. Which he didn't hesitate to freaking kiss, and I pulled it away quickly, contemplating if maybe I really did catch fire. My insides clenched and rumbled as something took flight deep inside.

Well, it didn't take a lot to get my butterflies going...

Hussies.

"I think you lost, Wildflower." He leans into my space. His mouth hovering a breath away from mine as my own breath catches.

His woodsy scent is so much stronger now, and I think if I wasn't already poisoned from eggs, I'd definitely blame it on him.

"I'm going to kiss you now."

"No, you're not."

"Yes. I am. Come on, Wildflower, pay up."

My breath catches once again. The walls crumble, and my eyes fix on him as I try to understand this absolute stranger.

He is so weird but enchanting at the same time. I should've walked away long ago, but my feet can't seem to move away from him and the nonsense he spews.

Jacob gave me more in the span of ten minutes than Brian and Justin did in all the years I dated each one of them.

He studies me with that little smirk on his face to see if I will "pay up" but my brain can't catch up to a single thing that is going on right now. And then his lips are on mine. They are soft and sweet from whatever it was he drank. Or maybe it's just him. I assumed he would go all in right away, go for one of those deep tongue kisses, but he is being a perfect gentleman, being gentle and sweet.

Too bad I wish he wouldn't be right now.

I don't know Jacob, yet I've never felt more desired. I know what I want right this second. And I am not one to deny myself this. Not now. Not when my walls haven't been up yet.

"Let's go." I take the last swing of my beer and get up while Jacob is watching me with one eyebrow raised.

"And where are we going?"

"To have sex."

I have to give him credit; he doesn't stumble upon my words, and his eyes stay in their sockets despite my boldness. Instead, they shine with more excitement and lust.

"Just like that?"

"Yes, just like that. Oh, wait? Did you expect me to sit around for maybe another hour, melt from your sickening sweet words, and throw shy, suggestive glances your way? And maybe also twirl my hair around my finger a little for extra effect while I wait for you to come up with a super innovative invitation to your bed and then even blush a little at your offer?"

"You forgot to play with a straw of some fruity drink."

"What?"

"Girls also play with their straws to draw our attention to their mouth and fingers."

"Damn it, I knew I was doing something wrong in my life. I've never played with a straw." I snap my fingers dramatically and fake sigh.

Playing with a straw...what a crock of bullshit. Are girls really that stupid nowadays? Are they relying on a straw to land a guy? Idiots, but apparently, men eat it right up.

No wonder I keep failing at this whole relationship game. I don't play with straws.

"Wildflower?" Jacob snaps me out of my tiny brain rant. Somehow, his stupid nickname is already stuck with me.

"Hmm?" He is out of his barstool and pushes me back into mine, towering over me in a flash. His strong, veiny arms grab it for added effect, and I have to swallow a thick lust lump in my throat. God, what those arms could do with my body.

Can we get out of here yet? Or maybe he's not interested. He never did respond to my proposition.

Just as I'm about to tell him to back off so I can go add to my pathetic future eulogy, his right hand clasps over mine, engulfing it in his strength and power, and places it right over his crotch.

His hard. Solid. Large crotch.

Oh. My. God. I'm touching his rock-hard dick through those tiny rubber ducky shorts he is wearing, and I can feel every glorious inch of him resting against my palm. Jesus, I hope I'm not drooling over here.

"Do you feel that?" I nod. "Does that feel like I need you to twirl your hair, throw shy glances, or blush? Or God forbid, play with a straw?" He doesn't let me answer before speaking again. "No, I don't. Because the second I walked through those doors, I wanted you in every possible position, and I was willing to learn some new ones if it meant I could have you more times tonight. So, no, you are definitely not doing it wrong. Now, finish my drink, and let's get out of here."

I swallow again, my heart rate suddenly jumping into dangerously close territory to a heart attack, and the desire to have him in all those *positions* is stronger than my need for the next breath.

"Why do I need to finish your drink?" I ask, curious what his weird concoction has to do with us having mind-blowing sex. Because a guy like that will surely deliver.

"Trust me, you need the extra help. Because I plan to do naughty things to your body tonight. Naughty, dirty things." The cute, gentle Viking with gentlemanly kisses is gone as his eyes turn black like the midnight forest and his dirty words take on a new edge. "Finish. My. Drink."

I take the glass and let the sugary, red liquid flow down my throat. "Because those naughty things? Those won't be cute or gentle. There will be no lovemaking. No mercy. The ones that will make you moan and scream and beg for me to stop. But I won't. Your smart mouth thought you could be in control here. Well, think again. I will keep you sore for the whole week straight, Wildflower." He leans in, whispering into my ear, and my traitorous body reacts with a wave of goosebumps over my skin. Goosebumps and wild, hot fire under every inch of my skin.

What have I gotten myself into?

# 3

## *Joy*

*"Follow your bliss, and the universe will open doors where there were only walls." — Joseph Campbell.*

I don't remember the drive over here. I don't remember what type of car we were in or how far away his place was. I don't remember if I locked my rented Lexus or not. I don't remember seeing any buildings on our way here because the tension rolling through both of us hung heavy in the confined space. I could feel the heat coming off his body as mine was shuddering from the hand he placed on my thigh.

Never knew a hand on my thigh would be all it took to turn me on. But it's not just any hand. It's big and veiny and strong. It's the kind of hand you dream about wrapped around your throat, the one squeezing your breasts and using to fuck your pussy.

The heat from his touch is searing through my skin, straight to my bones. He is only holding onto to my leg, yet I feel him everywhere. It's like a shockwave running through my body.

The drive could have been awkward, but I don't remember a damn thing because as soon as the engine is off, his lips are on mine. Crushing me with hunger, I have never felt before. And not a trace of that cute kiss anywhere in sight.

It's as if we were suffocating our whole lives, and now our first breath was finally delivered. I've never been kissed like this. I've never needed someone else to survive.

Come to think of it, I'm having awfully a lot of firsts for a messed-up trip.

His lips are soft and gentle as he molds them against mine. His tongue slowly but confidently tracing each groove, silently asking—no, demanding—permission to enter my mouth. And I grant him what he wants, opening and welcoming him. And as soon as my lips part, his tongue is playing with mine in a matter of milliseconds. And what a play it is.

I'm pretty sure I moaned from the touch of his lips alone because of this kiss.

This is the kiss I've dreamt of. The one I've silently wish for upon every star in the night sky. It's slow, sexy, and erotic, yet strong, passionate, and wild. It turns every fiber of my body inside out, igniting the dusty corners. The one that has my heart clawing its way out, ready to jump into his strong, warm hands.

Somehow, we make it out of his car, and we end up inside his house, but as soon as the door closes behind me, he rips the shirt I was wearing off my body, and with one swift move, his hands trailed over the exposed skin of my waist a second later. Eliciting goosebumps on their way.

It's dark and warm in his home but scorching hot and bright inside my body. His every touch only adds more fluid to the already fast growing inferno.

Jacob pushes me against the front door, and with one free hand, cups my face while kissing the life out of me, while the other hand starts making its way up towards my breasts.

With one strong tug, both of them are spilling out of my bra, and his hot palm presses against my hard nipples, gripping the soft flesh and making me moan into his mouth.

"Wildflower, you have the most beautiful tits in the world. Fuck...they are so soft and perfect," he growls.

My girls are not small, but they fit into his palm so perfectly, and for once, I am grateful for my over-the-top C-cup.

Jacob's hand snakes around my waist, and he pulls me painfully close to him while his mouth takes one nipple into his mouth. And now, I'm glad for the extra support because my knees can't hold me up much longer.

He nibbles at it, following with a gentle flick of his tongue over the bruised flesh, making my nipple pebble from his mouth even more. My hands reach up and grab hold of his long, blond hair, digging into the soft locks with reverence, and I hear the deep rumble of approval rolling off him. I've been dreaming of doing it ever since he sat down next to me.

The contrast between his scratchy beard on my sensitive skin and his soft hair in my hands sends me into a tailspin. And I think it drives him just as crazy because suddenly, my feet are off the ground and wrapping themselves around his waist while he is carrying me to his bed. Or at least I think it's a bed. His lips never leaving my skin—kissing it, nipping at it with his teeth, and sucking it in, definitely leaving hickeys for me to find tomorrow, but somehow that knowledge only makes me go crazier with need for this strange man.

Jacob lays me down and steps away. "Look at you." He gestures with both his hands to my half-naked, panting body. "If this is not perfection, I don't know what is."

No one has ever said those words about my body before. No one.

"Jacob. I need you now. Right now," I say, channeling my authoritative, doctor voice the best I can, but he's not having any of that.

"Oh no, boo. You see..." He gets on his hands and knees and starts crawling over me like the most dangerous and vicious predator. "You might be big and important out there..." He hitches his thumb to point outside. "But in here, in my bed, I am the one in control. I am the one who commands your body, and you will obey me, Wildflower."

As soon as the last word is out, his hand clasps around the front of my bra, and he rips it off my body, making me gasp from the sudden action, and I feel a gushing flood hitting me down below.

I am soaking wet for this man.

That shouldn't be so hot, but it is. His caveman attitude is the sexiest thing I've ever experienced, and I am all too willing to give up the reins to him. Why I am allowing this complete stranger to do all this to me is beyond me. But for once...for once, it feels amazing to let someone else be in charge. To let go of my control. Even if it's for one night only.

Jacob throws what used to be a five-hundred-dollar La Perla bra to the ground and moves toward my slacks. In another swift movement, they are gone, and he discovers I don't like to wear underwear.

His eyes immediately fixate on my bare, glistening pussy, and his tongue darts out to lick his bottom lip.

Jacob may be in control here, but it's my body that holds the key.

"I fully approve of this," he says and brings his middle finger to my swollen clit, torturously slowly dragging his finger through my folds. "Although, I'm grateful I didn't know you were bare at that bar."

"Why?" Is that my voice? When did I ever sound so lustful. So weak...so needy.

"Because I'd have taken you right in that bathroom like a horny teenager instead of savoring your pussy in my bed." I whimpered in response. "So wet, so ready, so perfect." He drags his finger one more time and dips it inside, pushing it as far as it can go, making me squirm.

"More," I rasp out. "I need more, Jacob."

"Do you now? Well, you have to be a good girl and say please." He licks my lips.

Fuck... I've never been on this ride before, and I think I missed out on a damn lot because hearing him command me, ask me to be his good girl and say please, completely undoes me, and I find myself not just asking but begging.

"Please, please, Jacob, please!"

"Look at that. Such a good girl I have here," he praises me. His words alone bring me closer to an orgasm, but then he suddenly drops down to my pussy, impales me with his large three fingers at the same time, and sucks my clit in, while fucking me with his fingers and mouth mercilessly.

"Oh, fuck..." I scream out.

"My name."

"What?" I'm so lost in the moment; I have no idea what he's saying.

"Scream my name, Wildflower. Scream for the whole forest and ocean to hear. Let them all know who is bringing you so much pleasure."

"Jacob..." His name leaves my mouth uncontrollably, and I chant it like a mantra while he's working me towards what must be the most epic climax of my life.

My hands are gripping whatever flash of his I can reach, scratching and scraping at him. I need him to feel what he makes me feel.

He makes me *feel*.

Period.

My hips are moving in sync with him, and within seconds, I explode all over his tongue and fingers as he curses. "Fucking hell, Wildflower, you taste so fucking good. Your cum is my new favorite dessert," he says, and I die.

His fingers are still inside me, still pumping through the last waves of pleasure, and then it gets to be too much. I try to squirm away from his touch, but he's not having it.

"Jacob, I can't. I can't."

"What do you need to say?"

Fuck, what do I need to say? "Please!" I yell out, remembering his instructions.

He stops and lifts his head up. "Good girl."

My inner muscles clench around his fingers that are still inside, and a wicked smile tugs on his glistening face. It is wet from me—that's my orgasm all over him.

Jesus, have mercy. I've never been so turned on in my life, and I just came.

"You like being a good girl, don't you?" He takes his fingers out and brings them to my lips. "Why don't you show me just how good you can be and suck yourself clean off me."

My lips part of their own accord, completely ignoring every alarm I have set up through years of dating and sex. I never give up control, and yet here I am, doing something I've never ever done. Something I've never even imagined doing before.

He slips his wet fingers inside my mouth, and I wrap my lips around them, tasting myself.

I've never even kissed a guy after he went down on me. It always felt so gross, and now I want to smack myself for missing out. Because this is a whole other level of hot. Another first for me at the hands of this man.

But maybe it's only this good because it is *this* guy doing it to me...

Jacob's mouth parts as I start sucking his fingers harder and faster, wishing it was his cock. Although I've never wished for such a thing, I don't like giving blowjobs. I don't. But now I feel like I physically need to!

"Oh hell..." He pulls his fingers out real fast and climbs off my body, leaving me in a sex haze.

In one take—like what you see in movies—he takes his shirt off and sends it flying to the ground.

Oh, sweet Lord. His chest is covered in tattoos. He is sporting an eight-pack, and this guy has the most defined V-line going down into his groin I've ever seen.

My mouth waters as my pussy floods once again. This is one fine man. A Viking in its true nature.

His green eyes are trained on mine, and there is no breaking this connection between us. He unzips his shorts, and I find someone else who likes to go commando.

But that's not the important bit here. No, sir.

The important thing, or should I say *unreal thing*, is his large, thick, and very angry cock. He sees my stunted expression and smirks, knowing exactly what I'm thinking.

I've never seen a cock so gorgeous, and I've seen a lot throughout my years in medicine.

I clear my throat as he starts climbing back up to me.

"I'm a doctor; I know what fits and what doesn't and that—" I point to his dick, "That won't fit in my vagina."

"You're so sexy when you say vagina," he tells me. "But it's not going into your vagina. Yet."

"It's not?" I sound almost disappointed when I should be grateful for not needing stitches later.

"No, Wildflower. You are going to suck my cock first, won't you?"

Oh, fuck…I will, won't I? Because suddenly, I am a whore for his dick in my mouth. I nod like an idiot as he climbs all the way up, straddling my chest with his strong, hairy thighs wrapped tightly around me. I want to touch him. I want to touch him everywhere. And it looks like we are starting with his cock.

Jacob grabs his shaft, pumping it a few times with those sexy, sinful hands, and slowly drags it over my swollen lips, smearing his precum over them. "Open."

And just like that, my lips part, and the smooth head of his cock sinks inside my mouth. He is so large, I'm afraid I'll have a dislocated jaw after this blowjob, but ask me if I care…

He groans as I start to suck and lick the underside of him. His hands find their way into my hair, and he clenches it hard, keeping me right where he wants me, and I moan in agreement.

"You like that? You want me to fuck your tight little mouth like that? Hard and rough? You want to choke on my dick, Wildflower?"

He pushes in farther, making me gag, and tears spill from my eyes, but I find myself nodding vigorously.

I want it.

I want it all.

I want him to use my body the way he wants. I want to be good enough for this stranger.

"Fuck, my good girl, you will be the death of me tonight," he says and proceeds to thrust into my mouth just as he said he would.

With one hand in my hair, the other one grabs onto my breast as he rides my face hard, and I get no breaks, no time to catch the saliva spilling around his shaft, and I feel it dripping everywhere, but neither of us cares. With his body up on top of mine, I have easy access to his ass, and I grab it with my hands, needing to touch and feel him in every way. Jacob throws his head back and groans.

His previously gentle green eyes are replaced by two raging storms and the happy weirdo from the bar is nowhere to be seen, but I like this version of Jacob.

This one speaks to my broken soul.

This one understands me. And might be fluent in the same language.

I feel his cock thicken inside my mouth, and just as I'm preparing myself to swallow each drop of his cum as he did mine...he pulls out, flips us around so I am on top, and, without a second thought, pushes himself into me.

"Agh," I scream. "Jacob...fuck..." I brace my hands on his chest.

"Fuck, indeed," he growls out. "Fuck, you are so tight, Wildflower. So fucking tight."

He shuts his eyes hard as he keeps his strong hands on my hips, making sure I don't move an inch.

As if I could. As if I have any room to move.

The unexpectedness of his action took the initial sting away, but now I feel all of him. I feel him deeper than anyone else I've ever felt before. I feel him reaching part of me that shouldn't be reached yet with each second, the pain morphs into pleasure.

Without moving me away, he gets up, using those ridiculous muscles of his, and sits up to meet my body.

"I've never felt a pussy like yours, Wildflower," he says and sucks in my hard nipple, making me moan and move my hips involuntarily. "Stop." He halts my movements. "Stop, or else I'll come right this second. You just sucked the life out of me, and now I'm inside my personal heaven, and I just need a minute."

Oh, he needs a minute? Well, he ain't getting one because I need to get fucked by this man right this second. I fight against his grip and shift my hips again, eliciting a growl out of him.

"Wildflower," he says as a warning, but I ignore it and keep rolling my hips around his cock.

Fuck, but that feels good. So, so good. My eyes close in pleasure but are forced open when he smacks my ass, and I feel the hot sting against my soft flesh.

"Ouch!" But Jacob doesn't respond. He flips us again, and this time, I'm on the bottom as he towers over me.

"Not a good girl. A bad one," he says and thrusts into me hard, knocking the air out of me. "Yes, boo, two can play this game. You want it, I'll give it to you."

And so, he does.

He fucks me just as hard and rough as he did my mouth. Even more so. He wraps himself around me, using my body as an anchor to push inside me as deep as he can. My nails dig into his shoulders and back, trying to tattoo themselves into his skin forever. And within seconds, I feel my climax build up again as I fight against it.

No, not yet. I want to hold on a bit more. I want to feel his cock inside me a little longer because God knows I won't find another one like this ever again.

"Take it and give it to me," he hisses into my ear. His voice is husky and coarse as he fights his own orgasm. "Come right this second, Wildflower," he commands me, and my body obeys.

It freaking obeys instantly, clenching around him and dissolving in helpless ecstasy.

The climax is so strong my vision goes black, apart from tiny white spots here and there, and I moan and scream and scratch at him.

"Fuuuuuck..." he drags out, quickly pulling out of me, and I feel his hot cum, coating my breasts and stomach in long, thick stripes.

Condom.

There is no fucking condom.

Oh my God. How could I be so stupid.

"Jacob," my voice is full of alarm, but his gaze is firmly fixated on the mess he made of me.

"Fuck, boo, that was so goddam hot, but I'm sorry. I got caught up in the moment. I swear I'm clean. I get tested monthly, and I've never not used a condom before. You're the first." His words somewhat calm me down right away.

I was special enough, desirable enough for him to lose his mind...

And fuck, but it was so hot—it is, so hot—to be covered in him.

"It's okay, I'm clean too. I got tested after the last bastard, and I'm on birth control. We should be fine."

"Good." His body finally gives way, and he slumps, crushing into his own release and giving my body his full weight. Even exhausted, his lips find my skin, and he kisses my neck and my shoulder gently. Those gentlemanly kisses are back.

What a drastic difference between now and just a minute ago.

"I'm sorry if I was too rough. But you were such a good girl, taking all of me."

I groan in response.

"No, you were perfect. *That* was perfect, but you need to stop saying that. You're turning me into someone I don't recognize."

"Is that a bad thing?" he asks with another soft kiss, and I feel shivers running up and down my body from his loving caress and tickling beard.

And this is where my brain finally snaps into place again.

No love. No loving touches. Just sex. Rough and hard.

"You're crushing me," I tell him in an attempt to get him off me because this was getting a bit too much when, in reality, I'd like to keep his weight on me forever.

This wasn't just good sex. This was the sex of all sex kind of sex. The epitome of pleasure, and I'm already hating myself for falling under his charms in the first place and allowing myself a taste of what it could have been versus what I've always had.

Mediocre.

And I don't want to go back to mediocre.

I never knew sex could be like that. I am thirty-one years old, and my sexual activity was limited to two—now, three men. And two out of the three wouldn't be able to hold a candle to this one!

But I'm not staying in this town. I can't. I won't.

Jacob begrudgingly rolls off me, but instead of just laying by my side, he rolls me on top of himself. "There, now you're crushing me. And I don't mind in one bit."

I should fight him on this, I should push him away. But I don't.

We are sticky, dirty, and sweaty, but...this feels nice.

Very nice. Too nice for my walls, and I started to get up to get cleaned off, only to be pulled right back to where I was.

"Stay," Jacob says softly. "We are about to do a lot more of that, and I quite like the thought of my cum on your body. In fact, next round, I just might spread it all over your heavenly ass, marking it with me, and in the end, for good measure, I'll spill what's left down your throat. How does that sound?" he asks as his fingers draw soft, gentle circles over my naked back.

All I can think of is that it sounds like the best night of my life. The best, craziest, and probably full of regrets for me to agonize over later night.

So, I lift my head a bit and say, "Yes, please."

And we proceed to do just that. With Jacob taking me over and over again until I can't feel my legs anymore, until my whole body is sticky and messy from his cum, and we are in a half-conscious state.

---

"Why is your shower so small?" I look around the place, and I think I'm only now actually seeing it for the first time despite being inside for over an hour.

Jacob flipped some lights on, and now I see that his kitchen is in his living room, and his shower door opens right next to his fridge.

"Why is everything so small?"

Jacob shrugs and turns on the water in the tiniest shower stall I have ever seen. It's tiny, but it is beautiful. The emerald-green subway tiles line the walls with copper fixtures, elegantly adding to the charm of it.

I'm not even sure two people could fit in there at the same time, yet he is pulling me inside along with him. "It's a tiny house; it's meant to be small."

"Tiny house? You live in a tiny house? This is a tiny house?" I shriek, my questions making zero sense.

"Yep, now get in, boo."

"Oh, great, another nickname for me." I roll my eyes at his wide grin but take his hand and step inside.

Surprisingly, we do fit in here together, but it's an extremely tight fit. After a few seconds of soaking under the water, I reach for his body wash, but he slaps my hand lightly, taking the soap away from me.

*Gee, fine, you can have it first; I guess you are not as gentlemanly as I thought you were.* But when he opens it and lathers his loofa with it, it's not his body it touches. It's mine. And I freeze.

Jacob is washing me gently and thoroughly. He uses light pressure to get his dried cum off my breasts, and as soon as the soap is washed off, he lowers his mouth to my nipple, sucking it in. I arch my back into his touch, and his other hand climbs over my wet body to cup my other breast, lightly squeezing it, and I purr into him.

I fucking purr.

What the hell is wrong with me tonight? But once again, I can't stop.

He keeps playing with my tits, and since the stall is so "spacious," we are pressed together, which means I feel his erection growing hard once again.

"Oh my God, are you even real?" I ask, apparently out loud, when I meant to do it in my head because he snickers with my nipple in his mouth, and reaches for his cock, lining it up with my swollen pussy.

"It's all you, Wildflower. It's all you. Now spread your legs, and let me have you in this shower. I want to think of you when I am all alone, fucking my fist while dreaming of your tight pussy."

Oh, Jesus…I try to widen my stance, but this is a fucking tiny house. There is only so much spreading I can do, but he finds his way in and surrounded by emerald-green tiled walls, he fucks me just as hard as he did on his bed.

With groans and moans, we both come for God only knows what time tonight, and Jacob goes back to cleaning me up. And then something wild possessed me to return the favor.

I grab the loofa from him and soap him up.

I've never done this.

I've never even showered with another man, let alone this intimately.

Jacob is doing something to me. He's using some weird voodoo magic on my walls, crumpling them to the ground, and there is not a damn thing I can do about it.

What an easy prey I am.

But it's just one night.

I can be someone else for one night. I can allow myself to feel for one night.

I'll go back to those walls and locks tomorrow. I'll go back to my solitary life tomorrow.

We get out of the shower, and Jacob takes care of me once again. He dries me with a weird scratchy towel, explaining that it comes from natural shit, and that's when I remember I'm in the weirdo town. Of course, his towels would be made up from seaweed or something along the lines.

Once I'm dry, I go looking for my clothes, but he stops me. "Where do you think you are going?"

"To my car."

"Nope, I don't think so. Up you go," he says, gesturing to a staircase I've only now noticed. "Let's go sleep the few hours we have left in this night."

"I'm not sleeping with you," I say with dead assurance.

I've never spent a full night with a man. Not ever. And every warning bell in my brain is going off that I should definitely not start with this one.

"Well, I think you already slept with me if you want to get technical, and now, we are just going to rest our heads together on some comfy duck feather pillows and shut our eyes to let the dreams take us places."

"You are so weird, Jacob." Something passes over his face when I say that, but he wipes it off really fast, replacing the uneasy reaction with a wide smile.

Deciding that it's a losing battle, I tell my brain to shut up and climb up the stairs, only to hit my head on the roof. "Damn it. Why didn't you tell me you live in a tiny house? And why live in one anyway?"

Jacob climbs in after me, fully naked, showing off his glorious body, and I drink it in again. Storing it in my memory for future vibrator date nights. "This house has everything I need. Why would I waste resources, contaminate the Earth, and pay obscene amounts of money for a mortgage when it's not necessary. And you and I didn't exactly have time to discuss my living arrangements." He winks at me, and my insides clench.

Come on, how much more sex can you want, body?

My vagina screams, *With his cock? Twenty-four-seven, please!* Shutting the whore up, I switch my mind to the previous conversation.

"Oh, you are one of those," I tell him with an eye roll.

"Nope, Wildflower, there is only one of me. Special edition."

Fuck, he's right, isn't he? He is one of a kind, and I'm the lucky damsel in distress who got to experience him tonight.

One night. That's all.

I thought sex with Justin was good, but boy, was I wrong. He's got nothing on this sexy stranger.

I turn around, guiding my body to the very edge of his tiny bed in an effort to put as much distance between us as possible, but apparently, Jacob has other plans.

His big, hairy, muscular leg slides over mine at the same time as his arm wraps around my waist and hauls me to his chest.

"What are you doing?" My voice sounds scared, nervous, and a bit frantic, and I don't like it one bit. I'm used to being the one in control. Not the other way around.

"Shhh, sleep, Wildflower," his soft voice whispers into my ear, kissing my temple, and just like that, I melt and obey his command, closing my eyes and falling into a deep, sated sleep.

Sleep. Not love. Definitely, no falling with the L word...

# 4

# Jacob

*"Make your weird light shine bright, so other weirdos know where to find you." — Unknown.*

Warm, soft body, a different than mine hair, baby snores...

My eyes fly open as my brain catches up to my fast-hardening cock. A certain Wildflower is sleeping soundlessly in my bed. In my arms with her curvy, naked ass pressed into my groin. Fuck...what a night this was, and if I didn't have to get up for work right now, I'd stay here watching her sleep until it's time to kiss her to wake up, then kiss her again down below, enjoying my breakfast and serving her hers right after.

I've never entertained the idea of calling in sick to stay home...but I am today. Because last night, I met the most perfect woman in the world, with her darkest brown hair, constantly frowning face, and "sparkling" personality.

The same one I am contemplating waking up at five-thirty AM only after we had about an hour of sleep.

I am not ready to let go of her.

Who is she, and how long do I have to beg at her feet for a chance with her? To have her here, splayed over my green pillow and in my home.

Because I will beg and cry and throw a pissy tantrum if I must...but I *will* have this girl. I've never seen someone more beautiful in my life. Someone who made my heart skip a beat.

You see, I had a feeling I needed to go to LPs last night. Granted, I have that feeling almost every night, but last night, it was especially annoying.

All my beer randomly disappeared from my tiny fridge. All of my extra organic, homegrown snacks fell through some magical hole, and the dinner I was so excited about fell face-first to the ground. It was as if the universe was calling out to me, nudging me to come out and meet my future wife.

And as soon as I stepped foot inside the bar, I felt this crazy pull toward her. And let me tell you, you don't ignore a pull like that from the universe. I am no stranger to striking up a conversation randomly with anyone and everyone—locals, and tourists alike—but this felt different.

It felt like destiny. Like a rainbow arched over her head full of that long, dark brown hair, and unicorns started popping out of it. But nothing prepared me for the shots that were fired. My heart shot out as soon as I slipped into the seat by her. No, as soon as I stepped into her vicinity.

Her rich smell, her brilliant eyes, her curvy figure. They all called out to me, and suddenly, I felt the world tilted on its axis, and now, instead of physics, it was her who kept me walking, breathing, and living.

Same as her hair, the dark eyes called out to something deep inside me. The intensity of those magnetic pools matched their dark color. They threatened to pull the parts

I had long ago buried and put a nice monument over, but now I am ready to wake up from my hibernation and call her my wife.

Yes, fine, I am joking about the whole wife thing. For now..

At least until I can make sure she stays here in Loverly. And I need to make sure of that.

Somehow.

Because she stole my breath and refused to give it back. Her kisses were pure fire and passion, engulfing me wholly and bringing out the hidden parts of my soul out.

The controlling freak parts. The beast who needs full submission. I've buried him, and she dug him up with her pristine French manicured nails.

And the best part? She craved my control. She relished in it, even if she won't admit it. And now that I've had the taste of my old lifestyle, I want more.

I need more.

Last night with her was...it was an experience.

Each move, moan, and thrust felt familiar. Like we have done this dance a million times before. Like we are two pieces of one rainbow, connecting through all the clouds. Like she is mine and has always been mine.

Fuck it. She will be my wife—all jokes aside. And I don't intend on breaking this promise.

But for now, I have to leave her without even knowing her name or having a way to contact her again. The stubborn vixen wouldn't give me anything last night, and the only thing I need to rely on is God and whatever power exists to lead her back into my life.

My wildflower doesn't seem to want to be caught. She is just what her nickname suggests, wild. But not in an I'm-up-to-anything wild, no, she is more of an I'm-perfectly-fine-on-my-own or touch-me-and-I'll-bite-your-head-off wild. And I don't want to spook her.

I like my head.

Both heads...

I'm trying to be really careful not to wake her up at five-thirty in the morning, reluctantly sliding my arms from underneath her and untangling our perfectly collided feet to get up. I've only had about an hour of sleep, but if I could do it again, I would take off my shorts right now and climb her like a clinging koala.

Yes, a clinging koala because they are cute and cuddly, and those are the same characteristics I have going for me since there is nothing else I can offer. What could this siren want to do with me? A simple guy living a simple life in his tiny house on the edge of the best—yet, most unique—town.

What could a guy like me offer a woman like her? She mentioned something about being a doctor, and I nearly died...oh, the irony.

Nope, I need to snap right out of that nightmare. The Jacob from five years ago doesn't exist. That sullen, unsatisfied man is long gone, along with his big ass house, a six-figure salary, and a bitch of an ex-wife.

Everyone in Loverly knows me as a happy-go-lucky guy, and that is who I prefer to be. That is the person I am today.

Today, I have peace to offer. Life. Freedom.

This town gave me a new chance, and I'll be forever in their debt—not that they ask for anything. These people here are too pure for the horrible, vile world out there, and I'm very much content with staying with them for the rest of my life.

Now, if I could get a certain wildflower to share that life with, well... I'd be all set.

I take one last look at the woman who possibly changed the course of my whole road ahead in the blink of an eye. I take in her curvy ass, barely hidden by my blanket, the one I'd very much like to sink my teeth in. I glide my eyes over her delicate, yet sharp, facial features. The fluttering eyelashes, the slightly propped open mouth, and soft baby snores coming from it.

Oh, how I wish I could climb in behind her, nuzzle my nose into her hair, and softly kiss her wake-up, followed by softly nudging something else into her. But my town needs me this morning.

With all twenty of my fingers and toes crossed, I make a wish to see her again and step out into the morning breezy air. It's filled with salt and seaweed and crashing waves I'd love to hit up.

Maybe later, after work.

Maybe I can talk to Miss I've-got-a-stick-up-my-ass to join me, if she's still here. I snicker to myself at the thought. Wouldn't that be something. This girl doesn't seem to know what fun is if it were to hit her right smack in the face.

She is grimly sarcastic, pessimistic, stubborn, and in control.

Although, she seemed to be quite content in giving up some of it last night. And Jesus, her personality of a Grinch turns me on like no one has ever did before.

Because I have a feeling underneath all that green fur lies a diamond.

My diamond. And I will find it.

"Jenny, don't you think our Jacob looks especially radiant today? The yellow aura surrounding him is just blinding."

The little bar-owning old hippy, Willow, who witnessed me with my girl last night, smiles slyly as she speaks to her best friend, Jennifer Levine.

There is absolutely nothing as serious and important as gossip in Loverly Cave town. Especially if it's love gossip.

It's basically a religion over here.

I have no doubt that my visit to Willow's bar last night was all over the Love Hive, our town's gossip site. Heck, they might be planning our wedding already, and I am seriously contemplating enlisting their help.

"He does look extra happy today, Willow. You are right," Jenny confirms with a happy nod and grins my way too. "Jackie, have you met someone?"

Good thing our town is there when you need them to be. Hey, they even talk for you, so you don't have to stress about it. Just look at Willow, who is doing precisely that for me right now.

"I think he has, Jenny. And it was a new girl. I've never seen her before, but she did look familiar for some reason."

At those words, all of a sudden, Mrs. Levine shoots up, straightens her back, and looks even more interested in the conversation. "What girl?"

"Her name is just at the tip of my tongue." Willow gestures to her mouth as if she can literally taste it in there, and now, she has my full, undivided attention. "Oh, rainbows, I had one too many Mellow-yellows last night. I can't remember, but she had beautiful dark hair and dark eyes but a deep gray aura surrounding her." Willow sighs as if Wildflower's mood affects her personally. "Jackie, I hope you got her spirits up." She wiggles her eyebrows at me, and I'm fighting really hard not to grin.

"Come on, Will, you know I don't kiss and tell." I wink at the pair of my most loyal morning trainees.

# MEET MY WIFE

I swear, on my shark slides, I see a light bulb go off in Mrs. Levine's head. "Willow, call in code Pink Mist," Jenny says cryptically, gathers all her equipment, and rushes away with her friend, following closely, fast and with bulging eyes.

What in the world just happened? Usually, I can't get these two plus Mrs. Colson—my best friend's mom—to leave me alone, trying to pair me up and give them step-grand-babies. Their words, not mine. And today, as soon as they learn I've met someone, their neon-colored suits catch fire, and they run away.

The morning passes in a crazy rhythm, and by the time I'm freed up—thankfully sooner rather than later—it's nearly noon. But without even going inside, I know. I know she's gone because the pull isn't there.

Her piece of the rainbow is missing.

Fine, Wildflower, I'll chase you down. And when I catch you, there will be no more leaving...

Jacob: **I am not okay...**

Alec: **If this is you telling me you're not coming to work today, I'm not accepting it.**

Jacob: **I am not okay...**

Alec: **You said that already, yet I'm still not giving you an out from your tattoo appointments today.**

Jacob: **I am not okay...**

Alec: **Jesus, fine, what happened?**

Jacob: **I think I met my future wife last night.**

Alec: **Um...**

Alec: **In your dream?**

Jacob: **In my bed.**

Alec: **Get your ass to You Know You Want It, I need to hear this.**

Jacob: **I am not okay...**

Alec: **I don't think much will change if you keep repeating it. But does me saying a fresh copy of your favorite magazine came in makes it better?**

Jacob: **Fashion Linc?**

Alec: **Yep, along with a heartwarming note from Landon. I still don't understand how you managed to have a magazine-owning billionaire as your friend.**

Jacob: **Excuse me? Have you met me? I'm amazing, who wouldn't want to be my friend?**

Alec: **I'm going to guess that future wife of yours.**

Jacob: **Damn it, you had to ruin it for me, didn't you?**

# 5

# Joy

*"Love takes off the masks we fear we cannot live without and know we cannot live within." — James Baldwin.*

Something really warm heats up my cheek, making me squirm and try to escape whatever is trying to wake me up from the best night of my life. I'm on a cloud. It's green like fresh moss and smells heavenly. Like a forest after the fresh rain, mixed with salty ocean air. It's too warm and too springy for Chicago, isn't it? And just like that, my eyes fly open as I rush to sit up, only to hit my forehead right smack on the ceiling above—or rather, next to—my head.

Tiny house.

I'm in a tiny house where everything is cramped, and I keep hitting myself on the walls. The house that has more natural light flooding in through the walls than the actual walls themselves. The one with a tiny kitchen in the bottom, a small couch on which I had a gazillion orgasms last night and didn't even notice the size of it.

I'm in a tiny house that belongs to the sexiest weirdo I've ever met and who is nowhere to be found. Thank God.

I'm alone in his bed, feeling more sore than I have in all my life. I'm not particularly athletic, and the gymnastics this guy had me do last night are going into my personal Guinness World Records. Because it was that good.

So good I'm embarrassed to admit I was looking for a morning "workout."

Maybe I need to practice more one-night stands? Only I highly doubt I'll ever find anyone even close to my Viking.

*My Viking*...one hot night, and Joy lost her mind. Great.

I sigh and stretch—as much as it's possible here—and when my eyes finally adjust to the new shining day, I find a little note on a bright yellow paper lying on the pillow next to mine.

**Good morning, Boo,**
**I had to go to work early this morning. Please feel free to help yourself with anything you need here.**
**I'll be back soon.**
**My number 831-303-3131**
**Your future husband,**
**Jacob**

I scoff at the audacity of this man, but I'm also smiling like an idiot. Yeah, I am smiling. I'll work on those wrinkles later. Even his number is weird. There is something about him I don't understand.

Well...a lot. There is a lot I don't understand about Jacob. The guy I met at the bar was silly and hot as hell, but the one I got to see in bed was a total controlling beast, ravaging my body mercilessly, and then he went back to the weirdo I first met.

And let's not forget this house.

Yeah, Jacob is…is something else.

I've never considered the life I have to be unfulfilled, boring, or empty. But waking up alone in his bed, suddenly I'm questioning everything because the way he made me feel last night—from the bar through our sex marathon and ending with sleeping in his arm—well, I've never felt that before.

I'm not even sure *what* I'm feeling.

Satisfaction?

Pleasure?

Exhaustion?

Companionship?

Understanding?

…Affection?

Whatever it is, it's time to throw it off the cliff and go back to the comfort I know. *To be in the know.* To be sure of what I have.

To be alone…

I thought I would get murdered by a weirdo in this town; instead, I got wrecked by one.

I rush to put my clothes back on, which proves to be slightly difficult since they are nowhere to be found.

And I mean that literally! My pants and blouse are gone, and trust me, I've looked everywhere in this matchbox of a house, running around naked like a lunatic.

Jesus, if someone from my work could see me now, they would frame it for eternity. Doctor Joy Levine is naked in a tiny house in the middle of nowhere. Which is another question on its own. Just how the hell am I supposed to get to my car? I don't even know which way to go.

But wait, it gets better because my phone is dead freaking turkey out here with no service, and I am contemplating going up to that tree out there and asking for directions.

Yes, I've gone mad. I know.

*Breathe, Joy. In and out.*

But seriously, where the hell are my pants? And no, I'm not looking for my bra; I accepted its eminent death last night.

You ask why am I rushing to leave and not waiting for Jacob to show me a way out of the woods? Well, the answer is quite simple.

I cannot, absolutely *cannot* see that man again. He does things to me. Things I don't want him to do, things that need to stop happening.

Things like heart skipping beats, sane thoughts falling to the ground, alien smiles popping up on my face, those damn hussies—aka, butterflies—messing up my insides and hope building up.

The last one is the worst of them. Hope is a deadly weapon, and I'm not talking about my sister. Although that girl is nuclear to my life. If she'd met Jacob, she would probably have stolen him from me, too. Just like she did Brian.

Fucking hell...

A, Jacob is not yours, Joy.

B, I thought you had let go of that hurt a long time ago.

Clearly, someone was lying. Whether it was my consciousness or my heart, I haven't decided yet.

But the point stands. I'm never good enough, and allowing any kind of hope to swirl around in my head won't end pretty. So, getting the hell out of here is essential to my life.

It was one hot, mind-blowing, fantastic night of my life. The end.

After another five minutes of pointless looking, I find out that Jacob is a health nut, has zero coffee in his house—seriously, what kind of monster doesn't have coffee?—he uses natural deodorant, and he is a psycho. I knew he was too good to be true because who in their right mind has so many rubber ducky-themed things? Yep, he is insane.

Oh, and also, my clothes apparently took a morning stroll without me.

Fantastic.

Rubber ducky clothing, it is.

I quickly pull on one of his T-shirts, completely ignoring the shiver running up my body at the touch of the soft material and the smell surrounding me. Nope, I'm not noticing that woodsy scent at all. Nope, it doesn't make me want to climb walls, not one bit. And nope, I will absolutely not sleep in this shirt for the rest of my life, never washing it so his smell stays where it is.

*Seeeeee*, things. He's doing things to me. Or maybe it's the lack of caffeine in my body. Yeah, let's blame it on that.

I groan, grab a pair of his swimming shorts, because those are the only things that have a string I can pull, make sure my pantyless ass doesn't show itself to the rest of Loverly, and get the hell out the door. But stop immediately as my lungs fill with fresh air.

Fresh, ocean air. Wow. I take another lungful of this ecstasy. A little cold, a little salty, a little perfect.

I need to go, but my feet won't move as my eyes take in the scenery in front of me. Last night, I arrived late and wasn't able to see the absolutely stunning view below.

Jacob's house is apparently nestled inside the woods, but right on the cliff at the same time, and only a few steps away from his front door, I can see the town down below.

Well, that makes it easier to find my way back, but I'm still not moving, mesmerized by nature around me. The vast, dark ocean with raging waves crashing against the rocks and caves scattered around the sandy shore. The huge, tall, imposing cave stands guard over its town. The colorful buildings of the said town. And behind me, the green, deep forests, climbing up the mountains around us.

How is this place real? How can two different worlds exist together in perfect cohabitation? A harmony.

As my head swings around to take it all in, I zoom in on the house itself, which I didn't really see from the outside until now. How could I miss it all last night is still beyond me, but I guess a hot weirdo Viking can do that to a horny girl.

The front is covered by actual walls, and that is why I hadn't seen the ocean before since I was looking out the back wall, which is all glass and faces the green trees.

The house is definitely tiny. Like a minuscule version of a beach cottage. He does have a fairly large porch with chairs and a table sitting out front, as well as a small fire pit, though.

Suddenly, my brain decides to come up with a small trailer or more of a teaser of what a night looks like here with a soft blanket—or his arms—around me and warm flames flickering around us. The touches and kisses we would share. The sex we could have right in the open under the shining stars since there is absolutely no one around here. And in the morning? In the morning, I'd sit right at the same spot with a scorching hot coffee in my hands and a book on my lap, reading to a heavenly view.

Oh hell...here it is again.

*The things.*

The worst ones.

How do I get my brain to delete the last few thoughts it had? Is that a thing?

I need to look into it as soon as I get back home.

Shaking my head to dislodge those sickening ideas, I finish looking around.

There are at least three surfboards stacked against the frame, and it doesn't surprise me one bit that Jacob surfs.

It actually makes perfect sense. And also solidifies how different we are. The only thing we seem to have in common is great chemistry. That's all.

And I've already had enough of physical-only relationships in my life, so spotting the gravelly road, I take off. Most likely looking like a complete idiot with my hair wild and everywhere, wearing a man's t-shirt and bright yellow swim trunks but with heels on my feet and clutching my Coach bag.

Let us pray that residents of Loverly Cave enjoy sleeping in, and that nine AM is too early for them to stroll around.

Of course, it's not. They are all up and watch me flee the cliff like the most fascinating show.

And I do mean all. Why are there so many people in the square? Do they have some kind of town meeting today? It would be just my luck to stumble upon them today of all days. They all keep smiling at me.

Why are they smiling? It's unnatural to smile so much. No one could be that happy, but then again, they could be smiling because I look like a real-life clown. A very convincing impersonation.

It takes two, no, three grueling hours for me to hike downhill in my heels until I reach the first civilization. Okay, maybe civilization is a bit of a stretch here, seeing as this is pretty much a fancier village, but whatever.

And fine, it was more like fifteen minutes, but the point stands—it was horrible. Not only am I not athletic, but I am also extremely sore from last night, and I literally needed to hold my vagina with my hand to stop the heavy feeling in there. What is that anyway? Why does it feel so weird? And to add to my misery, my phone refuses to work in this town.

Plain and simple. I have no service. Not on that damn cliff and tiny house, nor down here in the valley, so I'm pretty sure I'm lost at this point without my Apple Maps.

This town is literally two by two, and I managed to get lost in it. It also doesn't help that all these buildings are blindingly bright and colorful, and no, I don't mean they have pretty flowers hanging off the windowsills. Nope.

I mean, the whole thing is painted either pink, yellow, green, blue, or any other color imaginable. I think I'm getting dizzy.

Just when I'm about to scream and drop to the ground in despair, I catch sight of my rental and run towards it.

Thank God. I was a second away from a mental breakdown, and I don't do breakdowns of any kind. Locking myself quickly in my car, I drop my head to the wheel and take a few deep breaths.

This has all been too much for my very orderly and well-organized life, and I need a minute—no, hours—to calm down before I face my parents.

I also need to change and get some damn coffee into my system.

But before I even started the car, my phone decides to start working now. Now!

Useless piece of garbage. Where were you an hour ago when I needed to call an Uber, huh?

I pick up my phone and see Zoe's name flashing.

"Jesus Christ! Did you get abducted? I've been calling you nonstop!" My assistant slash new best friend, who clearly feels extra familiar with me, yells at me, and I have to pull my phone away from my ear.

"No abduction, just stuck in the weirdest town on planet Earth where apparently my phone has a mind of its own and works when it pleases."

"Well, good for you to be all nice and cozy over there," she snaps at me.

"Okay, Miss Joy, one-point-oh. Who pissed on your cadaver this morning?" I ask, surprised because Zoe doesn't ever raise her voice or get mad. It's always me who's the bitch of the lab. She exhales loudly and, I think, sniffs. "Zoe? What's wrong?" I don't have many people I care about anymore, but this girl has made it onto the list.

"The shit has officially met the fan over here."

"Zoe, time is expensive. Get to the point. I'm not into suspense."

"There was a formal complaint filed against Justin for sexual harassment." I swear my whole life freezes at this moment. Everyone stops walking, the ocean stops moving, the air sizes, and my lungs collapse.

"What?" It's barely a whisper.

"Yeah, apparently you and I, and, oh, his *wife* weren't the only women in his life. Seriously, how did his dick not fall off?"

"Zoe, I need you to focus. We can discuss Justin's ugly dick later."

"Promise?"

"Yes, I swear on my favorite scalpel. Now, explain."

"I don't know much. It's mostly rumors at this point; you know how that family is. Reputation is everything, so I'm assuming they are trying to snuff it out as soon as possible. But I overheard a few students discussing it this morning in the lab." Zoe goes quiet for a few seconds. "She's a young student. Very young, from what I gather."

"Oh, fuck..." I drag my hand down my face, rubbing a bit too hard as if I can somehow rip all this news off myself.

"Yeah."

"This is not good. So not good."

"Joy?"

"Yeah?"

"What's going to happen to us now? Are they going to find out we were with him, too? Jesus, this is so embarrassing. I can't stand staying here."

"Stop. Breathe. No one is going to find out anything. I think. I hope. Like you said, they will try to bury the story as soon as possible, and I don't think anything will come off of it, but keep your ears sharp, and I'll call some other doctors to see if they heard anything. Okay?"

"Yeah, yeah, okay. But if anything, I'll be coming out to hide with you. Just so you know." Her comment sparks a warm feeling in my chest. Zoe is my friend, and she wants to stay close.

"No problem. Come check out the sexy weirdos anytime."

"Sexy?"

Oh shit, I let that one slip, haven't I?

"Um, yeah, well, no. Well, I don't know. I've only seen one."

"Dr. Levine? What are you not telling me?" Her voice turns coy as if she knows what I've been doing this morning, and since she is pretty much the only person I can talk to, I end up spilling the whole story to her, from the plane ride of hell to the morning hike in heels.

I'm not one to share. Ever. But Zoe is different. Zoe, I can trust. That girl has been through the same smelly crap as I have.

"Oh my God. Please tell me you're seeing him again! Also, I need pictures! Let me live vicariously through you since I've decided to swear off men at the moment."

"No and no and no again."

"That's a lot of no's." She chuckles. "What's that last one for?"

"For you swearing off men. Don't let one horrible experience dictate your life."

She scoffs. "You're the one to talk."

"Yes, I am. I had two strikes. I win."

"I don't like this competition."

"I don't either. But it is what it is. Now, go finish the reports and send updates about our insatiable kitten—aka Justin—over here."

Zoe bursts out laughing.

"Will do, boss, and I am still expecting that picture. Also, please do us all a favor and fuck him as much as you can."

I go to tell her off, but she quickly says bye and hangs up.

No can do, my dear newfound friend. No, I can't do that. I wish it would be as simple as I try to play it off. I wish it was really the one-night stand I had set out to have with him. But somewhere during that night in his tiny house, we stopped being strangers, and he became the most dangerous creature in my life.

Because if I see him again...I might not be strong enough to walk away a second time.

# 6

## *Joy*

*"I love you no matter what you do, but do you have to do so much of it?"* — *Jean Illsley Clarke.*

I've never felt more disorganized in my life. My head is all over the place, and by the time I make it to my parent's house late in the afternoon, I am one big ball of nerves. The six hours I took to calm and collect myself did absolutely nothing for me. I even left the town as a whole and drove two hours to Santa Cruz just to unwind and find coffee, but nope.

My mind is still going hard at it with everything that has been dropped into my life this past week. Justin's lies, Dad's cancer, Jacob's hot sex, a new fear of what could pop up with the allegations that were filed against my ex. And now I can add seeing a very familiar, very old, beaten-up Toyota with fading red paint, parked in front of the house I am trying to get to.

My heart rate picks up, and my palms sweat.

*Breathe, Joy. In and out.*

There is no way that could be Hope. There is no way my younger sister could be here right now, and even if she were here, I highly doubt she'd still be driving her teenage car, the one our parents bought her as a gift when she got her license at sixteen years old.

No, someone on this Positive Street just has a taste for old junk. Yes, that is the name of the street my parents live on. What? Are you surprised? I'm not. I am grateful it's not something worse like Holly-Jolly Drive or Unicorn Avenue.

With another shake of my head, I get out of the car, looking at a house that almost gives me whiplash. How could my parents replicate our place from Ohio almost to a tee over here is beyond me, but I won't lie and say it doesn't bring tears to my eyes.

Those years I spent at home were happy, carefree times, with crazy Sunday dinners, annual RV trips, and so much love. Those were the years when I had a family, and now, looking at this small, white shiplap house with bright blue trim and the front door in a vomit-yellow color, I can barely hold myself together. The colorful theme of this town has rubbed itself off here as well with the million tiny, colorful flowers my mother planted everywhere. And when the slight breeze passes through, I hear the silly wind chimes greeting me.

My mom and her wind chimes. She always had them in the front and back yards, driving Daddy mad.

I don't cry. I won't cry. I am just exhausted and possibly still drunk off of all the orgasms I had last night.

I step on the path laid out in natural-colored stepping-stones mixed with gravel and close in on the door. Only when I get closer do I take a step back.

A voice. There is a voice I haven't heard in over ten years. I look at the old car parked by mine and back to the door.

*What has happened to you, Po? How come you are still driving that piece of shit?*

No, none of it matters. Her life doesn't matter to me anymore. Sure, she is here for Dad, and I will deal with it. We are adults and won't even have to see each other all that much. Right? We can be civil.

Without thinking much longer, I pushed inside and lay eyes on my little sister. A sister who looks like she is about to pee her freaking pants, and her identical to mine brown eyes widen in fear. Jesus, it's like she expects me to slash through her with a knife, and that's what makes me angry.

Not seeing her again after so long, not even the fact that she tore my life apart ten years ago. No, I am hurt by her reaction *now*. My jaw clenches in an effort to stop myself from those pointless and unnecessary tears. She was my best friend, and now she acts as if I am the enemy here.

Fucking phenomenal. But if she wants to play the victim here, then so be it. Ignoring her completely, I call out to the two people I came to see. "Mom, Dad." My tone is hard and wary.

"Joy, honey." Mom smiles wide at me and runs up, embracing me in one of her mommy hugs. The ones that made everything better no matter how old I was. The ones I have missed and didn't know I needed until now. It's the hug that threatens to undo me right here and now. "You made it!" she adds, patting my cheek.

"Of course, I made it!" I untangle myself from her warm embrace because a second longer, and there will be no going back. I'm already too raw. My armor is too beat up, and I need to amp up the security gates, so I return my attention to my father, who is looking between all of us and shakes his head. "Dad, how are you feeling? Tell me everything. What is your diagnosis exactly? Because mom was super vague over the phone. I spoke to the oncologists at my university, and they are willing to consult you; I just need to send them your patient file."

I try to jam as many questions as I can in one breath. I need to know. I need to know my Daddy is okay. I can't lose him or Mom. They are all I have left.

Well, I guess I have Zoe now, too. At least something good came out of my broken relationship, but that's beside the point right now.

I am looking expectantly at my parents but noticing only a slight flinch and a grimace on my mom's face and a total amusement on my dad's.

"Is anyone going to answer me?" I press because this game of mute is really not my thing right *now*. Realizing I only have one option left, I turn to Hope and ask her. "Do you know anything?"

She gulps, shakes her head, and answers me without really looking into my eyes. "No, I just got here a minute before you did."

I suck in a sharp breath, not catching myself fast enough. I hate to give away what I am feeling, but hearing her voice is like a gut punch. The last time I heard it she was getting into that very same car that is parked out front with my boyfriend in the passenger's seat and said, "Bye, Joy."

Despite it being so long ago, I remember every detail vividly. I remember every syllable and face expression. I remember Brian's empty eyes and the voice of doubt rising inside my head.

If you want to hear that story, head over to Hope. I have no intentions of revisiting a very much closed door. I tossed that key into Lake Michigan a while back.

Hope was always beautiful with her long chestnut hair and dark brown magnetic eyes. She was always slim—at least two sizes slimmer than me—and held every boy's attention in Flitzburg. So, when I saw my own boyfriend with her, all I felt was that very familiar feeling of not being good enough.

Not slim enough. Not pretty enough. Not ready enough to change the course of my whole life and run away with a boy. Yes, Brian offered to go with him, before he took Hope with himself, but I was set on going to medical school and had no plans of traveling across the country as he tried to make a name for himself on the big stage. I wanted to, but I couldn't.

I have worked through my issues—well, most of them—over the years, and at thirty-one, I love my curvy body, I value my brain over my face, and I was ready to start a family with the one I thought I loved...but he reminded me I am not good enough for *that*.

But Hope? This new Hope? This new voice? It's not her. It's so small. So uncertain. So...broken... It's like she has worked through something as well, but I don't think she was walking in the right direction.

What the hell is going on? That protective older sister in me wakes up from her decade-long sleep and demands answers, but I won't voice them. I can't. I'm too raw, and at this point, no one knows what can come out of my mouth.

*Just remember last night...*

Yeah, no.

When the silence stretches some more between all of us, Dad speaks up, breaking the spell between me and Hope. "Jenn, you better start talking." He gives her his signature "I told you so" look, and she squirms under his warning, wiggling her nose from side to side and picking up the plate with fresh, warm cookies. Almost as if she is using it as her shield.

Okay...

I haven't seen them since my graduation from med school. They came out to be there for me and wore their proud smiles as I walked across the stage in my cap and gown with a million extra cords around my neck for all the achievements I'd made throughout my school years. But these two are quite a pair and my forever role models. They fell in love in high school, and afterward, Dad never left Mom's side. They know everything about each other, and what's most important, they are a team. A real, rock-solid team. A perfect pair where Dad is the calm and collected one, and Mom is dramatic and expressive. He is her gentle giant in his big, burly body, and she is his mischievous pixie who is still very much in shape after all these years.

Finally, Mom breaks her silence.

"So, you see...I might've exaggerated a few things here and there," she says slowly, not making eye contact with us.

Every alarm I have in my head is starting to go off, and my back snaps upright with my hard gaze narrowing on her. "Mother. What exactly did you exaggerate?"

Now I understand why she has those cookies clutched tight in her hands as she squirms some more.

A perfect shield. The little woman with graying hair knows it's our weakness.

"I might've blown your father's illness a tiny little bit out of proportion."

Dad humphs and rolls his eyes at her statement.

"Dad, do you have cancer or not?" I ask, my anger flaring up once again. So help me, God, if he says no right now.

"Nope," Dad says easily, and I literally hear my and Hope's jaws falling to the ground with a loud thud.

"Mom!" we both yell out in outrage and share a look between each other. The one we used to have all the time when we were kids. The one that means, "Can you believe this crap?" but I quickly look away. I have too much to deal with right now to get lost in pointless memories.

I turn back to Mom, shake my head, throw my hands up, and scream, "Unbelievable. Un-fucking-believable."

"Why would you lie about this?" Hope asks with an almost heartbroken expression on her face. That girl always wore her feelings on her sleeve. Not as much as our youngest sister, Grace, but Grace is a wild card. She can play the room, while Hope has absolutely no poker face.

"I told you this will blow up in your face," Dad says point blank to Mom, who is now partially hiding behind the couch, still clutching those damn cookies.

"Girls, girls, stop. Daddy does have issues, and you never know when something more severe could come up. Isn't it better to be around, just in case?"

"I have mild arthritis, Jenn. I'm not dying from it, as far as I know."

I don't know whether I should laugh, cry, yell, or beat someone up right now.

"Mom, have you lost your mind?" I asked her loudly, yelling, it is.

"Oh my God, Mom, that is so not okay," Hope adds, with throwing her head back. And no, none of this is okay. None.

Oh, Jesus Christ. I could have avoided sulfur poisoning on that stupid airplane ride here. Yes, I will focus on the sulfur poisoning from those rotten eggs because I am not ready to focus on last night's events that could have never happened if I hadn't come to Loverly.

I am not ready to admit how that makes me feel.

So, once again, I settle on yelling. "It's this stupid town, isn't it? Is this town some kind of a cult? Do they have you sit in circles, smoking weed and creating elaborate lies to get your unsuspecting daughters here?"

"Told you." Dad kicks back in his recliner, watching the free show we are putting on for him. The only thing that could make this whole scene even more dramatic is our youngest sister.

"Oh, stop it, Rick. I missed our daughters, didn't you? Plus, we need some fresh blood in this town. The testosterone levels are too high. And no, Loverly is perfectly normal."

I pinch the bridge of my nose in an effort to rein in the fury.

Newsflash: It's not working.

"Please don't tell me you made me leave my job at the most prestigious university in the country, working as one of the highest-paid pathologists with my own lab, research team, and students to come to this God-forsaken hippy town to entertain the horny males who seem to be stuck in their teenager stage, despite being the physical age of thirty." The words slip out of my mouth uncontrollably because I fucking did it.

I played into her hand without knowing and did entertain the horny male population. Fine, one horny male with a teenage brain. And just like that, fear grips me.

"I am so not staying here," I add quickly, pointing the finger at Mom.

"Oh, honey, you will have to pay all these taxes if you sell right after you bought the house."

"Mother!"

"Nooo," Hope groans.

"Let me guess, you bought a house here too?" I asked her, already knowing the answer, because this is our mother we are talking about.

The woman doesn't half-ass anything.

"Yeah, this morning. I'm assuming you did as well," she says, confirming my assumptions. Fucking great.

"Yep. Paid in full. One lovely Nina Colson had only one available cottage for sale."

"Same," she blurs out, and I shoot her a confused look. She drives a piece of shit on the wheels, which is almost as old as her, but she had enough money to buy a house?

"You've thought of everything, haven't you?" Hope asks Mom and breaks my train of thought.

"And look how wonderful that turned out." Mom smiles overly eagerly at us. "You needed to get away after that breakup, and what better place to heal than here?" she says to Hope, and that statement does nothing but fuel my need to know what that piece of shit did to my little sister.

And just like that, I have to bite down on a groan, because look at me. Life teaches me nothing, and here I am, ready to lay myself down for her as if nothing had happened before. As if she didn't crush my heart and run over it with her car without ever apologizing or even explaining herself.

I am about to start with all those questions that are burning me from the inside out when Mom douses me in a bucket of ice-cold water.

"Did you, by any chance, run into Alec or Jacob on your way here? Such lovely boys." She muses dreamily, and I have to blink a few times to get my nerves under control, but I see a wicked glint in one of her eyes. The one that is aimed at me, and now I am the one squirming.

Fucking hell. I don't do squirming, yet here we are. And that glint? That's the most dangerous thing you can ever see. Because it can only mean one thing.

She knows. She freaking knows, and now I am a dead woman walking.

"I did, in fact, run into both of them," Hope answers without realizing what kind of turmoil is raging inside of me, and her admission only adds fresh fuel to my fire.

Of course, she ran into him. Of-fucking-course we found the same exact guy in this town. I refuse to swallow the ugly lump now stuck in my throat at the thought of her with him. With my Jacob.

Not mine. Never mine. It was a one-night stand, and once I leave tomorrow, she can have him. She can have yet another one of my boys.

"You did?" Mom asks her, looking as if Hope just told her she is pregnant with triplets.

Hell, maybe she is. Maybe she and Jacob shared a wild morning or lunch together, and now his inhuman dick inseminated her with his inhuman Viking sperm, and she will have his blonde Viking babies.

"What did you think? Who do you like better? Oh, I'm so excited right now. Oh, we should invite them over for dinner, and I also heard Luke is in town!" Wait, what? What does she mean, *them*? The only name I heard was Jacob's, and now I guess this Luke guy, whoever he is. But was there someone else I missed?

She shoots me another look, this time less subtle, confirming she does indeed know where I spent last night, and I need to change the subject as soon as possible before all my dirty laundry is aired for perfect Hope to see. "Mother, calm down your horses for a second. This is not about boys. This is about you lying to us to get us to come here."

"Oh, poopie crap. I did what I had to with such stubborn daughters. God only knows why I deserved it." Yeah, of course, we are the issue here, and I am about to get into it with her when the free show for Dad, who is rocking lightly in his chair with his hands clasped on his small belly, does get better.

A fancy, sleek, black Rolls-Royce pulls up to the house, parking crookedly next to my Lexus, and we all watch stupefied through the huge front window as a tiny figure wearing an all-white, extremely puffy white wedding dress, looking like a marshmallow on the Fourth of July is rushing out of the said car.

The marshmallow that holds an uncanny resemblance to my little bitty sister, Grace. She hikes up her monstrosity of a dress, showing off her sparkly high heels with a bow on top, and runs to the front door with her ridiculous, cathedral-length veil trailing behind her.

And for God knows what reason, still holding her equally monstrous bouquet of crisp, white roses as if her life depended on it.

Well, that's what I call an entrance, and I save it for the baby of the family to render everyone freaking speechless. I don't think either one of us has moved a millimeter apart from Dad abandoning his recliner to get a better look out the window.

Within a few seconds, Grace breaks in through the front door, stumbling with all that puff around her and greets us as if nothing is wrong and we have met up for one of those Sunday dinners ten years ago.

"Um, hi, everyone...I guess."

I have to hand it to her; she at least has the decency to look away from our stunned faces and opened mouths.

Confront my sisters or parents? Sisters or parents? Yep, parents, it is. I eye Grace for one more minute, take a deep, much-needed breath, and point my finger at the runaway marshmallow. "We will get back to this. For now, Mom, Dad, what the hell?"

My Dad seems to be in some sort of shock, and hell, I don't blame him, but my words seem to bring him back. "Girls, I told you, I had nothing to do with this!"

"Way to be a team, Rick." Mom sends a death glare at him. "Go ahead, throw me under the bus. Let the hungry wolves tear down your wife."

"Too dramatic, darling." He doesn't even bat an eye at her dramatics, being way too familiar with all her lines for decades now. How he put up with her is beyond me, but I guess they call it love.

A bunch of weirdos.

"What's going on? Dad, are you okay?" Grace looks from us to Mom and Dad, confused.

"Jesus, please tell me Mother didn't ruin your wedding with her scheming. And by the way, a wedding? Really, Gracie bear?" Dad sounds offended and borderline pissed. Again, can't say I blame him at all. And although I understand why Hope and I didn't make the guest list—even though it still stings a bit—Mom and Dad should have been invited.

I have a thousand questions for these two, but I'm not sure I will be asking them. We all chose to live this way, and I am not sure my beaten-up armor can take any more hits if they refuse me right now.

Gracie scrunches up her nose, which she only does when she feels ashamed of her behavior. As she should.

"If it makes anyone feel better, I didn't go through with it," she answers with a fake smile and directs her gaze back to the hardwood floors down below. That damn bouquet is still in her hands, and I am just itching to come up and slap it out of her hand.

What kind of man was she going to marry if she ended up running away from the altar? What the hell happened to my sisters?

Screw it, armor be damned, I need to know, but not just yet. We have more pressing matters at the moment.

"One question," I say to Grace. "Did you also buy a house here?"

"What do you mean 'also?'" Grace furrows her eyebrows. "I did buy a house. The only cottage that is available on the beach. Lovely Mrs. Colson sold it to me for a steal." Our youngest sister looks so proud and excited I almost feel bad for ruining it for her. Almost. Because she didn't feel bad about ruining my life.

"Did you just say a cottage on a beach?" Hope asks naively, thinking it was only me and her who got roped into Mother's elaborate schemes, and I almost scoff.

I can't see Grace's face as she turns to Hope, but whatever Po sees makes her flinch.

"Yeah," Grace answers.

"I bought a cottage on a beach," Hope says, pointing a finger to herself.

"So did I," I add, holding back the snarky comments I wish to say right now. Instead, I send another scolding look at Mom. "Mastermind. Evil, scheming mastermind."

"I'll take that as a compliment," Mom tells me with pride, tilting her chin a little higher.

"Mother, you realize how bad this is? You need to go pray in every church there is so that God doesn't punish you for those lies. To even think about saying something like that out loud!" Hope, being the hopeful little creature she is, thinking our mother feels even an ounce of remorse.

Hilarious.

# MEET MY WIFE

"What do you mean, lie?" Grace asks Hope, more confusion laced in her tone.

While I am mentally counting to ten a few hundred times, Hope catches up with our youngest sister on all the lies. Grace's blue eyes, which she inherited from dad, and I was always jealous of, grow larger as her face paler until she slumps down to the floor in her puffy dress, using it as a cushion.

"I ran away from my own five-hundred-thousand-dollar wedding to be here for Dad because I thought he was dying." She covers her face with her hands.

"Poopie crap, honey. You ran away because that Dickerson asshole of a fiancé you had was no good for you. Thank God I called and interfered before it was too late," Mom says casually. And by the look on Grace's face, she didn't expect Mom to know it.

"How do you know about this? How do you know about Peter?" Point in case. Please, call me the all-powerful, all-knowing J.

But then, Mom turns to me, and I feel ten-years-old all over again. "And you, you have absolutely no life in that lab of yours. Look at you, in your thirties, stunning and slowly dying a lonely death because that professor you are in love with is not available."

What. The. Fuck?

Scratch the previous statement. You can call my mom the all-powerful, all-knowing J. I feel the strong pounding growing in my head, all the excitement finally catching up with my body.

"I'm not—" I start to protest, but Mom is not done with us yet, and now it's Hope's turn.

"And you finally opened up your eyes and saw Brian for who he really was. A cheater, a scumbag, and not worthy even of a pinky of any of my daughters." She humphs. "Hiding you away like you are some kind of a slave or a dirty secret. Not on my watch. Not anymore."

I am not sure if I want to know how she knows all that, but I am ready to bow down at her accurate description of my—and I guess, now Hope's—ex.

Knowing we all have questions, she simply says, "A mother always keeps tabs on all her children. Now, go unpack those cars of yours, bring your stuff into the spare bedroom, and come help me make dinner."

And just like that, I am thrown a decade back to the time when we were one happy family, cooking dinners together and laughing at all the silly things.

"Oh." Mom suddenly stops and says, "And welcome to Loverly Cave Town."

# 7
# *Hope*

What am I supposed to do? Where should I go?

I want to stay, but what if I don't win the bet?
What if he penetrates my newly formed rules?
And my sisters? How can I ever look them both in the eye?

# 8
# *Grace*

I knew my life was going up in flames as soon as my eyes landed on him, so I ran away, but fate is a manipulative asshole...

He is here...

# 9

# *Joy*

*"There must be millions of people all over the world who never get any love letters. I could be their leader." — Charles M. Schulz.*

Can I press the rewind button? Is there a way to go back a few days? No, scratch that, three years back, or maybe even ten...?

Mom retreated to the backyard and not-too-subtly pulled Dad along with her, leaving the three of us in the funky living room. I hadn't even really gotten to look around when I first walked in, but now I spot all the family photos crowding the walls and the large, picturesque windows looking out back to the mountains. The same mountains I looked at from the window of Jacob's tiny house.

There is a comfortable-looking but just as ugly as our old cat back in Flitzburg, orange tweed couch, and Dad's recliner in the same shade standing in the middle. The floors are a warm, natural oak wood, and overall, the space feels welcoming. Of course, it does.

Unfortunately, the same cannot be said about the three of us. What do I say? Do I even want to say anything? Is it going to change anything? Probably not, so why waste my own energy?

"Are you guys staying here?" Grace ends up being the brave one and speaks up to us, but I scoff right away at her question.

"No fucking way. I'll rent out the house I bought until I can sell it, and I'm out of here. I can't believe I dropped my whole life for a lie." What I leave out is that it seems to be an ongoing theme for me.

The lies. The deceptions. The fake stories. I shake my head one more time, firmly set on leaving as soon as I can find some renters, and look to Hope, waiting for her answer.

"I'm staying," Hope says with confidence and what seems to be some kind of internal resolution. Of course, she will stay. If there is a chance she has met Jacob, I can't blame her for wanting to give him a try.

I can't, but I will. I let the irrational jealousy place me in a deadly grip and cloud my vision with green, stinky smoke while Grace looks up to Hope as if she is an angel walking on water.

"You are?" Grace asks, surprised. "Is running away not your motto anymore?"

I almost snort. That's more like it. That is the Gracie I remember, and I expected Hope to fire off a snarky comment back, yet she silently drops to the ground next to Grace and looks so damn broken, it's hard to remember why I' was mad at her in the first place.

"I have nowhere else to run to," Hope says, biting her lips nervously. "I'm staying. Are you?"

"I think I'll stay too. I kind of burned the bridge in New York in an epic way." She smiles softly, pointing to her dress.

"Nowhere to run to either." And we are back to the angels walking on water.

Jesus, I need to get away from all this goo threatening to undo me. I cannot be undone. I like my life and myself as I am.

Strong. Confident. Impenetrable.

"This is all very cute and sickeningly sweet—I think I might throw up—so I'll leave you to it." Without another glance at my two sisters, who seem to be hitting it off again, I stride out of the house. I'm not like them, and I never have been.

I'm not carefree and easygoing. I don't forgive easily. And I definitely don't forget. Yet, I'm not sure why I'm so pissed right now because I did forgive Hope and Grace. It has been long enough for me to move forward.

*You know exactly why you are angry right now, Joy.* History is repeating itself, and I don't wish to stick around watching it unfold. Again.

I like to think I am so strong that nothing can phase me; nothing can puncture through my steel walls, yet here we are. One night with a complete stranger who isn't even my type has me acting like a jealous psycho.

No, it will be better for everyone if I am gone. They can all live happily ever after in Loverly Cave, and I will be rotting next to my corpses back in Chicago. Grabbing a few necessities out of my car, I come back inside to find my sisters chatting away and smiling at each other.

*Breathe, Joy. In and out.*

"Joy," Hope calls out to me, but I can't look her way. I can't look into her eyes and see the future she will have. My future. Once again stealing what was meant for me.

"J," Grace uses her gentle voice. The little shit knows the magic it holds on me and it always worked to get me to do anything she wanted and take the blame for her mistakes when our parents would inevitably find out about the broken plates. The ones Grace needed to grab for her dolls, but her little fingers couldn't hold onto them, so I told Mom it was me who broke them and had to wash the dishes for the next three days.

Or the chickens she set free because apparently, at night, the tooth fairy gifted her with animal mind-reading powers instead of a dollar, and the chickens told her they were sad in their coop, and I ended up running all over Flitzburg catching each one.

And let's not forget her first date on which she lost her virginity. I had to sit in the car waiting to pick her up, but somehow, the idiot teenager she was with kept her busy for a really long time, and we ended up coming home around midnight, for which I took the blame, saying I needed to see Brian.

So, the point is, I am not falling for those tricks anymore. Nope.

"I have zero desire to talk to either one of you," I tell them, planting myself on the neon couch with my laptop, but of course, they don't get the memo I'm trying to work in silence.

"Come on, we are sisters, and we are stuck together in this town for some time. Can we try to make things right?" And with that gentle voice again.

I lift my eyes up to her, wearing my impassive mask, and ask something I've wondered about my whole life. "How does it feel to live in a realm where unicorn crap tastes like strawberry ice cream?"

I make a mistake glancing at Hope, who is barely containing her laugh, and I feel my own lips pull up to a tiny twitch. Stop. No smiling.

"Oh, you are so hilarious, Miss Joyless." Grace folds her arms and pouts like the baby she is.

It was cute when she was five, not so much when she's twenty-seven.

"And it tastes delicious, if you want to know."

"Good for you," I say without looking her way, pretending my empty screen is the most fascinating thing in the world.

"Do you want a piece?"

"And take a chance to become as insufferable as you? No thanks."

"Joy, that was mean," Hope chastises me quickly, and I quirk an eyebrow at her.

"You want to talk about mean, Hope?" She flinches at my delivery, but somehow, with that one phrase, she has undone my composure, and I end up spilling it all out. The words I craved to say all those years ago.

"Mean is dating your sister's boyfriend behind her back. Mean is running away with the said boyfriend. Mean is breaking someone's heart and stomping all over it. Mean is leaving me to deal with the mess you left behind while you enjoy the glim and glam of your new celebrity lifestyle."

"Joy," Grace hisses, the gentleness long gone as she shoots me a death glare.

Yeah, *I am* the bad guy here. Always.

"What? Am I saying something that's not true? Our sister didn't trade her boring, stuffy life with us for the glamourous one with that bastard and never turned back?"

Hope snaps her identical eyes to mine, and for the first time since seeing her, I get a glimpse of the old Hope. "None of what you said is true! None of it. You think I'm such a villain? That I stole your life from you? Well, let me fill you in on the life you missed out on. My blind love left me in shackles worse than those in prison. For the first five years, we lived in my old beat-up car. The same car you see parked out there. The same car Mom and Dad bought me. Yes, I'm so fancy and rich that I still drive it. I never got to go back to school. I don't have a degree or any work experience except being Brian's Dobby. You think when he finally made it things changed? Not in the slightest! He never made our relationship public because it could 'ruin' his image." She gives me the air quotes. "I was always in the shadows. Up until a day ago when I walked in on him fucking his new manager and yelling for me to get the hell out."

Oh hell, I am going to rip his balls off and dissect them on my table to see if there is an ounce of humanity in him after all.

"So, what I believe you want to say is "thank you" for saving you from my life. For having an amazing job at the best university or wherever it is you work at. You. Are. Welcome. Joy."

Suddenly, the air is thick and heavy. Tears are streaming down my sister's beautiful face as she allows us to see all those broken parts of her heart.

Why is life so cruel? Why did we have to go through all this pain? Why couldn't at least one of us be happy? And how could I possibly say thank you when I see what he has done to her...I would trade places with her instantly so she would never have to go through that heartbreak.

"But I am sorry for hurting you in the first place," Hope continues, her bravado gone, and she is back to small and broken. "I know you won't believe me, but I didn't know you guys were dating. Brian never told me. Yes, I refused to believe Grace when she brought it up, instead blaming her and calling her a liar. I found out after we were on the road already, and I saw the text messages between you guys."

Fine, I guess I could believe that story, since Brian and I never acted like a couple out in the wild in the first place, and I am pretty sure the rest of the town thought we were just friends. Well, at least that I only saw him as a friend since he was more than happy to go all out. But public affection was never my thing. It still isn't.

"Why didn't you come back home then? When did you find out?" Grace asks quietly.

"How could I? First of all, he fed my gullible brain some more fresh lies that I willingly believed, and even if I didn't, I was so ashamed of my behavior on that last day that I could never come back and face you guys. I decided to go all in and keep believing what I was shown instead of the truth." She sighs.

"I think part of me always knew Brian was a liar, but I turned that part off to protect myself until I could no longer keep my eyes closed. I was never as strong as Joy or as happy and positive as you. I wasn't the beautiful one out of the three or the smart one. So, when a boy like Brian took notice, I did everything to keep his attention, including shunning you all and living in a blissful layer of crapville."

"Oh, honey..." Well great, I guess it's a family meet-up with Mom back in here.

"Huh, fine. I guess you served your penance," is what I say instead of running up to her, wrapping my hands around her shoulders and crying alongside. And I watch as her heart break once again from my stupid words.

The words that aren't true, but I need to keep saying to protect my own heart.

"You know what, I'm out of here. I should have never come back." She jumps up and flees the house, but the marshmallow—also known as Gracie bear—is fast on her heels.

"Joy Levine!" Here it comes, the scolding. Seriously, what is it with this family and their use of tone on me. Why does it always work, too? "I know you are better than that. I know you don't hate your sisters, and I know, given the chance, you would take on all their burdens, so why won't you just let go and let them take on some of yours?"

*Breathe, Joy. In and out.*

This woman knows way too much and somehow sees inside my head, too. But she is right.

I don't want to live in this misery anymore. I have been alone for so damn long; wouldn't it be nice to have some company? I set my computer down and followed Grace and Hope outside, catching the end of their conversation.

"Please, I was always the smartest one out of the three. You two just never gave me a chance to prove it." Gracie rolls her eyes at Hope, and I am glad to see the stupid bouquet is finally on the ground.

"Aha, says the sister who ran away from her own wedding." They spin around fast to see me standing at the door with my arms crossed but a small smile tugging on my lips. In Joy speak, I am full-on laughing.

"Not that I care, but I am dying to know what the hell happened there." I gesture to her dress. "So, both of you, get in here. Oh, and Hope?" She looks up to me. "I forgive you."

Many might ask how could you forgive your sister so easily, so fast?

Trust me, there was nothing easy or fast about it. Nothing.

But years do heal things, and with each one, you realize how menial it all was. How stupid it was to keep a grudge with the two most important people in the world over a guy.

No guy is that special. None. I don't care what anyone says.

Did we go wrong about the whole situation? Hell yes, but what did you expect three teenagers to do? Be adults?

No matter what those romance novels say, we are not that mature at that age.

In a flash, Gracie has me and Hope in a tight embrace as she hugs the life out of us while we also suffocate on her wedding gown.

"Grace, I swear, if you don't let go of me this instant, I will kick you," I threaten her. I might be on my way to mending our relationship, but hugging is somewhere around step twenty-five in my recovery plan.

"Go ahead. See all this tulle? It's bulletproof," she says and squeezes us harder, speeding up that number to two real quick.

"Jesus, Gracie, you will suffocate us."

"Deal with it."

"Awww, my girls." We hear a teary mom whispering from the house.

# 10

## Joy

*"Don't look at me in that tone of voice."* — Dorothy Parker

I might have settled on temporarily moving into this weird town. I might have settled on leaving my precious research in the hands of another person. I might have settled on reconnecting with my sisters and the fact that our mother is, in fact, insane.

But...

I have not settled on the fact I have to share one tiny room with one small bed with said sisters. Yes, one room for three people who haven't seen or spoken to one another in ten years. When we all stepped foot in the cottage, the groans and desires to go see our "one-of-a-kind" cottages were loud and clear. Except, Mom wouldn't hear of it. Saying it's a mess and we have no furniture there.

Little scammer thought of everything!

I also can't settle with the fact that I'm still internally biting my nails, trying to figure out how Hope had met Jacob already and how into each other they are. All throughout dinner prep and the eating part itself, I'm trying to shut down those haunting thoughts. Especially since it shouldn't matter to me.

But since when does my brain do as I ask? At least it's nice enough to spill the horrid details of my life as Hope and Grace bombard me with questions. *Thank you, brain.*

There is no way I am sharing my embarrassment of a love life with them. So, I'll just focus on theirs since it's as entertaining as mine is. And it just got even better.

We are about to enjoy the fresh peach pie when we hear knocking at the front door.

"Oh, I'll get that; it must be Nina. She lives next door," Mom says, pushing herself out of the chair as if the house is on fire.

"Ooh, ask her about our keys," Hope adds, and we all nod because living here as one happy family is testing my patience already.

Two hours into the freaking reunion.

"Good evening, Mrs. Levine; how are you this fine evening?" A male voice I've never heard before sounds from the entryway, and Grace and I perk up as Hope pales.

"Alec!" Jesus, Mom is happier to see this stranger than she was us based on the high pitch and the beaming smile in her voice.

"Who's that?" Grace asks, getting up herself to see who that sexy voice belongs to. Because, yes, it is sexy. Even if his cheeriness reminds me of Jacob's a bit too much for my liking.

Suddenly, Hope jumps out of her seat and plants all her limbs across the door, opening it like a goddam starfish and guarding it like her life depended on it.

"Um, Po? Are you alright?" I asked her. My confused facial expression mirroring Dad's and Grace's.

"Yep. Totally. I'm perfectly fine," she squeaks out too fast.

Yeah, I'm not buying that one, sister, and I am about to question her some more when this new guy at the door becomes my new favorite person. *Sorry, Zoe.* This guy just gave me a new breath, so he wins.

"Is my girl home?" he asks, and we all freeze with our wine glasses and forks full of pie lifted midway, but it is Hope who goes from pale to cadaver gray. She closes her eyes and takes a sharp breath.

Well, it looks like my trip is finally paying off.

"Why...I have three girls at home right now; which one of them belongs to you?" If I were Hope right now, I would literally pack up my shit and flee. Because of the tone that Mom just used? That tone means problems...for Hope.

And she knows it; even if she was missing out on it for a decade, it is not something you forget.

It means Mom has already planned how many kids they will have and when. Also, she has most likely picked schools for the said kids and created a schedule for who picks up Wendy-Lou from dance rehearsal at three and who goes to get Jimmy-Joe from karate at five.

"Oh, Hope, of course," he answers, and I let out a breath I wasn't aware of holding. It's not Jacob who wants Hope. It's this Alec guy. My new favorite person. And what looks like a death of peace for my sister.

This is exactly why whatever happened between me and my sexy weirdo can never be repeated or spoken about. Never. I am not looking for meddling in my life.

I am not looking for two-point-oh kids and a white picket fence.

"I officially hate this day. This town. This month."

"Sheesh, don't hold back, now." Grace rolls her eyes as I narrow mine on her.

"Don't even start," I snarl back because my normal ability to talk is being cut off by this ridiculous push-up sports bra.

Have you ever seen this crap? A push-up. In a sports bra. Do women buy these for actual working out or to show off their titties to gym jocks? Oh hell, scratch that question. Please, for the love of everything, dear brain, forget I ever asked that because this particular push-up abnormality belongs to my mother, and I do not want to know why she bought it.

No. I've had enough of her this morning, and that is saying something as it's only six-forty-five AM.

"Hey, you aren't the one Mom woke up with a slap to her ass and called herself a bitch, okay?"

"Yeah, I'm the one she woke up with her neon-clad ass in my face, so I win." I point to myself as I try to keep this car on the road.

"You all are lucky I didn't bring my garden hose to wash you out of that bed," Mom adds from the backseat. "And my ass looks fabulous, thank you very much."

"Oh my God. Mom, please stop. My filter function isn't on yet, and whatever you say right now will most likely stay in my brain forever, and there is no way I want *that* image stuck there."

Thankfully, she only humphs in answer, and I silently pray someone will rent my cottage out as soon as possible.

You ask what I could possibly be doing praying this early while I am on vacation? Oh, don't let me keep you hanging.

Not even twelve hours after I promised to stay in the shadows and live quietly in this town for however long I must, the plan is out the door. Scratch that, it's burning up like a sausage on a hot skillet because come six in the morning, I have been forced out of the bed I shared with my crazy sisters—who don't know the meaning of sleeping on their allocated section of the bed—by our even crazier mother.

As if being kicked and humped all night by an evidently very horny Hope wasn't enough, I got to enjoy Mom, dressed in all neon, colorful polyester, and a high-top ponytail on her head, yelling for us to get up for a town workout. Yes, it's a thing here. And at this point, I won't be shocked if someone tells me they don't sell real coffee here.

Jesus, please, I will go to church. I will pray every day, but do NOT let this be a thing here. Or else I will be next on Zoe's table, waiting for my dissection to determine I died from lack of caffeine.

To make my life even better, I was forced into Grace's two-sizes smaller leggings because I don't own any myself. Which, according to my youngest sister, is a crime against Lululemon—whatever the hell that is—and my ass. Her words, not mine. She then took my credit card out of my bag and proceeded to spend five-hundred dollars on spandex mixed with polyester for my ass. Then I was pushed out the door with my boobs falling out of the stupid push-up sports bra that Mom lent me because, once again, I don't own such stupid crap.

And now, I can officially submit my application for the most stuffed sausage of the year.

I drew a hard-ass line when I saw Hope trying to get us into her tin can on wheels. No way was I getting into a car that she lost her virginity in to Brian. Nope.

So, two minutes and a million groans later, everyone was packed into my SUV, and I was instructed to drive to Love Street, having my basic human rights to coffee or a sip of water declined. And when I tried to check my phone for work updates from Zoe, Mom slapped it out of my hand, saying, "This is family time, not slavery to the dead." And that was that.

Monsters. I am related to monsters.

And that brings us here. To the mother-effing town square where hundreds of happy, neon-wearing weirdos are participating in some kind of cult, right in the middle of it.

"You're lucky we made it on time, Joy," Mom throws at me as those hundreds of colorful blobs—aka locals—crowd us like it's Black Friday and we are the hundred-dollar PCs.

"Yeah, so lucky." I don't even try to hide my sarcasm because things are going from bad to worse to a fucking disaster as I get tossed from one embrace to another.

But even *that* is not the best part of this lovely morning. Not even close. Because when I said we are entering the disaster zone, I meant it.

Him.

Shirtless. Shirt-fucking-less.

I am staring at the one set of eyes—and muscles—that I should absolutely avoid. I am sweating, swearing, and drowning in lust at seven freaking AM.

Jacob...Jacob slash my-wet-dream-I-can't-taste-anymore is standing on some kind of a podium without a shirt, exposing his fine male anatomy to the whole world. Wearing only one of those stupid short shorts he owns—this time, they have dancing duckies on them—and his hair is tied in a loose and sexy-as-fuck bun.

There is literally half the town in this square, setting out their yoga mats and chatting away, but it's as if someone took his face by force and shifted it until it was trained right on me. Those moss-green eyes drilling into mine and slowly moving down my overly exposed body with a sinful lick to his lips.

He might as well have licked my pussy directly; the effect would be the same.

It's the veins. It's the fucking veins and those tattoos on his arms. The sudden rush overtakes my senses, and the only thing I am able to think about is his body over mine in that tiny house while he unleashed his secret beast on me.

It felt like hours pass as we watch each other, documenting each micro-move standing across the whole town square from one other. My eyes roam over the glorious muscles available to my hungry eyes as heat crawls all over my body, and I have to clench my thighs together to prevent my vagina from drooling.

If I were the genius I claim to be, I'd have packed my shit and left this town the moment I saw him again.

But apparently, all the awards, certificates, and degrees decorating the wall in my office are fake. Because I'm as dumb as a bell and as horny as a bunny.

Are bunnies horny?

*Oh, hell...Joy! You cannot crawl into bed with the hot Viking again. No. Look away. Stay away. Wipe the drool off your vagina.*

I force my eyes away from Jacob only to watch the next horror show unfold in slow motion as my mother volleys her eyes between us, and a light bulb goes off on top of her scheming head. If I had my suspicions before, now they have been confirmed.

She knows, and I'm screwed ten ways to Sunday.

# 11

# Jacob

*"The great question which I have not been able to answer is, 'What does a woman want?'"* — Freud.

Is this a hallucination? Am I really seeing my little Wildflower standing across the square wearing leggings that mold her ass better than her own skin? Am I really witnessing those glorious tits spilling right out of that way too small for her—*my girl's* bra?

Where is Alec when I need him to pinch and kick me awake? Or at least be the good friend he is and confirm my visions. No, he had to stay and tattoo someone at the crack of dawn. Best friend, my ass. Next time he comes to me for advice to charm his girl, I will tell him to kick it.

Okay, I won't say that. I will still help the idiot I love to get the girl he apparently fell in love with at first sight... Like I said, he's an idiot but the best one.

Alec Colson is my ride-or-die, and when the said girl walked into our tattoo shop yesterday, the guy lost his shit. I mean that, literally. I basically had to wipe his drool off the counter, and I will admit, I nearly had a stroke myself when I saw her.

Hope was her name, but I could swear I was seeing my Wildflower, only a bit different. She had the same dark eyes, but they lacked the intensity my soul craved. Still the same dark hair, but it didn't have me in a chokehold like Wildflower's did. Similar body, but all the mouthwatering curves were missing.

Don't get me wrong, Hope is gorgeous. Beautiful. But she wasn't her. Only someone who looked like my Wildflower, and apparently, she was sent here to make a fool out of my best friend and a dead man out of me because I'm having hallucinations.

Yet, there they are. Standing side by side with a smaller one on the other side of Hope, warding off the locals with strained smiles and rigid body language. Sisters. They must be sisters.

Would you look at that? Wildflower is real, and she is back. And she watches me with the same intensity as I watch her.

*Thank you, Universe. I owe you one. How about a month with no electricity?*

The other question, though, is, how in the world am I supposed to lead this workout when my dick is trying to show off his superpowers to Wildflower? My ducky shorts are doing a piss-poor job of hiding it. I swear, I see her eyes flick over to my cock before she snaps her gaze away, and I watch as her hot ass sashays through the crowd where her family has set up their mats.

The sight absolutely does not help my very uncomfortable situation, but somehow, I tear my eyes off her long enough to calm my erection to a semi-hard ,and proceed to make the town sweat. These morning workouts have become so much more than just some simple physical activity or my morning job. It's bonding time, healing, and therapy wrapped up in one. And usually, I stay behind to listen to whoever needs a minute to talk, but not today.

Not when I am on a mission to finally know her name, her number, and the date we are getting married.

She avoids looking my way for the whole hour, while I might have been flexing a little harder today. I still caught her glances—her many, many glances.

I hurry through the crowd before someone gets a chance to pull me or before the Levine's pack up. I reach them just in time to see my Wildflower lying on the ground, eyes closed, mouth open, and her tits covered in a glistening layer of precipitation while they are also rising up and down from her still ragged breathing.

Hmm, we need to work on that endurance, boo. And I am so looking forward to that.

Not that I am not enjoying the hell out of watching her right now. So spent, wet, and vulnerable. Just like she was the other night in my house, underneath my body, in my shower.

Anddddd we are back to rock hard.

I clear my throat, alerting the wild thing to my presence, and she shoots up immediately while the rest are giving me pleasant smiles. "Good morning, beautiful Levine women. So glad we are adding three gorgeous faces to our town."

"They are lovely, aren't they?" Jenny beams at me with a knowing grin, and I am putting two and two together from yesterday. Yep, she knows. She knows about us, and I can't be mad about it. I will use anything I can to win another night or ten with her daughter.

"They sure are," I agree with her while the said daughters throw me a mixed variety of looks from *You are a shit liar* to *Shut the fuck up*. That last one from my Wildflower, and the stupid smile on my face only grows larger.

*Look at her! So sexy! Flushed, panting, and sweaty.* Is there anything more beautiful?

"They came out of me," Mrs. Levine casually states, and I nearly fall over while my girl is choking on the water she's trying to drink when her mother made the statement of the year. If I wouldn't have been thinking about Wildflower's tight pussy at this moment, I might have found it funny. Alas, I was, and now it's just weird. And I hate that word, but if the shoe fits...

"Jesus, Mother," she finally says after the fit passes.

"Well, you are one of the most beautiful women in this town, so I'm not surprised at the least." I try to salvage the situation and roll it back onto the safe track. "Hey, Hope. Nice to see you again," I say to her.

"Hey, Jacob. Nice to see you, too." She smiles at me. What a difference between these two. One can't help but scowl and snark at me, while the other one is all nice and sweet. Yet I feel absolutely nothing for this sweet girl. Not a thing.

No, I want that little witch barring her teeth and choking on my cock.

*Fuck...*I banned those types of thoughts five years ago, and for some unfathomable reason, this woman brings them all back. I don't want to be a gentleman with her. No, I want my fire to be consumed by her gasoline because it seems to be the only brand my inferno craves.

"I guess those sisters of yours did make it to Loverly, huh?" I ask Hope, remembering our conversation yesterday where she told me her sisters lived on the other sides of the country, so I didn't bother putting two and two together.

Sloppy mistake, Jacob. But mind-blowing sex will do that to you.

"Oh, yes, let me introduce you." She hurries over to the one I don't know. "This is my younger sister, Grace." She looks just like Hope but with crystal blue eyes and a bit of their mother's mischief gleaming in them. We smile and share one of those quick obligatory hugs when Hope continues on. "And this is my older sister, Joy."

No. Fucking. Way.

No way is her name, Joy. *Oh, man, please keep it together, Jacob. Do not laugh. Don't you dare!* And by the look of Joy's murderous face, I can tell she knows exactly what I am thinking.

*I love you, Universe, but sometimes you are twisted as fuck.*

"Joy?" I ask her, biting my lip and scurrying over to share a meet-and-greet hug with her, but my Wildflower is having none of that. Her hands shoot up in front of her, blocking my way to her half-naked body.

"Don't. Even. Think. About. It," she grids out, but those dark eyes are not looking into mine. Oh, no. They are occupied by watching my own naked torso, and I can't help myself when I flex a bit to give her a better show. With a quiet but sharp inhale, she finally looks up to see me smirking.

"Not a hugger, are you? That's okay, you'll warm up to them...and me."

If only looks could kill, I'd be twenty-feet under.

Deciding not to test my luck just yet, I change the subject. "Ladies, I also came by to hand out your car patrol schedules for the next month; I added you all last night."

"Car patrol?" Grace asks, scrunching up her forehead.

"Yep, maybe you noticed we have three special cars driving around. One is our Motivation Car, to walk you through a crisis and give you the right kick your butt needs to keep going. The second one is the Hug Car; that one is self-explanatory. Sometimes, we all need a hug. The last one is the Love Car; it's there to offer some advice or a shoulder to cry on—no shame in that—or to simply sit with you when you are lonely. So, whenever you are in need of any of those things, you just flag the car, and its service is at your feet. And we, as a community, have rotating schedules for those." I pull out the papers from my pocket and hand it to them. The mayor told me we were getting three new residents so I could make the appropriate changes in the rotation, but I had no idea who those residents would be.

"Okay," Hope says as her and Grace accept the new responsibilities, but when I turn toward Joy to hand her hers, I am met with yet another scowl. "Here is yours, Miss Joy."

"I'm not taking it." Oh, here is my favorite grumpy girl. It's okay, I can take you, boo.

"Why not?"

"Because I'm not staying here, and even if I were staying, I'm not doing that crap."

"Not staying? What do you mean?"

"Do you need me to spell it out for you?"

"Nope, Wildflower, no need because I know you'll stay!" I feel four sets of eyes watching us closely and many others watching from far back, and I know it is only a matter of seconds before this conversation will be posted on Love Hive for all to see and scheme away.

"A wildflower?" Hope quietly muses to Grace.

"More like a cactus." Grace scrunches up her nose. "But sure, wildflower works as well. They do have those pokey kind growing out there in the wilderness, don't they?"

"You do know I can hear you, don't you?" Joy says to her sisters, but her eyes are narrowed at me.

"Hmm?" Grace feigns innocence, and I see the eye roll along with some eye twitch Joy is trying to hide.

Grace and Hope say something else as they turn to run away from their explosive sister, but I'm not listening. Every sense in my body is honed in on *her*. My ears are tuned in to her rapid inhale and exhale, my eyes to her flaring nostrils and murderous glances. Everyone else is gone. I can't see or hear them.

"Jacob," she says in a warning tone.

"Joy," I answer with a smile. "I must say, we need to work on this."

"Work on what?" she asks, fuming, but as I take a step towards her, the anger morphs into something entirely different. Something very close to lust as the tip of her tongue peeks out to lick her bottom lip, and my dick is trying to jump out, asking for his turn.

"Get your dirty mind in check, boo. I am not talking about working my cock in your pussy." I hear her gasp softly, and she starts to stutter out a response when I keep talking. "Fine, fine, we can work on that also." I sigh as if bending this woman over and taking her the way I crave is a hardship.

Joy's cheeks are now pink once again, but this time, it has nothing to do with the workout at the town square we just had. No, this time, it's all about the workout where she screamed my name as she came all over me.

"Y-you—" she starts again, and I interrupt her again.

"But I was talking about your beautiful face in constant frowns. You should smile more." I send her a smile of my own, and pray her dark, witchy eyes really can't kill me. I'm not ready to go yet.

"I don't smile." She folds her arms at her chest. Oh, hell, her tits are pushed up...

*Think about rubber duckies, Jacob. Rubber duckies.*

"I beg to differ," I repeat the same line I used the other night, and predictably enough, she starts to open her mouth and tell me she doesn't care, but I beat her to it. "Don't say it." She purses her lips shut and glares at me. "I got the memo the last time." And I must have a death wish or simply desire to see her rip my head off because I wink, step in closer, and add, "It's just that *I* don't care. I will make sure this gorgeous face lights up with as many smiles as possible. And moans. Definitely more moans."

Joy is still flushed, but she clenches her teeth together, balls up her little fists, and says, "You know what? I might have considered another night with you, but now? Yeah, now I'm all done."

"Are you?" I taunt the beast some more. "Are you really all done?" I take another step closer because she keeps scurrying away, almost touching her breasts with my bare chest. I feel her heat, her desire, her rapid heartbeat. "Are you trying to tell me if I slipped my hand into those leggings—which, by the way, you look delicious in—I won't find my girl all wet and needy for me?"

"I will give it to you, the level of your audacity is atrocious."

"I call it confidence."

"In getting any girl you want into your bed?"

"Not any girl. I don't want just any girl. I want my future wife." I never knew a person could roll their eyes as far back as she is right now.

"Jesus, how did I happen to find the weirdest weirdo out of this whole town?"

"You are lucky like that." I flashed her another grin. "Want me to prove that I will be the best hubby?"

"No."

"I knew you'd agree," I tell her while she counters with, "I didn't."

I keep going. Joy just doesn't know she wants me in her life yet.

"So I will give you fifty reasons why you should marry me."

"Fifty?" Her eyebrows shoot up.

"Yeah, you are right. We better make it a hundred."

"You are ridiculous. There won't be even one."

"I'd say my *perfect* dick has already taken the first one." I smirk as a flash of heat passes through her eyes and body.

"Joy?" Mr. Levine calls out to his daughter, and we jump away from each other so fast we nearly trip over our legs.

That's right. We are in the middle of the nosiest town with all the nosiest busybodies watching us like their favorite TV drama—or erotica. Really, it could be either one.

Joy coughs, clearing up her throat. "Yes, Daddy?" she asks him, sounding like a completely different person.

And apparently, my cock doesn't care that she is talking to her actual father, the one who is watching me with narrowed eyes because he decides he wants to be called "Daddy" by this girl.

I need help.

And beer.

And to have sex with my Wildflower.

I prefer to start with that last one, seeing as I am about to die from a permanent hard-on.

"Your phone, honey. It was going off a few times," Mr. Levine tells her, and she takes it from him; her demeanor clicks right back into that hard and cold persona.

"Shit..." she says, trailing off and rushes away from me without another word. Her phone is already at her ear, and it doesn't look like good news.

It's okay. I will be here to comfort you, my Wildflower.

**Love Hive:**

Fforall: Did you all see that?

Freeman1: Are we talking about operation Pink Mist? Or Deer and the Hunter? I also spotted Ashes sending heated looks to our Bride.

Cookiej: Oh, oh, my grandbabies' meter is spiking all the way up right now. Could this day get any better?

RickyL: I just got them all back.

CookieJ: Ricky, don't pout. It doesn't suit you.

# 12
# Joy

*"Our relationship is like a walk in the park, Jurassic Park."*
— *Unknown.*

"**O**h, my sweet Saturn, Mars, and Pluto! Where the hell have you been? Did you end up getting abducted by those weirdos you claim to live there? I have been calling you all morning! You'd think after leaving fifty-seven voicemails screaming like a banshee, one-hundred-thirty-five messages with angry emojis, and a dozen emails saying 'URGENT, LIFE OR DEATH' in the subject line, you would respond...but, no!" I literally have to pull my phone away from my ear as Zoe continues yelling at me.

She has been going at it for the last three minutes without letting me say a word, and obviously, she has a whole speech prepared, so I might as well sit down, calm my stupid vagina and clear off my lust haze from the encounter with Jacob while my assistant has her five minutes of fame yelling at *me*, over the phone.

Not sure what is going on back home because, in her rant, she hasn't explained a thing yet, but my brain is not capable of analyzing Zoe or her menstrual cycle—which is clearly affecting her—right now.

No, we are still hung up on the half-naked Viking who is getting way too comfortable around me after knowing me for all of twelve hours, maybe less. Somehow, this man is capable of getting under my skin and refusing to be intimidated by me. Somehow, every word that comes out of his mouth is some sort of secret code to breaking mine. Somehow, I lose absolutely all control around him, and if not for my father back there, I'm pretty sure in the next minute or two, we would have been fully naked.

Forget the audience and my parents standing a few feet away. Forget my rules and principles. Forget I said no more sex with Jacob, because the only thing running through my head is how much I want him and his secret dominance. The side he shows in the bedroom alone. Because the guy leading the workout this morning? That is not the same guy I slept with a night ago. No. And this is where the scientific part of my brain leads me into trouble because it is dying to analyze him, to research, poke, and probe until we know which Jacob is the real one.

Is it this sweet goofball joking around with all the grandmas in the square, or is it the one who showed no mercy in the dead of night?

No, Joy. There can be no touching the specimen. Touching hazardous specimens can lead to death, and I think I am only now starting to live. So, I will conduct my research from afar. I don't have to touch it. He will be like the Louvre Museum in Paris. Look, but don't touch. Admire, but stay away.

Of-fucking-course, he chooses this exact moment to look at me, sitting on the sidewalk, and fucking wink! Now. When I'm trying to talk myself into not touching the man.

Jesus, this might be the most complicated research I have ever conducted, and that is saying something.

"Are you even listening to me?"

Oops. Zoe is still on the phone, and I have completely forgotten because, *come on*, ogling sexy men sounds so much better than listening to her bitching about work.

"Aha. I am." I lie.

"Really? Because I just told you Justin is getting prosecuted for the sexual assault charges, his wife has filed for divorce, and he has been sacked."

"What?" I screech loudly enough for every remaining member of the morning workout to turn around and stare at me. Jacob included, and his eyes are narrowed, brows furrowed, and I think he almost looks...worried?

Turning away from all the prying gazes, I focus on Zoe. "Please, repeat all that again but slower and with more details this time."

She sighs dramatically but starts talking, nonetheless. "Apparently, a lot more girls have stepped up after the first claims started to seep through and spread over the campus. So, they came forward, and now Justin is in deep shit."

"Well, fuck..." I muse.

"Yeah. Fuck indeed. What if this comes back to us?"

"Stop freaking out. Nothing ties us to him unless we decide to speak, and as much as I'd love to bury that bastard even lower, I don't want to be involved and to have my name associated with him in any sentence."

"Me too. I am just starting my career; he's messed with it enough. I don't want to give him any more power over my life." Zoe sounds defeated, but only for a second because all of a sudden, we are back to ranting. "Fucking asshole! When did he even have time to fuck so many people? Between you, me, and his wife, you'd think the fucker was satisfied! But nooooo. It was never fucking enough!"

I wonder how many times she can manage to say the word "fuck" in her little speech? So far, we are at four, but she has more to say.

"Fuck. Fuck. Fuck!"

"Zoe, Jesus Christ. Will you calm down? Are you on your period or something? I've never seen you so wound up."

"Yeah? Well, maybe it's because my life is about to fucking implode! And no, I am not on my period!"

"No, it won't. I will protect you. We ignore all the whispers and gossip and stick to what we do best. Work. Science. Dead people." I stop, thinking for a second. "Actually, why don't you come out here? For a week, until the dust settles there?"

"Is that really you saying that? Maybe you are the one who is on her period or something because the Dr. Levine I know would rather tie me to the desk than let me have a week off when our research is in its peak stage. Seriously, what is going on over there? You sound different, and it's only been two days."

"Nope. Nothing is going on. Everything is perfect, and I will be out of here next week or as soon as I find some renters for my place."

"Renters? Isn't your dad sick? You're not staying for him?" She sounds confused, so I fill her in on the events of yesterday, using the CliffsNotes version and skip the details pertaining to a certain blonde, goofball anomaly.

"Okay, after hearing all that, I have a new appreciation for my life and my family. Thank you, Dr. Levine, you are a true healer," Zoe snickers into the phone.

"Oh, shut up, why don't' you?"

"Aha. Well, I guess I will see you soon?"

"Yes, and keep me updated on the Justin situation."

"Will do, Joy. Also, the report is in your inbox. Bye."

"Great. Bye." And that is why I love Zoe. No sappy goodbyes, no miss you's or love you's. Only science and facts. I'll consider her earlier rant part of the freak out.

I turn my head back to the square, and Jacob still has his eyes trained on me. The way he watches me is as if he is an X-ray scanner or, better yet, an MRI machine, and I am a substance composed of one cell he can easily see through.

He looks at me like he wants to know all my secrets and won't rest until he does. He looks at me like I am *his*. Like his stupid reasons for me to marry him are valid and true.

Oh, hell...I need a cold shower or, better yet, a dip in the freezing ocean.

Mom: **My dear favorite older daughter, in your attempt to flee our sweet boy, Jackie, you forgot your parents at the town square.**

Joy: **Fuck...**

Mom: **Yes, fuck indeed. Don't worry; we are getting a ride home. But don't think you will be getting away without sharing with your mother about your future husband.**

There is so much to unpack in that one little text, and I don't know whether I should start with the casual "fuck" everyone seems to be throwing around today, her thinking I am running away from *Jackie*...or the fact that she just mentioned something about a future husband.

You know what? Ignorance is bliss, so avoiding it all, it is.

Joy: **I am so sorry, Mom. Some things came up at work, and I wasn't thinking.**

Mom: **I know what you are doing, and it's not working.**

Mom: **When were you going to tell us about you and Jacob?**

Joy: **I have no idea what you are talking about.**

Mom: **I can see you blushing through the phone. You were always a bad liar, Joy.**

Mom: **Ignoring me won't work either; we are pulling up.**

Joy: **What? What were you saying? Sorry, I don't have time to read my texts with all this packing I am doing. Need to catch the next flight to Chicago.**

Joy: **Oh, and don't play the innocent one here...We know about the Love Hive. And Hope is on a war path.**

If I ever leave my parents—specifically my mom—somewhere alone again, please smack me upside the head. Because that woman can't take a step without scheming and plotting.

Guess who the good soul was giving them a ride home?

Ding, ding, ding...winner, winner, chicken dinner. It was the one and only Jacob, aka Viking-I-am-trying-to-stay-away-from. Can't a girl get a break around here?

Apparently not.

"Wildflower, I brought our parents' home," he calls out loudly with a smile that is audible as they walk through the front door. I am doing my damn hardest to keep the scowl look on and the stupid smile that is threatening to appear at the sound of his voice off.

What the hell is wrong with me? I don't smile!

*Breathe in, breathe out, Joy.* It's just this town. It's something in the air here, probably some voodoo hacks and tricks to turn your sensible brain into mush and fill it with weirdness. Yeah, I am getting the hell out as soon as possible.

"Joy?" I hear Mom call out, and with a sigh, I get up and leave the room to face the music.

"Yes?" I ask as they come into view.

"Oh, goodie, you are home. I hope you didn't forget Nina is giving you girls your keys in a bit."

Can you strangle your mother and not go to hell—or prison—for that? I'm asking for a friend here. A friend who has a very strong urge to do just that because said mother didn't just share some useful information. *No*, she just threw a juicy bone to the one man I hoped wouldn't find out about my home purchase in Loverly Cave.

Guess that ship has sailed now because his grin is wide and bright, and I swear he is bouncing on his toes from excitement. How the heck did I end up sleeping with this guy? Where are my usual suit and tie, clean-cut guys?

"Keys? I didn't know anyone was renting in Loverly," Jacob states, looking at Mom and me. And I am trying very hard to use my mental powers to tell Mom to shut up.

Of course, she doesn't...she understands very well what I was trying to say without saying because that Cheshire cat grin she has going is more than telling. "Oh, no, Joy and the two others bought houses. The old cottages on the beach."

"Really? Isn't that wonderful?" Jacob smiles at me, and I feel my eye starting to twitch.

"Yes!" Mom claps her hands together. "Daddy and I are so excited to have our girls home, but I worry about them. Those cottages need so much work done. Maybe you can stay with us for a little longer, Joy? Or maybe you can stay with Jackie for a few days while we clean up your place?"

Thank God, I'm not drinking anything because I sure as fuck would choke on it right now. So, my body settles for a nervous hiccup. "A, I am not sleeping with my sisters another night, even if you were to pay me. Or if the house I bought is crawling with cockroaches. B, I'm not staying with *Jackie* here either because..."

Damn it...why? Why can't I stay with this sex on a stick again?

"Because..." Jacob taunts me.

"Because I can't," is my brilliant answer. I guess that higher education really does come in handy.

Amazing, my inner sarcasm is on.

"Well, then, why won't you just help our Joy here clean up and remodel?" Mom comes back swinging with her helpful ideas *once again*.

"Mom, I am thirty-one years old. I am quite capable of doing it on my own like Grace and Hope will be."

"A, I know how old you are. I am the one that pushed you out of my very small—"

"Mom!" I cut her off before she goes any further, and she just humphs at me like I am the insensible one here.

"And B, Hope has Alec to help her, and Grace is not alone either. Or she won't be, if all goes according to plan."

"Plan?" My eyebrows shoot up. "Please tell me you're not making any new schemes." I close my eyes and place my hands on my hips.

"New? No, nothing new," she answers, and I feel like there is a loophole somewhere there. "Anyway, Jackie, you're going to be a good boy and help my favorite oldest daughter, right?" She bats her eyes at him, and even if he didn't want to do this himself, he sure as hell wouldn't be able to say no to that woman.

No one can.

"Of course, Mrs. Levine. How could I leave my Wildflower all alone?" He winks at me. He freaking winks.

But that isn't the problem. The problem is the idea that he's put in my mom's head. I mean, I am sure she already had plenty in there, but he is just feeding the monster and patting it on the back at this point.

"Oh, my sweet boy." She gets on her tippy toes to ruffle his hair and pat his cheek lovingly. "Please, call me mama."

That eye twitch I had going for me? Yeah, no more. We are at a full-blown seizure now.

# 13

# 50 Reasons

Reason #2:
*Jacob: "Let's start with the most obvious one. I'm stupidly handsome, hilariously funny, extremely loyal, and I will generally just make your life so much better."*
*Joy: "Wow, what a rap sheet. Sounds like a list you come with to see your therapist."*

Reason #7:
*Jacob: Being married is like dating, only you don't have to drive home after the date. Saving gas and all that.*
*Joy: Because this town is so big...*

# 14

# Jacob

*"Before you marry a person, you should first make them use a computer with slow Internet service to see who they really are." –Will Ferrell.*

Did I mention before how much I love Mrs. Levine? I mean, that woman is practically my guardian angel at this point, and her wish is my command. Especially if it pertains to a certain wildflower of mine.

After angrily stomping out of her parents' house, Joy got into her car and drove off so fast that the tires left black, distinctive marks on the driveway. What a joy my Joy is. She was fuming mad, and any normal guy would stay away. Good thing that's not me.

I can't stop following her. I can't seem to leave her alone even though I know she wants nothing to do with me. Well, maybe she wouldn't mind another hot and heavy session in the sheets, but that's it.

I'm not the kind of guy Joy normally dates. I don't know her, but that bit is very clear, and I'm not sure how I feel about it.

I'm not sure why, all of a sudden, I'm questioning leaving my old life behind even though I know it was the right choice for myself and my sanity. No, there is no going back, and I will just have to persuade Joy that happy, surfing weirdos are her new kryptonite. One happy, surfing weirdo. Me.

Getting into my car, I quickly follow behind her but decide to make a quick stop at Fifi's to get some supplies. I am very much surprised that those cottages were sold to the Levine sisters. The beach huts were empty for years before I got into town, and no one has been able to occupy them while I have been living here, either. No matter how much anyone offered, the town always said no.

They were like monuments of sorts here, and how they finally got sold is a mystery.

They are amazing homes, but they are falling apart and need more than just a facelift, so I grab a few things and make my way there. I see Alec's gleaming red truck already parked and the girls standing on the sand in front of the three cottages, looking up to them dreamily.

The first one is in a washed-off blue color. The second one is pale pink, and the last one is in what used to be a bright yellow tint. They each come with a small wrap-around porch, beat-up wooden pathways into the beach, carports in the back, and stale scent.

But the thing about old bones...it makes for the perfect future. These houses come with their own energy and history. Every person who lived here before left some sort of footprint and happy memories for us to enjoy now.

The girls quickly notice my appearance, and I take in three different expressions. From curious Hope to excited Grace to scowling Joy—my now favorite expression.

"Hey, boo." I wink at Hope, deciding it won't hurt to taunt my little beast some more, and when I glance at her, I almost shiver. Yikes. There she goes with those glares.

"Oh, come on," Grace groans out with her hand up to the sky. "She gets two for the price of one? How is that fair?"

"Don't worry; there is enough of me for all three of you," I tell them with a grin. I am happy to help each one, but I'm here for Joy. My Joy.

The one that clenches her jaws, glares once more for good measure, and says, "I'm all good, thanks." And then quickly disappears behind the front door of the pink house. Oh, man, of course, that one is hers.

"Ahh, that woman will be my wife." I think I said that out loud based on the sounds of the dropping jaws around me.

"Jacob, I really like you; I'd like to consider you my friend, so I feel like I need to warn you. If you ever say that to Joy's face, she will cut off your balls and make turkey stuffing out of them."

Ouch, she definitely might, but I don't think it will be for saying that. I think it might be because I'm over here chatting and flirting with her sisters, and the hopeful idiot in me wants to believe she is jealous.

"Nah, she already loves me."

"I think he's insane. Do you think he is insane?" Grace whispers.

"Definitely," Hope agrees with her.

"Jacob, what are you doing here?" Alec storms out of the blue house, which I assume is Hope's, and stares at me, silently asking 'what the hell?' You see, last night, I gave him some tips on how to get Hope to fall in love with him, and I think he's assuming I'm here to mess it up.

No, buddy, I am here to woo my own Levine sister.

"I came to help my boo here, of course." I motion in the general direction of the houses. "And relax your balls. I know she's yours; I'm simply being a good friend."

"You better." Alec shoots me a look.

"Well, if you don't need him, I'll take him," Grace quickly says, and I don't even have a second to think about it as she drags me towards the farthest house.

"Jackie." We both stop Joy's overly sweet tone, and I have to blink a few times to catch up to what my ears have heard.

Joy's standing at her door, arms crossed at her chest, and despite the sugary tone, her eyes are as green as they come. I have to bite down on my lips to keep the amusing smile off my face. Because I think my Wildflower is indeed jealous, and I think I am in heaven.

"Yes, my Wildflower?" I ask her as Grace volleys her eyes between the two of us.

"You wouldn't be disobeying *Mama's* orders now, would you?" The way she said mama's is meant to taunt me, but I'm not the one to skip on fun.

"No, definitely not. Disrespecting my future in-laws would be a shame. What if they get pissed off and refuse to babysit our children while I take their mommy out to the woods to do inappropriate things to her?"

"I feel like I'm missing some vital pieces of information right now," Grace muses and reminds us of her presence. In all honesty, I completely forgot she was standing next to me and holding on to my arm because when my girl is in the vicinity, everything else ceases to exist.

Jesus, it has only been a couple of days, one hot night, and a handful of heated, full of jabs-conversations, yet I am losing it. I didn't feel even a fraction of this magnetic connection with my ex, and she was the one I actually married...

I didn't feel this visceral need to be around her, to just sit and stare at her and make sure she was real.

"Sorry, Grace. I wish I could help, but as your older sister kindly reminded me, I am not allowed to do so." Grace pulls her brows together.

"What? Why?"

"Something about how she has it all planned out, and I just might be scared enough of your mother to listen to her."

"Oh, for Harry's sake!" She throws her hands up and stalks away toward the yellow and last house without another word. I pop an eyebrow and look at Joy for an explanation, but she just shrugs.

"Don't mind Grace, a flare for theatrics runs in her blood. Also, she is a Potterhead." I match her shrug and walk up to Joy's porch with supplies.

"What are you doing?" She stops me before I get a chance to enter her home.

"Coming inside?" The moment those words leave my mouth, a light pink hue splashes over her cheeks, and I smirk. "And they say men only think about sex, but for you, my wildflower, we can practice that kind of coming inside, too."

"Bye, Jacob." In one swift move, she turns around and tries to slam the door in my face, but I block it with my foot.

"You won't even invite me in?"

"No dogs allowed."

"Hmm, and what kind am I?"

"The most annoying one. A Chihuahua, probably. Those things never shut up or leave you alone. They are also highly untrained and pee all over the place," Joy states, still trying to close the door. Unsuccessfully, I might add.

"And here I thought I was more of a golden retriever. Friendly, funny, and loyal to a fault. Oh, and they are also such cuties."

"Don't flatter yourself, *Jackie*. I'll give the friendly point to you, even though I might consider you more obnoxious and invading, but fine. Funny?" She scrunches up her nose, which is almost too adorable. "Yeah, no, don't see that one. As for loyal, I don't know enough about you, but there is no such thing as loyalty in men's vocabulary."

I narrow my eyes slightly, trying to interpret her words. How many times have some bastard hurt her to earn such venom in regard to that word? But I decide to skip that thought for now, filing it away for the future. "You forgot, cute."

"What?" She looks at me, confused.

"You forgot how cute the golden retrievers are."

"There is absolutely nothing cute about you, Jacob." Damn, this woman and her sharp tongue. I can't seem to stop thinking about it since I let her graze me with her blades nonstop, and I love every second of it.

I take a step closer, her hands no longer trying to shove the door closed, and whisper into her ear. "Stop being so mean to me, or I swear to God I'll fall in love with you."

Grace: **I would like it to be known that I hate you both a tiny bit.**

Hope: **What else is new?**

Hope: **We have heard this song and dance since you were about 3.**

Hope: **But out of curiosity, what is it about this time?**

Grace: **You both have hot man hunks helping you out while I'm slaving away on my own.**

Hope: **Wait, didn't Jacob go with you?**

Grace: **Nooooo, apparently, he isn't allowed.**

Hope: **Huh???**

Grace: **Idk, ask Joy. She's the one who stole him from me.**

Hope: **Joy? Learning from the best?**

Joy: **If I never respond, will you stop bothering me?**

Grace: **Nopeeee.**

Hope: **Highly doubt it.**

Joy: **\*Unimpressed emoji \* All questions should be yielded to the evil mastermind.**

Grace: **Mom? Is that the mama you guys were talking about?**

Joy: **Aha.**

Grace: **In that case, I'm fine not knowing.**

Grace: **Did you both at least lick your hunks yet?**

Hope: **GRACE!!!!**

Joy: **Fucking hell, Gracie!!!! Now my shirt is wet.**

Grace: **OMG. Did he come on you???**

Joy: **What the hell??? Are you normal? You think I'd be texting you idiots if I was having hot sex?**

Joy: **And come on my shirt? What the fuck?**

Grace: **Hey, I'm not kink-shaming anyone. We all have our needs.**

Joy: **Jesus Christ. You need help just like mom does.**

Joy: **No, you need more!**

Joy: **Hope? Got anything to add?**

Joy: **Hope?**

Grace: **See? She is getting her lick in. Go get some, too.**

Joy: **No, can do that. Also, quit whining, Gracie. I'm all alone, too, and you don't see me soliciting your text messages.**

Grace: **Why? Did you send him away? Why don't you let him help you? Support you?**

Joy: **The most support and help I've ever got was from my bra. Not a man.**

# 15

# *Joy*

*"Love is an electric blanket with somebody else in control of the switch." — Cathy Carlyle.*

To say I've been off kilter the whole day is not to say anything. Because the most fascinating and frustrating research subject, along with his sexy body and that absolutely perfect ass in his tiny shorts, has left me standing alone at my door with a whole bunch of painting supplies at my feet and my heart in my vagina.

How could I possibly call that man *cute?* What kind of word is that? He can't be cute when he is stupidly hot, alluring, magnetic, and completely irresistible.

His parting words have settled in the bottom of my stomach, ignoring all reason and my insistence to vacate the premises.

*Stop being so mean to me, or I swear I'll fall in love with you.*

I try to clean up my very old, very beaten-down beach cottage, but those words would come back, haunting me every minute, making me ignore my new project.

The cottage is in pretty good shape overall—apart from the hideous hippo-pink exterior—but it needs a major facelift before I can rent it out.

It's technically a one-bedroom, one-bathroom. However, there is a hidden upstairs attic room, which could be turned into an amazing office, family room, or even a bedroom. But every time I look at that hideous palm tree wallpaper, peeling here and there... every time, I glance at the puke yellow cabinets in the kitchen with its doors hanging off the hinges... every time I try to sweep the floor, which has a multilayer of dirt stuck to it, I remember it. That one word. *Love.*

I know he said it as a joke. I'm not an idiot to assume otherwise, but no one has ever said that to me before. No one but my direct family. And for some stupid, unreasonable reason, my cold heart decides to stick with it.

Logically, I am smart enough to know such a notion doesn't exist anymore, but pathetically, I still cling to the hope I might find it.

Oh my God! This town is getting to me already!

The rest of the day was as productive as the first half, meaning I didn't get shit done because my head was filled with nonsense, but at least I got some basic furniture. And now instead of unscrewing old cabinet doors, I am being dragged by my pixie of a sister—aka Gracie bear—to the bar.

It's evening, and the sun is halfway down, creating the most beautiful evening sky, and I'd love to just sit on my porch in my new, cheap camping chair, admiring it, but apparently, "We need to unwind," she said. And I didn't have the heart to tell her there will be no unwinding for me. Not until I'm out of here. And once I see *where* she planned for us to unwind, my body tenses up even worse, stiffening my neck, shoulders, hands, and feet.

Love & Peace Bar. *The* Love & Peace bar, the one I met him at.

The one that serves weird drinks, implanting weird thoughts in your head. Thoughts like how someone's lips would feel on yours. How big and warm his hands would feel on your naked body and how amazing it would be to be fucked by a blonde, hippy stranger.

Fine, it was probably all me and not the drink, but the point stands. I can't go in there. I dig my heels in right before Grace is about to open the front door, and the soft tunes of "happy" music are filtering through the cracks.

This is *not* your typical bar music. The kind that gets you all hyped up to drink and party, yet my body seems to think it's the music to get laid because suddenly, my reproductive system is high-fiving my brain and does a "we are getting lucky tonight" dance.

If I could slap my vagina, I would. I would also notify her that Pharrell Williams, with his "Happy" song, is hardly considered a sex tune, but do you think she cares?

Nope.

No, the bitch is only thinking about herself, pressuring my feet to start moving and allowing my little sister to drag me inside the bar.

I take a deep breath and quickly scan the room as soon as we are in, noting Viking isn't here, and I mentally chant, *"Take that, you little whore,"* to my vagina.

I swear, she is huffing in displeasure and folds her arms across her chest—lips? Oh my God! I need help.

I'm talking to my own organs.

But as Grace seems to find someone she wants to go to, I take in LPs once again. It's quite nice for a small-town bar, even with its funky-colored stools, all in mismatched designs and styles. The bar itself is impressive, and the drinks I had last time were perfect.

It's not one AM this time, so the happy song I heard from outside is actually being played by a real band made up of elderly locals. Who, I swear, are watching me behind their peace sign glasses.

Creepy weirdos.

Once I turn my head back to my sister, I see she is leading us back towards the booths and to one, in particular, where my other sister, Hope, is obviously enjoying her time with Alec.

"Grace," I hiss. "Let's not bother them."

But it's too late because she is already sliding into the empty seat, dragging me along with her. But at least I have a perfect view of the front door, and I can see every person that walks in.

*Are you hoping he does or does not open that door, Joy?* I hear my stupid vagina asking me. Yes, yes, I'm sure it's her being all needy and crap, not my brain or, God forbid, my heart.

"Are you sure this is the only bar in town?" I ask, narrowing my eyes at everyone inside to make sure I haven't missed him. But I already know the answer. He's not here.

There is no missing Jacob. That guy doesn't know the meaning of the words, under the radar or unnoticeable.

"Yes." Grace sighs and rolls her eyes at me because I have been a pain in her ass tonight. Starting with my "furniture" shopping until now. "I already told you this, and I also told you that you didn't have to come along with me. You could have stayed in your cottage on your sad blow-up mattress."

Aha, sure she did. Sure, she said, "I can go alone. I'll be all lonely, and some local might steal me, but I will go alone." Manipulative little vixen.

"My mattress isn't sad," I grind out because we've had this conversation a thousand times at the store already, and I'm not looking to rehash it once again. Yet, it seems I must. "It's a perfectly functioning bed for the little time I will be wasting in this town. And it would be plain irresponsible to let my little sister wander alone at night in this weird town."

"And what is so weird about it?" Alec asks me. I officially met him earlier today when he showed up to help Hope, and man, I don't blame my sister for having that permanent blush on her cheeks. This man is good-looking with his dark, slightly curly hair, bluish-green eyes, tattoos—of course—and never-ending charisma oozing from every pore.

"Everyone is too happy." I cringe. "It's unnatural. They are like *Trolls* on crack."

"Are you talking about the cartoon?"

"Yeah, that one." I point my index finger to him.

"Huh, interesting," Alec muses. "And no, no *Trolls* here, although I love that cartoon. We just live by——" He doesn't get to finish his sentence because someone else does.

Someone I was supposed to keep an eye on, and this lot distracted me. I was being an idiot, and now I'm paying for it by clenching my thighs and calming down my pre-cardiac arrest heart rate.

"Hakuna Matata," that someone says. *My* someone.

*No! Not yours, Joy. Snap the fuck out of it.*

I take a deep breath and lift up my head to meet the moss-green eyes belonging to Jacob, who is standing in all his careless gorgeousness, wearing a loose linen button-up shirt that does nothing to hide the art on his chest and matching pants set. I guess he owns normal-ish clothes, after all. Normal-ish because the look is complete with his shark slides.

He's looking down at me with a blinding, knowing smile on his bearded face. His hair is tied up in a loose bun, and my fingers decide to join my vagina's movement of "Let's get laid" by tingling and itching to dig into those blonde locks.

"Are you quoting *Lion King*?" Grace breaks our stare down, and suddenly, I have the urge to kiss and kill my sister at the same time.

"Yep, because that is the motto we live by here." He looks to Grace and turns back to me. "Not *Trolls*, Wildflower. Although, I'm personally a huge fan of Poppy. Best. Queen. Ever." The idiot grins at me, and I feel my cheeks flame up.

Of course, he heard the one slip-up I had. Screw it, yes, I love cartoons. There. It's out in the open. We all have our guilty pleasures, and this one is mine.

I know I'm a wild one with my choices, but honestly, it is the only thing I can watch. I would puke from any type of romance, roll my eyes at the fiction, and find mistakes in history and science. So, cartoons it is.

Alec and Jacob get into some kind of discussion where Jacob is pouting but don't ask me what they are talking about. My brain is currently leading my vagina's parade and waving "go home with him" flags inside my head as my eyes hungrily devour that little snippet of naked torso peeking out of his unbuttoned button-up shirt.

How could he be so hot? Why? Why do I have to find him attractive right now when my life is in shambles.

"Can we get back to the whole Hakuna Matata thing?" Grace breaks my train of thoughts again, and I quickly yell out, "NO!" There is no need to encourage him.

Somewhere in the back of my mind, the conversation they were just having makes an appearance through the lust parade, and I ask, "You guys are on a date? What the hell, Po?"

See? This man fries my brain, and I miss key information. I would be happy for Hope, but is she ready for something new?

I know I'm not, and I am not the one who just came out of the ten-year-long relationship. And then I look her over as if seeing my sister for the first time tonight. "And why is your hair green? Or is it blue?" Her hands fly up, looking for the colored part.

"Ooh, ooh." Grace jumps up and down in her seat. "I know, I know." But she doesn't get to answer as Hope shoots her a threatening look, and she smirks back.

"Told you, you should've let me shower with you. I'd get it all out." My mouth falls open at Alec's answer, and I have so many questions, but they all disappear as a warm, familiar body slides into the booth right next to me, pushing into me and setting me on literal fire.

If I thought my organs were having a parade before, now it is a full-blown riot.

"What do you think you are doing?" My words are clipped, my glaze is saying, "I am going to kill you," and my body sings in joy.

Fantastic.

"Sitting next to my future wife," Jacob casually states, and I have to bite down the curses I really want to yell out.

"What did you just say?" I master to say in a sort of flat yet deadly tone. This is not the first time he has brought this comment up, and now I am starting to question how serious is he?

I'm sure the others are watching us like a freak show, but I couldn't care any less. My whole focus is on a man who is dead set on making me lose my shit.

"You, me, wedding bells and babies." He smiles softly while I am bristling with fury.

Sex is one thing, but saying he might fall in love with me and that I am his future wife is a whole other story. The one I'm not looking forward to.

"Joy, please don't kill my idiot friend; he still needs to be my best man when your sister agrees to marry me," Alec says, snapping us from our own bubble. Yes, let us concentrate on my sister, who seems to be a great guy for her.

The drinks Alec and Hope ordered come, which happen to be a pair of Mellow-yellows, and as soon as the guys explain to my sisters about these cocktails being not just cocktails but each one holding "magical powers," my sisters pressure me to order something for myself. And it's not like I can tell them, hell no, I won't touch anything from that chalkboard of horrors that hangs above the bar, since no one knows what happened here a couple days ago after I finished Jacob's cocktail. So, I settled on good, old beer, much to everyone's dismay.

"Yeah, magic powers, alright. Those lead to bad, bad decisions," I murmur to myself, but of course, the one who is not supposed to hear it does.

"Do they now?" he whispers into my ear. "I happen to remember differently. In fact, I think you particularly enjoyed Eros Spell."

"What?" I hiss quietly, making sure others are preoccupied.

"Hmm, yes, you were being a very good girl that night. A very naughty, good girl." His words lick my insides. My vagina has passed out, drooling, and my heart is trying to wake her up with rapid beating as it fans over her.

He just had to go and say that right now. Didn't he? He had to call me *that*.

"I think we should try the Cupid's Arrow this time. This one is supposed to help you fall madly in love with me." The way he says it is so casually, yet hot and heavy, it makes my skin break out in sex hives. It's so easy for him to throw all these words around. The words that make my heart ache.

And I don't want it to ache. It has ached enough for one lifetime. *Breathe in, breathe out, Joy.*

"Since you three ruined our date, the least you can do is tell me everything I need to know about Hope," Alec says to us, but it's Jacob who speaks first.

"She's very flexible." I freeze. What. The. Fuck... "What? You asked me to tell you what you need to know. I happen to think this is vital information."

"I happen to agree," Alec says, but that ache I had going on? It is slowly morphing into fear and something resembling anger. "The question is; how do you know that?" Alec continues, pointing to him.

"Town workout, remember? I led it today."

"I need to get out of here," I think to myself, but based on all the eyes on me, I might have said it out loud, and now I need to come up with an excuse because feeling irrationally jealous and betrayed by my one-night stand is not an option. "I need to go back to normal people who don't consider flexibility as vital information."

"I happen to disagree———" Jacob thinks it's a great time to keep joking, but I'm done here. He is just like the rest of them, ready to jump any good-looking piece of ass, and I am not going through that again.

Enough is enough for me. Even if *I* was never enough for anyone. Oh, the irony...

"You still don't seem to grasp the concept of me not caring what you happen to think. No more talking," I cut him off, pinching my thumb and other fingers in a shut-up gesture, hoping he has some brain cells to understand me right now. My chest is heaving with the sizzling anger inside it. I have successfully shut down the fucking lust parade, and now, I only need Jacob to shut up.

"Wildflower, you wound me." Nope, no such luck.

"Enough, please. I'd like to have my turn to tell Alec how to woo my sister." Grace looks at me; somehow, she understands that I am a second from falling apart, and the sympathy in her eyes almost does me in, but I'm grateful she's come to my rescue, nonetheless. And she falls into an easy conversation, telling Alec all he wants to know about Hope, with me agreeing here and there, or shaking my head.

My beer is almost done, and I have successfully avoided the man on my right the whole time drinking it, but now an entirely different species of male stumbles upon our table, and we all freeze.

This guy is the postcard for tall, dark, and handsome. Except there is absolutely nothing "nice" about him. He looks pissed off at the world, and every fiber of me can relate to the feeling on a visceral level. He looks imposing and dark, with his broad shoulders straining in the simple black T-shirt. His dark hair is clean-cut and styled professionally.

He. He is who I would describe as my usual taste in men, but suddenly, I don't find him all that attractive. I mean, yes, he is fucking hot, but my vagina is not going on a riot for him.

I am waiting for some explanation of who he is, but it seems there is some kind of mute game going on between him and—weirdly—Alec. The new guy sends glares to Alec and then slowly moves his gaze to my little sister, Grace, who is currently trying to pretend she is a squirrel and hides behind my back.

I am not a small woman, but I'm not big enough to hide her from his darkness. Usually, I would be going all mama bear on him for looking at her this way, but for some reason, I won't. Something in him tells me he is not a threat to her. At least not in a malicious way. Maybe we share the same walls in our lonely ward; maybe it's the researcher in me doing her quick assessment of the data I am presented with, and all my answers point to one simple conclusion.

This guy, whoever he is, wants Grace. Like a beast on a hunt.

"Alec," the new guy finally says in a deep, throaty voice that normally would send any woman's panties into a wet mess, but mine are already ruined from the one I'm trying to ignore while he shifts closer and closer to me.

But Grace? That girl is having a full-on panic attack behind my back, panting and sweating while clutching onto my arm for dear life.

I mean, I don't blame her. Not really, and remembering our talk earlier when she mentioned something about coming without ever being touched, I am suddenly curious if he is the one with those superpowers.

Suddenly, it clicks. Oh, shit. The talk we had earlier...

Grace bites her lip and averts her gaze from us. Oh, yeah. This beast is it. I eye him up and down. Damn it, it must have been one glorious orgasm. I have zero doubts it was our mother who planned all this. She is the one who trapped her three daughters in this weird town with three irresistible men, and now, it's all her fault all of us are suffering from blue ovaries.

Well, I guess in Gracie's case, she got her reward, even though it is very unconventional. But an orgasm is an orgasm.

This guy could easily pose naked in those Firemen calendars all of my students own. All those muscles ripping through his shirt are a dead giveaway; he is fine underneath it. Very fine. Yet, I still feel absolutely nothing towards him. Nada.

Please, pray, do tell, my dear vagina, why in the world you are boycotting right now?

And then, as the front door opens, carrying in a light breeze inside, it blows Jacob's scent my way, and I am dying... I stiffen from his smell alone, but the bastard puts his warm, big hand on my jean-covered thigh, and I'm hyperventilating the same way Grace is, but in response to a completely different guy.

Yeah, I think I am going to kill our mother.

I should shake his hand off me. I should still be angry at his last comment about Hope's body, and I am, but the weight of his arm on me somehow soothes the pain. It's comfort.

"Luke," Alec responds to the stranger in a sharp tone I wasn't aware he was capable of. "What are you doing here?"

"I'm surprised you don't know yet, seeing as news travels faster than the wind in this gossip hole." Huh, I knew I liked you, *Luke*.

"Know what?"

"I'm the new chief of the fire department." And there goes my calendar prediction.

"You're what?" Alec yells in outrage, but everyone is too happy in this bar to notice, or they pretend not to, in hopes of hearing more gossip. Like those damn flies on the wall.

"Don't play dumb. It didn't suit you when you were ten, and it certainly doesn't add to your appeal today," Luke says with no emotion.

For anyone else, he would be a fascinating character to discover and learn about. But for me, he is not. From the moment he stepped up to our table, I was looking in a mirror but with a male face there. He has been hurt, and now his walls are impenetrable. Just like mine were before I came to this horrible, happy town.

Maybe Luke hasn't been here long enough?

"Why would you take a job in a—how did you call it—gossip hole?" He snaps his fingers at Luke, who sends him another scowl.

"None of your business," he says. "See you around," he adds, but those blueish eyes with a dark soul are resting on Grace once again.

I wish I could protect you, my little sister. Not from this guy but from a heartbreak waiting to happen...because I think you are already drowning in him.

Luke takes a sudden sharp turn and leaves us as the pin-dropping silence cowers at our table.

Hope clears her throat. "Um, who was that?"

"My brother," Alec answers with distaste.

"Brother?" Grace squeaks from the far corner she pushed herself into. "I mean, brother?" She tries again in a somewhat calmer voice, which is not fooling anyone here.

"Yeah, he hasn't been in town for seventeen years, and now he comes back announcing he's chief of FDLC? Fucking prick." Those F-words sound so sweet when these hippies say them.

And now, I want to taste it off of my Viking's soft lips while they are wrapped around my nipples and his cock buried deep inside.

No.

No more sleeping with Jacob. Here I am, worried about Grace's broken heart when I should be protecting my own.

"You know what? I need to go. I remembered something. I forgot to do something. Joy, let me out. I need to go. Now." Grace starts pushing me out violently, nearly sending Jacob to the floor.

"Gracie? Are you alright? Do you want us to come with you?" Hope asks her, but she just shakes her head.

"No, I'm fine. You stay. I'll go alone." With that last word, she flies out of the seat and out the door.

"She is so not okay. What the hell was that?" I ask, even though the answer is as clear as day.

"Remember the text messages earlier?" We shared a look, knowing full well that both of us had come to the same conclusion earlier.

"Care to let us in on the secret?" Jacob asks with his eyebrows raised.

"No," I say fast, and get up myself to leave. "I'll go find her," I offer because I am not staying in the same building with him for a second longer. At this moment, my family needs me, but all I can think of is Jacob while he is around, and that can't be.

No man is allowed that much space in my head anymore.

# 16

# 50 Reasons

Reason #13:
*Jacob: I am amazing at compromising.*
*Joy: Really?*
*Jacob: Yes.*
*Joy: Okay, burn your rubber ducky shorts because they annoy me.*
*Jacob: HOW COULD YOU?*

Reason #16:
*Jacob: If you don't want to be stuck at some work function, all you have to do is tell them your husband lost his rubber ducky, and they will let you go.*
*Joy: Aha, possibly forever.*

# 17

## *Joy*

*"Your mind is like a parachute, it doesn't work unless it's open" – Jordan Maxwell.*

Turns out, it is easier said than done. Staying away from Jacob proves to be nearly impossible in this small town. It's been a few days since I up and left from LPs, leaving Jacob behind. I saw him running after me, looking for me from the corner I was hiding in, and as soon as he was out of sight, I ran to my car, got in, and sped off towards the pink disaster I now call home, thinking I was safe.

Yeah...a fat chance.

My personal shark slippers-obsessed, tiny rubber ducky shorts-wearing stalker shows up at my front door at least three times a day. Do I open the door? Nope. Do I devour his fine ass through the upstairs window? You bet. But that is all I am allowing myself. Research from far away. Even though my vagina is pissed at me and refuses to orgasm from my own hands or even toys.

Apparently, one taste of Jacob's dick, and the bitch is hooked. Pathetic, weak organ.

No, I will not look at it from the psychological perspective since most anorgasmia issues stem from the mind-body connection. Absolutely not.

My mind is fine.

It's focused on fixing up this cottage and moving back home to Chicago, where my life is waiting for me.

What life, exactly? I have no idea but a life.

Zoe has been a wall for these past few days, so I don't know what the situation is like with Justin and those charges he got, but maybe it's for the better. I don't want to know anything else concerning Justin-lying-asshole-Hunt. Nothing.

In fact, I will die a happy woman if I never see his face again.

I would also die a happy woman if my little sister would leave me alone, but that one ain't happening for sure. Gracie has been a literal shadow of mine; she is always around, and when she isn't, she's texting me, bugging and annoying me until I give in to whatever it was she asked me to do in the first place.

We spent a whole evening unpacking the issues from that one night ten years ago. And my opinion hasn't changed. We were young and stupid, and communication was not our strong suit. But since we've both said our apologies, she has been her annoying little sister self again. And I'm not sure if she really wants to spend time with me or if she's simply avoids a certain beast the way I am my Viking.

That is how I found myself in a place that should be closed down due to health code violations. Because they violate my healthy need for caffeine. Sip of Love coffee shop owned by a love child named Julie. When Grace mentioned it to me,

I actually got excited, thinking I had finally found one good thing about Loverly Cave.

Wrong.

This is the worst thing about Loverly Cave town because these people serve mud waters, vitamin tonics, balance smoothies, mushroom concoction, and a whole bunch of other crap they have the audacity to call coffee.

And this is reason number one thousand-three-hundred-fifty-six why I am not staying here permanently. I'd die from caffeine deficiency. Yes, I am being dramatic, but can you blame me? When Julie stretched her arm out toward me, offering the mushroom coffee, I barely made it to the bathroom to throw up. Not only did it look like she went out the back door, scooped up some sewer water, and poured it into the cup, but it also smelled like it came from one.

When I returned from the bathroom, Grace rolled her eyes at me and gladly downed the whole cup of crap.

I, on the other hand, threw up again.

You'd think I had enough "fun" for one day, but no, my sister decided to put the final nail in the coffin and talked me into joining her, Hope, and Alec for a bonfire dinner at the beach. What she failed to mention is that a certain Viking would be in attendance also.

As soon as his feet hit the now cold sand, he stretched his arms wide and bellows, "Wildflower," loud enough for the whole beach to hear.

Involuntarily, my eyes snap up to his green ones, and I watch as a panty-melting smile graces his handsome face. His whole focus is solely on me as he prowls to the sand, and I feel those now very familiar hussies take flight in my chest and nether regions.

Jesus, can this man be a tiny bit uglier? Like, I am trying to stay away here, okay? And this, him, that smile, and body and the over-the-top-I'm-suffocating positivity is not good for me.

Add in his unruly, soft blonde hair, intricate tattoos, and that damn beard that felt better than a visit to a spa on my skin, and my legs are falling apart all by themselves.

Suddenly, Jacob disappears behind the small hill where I assume his car is parked, and a few seconds later, he reappears carrying a small potted plant. Its deep green leaves cling to a thin stem, but they are all standing upright. There are about three or four branches like that, and it sort of looks like a tiny forest, which he hands over to me as soon as he reaches us.

"This is for you, boo," he says, smiling, and I take the colorfully hand-painted ceramic pot from him, holding it as if he handed me an explosive grenade.

"It's a plant," I state the obvious, but *obviously*, my brain can't comprehend why he'd give this to me.

"I don't believe in regular flowers. They die. This way, my love can stay with you forever," Jacob smirks.

"Until I kill it," I deadpan.

"Ahhh." He clutches a fist to his chest dramatically. "Kill my love? Impossible! It's eternal, and so is the plant I chose. We both require very little to be happy, so you are perfect for us."

"I assure you, I'm not capable of even a 'little.'"

"Hmm, I remember quite well how 'much' you can give and take." The innuendo in his voice is as clear as a day, and Grace is eating it right up.

His wicked smile reaches my lady parts faster than I can put up a few more walls of protection. Before I can put myself back together, he shifts his eyes to my grinning sister. "Gracie." He tips his imaginary hat to my sister. "I now owe you a favor."

My gaze takes a sharp turn as it lands on the said sister, and she smiles sweetly at Jacob but has the good grace to look away from me.

"Fucking traitor," escapes my lips. "I cannot believe this! Did you bully me into coming here because he," I throw my thumb toward Jacob, "asked you to?"

"I don't know what you are talking about," she says while chewing on the inside of her cheek, and the urge to kill someone has never been stronger.

"Oh, I think I hear...yep, they are calling me," Grace points to her ear and to the pit where no one is making a sound and scurries away toward the fire faster than lightning, fearing my wrath would descend upon her in the next second or two.

At the fire pit, Alec—wearing one of his signature cut-off tank tops, a backward hat, and a blinding smile—is dragging wood into it, and Hope, who is barely containing her drool, sits on the blanket as she watches him.

Oh my God...do I look like that, too, around Jacob?

"I am stoked to see you too, boo," he continues as if I am not sending death glares in every direction. Without another word, I clutch my new plant to my chest and take off in the direction of my cottage, and this is the time I am grateful for living on the beach.

Fine, I love living on the beach, waking up to the sound of crashing waves and birds chirping away as they scout for food. This might be something I will miss in cement and brick-filled Chicago.

"Where are you and Bob going?" He catches up to me, matching my strides.

"I am going home. Who is Bob, and what is he doing? I have no idea. You, on the other hand, are going back there." I point to the blankets and bonfire.

"No can do. I go where my boo and our baby plant—Bob—goes." I stop abruptly, and he crashes into me.

"You named my plant?" For some reason, I feel offensive. It's my plant. I get to name him!

*Ridiculous. I know.* What else is new these days?

"Our plant. We are co-parenting. Should I move in? It will make visitations easier."

"Do you have a death wish?" I ask as we reach my porch, and I set Bob down. I fold my arms across my chest, which pushes my breasts up in that ridiculous tank top Grace made me buy and wear. Now I know why.

Jacob's eyes fall straight down there as his mouth falls open slightly, and I swear there is a bead of drooling pooling on the side of it.

"I have a wish, alright," he says after a moment, but his eyes are still glued to my girls, but for some idiotic reason, I am not doing anything to stop it.

I like his attention. I like to feel wanted. Especially by this man.

I know. I'm completely irrational and make zero sense, but whatever. Let me enjoy this for a little while longer.

"Can I make a request?" he randomly asks in the middle of a different sentence, and I feel my eyebrow raise in a silent "go ahead."

"When you kill me, can it be by suffocation? I'd like to be suffocated by your boobs. But I won't complain if it's by your pussy either."

"Oh my God, you need help," I say with a tired exhale to him, throwing my head back.

"Yes, yes, I do. Are you offering?"

"To kill you?"

"Aha." His head bobs up and down, his eyes glued to my body.

"Eyes up here, Jacob," I finally snap at him, pointing to my eyes with my index and middle finger.

"I can't," he says when he does look up briefly. His face literally looks tortured. "It's all so beautiful down here...I mean, you are breathtaking everywhere, but you have been hiding my girls from me, and now I'm aching all over, and my fingers are itching to touch them." He makes a grabbing gesture with his hands, flexing and relaxing his fist, like something you'd see a toddler do. "Can I touch?" He extends his hands out to me, and I quickly slap them away.

"Hands to yourself, Jacob." I pinch the bridge of my nose. "You have serious issues."

*He called you breathtaking*, my useless brain supplies.

"Mm-hmm and they are all below my waist."

"Hey, lovebirds, care to join us?" Alec calls out, and I'm about to tell them all to fuck off when Jacob interrupts me.

"Call us, JJ," he shouts, throwing his big, warm hand over my shoulder, and to my horror, my feet start moving as he walks us to the bonfire site.

"JJ it is." Alec grins while Hope and Grace look highly amused by the whole scene.

"Do not call us that." I throw his hand off and plant myself on the blanket beside my youngest sister.

"So, you agree there is an us?" His eyebrows are dancing up and down.

"My threat to kill you is still very much in effect, so I suggest stepping away from me," I tell him as I press my finger to his strong, warm chest and push him away. Silently swallowing my whimper at the contact.

Shut it, hussies. We are not touching anything else!

Jacob doesn't look fazed at all. My every insult rebounds off him like a bouncy ball, and I wonder how he does that?

How do you grow such thick skin to prohibit anything through it?

Or is it something else? Because I need to know. I need to master this skill.

"We have beer or ice cream, which do you prefer?" Jacob asks, looking up from the cooler.

"Oh, what kind you got?" Grace asks.

"There is strawberry shortcake, Oreo, rocky road, and popsicles."

"Heck yes, I'll take the rocky road." Grace fist pumps the air since they have her favorite flavor. I wonder if Hope's taste changed in the past decade.

"What about you, Wildflower?"

"Oh, you dón't have her favorite." Grace waves him off, and I shoot her another "I'll kill you" look she completely ignores as she opens her container of chocolate monstrosity.

"And which one would that be?" Jacob asks with a little glint in his eyes. This guy is good. Alec was all straight to the point and out there, but Jacob? He is creative with the way he gets his information. Sneaky. Dangerous.

"Birthday sprinkles," Grace mumbles out with a mouthful of rocky road.

The loom of glee and pure baby joy overtaking Jacob's face is worth my anger with Grace. His lips stretch into another panty-melting smile. "Boo? You were holding out on me? I knew you were my soulmate!"

"That was ten years ago. Grace got the wrong information."

"Naw, izs nat," she can barely talk now. My jaw slides to the side as I silently beg my little sister to shut the hell up. "Your freezer is stocked to the top," she says after finally swallowing her scoop.

"So, you're the ice cream thief?" Jacob asks me.

"No idea what you are talking about."

"Well, you see, Wildflower, birthday sprinkles happen to be *my*," he points to his chest, "favorite ice cream. And when I went to the store to get some today, they were all out."

Yes, fine, I bought out everything they had, but he doesn't need to know that. What? A girl needs to unwind somehow after watching his hotness I can't touch, walk around these streets every day.

"Sucks to be you, I guess." I shrug and hold my smile back.

"No, sucks to be you because now I am definitely moving in. How does tomorrow sound?"

"It sounds impossible."

"Busy in the morning?"

"Busy for life."

"It's okay, I can do all the moving myself."

"Jacob." I sigh, sounding exasperated.

"Are you tired, Wildflower?"

"Very."

"I think you have a deficiency." I quirk an eyebrow at him.

"Of patience?"

"No, of vitamin 'me.'" He winks and steps away as I roll my eyes. He grabs two beers from the cooler, handing one to me, and walks around the pit to sit somewhere on the other side.

Or at least that's what I assume.

"I'd totally fuck him," Grace says, puckering her lips and squinting her eyes at my Viking's ass as if she's seriously considering it. I choke on the very first sip of beer I take, causing it to spill from my mouth like a fountain, and I'm about to slap her up the head—not exactly sure whether from shock or irrational jealousy—when we hear a low, threatening growl behind us, and if you can imagine one of those scenes in the movies where suddenly you turn ramrod straight and the whole world freezes, that would be very accurate for us at the moment except I think Grace is about to puke all her rocky road out.

Slowly, very slowly, we turn around to see an imposing, larger-than-life Luke standing with his arms crossed at his chest and a scowl that has no rivals on his face. And it is directed at my little sister, who gulps loudly and exhales heavily.

"In case I don't live to see another day, I'd like you to know you were my favorite oldest sister, and you should totally go have hot, wild sex with Jacob," Grace whispers to me, but her eyes are on Luke. Not blinking or moving a millimeter away.

Okay...

In a flash, she is up and moving away from us, Luke hot on her heels.

"Where did Grace go?" Jacob asks as he drops himself right beside me on the spot that my sister just vacated.

"Wish I knew and that she'd take me with her," I mumbled to myself.

"Oh, well, I guess it's a double date," Jacob announces happily, clapping and rubbing his palms together, and both Hope and I say, "It is not," in unison.

"Fine, two single dates spent in the company of each other," he rephrases his statement, but the point still stands.

"Jacob." I pinch the bridge of my nose. "We are not on a date. There is no dating happening between you and I. And there will *be* no dating."

"You're right, we aren't dating. That's far too trivial for us. We are soulmates, after all, because come on, birthday sprinkles!" He taps his finger to his chin as I count to ten in my head. "Oh, I know," he finally says. "Let's call this the honeymoon phase."

"Is it your mission to piss me off?"

"I knew you'd fall in love with me. I'm irresistible." He smiles wide as if I didn't just say what I said. I take a deep breath, close my eyes, and place both hands on my thighs.

"No, you know what? I am not feeding your delusions. Nope." I decide sitting with my mouth shut is probably the best course of action.

The one that won't get me naked since, apparently, his stupidity is now a major turn-on for me.

I know. I need help. Please send your complaints to my vagina. Address: the soaking spot between my legs.

"Lovebug, I got you your favorite from Bagels and Love," Alec says, handing Hope a bag with a sandwich in it.

"I got my own food," she retorts back.

"I know, but I am trying to prove a point here, you know." He winks at my sister and drops himself to the blanket, but instead of just sitting next to Hope, he scoops her up, planting her on his lap and wraps his tattooed arms around her. She tries her hardest to hide her reaction, but everyone can spot that blush she is flashing from a mile away. Whatever these two have going on, I don't think she's winning it.

Hope and I share a look that says it all...we are screwed with these men.

Apparently, the boys got enough food—and ice cream—to feed an army, and we settle into a comfortable conversation as we devour it. Yes, fine, I concede that these people here can cook. Everything I have tasted so far is beyond delicious, and I'm not surprised to see Hope and me finishing up our vegan sandwich in the blink of an eye.

I'm so concentrated on the food, I completely miss what Alec and Jacob are talking about, but somehow, my brain decides to step in during the worst time.

"I feel like my dick is finally in shape. You know all that COVID shit messed with it," Jacob casually says, and I choke on the last bit of my food.

Can I eat or drink without near-death experiences for once in this town?

He reaches over and slaps my back lightly to help with the coughing fit I am having. I lift up my hand to stop him as it seizes.

"Oh, I know, dude. Same here," Alec agrees and nods along. "Alec Junior is finally feeling fine, isn't he, lovebug?" Finally, it is not me who is choking on food this time. Hope looks at Alec, then down to his "junior," and back up with an open mouth, yet nothing is coming out of it.

"See, Hope agrees." He winks at her.

"I do not!" my sister protests. "You and your 'junior' are on your own. I have nothing to do with that."

"Aha," Alec simply hums. "Sure, you don't." My sister's face grows red in the evening light, and I arch an eyebrow at her.

"No need to feel embarrassed, Hope. Alec's dick is a fine specimen. And if it makes you feel good, then that's all that matters," Jacob casually says while taking another bite of his sandwich.

"What the fuck am I listening to?" I ask myself out loud.

"What?" Jacob asks me with genuine confusion. "Are you trying to say my Antoine didn't live up to your expectations the other night?" Jesus, of course, he named his dick. I'm surprised I haven't heard about it before.

Immediately, all eyes are on us as mine are trying to disintegrate the idiot sitting next to me.

"Um, Joy? Is there something you forgot to mention to your sisters?" Hope asks me, but I decide to ignore it.

"Your dick did fine. Just fine. And we are done with this topic." I turn to my sister, who has a million questions written on her face. "No," I stop her before she spills her word vomit. "We are not discussing this. The end."

"Just fine?" Jacob's eyebrows shoot up. "I distinctly remem—" I cut him off with a scolding look.

"Don't worry, *big* buddy, Mommy didn't mean to offend you. She secretly loves you very much, Antoine. Her moans told us so." He pats the middle of his shorts as his dick twitches behind them.

I need more beer for this shit. "*Fine*," he mocks my tone. "And what's wrong with our conversation?"

"Um, it's inappropriate?" I bulge my eyes at him.

"Says who?" For the first time since I've met him, his eyes grow serious, dark, and intense.

"Everyone? The society? The etiquette?"

"Oh, boy. Here we go," Alec murmurs and shakes his head slightly, humor lining his features. "You have awoken the dragon, Joy. Congratulations."

I am about to ask what he means when the once-peaceful Viking next to me goes on a rant.

"Society," he scoffs as if that word is full of bile, and he can't wait to spit it out of his mouth.

"The damn society is a load of rubbish. They have set up all these rules for what is right and wrong. What is acceptable and not? What should shame us, and what should make us proud. But who's to say they are correct?" He turns to look at me again.

Something tells me I should keep my thoughts to myself, but he's looking at me expectantly, so I answer, "I'd say years of life experience would suggest they are."

"I'm not talking about the basic principles of life like don't kill, don't steal, and the rest of the Ten Commandments.

No, I'm talking about misconceptions. One old goon decided that burping in public is a show of poor manners, and now, anytime we see someone do it, we frown. When in reality, the acid reflux reaction is a sign of some underlying issue, and we should not be suppressing it. Our body is telling us to seek help, yet because we have been told it's just some rude thing to do, we ignore it."

When did Jacob get so smart?

"Someone said that a big house, a new fancy car, and a wife disfigured by plastic surgery is a show of status, class, and wealth, but is that true?"

I open my mouth to say something, but nothing comes out, and I close it again.

Truth be told, just before he said it, I did believe in that. I have a perfect example of that back home in Chicago. But now?

"What's really behind those big doors and fancy metal? Is the man happy with his fake wife? Or is she simply an arm candy to parade around other fake families? Is wealth measured in the amount of the bills stacked in your bank account? Does being rich instantly mean you are a good human being or that it grants you extra wisdom?

"Society believes that to show your intelligence level, you must go to school, college, university and so on, when in reality some of the smartest, most brilliant, humble people have never stepped a foot in such institutions."

"Yes, but you must admit school gives you more knowledge," I argue.

"No, I won't agree to that," he throws back. "We are all intelligent beings without old goons in stuffy classrooms telling us so. Most of us learn through life experiences. Yes, certain jobs require special knowledge, but not in the way it is provided these days." He scoffs again, and suddenly, my curiosity about this man spikes up.

He's not just a pretty face. There is depth in his thoughts, even if I don't agree with him, he doesn't succumb to public opinion, and all three of us are listening to him intently.

"You do realize universities are there to profit and stroke the egos of those who own it, right? If they taught for the sake of knowledge, we wouldn't have to pay these astronomical amounts of money in tuition," Jacob speaks with a certain level of disdain, and I want to dig into him and see what made him resent society so much?

"You went to a fancy school, didn't you?"

"I did." I nod.

"Because society told you to or you wanted to?"

"I wanted to become a doctor so of course, I needed to go to a good school!"

"Why? Would going to a smaller college change your knowledge? Or do they teach from some other textbooks?"

I should have a response, but I just blink at him.

"See." He points to me. "I bet you were too smart for that fancy university of yours. I bet you didn't even need it to become successful, but we are fed these preconceived notions about what is right and what is wrong and step right into the big pocket's traps."

"Did you go to a fancy school?" I ask him.

"No, I did not. Much to my father's dismay," he says the last part, and just when my interest takes on a whole other level, Jacob shuts down and changes the subject. "Anyway, the society sucks, and if I want to talk about my dick, I will. And you should, too."

"I don't have one."

"Oh, I beg to differ, Wildflower." He winks, and just like that, the happy weirdo mask is back on.

"You were right," Hope murmurs to Alec.

"Right about what?" Jacob inserts himself into their conversation.

My head tilts to the side as I watch him. I'm starting to get a better idea of this man. He is not as shallow as he would like us to believe. He's not just a happy-go-lucky guy...and my attraction to him morphs from simple physical to a deep-rooted problem which I am not supposed to have.

Lusting after him and wishing I could just sit and talk to him are two very, *very* different things. I'm off-balance. This isn't right; I'm not supposed to feel this way about men anymore. I never have, to begin with.

"Alec told me how seriously you take this society talk," Hope tells him.

"I just don't like being told what I can and can't be," he says to her.

"I don't either, but those chains are very heavy." My younger sister gets a faraway look in her eyes, and I know she went back into Brian-land. His shackles still weigh heavily on her shoulders.

"Then throw them off, dump them over the cliff."

"How?" she voices the question I have on the tip of my tongue.

"Simple. You live. You live each day like it's your last. You do what you love. You see who you want to see. You talk to who you want to talk to. You are enough the way you are, and if someone tells you otherwise, they are the ones who are lesser. *You* decide what is best for you, even if that best is frowned upon. They are scowling because they are too afraid to do it themselves and too jealous that you could."

*You are enough the way you are...*

My eyes lift up to his, and it's as if he knows he struck a nerve because those green stormy eyes turn soft. Jacob lifts his hand up to my cheek and softly strokes it while warm amber fires fill the darkness around us.

Instantly, there are no chilly winds, no ocean breeze, and soft waves clashing with the nearby rocks. There is no Hope or Alec. No one.

Just him.

Just my one-night stand turned into my personal kryptonite.

For the next week, I only have one task. *Stay away from Jacob, stay away from Jacob, stay away from Jacob.*

# 18

# Joy

*"People think a soul mate is your perfect fit, and that's what everyone wants. But a true soul mate is a mirror, the person who shows you everything that is holding you back, the person who brings you to your own attention so you can change your life." –Elizabeth Gilbert*

"Joy, honey?" I hear my mom's voice calling out my name. Apparently, she has let herself in while I am painting my room.

"In the bedroom, Mom," I call out to her, and a second later, she appears in my doorway.

"Goodie, I caught you this time," she tells me.

"I guess you did, but I will need you to leave that key to my place that you have made yourself without my knowledge right there on the bed," I inform her, my eyes still on the white streaks of paint on my wall.

"There is no key. Your door was open," the elaborate schemer replies.

"Sure, it was."

"Stop distracting me; I came here to tell you about dinner tonight. You have to come."

I stop. Red alert is going off in my head because nothing good comes from dinners at my parents' place. "Who is invited?" My eyes finally snap to hers, and I watch her carefully.

"Oh, the regular crew, you know, your sisters, the Colsons, some other neighbors," She waves me off casually. The neighbors, my ass. She invited Jacob, I'm sure of it.

"Sorry, can't make it, but it sounds like you'll have a blast without me anyway."

"Yes, you can."

"No, I can't. I have Hug Car duty later today. Sorry." I am not sorry at all, and for the first time since hearing about that stupid assignment, I am actually grateful for it.

I still can't believe I couldn't get out of it. The mayor.

The. Mayor. Of Loverly Cave, with just the most fitting last name of Loveton, came by earlier today and personally handed me my timecard. No, I am not joking; I haven't been smoking pot or drinking Mellow-yellows.

A hug car!!! It means I have to physically wrap my hands around someone else while they are leaking from their tear ducts onto my shoulder.

A fucking hug car!!!

Every time I tried to explain that I was not a real resident of this town, I was shut down.

Not to mention, the other day, as I passed by the entrance to the city, I watched them change the population number up top, adding four new members.

Hope, Grace, me, and Luke.

When I told them they got the wrong number, the guy shrugged and said *Jackie* told him it was four.

Whatever, if they want to keep climbing up there, changing the numbers every few days, then so be it. I don't care, and I am leaving. Soon.

Just for that alone, I am ready to kill Jacob. But that's a topic for another day, for now, I am grateful.

"Oh." Mom looks crestfallen, and my cold heart feels a tiny bit bad. That insufferable organ has been acting out ever since I arrived at LC, and I blame it for what I say next. "How about tomorrow? I can make it then."

Mom instantly beams at me and claps her hands together. "Yes, that would be lovely. Tomorrow it is, and oh, you are going to love Hug Car." I raise an eyebrow; my face says anything but impressed. "Fine, you won't love it, but it's not that bad. I promise."

"I don't believe a word you say, but I can pretend."

"Oh, I forgot to tell you something." She jumps up from excitement.

"What?"

"Last night I had the best dream! You were pregnant!"

My hand stops painting mid-roll, and I lift an unimpressed eyebrow at her.

"Was it a nightmare?"

Mom humphs at my comment, tils her head up in defiance, and says, "I'd like to consider it a prophecy."

"How very clairvoyant of you." I go back to painting.

"Where you got your grumpy genes, I have no idea," Mom mumbles to herself as she shakes her head. "Have fun today, and I will see you tomorrow." She kisses my cheek and leaves.

I note the empty bed, where she did not leave my key. I exhaled loudly; I'll have to track it down tomorrow. God knows what that woman can come up with while having unrestricted access to my cottage.

For the rest of the day, I lose myself in work, fixing, painting, scrubbing, and doing what I must to make this house as presentable as possible. I have already wasted way too much time in this town, and with the way Zoe has been blowing up my phone today, I can only imagine how much work I have waiting for me in Chicago.

Cold, grey, lonely Chicago.

No, I love my fifty shades of alone. That's where I am happy. Right? Then why doesn't it sound so good anymore?

My strange thoughts get interrupted by a text from my assistant.

Zoe: **Joy, call me back! This is about Justin!**

If there is one thing she could have said *not* to have me call her about, this would be it. I don't care about my ex. I don't care about his issues, complaints, or career.

I have Hug Car duty today, and I have to start in fifteen minutes, so Justin will have to wait.

I open the door to my car, throwing my purse inside, when I see a decked-out, tiny Smart car pulling up next to me. It's yellow, has rainbows all over it, and that cloud from the *Trolls* cartoon, extending his small arms for a hug as a gigantic sticker on the back windshield. At the top of the car, there is a sign saying, "It's hug time" –another quote from *Trolls*, and I fight the urge to roll my eyes. Let me guess, I am driving *that* for the next three hours.

But that's not the worst of it.

Nope.

Inside the tiny car is a hulk of a man, taking up far too much space in there and in my head, grinning widely at me as he waves me over. When he sees that I'm not making any moves to come closer, he steps out with that same smile, another pair of shorter-than-life shorts. This time, they are green and have silly emojis all over the fabric, and of course, his shark slides on his feet.

To be this carefree...

"Wildflower." His silky voice goes straight to the depraved lady between my thighs, who sighs in appreciation as if she just got her fix, but it was just one word out of the man's mouth.

Pathetic...

"Jacob." I steel myself, trying to keep those walls high so he doesn't get a chance to climb over.

*Fine, he already took a peek in between the cracks, but I've patched those up. No more peeking.*

"Come on, boo, we gotta start in five." He throws his head back to the car.

"We?" I think I heard wrong. My timecard only had my name on it, not his.

"You didn't think I'd leave you all alone on your first day, now, would you? Plus, you can't run away from me this time." I swear I hear the offended notes in his speech as if I just questioned his integrity and character.

And maybe I am questioning it, but only because there is no way someone can be this nice, happy, persistent, and kind. Nope, not real.

"Do you mean to say you are coming along?" I'm not sure why my voice creaks at the end there, but it does.

"Of course I am." He puffs up his chest. "Me, you—"

"Wedding bells and babies, I remember," I interrupt him and roll my eyes, but that stupid, sexy grin of his only grows more magnetic.

"I was going to say me, you and the Hug Car, but I definitely prefer your train of thought better."

Oh, Jesus Christ. Please add death by mortification to my eulogy. Why did I have to say that crap? No, you know what? It's all his fault. He's the one who put that thought in my head, so I'm blaming him.

Also, three hours in one small car with this man just might kill me, so I guess the list for my causes of death might be extra extended. I've spent the whole week since that bonfire night avoiding him, and here he is, thrusting himself at me full-force.

"Shall we make a stop at the town hall before or after the Hug Car duty?" he asks, winking, and I'm a second from exploding.

Pretending I didn't hear him and that his words didn't wake those hussies in my belly up, I grab my bag from my car and stomp over to the driver's side of the yellow blob.

"The silent treatment," he says, still smiling as he walks over to me. "Look at that, we aren't even married yet but going through the usual crap it comes with. I like it," he proclaims, and I raise an eyebrow at him.

He likes it? Who likes this?

"What?" he answers my silent question. "You are getting me prepared for what life with you would be like."

"You are impossible; you know that?"

"And you are more beautiful today than you were yesterday," he says, kissing my cheek. And I simply melt. I melt like an ice cube in California heat. From a simple compliment.

"Ha." He points to me with glee. "And just like that, the conflict had been resolved. See, practice makes perfect. Now, why don't we also practice some post-fighting sex? I heard it's magical."

"If you don't get into that car in the next ten seconds, I'm leaving without you, *hubby*."

He looks up to me with an open mouth and glinting eyes. Shit. This is all a joke, but suddenly, it doesn't feel like one.

That term of endearment rolled off my tongue way too easily. Like it was always meant to be said to him.

"Wildflower, I'll carry this moment for the rest of our lives." The idiot clutches his hand to his chest, and I decide to go back to ignoring him and my stupid proclamation. I slide into the seat and start the car when Jacob jumps into the passenger seat. "Okay, we can do the town hall after the duty," he says as he buckles himself in.

Once again, I don't respond, but Jacob isn't fazed by my muteness. He fills all the gaps himself, sometimes even answering his own questions as if I did.

After about fifteen minutes of patrolling around the streets of LC, I finally can't take any more of his chatter.

"You know why I picked pathology?" I ask him through gritted teeth.

"I don't think you ever told me, no. And by the way, I am not offended you didn't tell me about your profession yourself. I mean, not really. Because mentioning it while I was about to fuck your pretty pussy, didn't count. Thankfully, Love Hive filled me in." He places the palm of his large hand on my bare thigh—because I'm an idiot who decided to wear shorts today—and immediately, all thoughts disappear from my brain.

I can only feel it. Feel his warmth, heat, and strength. Feel him. And I don't want to *feel* him. He was a one-night stand with a stranger I was never supposed to see again. Yet here I am, dying inside from his mere touch. And his words. Those are not helping, either.

"Joy?" Shit, did I space out? And this is why I can't stay around this guy. This is why this golden retriever slash Chi-

# MEET MY WIFE

huahua mix, who is trying to work his way into my bed once again, is staying out in the backyard.

Ignoring his hand, which is still on my damn thigh, I go back to our conversation. "Because the dead don't waste my time on unnecessary chatter. They speak with their bodies."

"I can speak with my body," he adds cheerfully, and I mentally beat myself up for walking straight into that one. But there is a slight addendum of my own to his statement.

"No, you can't," I tell him.

"Why not?" He turns his whole body to look at me, and I fight the urge to look back. To see those green eyes trying to understand me.

So, I just click my tongue and make an unnecessary turn to give myself something else to do. "Because you don't speak with it, you scream, and I don't have time to get earplugs."

Ain't that the truth.

Only I avoid the fact that my hearing has been damaged, and I only seem to function on higher decibels these days.

The only volume my body seems to be interested in is his loud and dominating one, but that's okay; I will adjust and get hearing aids if I must.

From the corner of my eye, I see his devious tongue peeking out and licking his bottom lip. Like a Pavlovian dog, my core ignites at the sight. Instantly, I'm throbbing everywhere and fighting to keep my breathing normal. I should find a psychiatrist around here.

Me and my vagina need help.

"I happen to remember you were the one doing all the screaming while I talked."

Damn it. Damn, this man and that sex voice he is using right now.

I don't want to be sitting here thinking about his huge penis. Nor do I want to have shivers running through my body as it remembers the way he filled me deep and then deeper and then even more deep until all I felt was him.

He was in my vagina, belly, mind, toes, and fingertips. In and through every tissue inside me.

"Memory loss. Sorry," I somehow manage to push that out of my mouth, sounding semi-normal.

"That's right. It was only *fine* for you. I guess my good girl needs a reminder, doesn't she?"

I squeak. I fucking squeak, and he catches it like a lion stalking a lamb.

Since when do I have a praise kink? And not just *have*, no, him using those two words on me completely sears my brain, and if Jacob were to say jump, I'd jump right this second.

"Wildflower, you need to make a U-turn. I would love nothing else than to drive into the forest up ahead and fuck you until you remember exactly how loud you can get and how *fine* it was, but we still have over two hours of Hug Car duty."

*Ice bucket, meet Joy.* Thank you, Jacob, for bringing me back to life. Even though my vagina is back to wailing.

"Keep your sick fetishes to yourself," I tell him as I make the U-turn back into the city. How the heck did I drove over here without noticing is beyond me.

Again, it's all his fault.

"I can't, because you will feel left out. I know how much you enjoy them." Sick bastard and I might be the one sharing his cell after all because, hell, yes, I would feel left out.

One-hundred-eighty agonizing minutes later, I'm back home. I survived seventy-six hugs in the span of three hours, and if I thought *I* was the one who needed help, I was wrong.

These people do.

They all need help...and Jesus.

It was as if suddenly the damn broke loose, and everyone decided it would be a great day to sob on my shoulder, jump into my arms from unknown happiness and squeeze my body so close to theirs, I could literally feel their every muscle.

I need ten showers to wash this horrible day away.

Not only was I forced to endure strangers thinking I cared about their personal lives, I also had to fight the desire for the man in the seat next to mine. In the end, I couldn't spend a single extra minute with him, and when he was accosted by some older guy who didn't know the meaning of clothes, I slipped away, dialed Grace to pick me up, and stayed hidden until she arrived.

I mean, I know all this is hilarious, seeing as we live in a small town, and he knows exactly where to find me, but a girl's gotta do what she's gotta do. I also know how mature I am, acting like a real intelligent woman with multiple degrees.

But whatever.

I'm exhausted, dirty, hungry, and horny for my Viking. And all I can dream of is one comfortable mattress with green sheets and a ceiling right above your head. Instead, I get curious, gleeful Grace littering my camping chairs, an empty fridge because the thing stopped working, and a sad, lonely blow-up mattress.

"So? How was it?" she asks, bouncing on her ass like the Duracell bunny she is. Gracie is the one who is perfect for all these car-duty things. She is a people person. I am the science geek, and Hope has always been the walking organizer—hence the predicament she found herself in with Brian.

"It was absolutely horrific, terrible, and I will most likely have nightmares from too much skin contact." I sit in the chair next to hers.

I pretty much have a whole dining room set up. A mini fold-out table and three chairs. See, I was nice enough to buy one for each of my sisters.

"It couldn't have been that bad. I have my first car duty in a few days." She scrunches up her forehead, and I exhale a tired breath, sinking deeper into the sagging fabric.

"I'm sure you will love it. It's just not my thing. Plus, I had to share the car with the Viking, and that was torture on its own."

"Who is this Viking? It's Jacob, isn't it?" Oh, hell, I've let it slip, and the extra kick in her tone suggests I am not getting off easily from this one, so I might as well throw her a bone.

"Yes, it's Jacob. He was driving with me today. Something about not letting me be all alone on my first day," I try to say as casually and as indifferently as possible despite the fact that I literally just said it was torture.

*Please, please let this go, Gracie.*

Of course, she won't. "Spill it," she says, and I lift my head up to see her narrowed eyes on me.

"There is nothing to spill. He keeps annoying me, that's all."

"Aha, and I'm a prima ballerina, Katerina Minaeva. I don't believe you. I know we haven't been around each other for ten years, but the Joy I know doesn't let people get to her, and Jacob clearly has." Look at her being a good sister who remembers stuff about me.

"I changed."

"No, you haven't." She snorts in answer.

"Yes, I have."

"Nope. I can do this all night, you know." Fuck, she totally can. One of those annoying little sister traits she's got, but I have one of my own.

It's called leave me the heck alone.

"Go for it. In the meantime, I'm going to shower and order some food."

"There's no delivery in Loverly."

"What?" I screech. "What kind of town is this?" The past week, I have been having dinners at my parents' house or making my own and haven't needed to go out to get anything other than groceries. Which I might add that I have done it ten minutes prior to closing time to avoid the townies, and this whole no-delivery clause is really going to be an issue here.

I'm done with mom's never-ending baby talk, and I don't particularly want to see the locals as I try to eat my food. I would keep cooking myself, but that requires a functioning fridge, which I don't really have anymore. The stupid, old junk really betrayed me *and* my birthday sprinkles ice cream.

"The kind that believes in sharing meals all together."

"Like I said earlier, they all need help." I sigh. "I guess it's time to lose weight."

"No need, let's go to the Peace-Out diner together."

"No, thanks," I say and push on the armrests to get up and leave this pointless conversation.

"What happened to you out there in Chicago?" Grace's question makes me stumble back down.

"What do you mean?"

"Exactly what I asked. What happened that you would rather starve than go out into the town and talk to people? What happened to you that you refuse to buy a normal mattress? What happened to our happy sister who has been replaced with this sad, scowling version?"

"She realized smiling hurts."

"But I've seen you smile with that Viking of yours, and anytime you speak of him, I see the sparkle in your eyes."

I start chewing on the inside of my cheek. Is she right?

Nope. I am not going there.

"Nothing happened. I am perfectly fine with the way my life is, and I don't need extra people or a *mattress* in my life to be happy. And Jacob...that is just from irritation."

"You are lying."

"How very clairvoyant of you to read my mind. Did you learn from mom?"

"And now you're deflecting."

"Jesus, Grace, give me a break. I'm totally fine. I have the best job in the world, my own state-of-the-art lab, and a great townhouse in Chicago. See? Perfect!" My temper is rising, slowly boiling over because Grace is picking at a knee wound, and I'm trying to bandage up and not get caught doing it by the running committee.

"You may think everything is perfect, yet I haven't heard a single thing about a loved one, a friend, or even a dog to keep you company. You're all alone, Joy, aren't you?"

"I don't need a dog to be happy," I spit out, folding my arms in protest to her outrageous claims. "And why do I need a man in my life? I make my own money, my own future, and don't need to rely a single moment on useless skin attached to a penis."

"Ha!" She jumps up as if I just proved *her* point instead of my own. "I knew it was about a man." She points to me. "Spill it! Who was he, and what did he do?"

"You know what? I think it's time for you to go." I get up, opening the front door, and motion for her to get out. "And I do have a friend," I add, feeling defensive.

"Is it an imaginary one, or do Hope and I count as your friends now?"

"Oh, how funny! You should consider a career in stand-up." I throw a sarcastic smile her way. "Say bye-bye, Gracie."

"You think your rudeness will somehow discourage me? Honey, I almost got married to the most selfish man on the planet. There ain't nothing you can say that I haven't heard before," she says but gets up from her chair, stalking toward the open door while I slouch next to it. "We are not done here." She gives me a look but shuts the door on her way out.

First thing on tomorrow's agenda, put the cottage up for rent.

How dare she insinuate I am not happy? How dare she say something is wrong in my life? She knows nothing.

I kick the door to my seventies-style bathroom with its rainbow-colored mosaic tiles all over the place open, stepping inside, and try not to throw up because this much color on such small squares keeps making my head dizzy.

Let's change the agenda a little bit. First is this bathroom demo, and second is renters.

I turn the water on in the shower, waiting for it to warm up as I strip naked with a bit too sharp tugs to my clothes. And tie my hair in a messy bun on top, pulling the small hairs in the process. It's not their fault my sister is an idiot who doesn't know anything about me, but nevertheless, I am suffering from it.

The steam is just about starting to fill the space, and I step inside, welcoming the boiling hot water on my tired skin. I like my showers, like my temper. Hot.

My muscles are just starting to relax, letting the tension from them seep down the drain with the water, when I hear a muffled knock on my front door. Since this bathroom doesn't have a proper ventilation system, I left the door slightly agar -which I am now regretting because the anger I just let out is back. Great, she is here to tell me more crap about my life, but this time I have something to say. Balling up my anger, I wrap the towel around my still-wet body and stride to the door, swinging it open. "You do—" but my words freeze on my tongue. It's not Grace standing in front of me.

It's a whole other set of complicated.

# 19

# *50 Reasons*

Reason #19:
*Jacob: You can warm your freezing toes on my toasty legs.*
*Joy: I would get lost in your jungle.*

Reason #20:
*Jacob: You will always have someone to scratch that one spot on your back that you can't reach yourself.*
*Joy: Fine, I'll give you that one.*

Reason #21:
*Jacob: You can blame your farts on me.*
*Joy: So far, the only one using that excuse is you.*

# 20
# *Jacob*

*"I would fight the world for you. Well, maybe not the world, at least the country. No, let's bring it down to the street. How about this? I will fight you for you." — Unknown.*

Apart from Joy cringing every time she had to give a hug to someone, I'd say the day was a success. I got to spend it with her, and that in itself is an accomplishment since the woman is hell-bent on avoiding me. For the whole week, she pretended I didn't exist, didn't open her door, and acted like a hermit, holing up in her home.

Ever since that bonfire night, Joy has been putting more distance between us. What have I said to make her back away like that? Or is she simply feeling this connection between us growing like wildfire like I do, and it scares her?

Maybe it should scare me, too, but it doesn't. Something that feels this right can't be scary. She's been pulling me in a little bit more every time I see her, and I'm not planning on backing out.

# MEET MY WIFE

I was going to crash tonight's dinner at the Levine's house and confront her about us. But she bailed before it even began. So, I did the only thing I could and tagged along for her Hug Car duty.

I'm a genius.

Except my Wildflower decided to play a little mute game, not gracing me with her beautiful voice apart from that brief exchange regarding her work and the sounds my body makes.

Best. Conversation. Of. The. Week.

Since the last one we had about my "just fine" dick did not make that list. There was nothing "just fine" about our night, and I plan on reminding her of that as soon as possible.

And I won't even complain that she is a pathologist. Really, it only helps me to understand the woman she is. The walls she has and the gleaming personality she wears as armor.

That's literally her job. However, I am confident there is more to her. More to her story. I am sure my beautiful Wildflower had her heart broken before; and therefore, she won't let me come close.

Tough luck, because I want *the close*. I want her like I've never wanted someone before, and even though the marriage talks are all jokes, sometimes it doesn't feel funny. No, the more I see and experience Joy Levine, the more my heart yearns for her.

I watched her give me the slip earlier, right after her time was up, while I was talking to a few of my friends, and I'd let her know that in an hour, I'll be exactly where I am now.

Knocking on her door.

In all honesty, I didn't expect her to open it, like she hadn't all other times, and I was prepared to stay here the whole night and maybe the whole day tomorrow until she *has* to leave her den and see me sitting here, but I got lucky. So freaking lucky. I will be planting twenty trees tomorrow morning to thank the universe for this gift.

I might also throw in a week with no driving.

Not only does she answer the door, she flings it open wide, stressing the old, chipped wood barely holding on to its hinges, but that's not the best part.

The absolute cherry on top is that she's naked. Well, almost naked, but the small towel she has wrapped around her curves does nothing to hide them from my hungry—starving—eyes. And I let them roam freely, getting their fill before she inevitably slams the door shut in my face.

I trace the small beads of water sliding down her slender neck. The neck, I want to sink my teeth in, lick the pain away and suck on the delicate skin until it's marked by me for everyone to see and know who she belongs to.

Damn it, I am only talking about her neck, and she already made the beast in me wake up once again. The beast who seems to come out and play only for her.

I can feel her anger seeping through her pores and her rigid posture, but that's not enough for me to look away. I'm not planning to be a gentleman right now. I simply can't. The thoughts running through my head when I watch the slight rosy hue color her skin demand I be a caveman, not the good, sweet guy. But that's not a blush. No, Joy doesn't blush. She sets others on fire.

My eyes travel lower where the tops of her breasts are slightly showing through the top of the towel, and if I wasn't fully hard before, I am now. Steel hard. Rock hard. Diamond hard. Call it whatever you'd like, the point stands.

I think she's starting to say something before she cuts herself off and sees it's me standing on the other side of her door.

"What are you doing here?" she grids out, already on her way to close the said door in my face, but I am faster and push myself inside her home. "Jacob!" she yells out as the door behind us closes with a thud, and she rushes after me.

I take in the bare white walls, the sad, plain, fold-out table, and the three camping chairs around it and frown. The whole space otherwise is unchanged. The kitchen seems like it has been here since the cottage was built, and its doors held on by a thread. I think Joy tried to wash the floors, but the layers of grime go too deep and most likely need to be changed out completely.

I don't care if she uses cheap plastic furniture or that her walls are white. I don't care she hasn't remodeled the space. I care that she's not living. Not enjoying herself. This is a mere existence.

We are all given only one life, and it needs to be lived to the fullest brink. It needs to fill us so much that we are busting at the seams. Why waste precious time on pragmatism and boredom? Why live only on necessities? And I'm not talking about being wasteful or buying expensive stuff. No, I'm talking about emotions, feelings, moments.

The thought takes my mind off her nearly naked body, begging for my attention, and I focus on *her*.

"What's going on, Joy?"

"I'd like to know the same thing!"

"This is not you." I motion around me, but the groan that comes out of her is loud enough to alert the town mayor of her displeasure with me right now.

"And you know *me* so well you can tell *this*—" she mimics my motion, "—is not me?"

"No, not as well as I'd like, but I can read your aura. And it's not all white and boring. You have so many colors around you, why won't you let them fill you? Shine through?"

"I think it's time for you to leave." She balls up her little fists.

"No," I state. "And you know what? I'm not asking anymore or giving you time to get used to the idea of us. I'm coming over tomorrow and helping you rip out these floorboards and the kitchen cabinets. Then I'm teaching you to live."

"Like hell you are," she protests, placing her hands on her waist, completely forgetting she is wearing only a towel, it slips a bit before she catches herself, but not before one of her soft pink nipples peeked out to greet me. And I'm back to those naughty thoughts.

Damn, this woman and her perfection of body for getting me off track.

Forget the remodel, we can talk about it tomorrow. Tonight, I want to have a conversation with her body. Her soft, lush curves and wet pussy.

The tantalizing slip has fried my brain, and I just let all her insults pass over my head. I'm not even listening to her angered jabs. I think there is something about being the same as everyone else and me being the pain in her ass and a few other colorful words that we won't be repeating when our kids ask how I met their mother.

On pure instinct, I move towards her.

"What are you doing?" Her voice is no longer angry; it's wary and a little terrified.

I lift up my eyes to look into her dark chocolate ones and find a spark matching my own in there.

Well, that's all the invitation I was hoping for. I take another step forward, and she takes one back. We keep playing this game until her back is at the wall, and she has nowhere to run. I caught her, and now I will devour my delicious prey.

"Jacob," she tries to say as a warning, but her voice is too breathless, too needy for me to back off.

"Joy." I match her tone.

"I don't like you," she says, but that lip between her teeth serves as a nice little contradiction.

"That's okay." I bring my thumb to her bitten lip and pull it out. "I'll do all the liking in our relationship. I'm good at that." She lets out a small sigh.

"You're like that gum that sticks to the bottom of your shoes and won't fall off."

"Fruity or minty?"

The tips of our noses touch, sending one of those shockwaves through our bodies, and I feel the fight leave her.

"What?" Joy breathes out.

"Am I a fruity or minty gum?"

"The disgusting cinnamon one." She narrows her eyes at me, her breathing growing heavier with each second.

"Mhmmm, an acquired taste one. I like that."

Without letting her get another insult in, I crush my lips to hers and get my taste of the sweetness I've been craving the whole week. If I'm the cinnamon gum, then she is the multilayered one, where each flavor unfolds as you chew it more and more.

She lets out a small moan, and it goes straight to my already aching cock. I have her pinned to the wall, crowding her with my body, but it's not enough.

Joy is stiff for the first three seconds, but soon enough, she melts into my touch, and I kiss her like it's the only thing keeping me alive. Like I need her to survive, and I'm quickly figuring out that I might. Her taste, her scent, and the tiny moans and whimpers are my new lifeline.

Within seconds, our kiss turns feral. It's teeth and unleashed hunger. It's hands all over our bodies. Her leg hikes up and curls around my ass, pushing me even closer into her heat, letting me know she is just as crazy for me as I am for her, but I'm not nearly as strong of a man. With one quick tug, the towel that was guarding her mouth-watering body against me is gone, pooling at our feet, and she stands completely naked and all mine.

"Fuck," spills out of my mouth in a husky voice as my eyes eat up every centimeter of her. "I almost forgot how stunning you are. Almost," I add and rip my shirt off my body, needing to feel her skin on mine with no barriers. Needing those full tits pressed into my chest as her sweet pussy rubs on my aching cock.

I need to lose the shorts, too, but I am too impatient to have her back in my arms.

Her breath catches as I crush her into my body. I feel her nipples turn into razor-sharp knives, and without another word, I pin both her hands to the wall on each side and drop my head to take a nipple in my mouth as Joy lets out a feral moan. She tries to wiggle out of my hold, but I'm not giving her that chance and pin the squirming body with mine. I need to have my mouth all over her. I need to kiss each millimeter of her sweet skin.

"Jacob, stop. Stop," she pleads, but her eyes are hooded, her tits pushing themselves up for my taking.

"Stop? You want me to stop?"

"Yes, no, yes." I tear myself away from her sweet mounts for a second, and she whimpers. "No, I changed my mind. Get back!"

"You seem to be under the impression that you get any say over here, Wildflower." I let go of her hands and palm her tits with both my hands. I take them hard, and she whimpers some more, but I swallow those with my mouth as I kiss it out of her. With a quick swipe, I lift her up and carry her down the hall to the only sort-of-bed I can see. Her lonely air mattress lays on the floor, and at this moment, it could be bare concrete for all I care.

"I still don't like you," she reminds me as I toss her to the makeshift bed.

"Good thing you don't need to like me to scream my name as I make you come on my tongue." I watch her mouth prop open as I duck between her legs, spreading them wide and relishing the sight in front of me.

Wet, glistening and swollen. Her pussy is weeping for me, and I'm all too eager to soothe the pain. I run my hands from her ankle up her thighs, using a feather-light touch, giving her an inch but not the whole mile, and my good girl squirms for more. She loves it when I give her more, doesn't she?

I keep torturing her until my fingers reach my personal heaven, and I drag my whole hand through her drenched folds, soaking myself in her. "Flawless," I whisper into her body as I trail the kisses up those legs, once again barely touching her golden skin, tickling her with my breath.

"Jacob," Joy pleads, but she knows what she needs to say to get me down there.

"Say it."

"P-please," she breathes out, giving away her control without a fight.

"Good girl," I praise her, knowing she needs it, loves it, and probably just got wetter from hearing me say those two little words. But she really is such a good girl, completely surrendering to me behind closed doors.

She can be as cold as she likes to everyone out there, that's her choice, but in here? In here, she is my wildflower. My perfect girl. Mine.

This is only the second time I am tasting her, touching her, fucking her, yet it feels like a homecoming when my tongue swipes through the soft, needy pink flesh of her, and Joy almost jumps off the bed at the contact. Her graceful back is arched high, pushing those unbelievable tits up for me. My hand moves up to her breast, lightly brushing the top of her nipple, and it pebbles beneath my touch.

I roll it between my fingers, pulling on it slightly and watching her head fall back as the other has a protective hold on her ass, squeezing and kneading it hard.

So hard, I am pretty sure it's painful for her, but Joy only whimpers louder as her pussy grinds into my face harder.

"That's right, Joy, use my mouth, fuck it, ride it, drown me," I tell her and dive back in. Slightly tugging on her clit, sucking, and literally eating her like the starved man I am. Her hands dig into my hair, and she fists it hard, pulling on me as she seeks out every bit of pleasure my mouth is giving her.

"OhmyGodohmyGodohmyGod," she chants almost in a whisper. "Jacob," she moans softly.

"Fucking love it when you moan my name. Again. But this time, scream it."

The mix of her wetness and my saliva is dripping down my chin, and her pussy, the sheet below us, is soaked through, and her hold on me nearly rips my hair out as her orgasm rips through her.

"Jacob!" The whispers are gone as she shouts my name, screams, and claws at my back, flying off the bed. I almost want to stand up, beat my chest, and say, "That's right, I did that. I made her come like that."

But there's no time for that. I need her right now. I need to sink into her tight, hot pussy right this second.

Ripping my shorts off, I climb over her, peppering her lush body with tender kisses as she comes down from her high. Still panting and moving her head from side to side as if she's lost in space.

"You make me crazy, Wildflower. Feral." I take in her dazed look and swollen lips from our kiss but chapped from her harsh breathing. "I will let you in on a little secret." I lay my body on top of hers, and she gasps.

I twine my fingers into her hair, pulling it apart from the makeshift bun she had there and softly running through it. I need to give her a bit of sweetness before I destroy her.

My mouth is right at the shell of her ear, and as I breathe, she shudders. "I have long buried this man, yet one look at you and he is back in full swing. No, not just back... I'm a hundred times hungrier now. For you." With the last word, I push inside her fast and hard, thrusting in fully, all the way to the hilt, and Joy yelps, taking in a sharp breath as her small, dainty fingers rip into my biceps.

I don't give her a warning or time to adjust. No, I want her pussy to strangle me the way she is now. I want her to remember this forever. That she is mine.

Whatever words she and I were going to say stay trapped somewhere in our throats. Her mouth is propped open, her eyes rolling back, and all I can do is grunt in pleasure and restraint.

I'm inside her. Her legs are wrapped around mine. Our lips are kissing. We are pressed tightly to each other with our chests connected, yet it doesn't feel close enough. I want to be consumed by her at the same time as I am occupying her every thought.

"Oh, fuck," she whimpers.

"It's a fine dick, right? Just fine."

"Oh, shut up!" she groans out.

She is tight, wet, and oh-so-welcoming, squeezing me with her pussy. "Joy, I love how hard you are gripping me, but I need you to relax, Wildflower, or else I will come in the next five seconds." It's as if she remembers to breathe again, taking a sharp, deep breath and melting into me. "Good girl, now let me fuck you like you deserve to be fucked. Hard, fast, and with all I've got."

I withdraw and flip her over, pulling her magnificent ass up into my face. "Fuck, every inch of you is too perfect. I thought not seeing your face would help, but no such luck." I bite into her very much bitable ass, and she hisses in response but doesn't run away. So, I do it again on the other cheek, kissing and licking it afterward.

Joy's back is arched deep like she is presenting herself to me, and I will gladly take it all. With one last kiss, I position myself behind her and thrust into her viciously once again while squeezing her ass, even with my hands, until they are white from the pressure I'm putting on them. And her ass is cherry red from it. I spread her open to get a perfect look at that forbidden fruit, her puckered, rosy hole. I trace my finger through it, and she pushes into my touch.

"My good girl wants to be fucked here? You want me there, Wildflower?" She only purrs in response, and I slap her ass. "Good girl. You'll get your wish. Next time. Next time, I'll have you there."

The way she sounds as I fuck her should be illegal. She moans and meows and groans all at once, with occasional curse words shouted here and there. Her back is shiny with some hard-worked precipitation, and I bend over her to lick up her spine, from her hips to her neck.

"Ahhh," she groans again. "You...you..."

"What, Wildflower? I what?" I ask as I grab her dark hair, tilting her head up to face me and kissing those delicious lips while my other hand reaches for her clit, stroking through her.

"You are p-perfect," she whisper-moans into my mouth, and I fall apart.

That one little sentence gets me undone faster than the taste of her. She said it the other time before, but somehow, hearing it from her again, when she knows me and I'm not some sort of one-night stand with a stranger, is a whole other thing.

I crush my lips to hers again as we grunt and moan together. My cock pulses deep inside of her as her pussy squeezes around me, milking every last bit of me into her.

We are pressed tightly together, her sweet ass glued to my groin as our sweat and come mix.

We collapse onto the mattress. Me still inside of her, and I try to move away so as not to crush her, but she wraps her hand around my arm.

"Stay. Just like this. Stay," she whispers, and I do exactly as she asks.

I don't want to hurt her, but I think she needs this—me—right now. And at this moment, this moment is the one I know my marriage jokes might not be jokes at all anymore.

She needs me.

I need her.

And I can't let go. Not now or ever.

I kiss her shoulder softly while she still tries to catch her breath, nuzzling my nose into her neck, and it's as if she's electrocuted. Joy jumps up, pushing me off herself, and scurries off into the bathroom.

I fall on my back, my arms spread wide as I stare at the ceiling. This woman. She is so utterly complicated and guarded, but it's a good thing for both of us I am a patient locksmith, and I'll find the right key.

Deciding I won't let her build those triple walls back up, I get off the bed and follow her into the bathroom, where she is just turning the shower back on.

"You came inside of me," she sneers at me.

"Uh-huh," I agree as I step into the rainbow paradise and relish in the hot sprays of the steaming water.

"What do you mean 'uh-huh?' You didn't use a condom again, but this time, you came *inside* me, you idiot!" Yep, those walls are going up faster than I thought.

"And? We're both clean. We covered that part last time, remember? So, what's the problem?" I step behind Joy, wrapping my arms around her waist, but she quickly darts out of my hold and turns to look at me with those daggers in her brown eyes.

"What's the problem? *What's the problem*? Oh, I don't know? Maybe the possibility of getting pregnant? And maybe you've fucked half the town since that night," she yells loudly, her unhinged voice ricocheting off the rainbow walls. "And stop touching me!" She slaps my hand away as I try to reach for her.

But I am nothing if not persistent. I reach out again, and this time, I haul her into my arms hard and fast, without a second of hesitation or time for her to sneak away.

Truth be told, I completely forgot we weren't using a condom again, until it was too late. That little rubber thing was the last thing on my mind, and I am well aware how irresponsible of me it was to come inside her. I should have wrapped it. But for the love of peace, I can't regret it. I cannot fuck this woman with any barriers between us. It's a hard no.

I am ninety-nine percent positive Joy is on birth control, so we won't have a gift in our hands in nine months, but oddly, that thought really pisses me off. As well as her comment about me sleeping with someone else.

I have known this woman for all of two weeks, yet I am ready to wife her up and have a kid together. I was always told how crazy I am, but I never understood anyone until now because right about now, I am planning how to steal her pills.

"Are you telling me you are not on the pill?" I hug her tighter.

"I am."

I should be glad. There is no way we could have a kid now, but I am not.

"See? Nothing to worry about then, and like I told you before, I haven't been with anyone without a condom for five years before you, and I certainly wasn't with anyone after you. If you haven't realized this yet, I am kind of hooked on you. But nonetheless, I think your cute ass needs to be spanked once again for thinking this nonsense." She stills in my arms, her breathing turning shallow once again, and I have no doubt if I were to reach lower, I'd find her more than ready for me.

"You haven't?"

"Aha, now relax and let me take care of you. I should treat you a bit before the next round."

By some small miracle, Joy doesn't complain but stands there quietly, letting me wash every inch of her body, kissing her neck, shoulders, back, and arms, but as soon as I reach for the lips, she shuts me down.

"I think I'm clean enough," she says and steps out of the shower, wrapping herself up with a towel. I quickly shut off the water and follow her.

"Okay, you got what you wanted now you can go," she says with a blank face, but mine is not.

I got what I wanted, and now I can go? What the hell is that?

"You think I came here to have sex, and that's it?"

"Well, didn't you? Don't you all?" Her stance is fierce and guarded, but the hand that is wrapped around the towel holding it in its place clenches a bit tighter as she speaks, betraying her real feelings.

Someone hurt my Wildflower and hurt her bad.

I'm not a violent person, I can't even kill a spider in my home, but at this moment, I would murder whoever it was. With kindness, of course. It would be all very sweet and bloody.

But she won't tell me anything.

Not yet.

"No, Wildflower, that is not why I came here. In fact, you are the one who attacked me with your mouth-watering nakedness, and I am just a weak man, I only have so little willpower. Especially when it comes to your beautiful self." I take a step towards her, and we go back to playing the same game that started it all.

Joy steps back. "Why did you come then?"

"I came because I wanted to see you. To be with you. To talk to you." I close the space between us and wrap my arms around her once again, giving her a deep, long hug. And I swear I feel her exhale in relief.

"What are you doing?" she asks, but it's no longer in an offensive manner. It's almost with relief.

"Giving my girl a hug."

"I'm not your girl. Let me go. I've had way too many of those for one day."

"No, you gave them. And now *I'm* giving *you* one. Let go, Joy. Let it all go. Lean on me, Wildflower." My words must break something in her because she does.

# MEET MY WIFE

She lets go. Then something completely unexpected happens.

Joy's arms slowly rise and wrap around my torso. Her movements are unsure, shy even, but she is hugging me back.

We cling to each other during sex, but this is different. This is intimacy. Trust.

This is a possibility of the future.

"See? Doesn't it feel nice?"

"Shut up, Jacob. Don't ruin it."

"There is no shame in admitting I make your life so much better, boo." I smile into her hair, and she groans.

"Anddddd, there he is." She pulls away from me quickly, and I want to punch myself for being an idiot who doesn't know when to stop messing around.

I always have this need to make everyone smile, but that isn't what she needs right now, and I need to fix it. I catch her hand as she steps away. "No, don't go. I'm sorry." But she slips her hand away and goes to the luggage that sits open in the corner of her room, pulling some clothes out.

I let a loaded breath out and do the same. Tracking down my clothing all over the place.

Once we are dressed up again, Joy goes into the kitchen, and I follow her like the lost puppy I am.

"Why were you angry when I got here?"

"I think you just answered your own question." She raises a perfectly groomed eyebrow at me.

"No, that's not it. You were angry before you saw it was me."

"I could smell you from a mile away, it put me in a bad mood then."

"Are you saying there's a connection between us?"

"What? No! No connection at all," she bristles.

"Hmmm." I tap my chin as I pretend to be in deep thought. "You know; I think there's some merit to that theory."

"I think you're an idiot, maybe there's merit to that one also?"

I ignore her comment. "You see; I always end up where you are! Like it's meant to be."

"My theory starts to become more and more real. How could someone so hot be such a weirdo?"

I hate being called weird. It's the only thing that can put me in a sour mood, but when it comes from her, I don't feel the painful, deep, punishing punch behind that word. No, when Joy says it, it's almost loving.

"I really like it when you stroke my ego like that."

"And now we can add delusional to the mix."

"Oh boo, there you go again." I flash her my smile as she sneers, but there is also a bit of shine in her eyes. Joy is not as immune to me as she likes to pretend, and those tiny cracks I am seeing here and there will soon grow into full-blown holes.

Joy gets cut off from whatever she is going to say by a violent knock at her door.

"Open up. Open up right this second, Joy. This is a life-threatening emergency," Hope is whisper-yelling at the front door, and Joy turns ramrod straight and pale as ash.

# 21

# *Joy*

*"The problem with life is, by the time you can read women like a book, your library card has expired." — Milton Berle.*

"**O**h my God...my sister is here." I turn my head from the door to the very disheveled man with his Viking hair in a messy, wet tangle, standing next to me and then to myself, noticing for the first time I never put on a bra after our shower, my hair is slightly wet, and then I look at both of us. As an us.

We look like the most domesticated, married couple. Lounging in their comfy clothes after work, sharing lazy kisses, and deciding whether we are having Chinese or Pizza for tonight.

Oh, crap, crap, triple crap. My sister cannot see him here. No. Absolutely not.

"What the hell is she doing here?" I whisper more to myself than the object of my torture. "Quick, hide, go! You have to hide!" I start pushing at his chest, nearly getting burned by all the electricity passing through us.

I shouldn't be having these inappropriate reactions to this man anymore. I've had sex with him twice. Two heavenly amazing times which were more than enough to get him out of my system. So, my dear vagina, please find another object for your stupid drooling, okay?

I can't sleep with him again. I cannot have my sisters or—God forbid—my mother find out about us. I cannot let him in any more than I already have.

The weirdo slipped under my guard when I was the most vulnerable. After he fucked my brains out and all neurons and synapses were severed. Of course, I blurted out too much. Of course, I opened the door to my life when I meant to keep it firmly shut.

But when his strong, firm arms wrapped around me just because...to simply to give me a hug and my skin touched his...

I felt the fight leave my body quite literally. I felt the stress of the past few weeks melt away, and only his steady heartbeat was my new compass in life. The comforting *thud, thud, thud* coming from his warm, broad chest felt like the only thing that could possibly ground me. It made me feel safe.

Why does everything feel so much better with Jacob around?

I think my every previous assumption of this guy was way off course. He is not a peace-loving, delusional weirdo. He's a sledgehammer, no, a bulldozer, running through my every wall and line of defense. He makes me feel very much off-balance. This isn't right; I'm not supposed to feel this way about anyone.

I never did, to begin with.

But I can attend my own philosophy class later when the coast is clear, and he's not here. For now, I need this man to hide the hell away.

"Why? Don't you want your sisters to know about us?"

"There is no us! But help me, God, there never will be if you don't hide right this second because I will kill you," I grid out before I can stop myself, and I just know he heard my little slip once again. Damn it.

"Fine, Wildflower, we can wait until tomorrow to tell them," he antagonizes me a bit more, but at least he is smart enough to stop right there. Just as Jacob is about to run up the stairs into an empty loft I have there, he bends down, plants a sickeningly sweet kiss on my lips, and takes off.

*One kiss. One little kiss and Joy is off kilter. AGAIN.*

As soon as his feet touch the upstairs floor, I rush to the door, opening it just a tiny bit. "What? What's going on?" I'm using hushed tones. No need for that man up there to hear more than he needs to.

"Let me in; what is wrong with you?" She pushes me out of the way, swinging the door right open, and steps inside like it is her God-given right. Whose brilliant idea was it to reconcile again?

"Hope! I'm busy; I can't babysit you right now."

"Well, that's great. Because right now, I need a sister, not a babysitter." She plants herself on the blanket I have on my floor next to the wall. "Oh, and call Grace for me. I left my phone at home."

I send a quick text to Gracie, and ten seconds later, Miss Hurricane herself bursts through the door.

"I got the nine-one-one. I'm here, I'm here. What's going on?" She drops herself next to Hope on the other side.

"I am so messed up," Hope tells us, dumping her head into her hands.

"Why? What happened?"

"I almost gave in. I almost did it."

"Did what?" We need to speed up this pity party. I have a very sexy man up there, just waiting for his moment to blow up my life as I know it, and he is just unpredictable enough to randomly come down and kiss me in front of these two.

"I almost told Alec to feed me his cock just now."

Grace squeaks, "You did?" Clamping her mouth with both her palms as, I yell out, "You did what?" But I freeze because, at that exact moment, there is a loud thump sound coming from up the stairs.

Yep, I'm pretty much screwed, but hell, if I will go down without a fight. So, I started coughing violently and very much fake to cover the new noises, and thankfully, my sisters were too concentrated on Hope's issues to notice anything else.

"I don't know how much longer I can hold it. He's so hot, and he does all these romantic things I never knew were possible, and he is so nice, and his smile and those eyes and the tattoos and his humor and the faith he has in me, and the freaking showers where he jerks off after giving me massages... It's all too much." Jesus Christ, woman, shut up. Shut. Up. "Oh, and he's just seen me naked, and then he fed me meatloaf."

"What. The. Fuck?" I can't even comprehend this conversation anymore.

"Oh, my God! Yesss, yes, yes, yes!" Grace fist-pumps the sky with a happy cheer.

"Grace? Are you insane? What are you being so happy about? Hope doesn't need a new relationship right now," I scold my youngest sister.

"Oh yeah? And what does she need? To mope around for years and years until she settles alone with twenty cats?"

"She just broke up with Brian! She needs time!"

*We all need time.* Not sexy, surfing, tattoo artists who work out daily and apparently know every trick in the book to get the girl. Oh, and the ones that are not below using orgasms as weapons.

Yeah, we all need time. Major time.

"No, she needs a hot tattoo artist to fuck her brains out," Grace counters.

"That is true." Hope points to her. "I do."

"See?" she says smugly.

"But it's also is too soon," Grace adds.

"See?" This time, it's me being the smug one.

"Whatever. If you don't want a relationship with the most wonderful, Harry Potter-loving, hot surfer, just have monkey sex with the man at the very least." Grace rolls her eyes at us.

"No! No sex! Sex complicates everything. One minute, you think it's the best idea ever, and the next, you are looking for him like he's your next fix." You taste it once, and here you are, standing in line for seconds. You might also come back for the third and tenth serving. Hell, you might just never leave.

Oh, for the love of...I really just said all that, haven't I? Grace and Hope peel off the wall in slow motion, narrowing their eyes at me.

"Is there something we don't know, Joy?" Grace asks me, but I am quick to pull that indifferent mask on for the show.

"Nope. I'm just saying that shit happens." I can practically hear Jacob upstairs, grinning and folding his arms across his chest.

I will never hear the end of this one.

My sisters bicker some more, but I tune them out, listening to that weird silent conversation I'm having with Jacob through the ceiling.

*We do have a connection. We do. I can't keep denying it.*

"Come on, Hope. It's just sex. You don't need to go and fall in love with him, but it's a crime against humanity to not take advantage of that prime specimen," Grace keeps her coaching, and it makes me snap out of my trance.

"Do you hear yourself? Do you realize who you are talking to? Hope cannot do casual. She was born with this nauseating idea of a fairytale love. There is a reason her name is Hope. She is living and working with the man, for crying out loud."

What I leave out is that none of us were meant for casual. The Levines don't do casual. Look at me and my one-night stand. I can't even do sex with a random stranger properly. No, I had to go and start *feeling* something for him.

"Joy, maybe you should let Jacob fuck you. You're way too uptight," Grace casually says, as my whole world drops, and based on the loud crash upstairs, so does Jacob's.

"Did you hear that?" Hope asks us, and I roll my lips, biting them hard to keep myself from screaming.

"Hear what? I didn't hear anything." The words come tumbling out of my mouth too quickly, and my two little sisters share a quick glance.

"I heard it too, Hope. Maybe we should go up and make sure our sister is all safe here?"

"No need." I jump up, placing both my hands up as if that would ever stop these two. "I'm all good. That was just a paint bucket...yeah, that. It fell. Okay, time for you two to go. Up, up." Please, just get up and go home. Please.

Of course, they don't. Nope, they take off towards the loft with me running after them, screaming and praying Jacob somehow learns the powers of invisibility, or my sisters go blind for a minute.

"Stop it; I said I'm all good. Where are you two going?" The words leave me as I climb up, but stumble into Hope and Grace, who are standing right at the edge, both wearing masks of confusion.

If I didn't believe in the higher power before, I certainly do now. I glance around the room but don't see him anywhere, and it's not like there is anywhere to hide here. The loft is pretty much empty, apart from a few paint buckets.

"Huh, well, this is awfully disappointing," Grace says and walks back downstairs with us following her.

Dear sister, you have no idea...

"Hope, go have sex with Alec and stop whining. A hot man wants in your bed and heart. I don't see any problems with that." She slams my poor door on her way out, sending me a narrowed glance right before.

I turn to my younger sister, and we share a few more words before she leaves as well. No matter what I say, I am glad to have them both back. And I will always be here to support them.

But now, I need to know where the hell did my man go. As that thought crosses my mind, I slap my face. *My man...*

I climb upstairs just as he hooks his leg over the window from the other side. He went out my window to hide? Oh my goodness, what I wouldn't pay to watch that. There is nowhere to stand out there. So, he must've been hanging off the framework this whole time.

I purse my lips, trying to keep the laughter bubbling inside of me from escaping me, but when he's all the way inside, and I see how red his face is, only one shark slide remaining on his feet, and how sweaty he is from all the restraint he put himself through to protect my secret, I can't hold it anymore.

It's an inappropriate reaction to this situation, but I can't help myself. It's as if someone busted through my dam. No one has ever done anything remotely close to this for me. No one ever cared enough to protect my wishes. And I laugh. I laugh like never before.

"This? This is what gets you to laugh?" He points to his disheveled self, his face in a serious mask, and I double over, laughing even harder. I have no idea why it's so funny, but it is. "Oh, I'm so glad you find this amusing because I intend to make you pay for this. Big time!"

Without another word, he pounces on me, and I let out a squeaky yelp as I try to run away from him, but he catches me before I reach the stairs and tackles me down to the bare floors. "Jacob," I squeak again as his sweaty body lays heavily on mine.

I might be trying to push him off, but I am not *really* trying. I love it when he does this. Love to feel his weight on mine.

"Now for that payment," he says with a sinful lick to his lips, and I don't feel like squeaking anymore. No, I am ready to moan his name again and again.

"You are coming to the town workout tomorrow morning, then we will go out for a breakfast date, then I will help you with the cottage, but you are not staying here another night. You are moving into the tiny house while we make this place habitable."

"What?" I screech. "This is not what I thought you were going to say," I pout. I fucking pout, and the bastard grins. Damn it, his smile is too beautiful.

"It's cute how desperate you are for my *fine* cock, Wildflower. But you were a bad girl, hiding me away, and you don't get to have any more orgasms tonight." He plants a kiss on my nose as he squeezes my breast, making me even needier than I already was.

"Asshole."

He grins some more as his lips travel down my neck, kissing and nibbling on my sensitive flesh.

I concede that my body wants him, and I'm too weak to resist it anymore, but how bad would it be to have some more mind-blowing sex while I am stuck here? As long as I keep the fickle heart locked up, I will be perfectly fine.

"I am not moving into your tiny house, though. Forget it."

"Yes, you are."

"Am not."

"And why are you so against it? Afraid you might fall in love with me if we spend time and live together?" Jacob challenges me with a tiny smirk.

I scoff, "There is absolutely zero chance of that happening. I don't fall in love. Especially not with hippy weirdos who wear shark slides and ducky shorts."

"Aha, sure." The kissing is back, and my mind turns to mush.

"Prove it."

"What am I, five?"

"No, you're a chicken." He bites my lower lip.

"Am not!" I bite him back.

"Then prove it."

"I am not falling for this."

"I think you already have," Jacob smirks and winks, letting me know we are talking about a whole other *falling*.

Oh, the audacity this man has...

But if I thought this was bad...I clearly had no idea what tomorrow would bring...

# 22

# *50 Reasons*

Reason #25:
*Jacob: You would never have to run down the hall for a fresh roll of toilet paper with your cute butt out. I'll be there to land a hand.*
*Joy: Hmm, maybe I should get a trained dog. It would save me so much hassle.*

Reason #27:
*Jacob: Wildflower, this is not the right way to squeeze toothpaste out. See, what would you do without me?*
*Joy: Use it the way I want to.*

Reason #30:
*Jacob: I solemnly swear to wake up at night to change our babies' diapers.*
*Joy: We don't have babies.*
*Jacob: Not yet.*

# 23

# *Jacob*

*"Love is being stupid together."* –Paul Valery.

Alec: **Asking for a friend.**

Alec: **Say, he saw his best buddy running away like his dick was on fire from a certain pink cottage in the dead of night. Then he saw a certain girl hurling something at him. Should he ask his buddy if his balls are still intact?**

Jacob: **A, you have no other friends other than me, so stop pretending, loser. B, I wasn't running away like my dick was on fire, I was running away before that certain girl changed her mind about giving me a chance. C, she was simply tossing my favorite shoe back since it fell off my foot while I was dangling off her second-story window.**

Alec: **Woah, woah, woah...**

Alec: **I have so many questions!**

Alec: **Wait, you didn't lose your shark slides, did you?**

Jacob: **Thank you for starting with the most important one. You know I'd be heartbroken if I lost those babies. And no, Wildflower found the missing shoe, hence the throw.**

Alec: **Phew, (wipes his sweaty forehead) you got me nervous right there for a second.**

Alec: **Now, what the heck were you doing hanging off of Joy's window?**

Jacob: **I was hiding.**

Alec: **From?**

Jacob: **Your girlfriend, Grace, and their discussions of your sex life.**

Alec: **Wait, what? I am so lost right now.**

Jacob: **Apparently, that's an ongoing trend for you...**

Jacob: **Seriously, man, give your girl what she wants already. Our strategy is working; you just need to push a little harder.**

Alec: **How the heck did we make this conversation about me and Hope when you are the one sneaking around with her cold-hearted sister?**

Jacob: **Because despite what you all may think; Joy will be my wife.**

Jacob: **Eventually.**

Jacob: **Very far, eventually, but it will happen.**

Alec: **And you are so sure, because...?**

Jacob: **Because I flick my hair and do that smolder face better than you.**

Alec: **You've got to be shitting me! She fell for that crap?**

Jacob: **It's not crap. It's a strategy. One I told you about weeks ago, yet you still haven't listened to me.**

Alec: **I think you are full of shit and will have your balls served on a silver platter soon.**

Jacob: **Do you wanna bet Joy will agree to marry me before Hope agrees to marry you?**

Alec: **What's at stake? *thinking emoji***

Jacob: **If I win, your yellow surfboard becomes mine, and you have to tattoo my name on your body.**

Alec: **Ahhhhh, you went for the kill. My baby. My surfboard. How could you! And if by some miracle you do win, I will tattoo your name on my ass, I hope you know that.**

Jacob: **Whatever you are into, man, no judgment.**

Alec: **Shut up.**

Alec: **If I win, I get your shark slides.**

Jacob: **No, you didn't!**

Alec: **I sure did. Also, you will join my dad in his naked and free parade.**

Jacob: **How about three parades, but my slides stay with me.**

Alec: **Nice to see you are already planning to lose.**

Jacob: **Never \*angry emoji\* You're on, Loverboy.**

A day later, I will be tattooing my name on Alec's ass..., but we will get to that.

*Love Hive:*

Tinyhousebigheart: I need help!

CookieJ: Your future mama-in-law at your service, my boy. What can we do for you?

Tinyhousebigheart: Can I call you Mama already? I've always wanted to!

Ninasunshine: Jackie, give us a moment here. Jenny started crying from happiness; she needs a moment. Oh, and she's sobbing out "Yes, you can call me Mama."

Tinyhousebigheart: Thanks, Mrs. C.

CookieJ: Okay, okay, I'm back. So, tell us the plan.

Tinyhousebigheart: Tomorrow, right after the morning workout, I need you to turn on the song for me when I give you a sign.

CookieJ: Send the song and consider it done.

Tinyhousebigheart: Thanks, Mama. You will make the best grandma!

Ninasunshine: Now we are all sobbing.

# 24

## *Joy*

*"Stick with me because I'll ruin your lipstick, not your mascara." –Unknown.*

A morning fucking workout. Why did I agree to this again? After the grueling, sweaty hour of torture, I question why I simply didn't tell my sisters that Jacob stopped by to say hi and send him out the door.

No, I had to hide him. He had to listen to the whole conversation and my admission to him being my fix, and now I'm paying for it. With squats.

I also have to endure every single person on this square staring my way. Do I have something on my face? Between my teeth? Is there a stain on my shirt?

Why? Why are they all looking at me?

Sure, they like to work out, but generally, there are a hundred of them tops. So, why is half the town out here today? At least I have Gracie with me. We both decided to let go of last night's discussion and move on. She has her issues, I have mine, and unless the other one asks, we don't interfere with each other's lives.

Can someone pass this memo to my mom, who has been winking at Jacob the whole morning? Clearly, she had no reservations regarding meddling in our lives. Zero.

"How much do you love me?" I ask Grace after we finish our last set of squats.

"If you are trying to get me to do something for you, I don't love you at all."

"Grace, focus. This is important."

She rolls her eyes at me.

"Fine, I love you a little. Let's see if it qualifies for what you need me to do."

I squint my eyes at her, contemplating how much I want to share. "If mom starts walking toward the stage or anywhere near Jacob, can you tackle her?"

"Okayyyy, and you can't do this yourself becauseeeee?"

"Because the stupid Viking turned my legs into jelly with this workout. The only thing I'll be tackling will be the ground."

"He fucked you the whole night?" she whisper-shouts.

"What?" I screech loud enough for people to look at me *again*. "No, idiot, I'm talking about this workout. The actual workout."

"Oh, how disappointing."

"Grace!" I almost growl.

"Fine, fine, Jesus, I'll tackle the poor woman who dared to give birth to you. Also, I hope he didn't hurt himself out there last night," she smirks.

Perfect, Grace knows.

"Thank you, my favorite sister, Gracie, for not saying anything to Hope when you saw my boyfriend hanging out the window," my little, annoying sister mocks me.

"I can't wait to go back to Chicago," I say, pinching the bridge of my nose. Thankfully, this delightful conversation gets cut off by my phone, and when I pick it up, I see ten missed calls from Zoe, at least twenty texts, and a few voicemails.

Crap, I forgot to call her back last night after Jacob left my place. I was so exhausted that I fell asleep right away. I scrunched up my nose and hit her name.

"JOY! OH MY GOD! FOR THE LOVE OF...FINALLY!!!" Zoe is yelling. No, not yelling, you can't call this yelling. She is screaming like a banshee, and I have to pull my phone away from my ear, just like I did the last time we spoke. This woman is going through some crazy periods.

"Jesus Christ, Zoe, did one of our cadavers come back to life?"

"What? No! What are you talking ab—" she pauses. "Oh my God, you're cracking jokes. That's it! The world is officially about to end. First Justin, then my stupid malfunctioning blood tests, and now you are making jokes. You."

Huh? Blood tests? What blood tests?

"Zoe, how many coffees did you drink today?"

"NONE! I can't have any coffee! Add it to the stupid, ever-growing list of issues in my life."

"What do you mean? What's going on? Will you finally explain?"

"Listen, there is no time, but you need to go! Run..." Just as Zoe starts talking, the first notes of "Sexy Back" by Justin Timberlake and Timberland start playing from the loudspeakers at the square.

I am so stunned by the choice of music; I don't hear whatever it is that Zoe is shouting into my ear. The only thing I do see is Jacob moving to the fucking song. Moving as in dancing as the whole crowd parts for him like he is Moses, and they are the Red Sea. And he is moving my way.

As in, I'm on the other side of this Red Sea, standing motionless and stunned because he is taking his clothes off.

He. Is. Taking. His. Clothes. Off. And dancing. Sexy.

Oh my God, please have mercy. Is he dancing for me? Striptease at eight AM with half the town watching?

That's it. He has officially lost it.

My phone slowly slides away from my face as my mouth drops because he is halfway to me, and he is no longer wearing a shirt, showcasing his glorious, tattooed body to all these eyes.

Close your fucking eyes! This is all mine! I want to shout to all the drooling faces, but I literally can't. I'm speechless. Utterly speechless.

Oh, no. Oh, no, no, no, no, his hand is not reaching to the string on his already too-revealing shorts. *But it is!*

He pulls the string, and my phone drops to the ground. The remnants of Zoe's screeching fading away.

The song is too loud to allow anything else to be heard anyway.

I'm hot. No, I am burning. Alive. Jacob's green eyes are on me the whole time as he dances, sexually touching his body and even grinding on the nearby pole. Jesus Christ.

Thankfully, the shorts are still intact, and my—fine, his—cock is safely hidden from the prying eyes of these crazies. He reaches me with the next three steps, and the heat of his body, his nakedness, and proximity fry my brain as they always do; only now we have an audience, and I'm not into exhibitionism.

Yet I feel his heartbeat, and all my worries go away. His body is rubbing on mine as I suck in sharp breaths and stand here panting. Jacob slips behind me as his nose drags over my neck. The palm of his hand slides over at the tiny sliver of my naked stomach, and I shiver. It's as if he stung me while his very hard cock is pressed against my legging-clad ass.

Please, God, tell me my dad is not watching this because I am a second away from doing something stupid.

I want to touch him. I want to lick his every muscle and beat of sweat. He is fucking insane, and I will rip him a new one for this later, but he is doing this for me. He is showing everyone who he belongs to. He is showing everyone that he wants me. Me.

He moves to stand in front of me, his eyes burning into mine as he bites his lower lip, grabs my hand, and stuffs it into his shorts.

I yelp and jump slightly.

He's not wearing underwear. There's absolutely nothing behind these tiny shorts, and now I am confident I will kill him later.

"Jacob." I want to sound mad, but instead, it sounds like a moan. Fucking amazing.

I mean, yes, touching him is amazing. He's hard, smooth, and velvety. Oh fuck, I want to drop down to my knees and feel him in my mouth.

I've never enjoyed giving blowjobs before this man fell into my life. Before his monster cock nearly choked me on that first night. I have always seen them as disgusting and degrading, but with him—for him—I want to take him as deep as I can and swallow each drop of cum he gives me. I want to show him what he does to me. Because he makes me forget everything.

Jacob makes me feel so special and desired like I have never been before.

"You need to stop," I whisper as his lips graze mine, he presses them softly, and I moan. "You are insane, and I'm mad at you." This time, he kisses me with more force. "So mad." He keeps kissing me, tracing his tongue over my lips, and I part them for him. Granting Jacob the access he wanted. I wrap my hand around him tighter, and he groans into my mouth. "I just might kill you later."

"Don't forget, I'd like to go with your wet pussy suffocating me."

"You are such an idiot." We are both talking into each other's mouths as we are kissing. No, we are full-on making out, for God knows how long. I vaguely notice the song isn't playing anymore, and I think the people are mostly gone, but we are rooted to the spot. Kissing and touching as if we were alone. As if this is all okay.

As if the world belongs to us. As if there is an *us*...

My whole body jolts at his touch. It's like pressing your hand to an electric fence. My skin grows hotter and hotter, sensitive and needy. My reproductive system gears up for a new riot, and this time, I'm not sure I'll be able to say no. He brought out his bulldozer once again to ruin whatever walls I had left. And I let him.

Our tongues slide against each other, desperate for more. There is nothing sweet or soft about us right now.

"Close your eyes, Wildflower," he whispers into my ear. "Do you feel me? Do you feel us? Let go, Joy. Lean on me. Be mine."

This man is ice and fire. As soon as our bodies clash, Mr. Nice Weirdo is nowhere to be seen. In his place is a beast who is out to break me, please me, and ruin for any future one-night stands. But then he goes right back to being the silly dork, the easygoing, funny guy with golden retriever vibes.

But you know what I love the most? I think I'm the only one who gets to see his hidden part. The one he said he buried.

I think that Jacob is all mine. Somehow, this crazy guy wants to be with me. The one who has never been enough for anyone, and I don't have any misconceptions about what we are. This is passion and lust and need. Not commitment and babies, but for the time being, I am his, and he is mine. And I'm about done denying myself this man, I want him.

"Yours." That is the only word I can utter.

"We need to go home, now," Jacob growls into my neck as my hand gives him one last squeeze, and I pull it away.

I should say no; I should be furious he just pulled this crap in front of half the town, and by now, I'm sure the rest is well-informed as well. But I'm not. And I am nodding yes as I enjoy this moment of insanity in our little bubble.

Until we hear someone clear their throat. Loudly. Rudely.

The offensive sound startles us, and we pull apart, but when my eyes meet the ones standing across from us. Just like that, all my euphoria, bliss, and happiness are wiped clean.

Because those eyes? They belong to Justin fucking Hunt.

The eyes that I adored and thought I loved for three long years. The eyes that are full of hate and anger and so many other emotions right now as they stare at me and Jacob.

And standing next to him is my boss, his father, James Hunt. And I just had my hand down Jacob's shorts and behaved like a slut in front of him. Fuck my life.

Once again, I'm speechless this morning, but this time due to an entirely different situation. What is going on? Why are they here? How did they find me, and what do they need from me? But as my shock slightly subsides, I notice Dr. Hunt's eyes are not on me. Well, not really on me.

He is looking at Jacob, who has his jaw set in stone, his teeth clenched so hard I can hear the tiny cracks all the way here, and his hand is squeezing mine tighter with each passing second as if he is the one who needs the support right now, not me.

"Son," James says, looking at Jacob and forget speechless...I'm dead. Yes, that's it. I am dead...

# 25

# *50 Reasons*

Reason #32:
*Jacob: You basically get to live with a free, hands-on vibrator. All orgasms you can have, plus, I will wash you up after.
Joy: Fuck...I can't dispute that one.*

Reason #34:
*Jacob: Double the hair products!
Joy: And this is a good thing, how?*

# 26

# Jacob

*"The secret of a happy marriage remains a secret."* — *Henry Youngman.*

What the fuck is he doing here? And with that waste of space standing next to him, nonetheless? Talk about boner killers. I haven't seen my father in five years, and I'd like to keep it that way until the end of my days.

I've spent enough time in his toxicity while he was feeding me his higher class-society-connections garbage day in and day out. I told him everything I wanted to say when I left Chicago, and I don't see what he could possibly want from me now.

"Son," he says, and I grind my teeth to the point of pain. I don't grace him with a response, but I feel Joy stiffen next to me.

Shit, this was not the plan for today. Everything was going so well; she enjoyed my little dance even though I was confident she would murder me.

I like this woman. I like her very much. I think I'm falling for her, and just now, it felt like she felt the same. She was kissing me in front of everyone. She has let herself go. She was living in the moment, and we were just about to get to the good part when my family decided to ruin it all.

I never wanted for her to see all this, to feel the animosity between us. Joy should live in a perfect world, one where she is the center of my universe, and nothing should dampen her mood. Yet here we are.

"What are you doing here?" I say through clenched teeth and tug my girl closer to me as Justin's eyes roam freely over her body. He doesn't spare me a glance, his full attention is on her, and I'm a second away from punching the asshole. What a nice little reunion that would be.

I can sense her discomfort, her hard swallows, and her heavy breaths. Justin is leering over her, and my skin is crawling with hate. She was supposed to be getting loved right now. Instead, she's being drooled over by an asshole.

"Apart from watching you strip half naked in the middle of the town and in front of one of the best pathologists in the county?" He arches his eyebrows. "I came here to talk. It's time you come home," my father, the almighty James Hunt, pronounces. It's a statement, the one I'm supposed to follow and maybe fall down at his feet while I'm at it, but those days are long over.

"No," I reply simply. "If that's all, we'll be going. We have other plans for today, rather than wasting time here with you two." I wrap my hand over Joy's shoulder, forgetting all about my discarded shirt, and begin steering us away from them.

"Stop being a child, Jacob." My dear old brother finally finds his voice.

"Why? So I can be as insufferable as you are, brother?"

# MEET MY WIFE

"Brother?" Joy's voice is bordering manic. She looks at me, then at Justin, then back to me. We are not very much alike in any way, so I can understand her confusion.

"Half-brother. Unfortunately." Justin is almost ten years older than me. His mother—my father's first wife—died when he was seven, and dear old dad didn't waste too much time looking for new arm candy, also known as the woman who gave birth to me.

I don't hate my parents. They gave me life after all, but there isn't much to love there either.

Anna Marie—the woman my father married—hasn't spent a day with me alone. And no, I don't call her mom, she doesn't deserve it.

As soon as I was born, I was handed to my nanny and brought out only when the press was around, and my parents acted like I was the reason for their existence. Their pride and joy.

Yeah, not even close...

"Half-brother..." she trails off, her beautiful eyes blinking rapidly.

"Cut it out. That's not all." Father's hard voice speaks again. "I said it is time for you to come home. So, pack up whatever you need. Better yet, leave all this ridiculous rubbish here, and let's go. You can wear one of Justin's suits while we travel."

I try very hard not to laugh at his ridiculousness right now. I click my tongue and turn back to face him. "It's cute how you think you can still boss me around. Let's go, Wildflower." I turn once again, but my father stops us. Again.

"Doctor Levine, fancy seeing you here. I thought you were dealing with family matters. Since when do those include my son?"

"Dr. Hunt, hello." She gives him a cold nod, but this is not my Joy. This is the stone sculpture I found at LPs that very first night. "And yes, I am dealing with family matters. My parents live in Loverly Cave." It's insane, but it is not surprising my father knows Joy. By the sounds of it, they work together, and I want to hit myself up the head for not asking her more about her job. Granted, we haven't been together that much, and she's a walking vault, but still, I should have made the connection sooner.

"Ah, I see. And how did someone like *you* ended up with my delinquent of a son?" And you ask why I left five years ago? Jeez, with praises like that, I could have stayed as his slave forever, couldn't I?

"Again, this begs the question, what are you doing here then?" I interrupt my father's inquisition.

"No hi for me?" Justin interrupts Dad. He hasn't moved his gaze from Joy a single second this whole time, and now he looks almost pissed.

There is a threatening sound coming from Joy, and I'm pretty sure she just growled at him. I love it, but something tells me there is a lot more to this story. A lot. And I will get to the bottom of this, but for now, all I want to do is protect and shield her from my family, from their evil ways and sick minds.

"You." I point to him, seeing how upset she is getting. "You don't talk to her and stop looking at her with your sick eyes, got it?"

Father cuts us both a look, and Justin shuts up. "Circumstances have changed. You are the last resort, so pack up and quit stalling. Do something right for once in your life."

"What exactly is it that I am supposed to do right?"

"You are to take over KePah University," he says with a clenched jaw, and I blink. Blink again and even probe my ear a few times to make sure my hearing is working.

"Come again?" I squint my eyes at him, and he rolls his. "You want me, me?" I point to myself. "The weirdo of the family. The useless scrap of DNA. The disgrace to Hunt's name to sit at the head of your precious university?" Joy slowly lifts her eyes up to mine, the steel walls completely gone, as she looks at me with so much compassion that it nearly breaks me. "Have you forgotten I have no interest in your bullshit?"

My father hasn't stopped clenching his teeth. "Like I said, the circumstances have changed. We should be having this conversation in private, not around my staff." Yeah, I figured my brilliant girl would be slaving away at his hole of a prestigious school.

I turn my head to Joy and pray she won't kill me for this. I mean, she always wants to kill me, but this time she actually might.

Fuck it, I'm doing it.

"Anything you have to say to me, you can say in front of Joy. I have no secrets from my wife."

The said "wife" sucks in a sharp breath and freezes. "Jacob," she whispers, but that whisper is full of threats and bloody promises. Yep, she wants to kill me.

"Your what?" Justin screeches. "Wife? Did I hear that right?"

"I know you are old, but you're not that old, brother. You heard me, alright. Meet my wife, Joy Levine. Well, future wife. I just proposed a minute ago. You might've caught some of it, and she said yes, didn't you, Wildflower?" I squeezed her shoulder in a silent plea.

"Mm-hmm," she murmurs as her nails dig into my side, and I jerk away slightly but glue myself back to her almost instantly. Apparently, my family is too stunned to notice anything else right now.

"Joy?" Justin barks at her. "Explain!"

"There is nothing to explain. Now, leave. We aren't planning to invite you all to the wedding."

"Really now?" Father squints his eyes at us, and I can tell he's not buying it.

"Yep."

"When's the wedding, Dr. Levine?" he asks Joy, who is on the verge of passing out or stabbing me with a knife. Not sure which one she's leaning towards at this point.

She clears her throat, "We haven't decided yet." She paints on a forced smile for my father.

"You wouldn't be lying to your headmaster, would you?"

"Of course not."

"So, you are trying to tell me that someone like you stooped down so low and fell for this..." he trails off as he watches me with contempt. "With a guy like Jacob?"

"What's wrong with Jacob?" Is there a hint of protectiveness in her tone? Or is it wishful thinking on my part?

"So much, my dear, so much. And the fact that you have to ask means you don't know him at all. Now, let's drop this stupid act and move on."

"It is not an act!" Joy protests, her own eyes blazing with fire as my mouth drops. "And I clearly know more about this man than you do, Dr. Hunt, because my Jacob is anything but a delinquent. He is brilliant and thoughtful and funny and loyal," she says with pride and an elegant tilt of her head.

Jesus, if she doesn't kill me, I might do it for her as a gift because no one has ever stood up to my family like this for me. No one.

I feel so much for her. For this fierce, brilliant, and stunning woman.

"Baby, how does September sound to you?" Joy asks me, placing her hand on my chest and looking up at me with an overly sweet, sugary smile plastered on her face, and I think Justin just threw up in his own mouth.

Hmm, *baby*, how deliciously sweet that sounded. Like music to my ears.

"I think it sounds wonderful, boo. Whatever you'd like. We can even make your dress in that rubber ducky pattern you love so much." Hell, I am going to die anyway, I might as well have fun while I'm at it. I only have to remember not to laugh right now.

"Aren't you so thoughtful?" she squeaks out, her jaw clenching harder by a second. "And you must wear those shark slides. We can also serve Cupid's Arrow cocktails since they brought us together."

"It was the Eros Spell, remember my love?"

"Oh." She softly smacks her head with her hand like she's the stupid one. "Of course, how could I forget our first night." The innuendo in her voice is more than obvious, and I tug her closer until she crashes into my chest. I look down to her lips as she does to mine.

What is going through her beautiful head right now?

Apparently, kissing me, because a second later, her hand wraps around my neck as she pulls me down to her mouth, and we clash in a passionate kiss. I can't help myself when this woman is in my hands. Pretend or not, I want her. I need her. My hand travels down her spandex-covered body until I reach her luscious ass and palm it, squeezing it hard and making her moan into my mouth.

I had just kissed her a few minutes ago, had her hand down my shorts, and now that I'm kissing her again, all those emotions—a hard on—are back. The world needs to go away because I am a second away from snapping.

"Enough!" Justin bellows from the side, pulling us from the show we were putting on. Only there was no acting on our part.

And...I liked it all a little too much. I could imagine the whole thing so clearly. Us in rubber ducky outfits, her holding a bouquet of wildflowers as her dark hair flies carelessly in whichever way the wind blows as we say our "I dos" under the Loverly cave. I could see the town enjoying some drinks from LPs and us starting our life together.

"Doctor Levine! Step away from him!" Justin is just short of blowing a fuse. "That is hippy filth you are kissing. How could you associate with such a waste of space?"

"Don't call him that." Joy surprises us all by the cutting sharpness in her tone. We are all taken aback by her comment, and when I turn to look at her, I see that strong, tough, smart woman standing with her shoulders back, posture straight as a rod, and her chin slightly lifted as if being in the presence of my family is beneath her. "You do not get to offend my fiancé in front of me when the real issue of your family is standing right here."

Jesus, if I thought I was falling for her earlier, now I know. I love Joy Levine. My fierce, unstoppable, gorgeous girl who just stood up to whom I believe is her boss to defend me.

And she called me her fiancé. Can we take a moment to memorize this forever?

My father's mouth uplifts into a one-sided smile—a smirk is more like it—as he watches her intently. "Yes, you could've made a fine Hunt," he tells her. "Well, well, if only this were true, I might've considered that you had finally done something right in your life. Still, I am impressed," my father mocks me with a cold smile. He claps his hands together.

"Now prove to your family that you are not a useless hippy for once and come back home with your wife. I'm giving you three days to pack up and make the move."

"We are not moving anywhere, I already told you."

"And what are you going to do when Dr. Levine has to return back home to her job? Oh, wait, you didn't think about it because despite this cute little show, you two don't have a future together, and there is no wedding happening." My father's smirk knows no bounds.

I quickly pull out my phone and start searching for what I need. Finding the first link that pops up, I enter our information and, with another click, send it to the Love Hive group.

With a smile, I turn my phone to face Dad and Justin. "Here, our invites have been sent out to the whole Loverly Cave. Now, both of you can leave us alone. And don't bother sending us a gift; our love for each other is already more than enough for us."

I take Joy's hand and lead her away from this shit show. While James and Justin Hunt send death glares our way, only I am fairly confident they are for two different reasons.

Once we are a few feet away from them, she mutters, "I hope you know I will be enjoying murdering you on our wedding night."

Grace: **For the love of Harry, if I don't get a second-by-second recount of everything that happened after the nearly naked and very hot man tugged you away like a freaking caveman, I will move in with you.**

Hope: **What? What happened? What have I missed?**

Grace: **When mom told you to attend the morning workouts, you should have listened!!!**

Grace: **Our sister just got the equivalent of a lap dance in front of half the town!!!**

Hope: **WHAT??? By Jacob? Is that what the whole town is talking about?**

Grace: **Of course, by Jacob. Who else is stupid enough to sniff around our cactus?**

Hope: **Tell me you got that on video.**

Grace: **Ugh, I wish! I was too stunned! You'd think Mom would give us some heads up so we would be prepared, but noooo. Only she gets all the fun here.**

Hope: **Mom? What does she have to do with Joy getting a lap dance?**

Grace: **You aren't seriously asking that question, are you? *Eyeroll***

Grace: **Breakfast. Tomorrow morning. We will have our monthly sisterly meeting.**

Hope: **Um, we don't have monthly sisterly meetings.**

Grace: **Now we do, lovebug. Attendance is mandatory. Tardiness is punishable by a week of sleepovers at mom's house.**

Hope: **I'll be there ten minutes early.**

Joy: **You will all have to wait until I kill that nearly naked and very hot man.**

# 27

## Joy

*"Love makes your soul crawl out from its hiding place."* –
*Zora Neale Hurston.*

"Don't. Don't say another fucking word," I cut Jacob off from whatever else he's about to say as we walk away from the literal scene of the crime. "What the fuck just happened?"

"Joy—" I hold up my hand to stop him.

"I thought I told you to shut up. I'm asking myself out loud. Not you." As soon as we reach my car, I lean against it and rub my forehead with my hand. "You're a Hunt? Jacob Hunt?"

"Am I allowed to speak now?" I snarl at him, and he gulps. "Yes, yes, I am."

"And you didn't care to mention that you are an heir to a whole fucking dynasty?" My hands are flying wild because there is no containing these emotions right now.

Jacob, my crazy, hippy weirdo, is a Hunt. Forget that, he is Justin's *half-brother*.

I mean, I couldn't make this shit up even if I tried.

"I don't exactly talk about those people, and I am definitely not anyone's heir." He crosses his arms across his chest.

"Get in the car," I instruct him as I open the driver's seat door and slide inside.

"Why? Are you taking me out into the woods to kill and dissect my body?"

"Jacob." I take a deep breath. "Get. In. The. Car. Now."

"Fine, fine. I'm coming."

As we start driving away, the severity of what just happened dawns upon me.

Jacob danced striptease for me in front of hundreds of people.

He is a Hunt.

Justin is in town.

I work for James Hunt, who is the biggest asshole in the world. No wonder his son is one as well, and I'm not talking about the one sitting in the passenger seat.

Oh, and apparently, I'm getting married to Jacob—aka dead man walking.

And all this happened in the span of twenty minutes.

Fucking fabulous...why didn't Zoe tell me Justin got the pink slip? Why didn't she mention anything about this? Oh, wait, she tried, but I was too consumed by the Viking sitting next to me to pay attention or really care.

Now, I'm paying the price. I should have shut my mouth and let them deal with their family issues, but when I saw my ex standing there in all his assholish glory, looking at me like I was his meal for tonight, something inside of me snapped, and I went along with that whole ridiculousness. Not to mention, I was seething with rage as they were spewing that garbage out of their mouth, insulting Jacob.

My Jacob.

Jacob, who is possibly the kindest, most loving, sweetest Viking in the world. Jacob, who clearly did everything possible to run away from his family and has no desire to be sucked back into that hole. I couldn't let that fly.

I should have. But I couldn't.

I felt anger bubbling up inside my chest, my stomach contents churning, and red clouding my vision. For some unreasonable reason, I felt overly protective of him, and I was ready to do anything to fight them off for him.

But now the fight is leaving me as reality sets in. My boss thinks I am getting married to his son. Well, no, he actually doesn't, but if I back out now, it will prove that Jacob and I lied. I'm screwed either way.

"What even possessed you to say we're getting married?"

"I don't know." He shrugs. "I guess I wanted to prove to dear old Dad I'm not such a screw-up, and I've got this extraordinary woman agreeing to spend her life with me."

Fuck...

At least now, it is blatantly clear why his views on society and universities are what they are.

"Joy," Jacob's voice is small and unsure. "I'm so sorry."

"I—" I open my mouth to say something. Anything. But there's nothing. I'm blank.

He says he's sorry, but I don't feel the need to forgive him because, truth be told, I'm not mad at him. Not one bit.

I'm not even mad he called me his wife. Shocked? Yes. A little excited? Also, yes. And I will not try to analyze it right now. But mad is not one of the emotions I'm feeling towards him.

I'm appalled with myself for working at KePah for so long, and not seeing what kind of people surrounded me. For loving Justin. For being a part of their toxic family—even if it was in a screwed-up way.

So I settle on, "I think we need to talk."

"Yeah, we do," he agrees, and we spend the remainder of our two-minute drive in silence.

As soon as the front door to my cottage closes, Jacob drops to his knees and wraps his arms around me, pressing his face into my thighs.

"What the hell are you doing?"

"Please, say you forgive me. Please! I know I'm an idiot, and I know I just jeopardized your career, but I won't be able to live with myself if my wife hates me," he mumbles into my leggings.

"Get up, Jacob." I try to pull on his naked shoulders, which is fruitless. I might as well be pulling up a two-ton stone. "Get up, now! And I'm not your wife," I demand.

"Not until you say you forgive me."

"That's peer pressure. It won't be genuine."

"I don't care," he mumbles some more. "I'll take what I can get at this point."

"Jacob! I wasn't mad at you up until this point. Get up this instant."

"You weren't?" His head pops up from my legs as he looks at me with those puppy eyes.

"No. I'm not mad. Can we just talk? That was a lot for one morning." I feel exhausted. My voice is exhausted. My brain is wiped.

"Yeah, yeah." Jacob finally gets up from his knees only to pull me down with him to the blanket I still have lying by the wall.

"I don't know how to do this," I admit to him, leaning my head back against the cold wall.

"Do what?"

"Talking. Opening up. I don't really have many friends, well, I have one to be exact, and we don't exactly do talking."

He looks at me with softness in his eyes. "Whenever I did open up to anyone, they staked a knife in my back, turned around, and left me mixing up fresh concrete to build more walls to protect myself in the future."

"I am going to guess that my brother was one of those people?"

I wet my lips. "Yeah. He was." I am expecting a scowl, anger, displeasure, annoyance, pretty much anything but the calm he is giving me. I am expecting an interrogation, instead he gives me his story.

"Okay." He extends his hand to me for a handshake. "Hi, my name is Jacob Hunt. I am thirty-two years old. I am a trauma surgeon by profession, but I haven't worked in the field for the past five years. My family owns and runs KePah University, but I didn't attend it myself. I resent anything and everything that has my family's name on it. I was always the black sheep of the family whom everybody liked to pretend didn't exist. I was married, thinking we loved each other when, in reality, my father had arranged that marriage in a way. He got her to make me fall for the scheme since she was from a proper social circle and made a good match for a Hunt on paper.

"We were married for all of one year until my ex realized I wanted nothing to do with the Hunt name and I would not be a part of that fake, rich society. That's when she decided to move on to the other Hunt brother and became his mistress."

My mouth falls open, my jaw hitting the floor.

Oh, fuck...yeah, sure, let's add another woman to the mix. Jesus, I'm so pathetic, thinking he loved me...

Jacob sees my face and adds, "Yes, the same half-brother who is a pathological asshole. In all honesty, it was his betrayal that hurt more than hers." He sighs. "I left my job and my home and went backpacking across America five years ago until I ended up in Loverly Cave, and for the first time in my life, I felt like I was finally home. Like I belong somewhere and people like me for who I am. For my weirdness and quirks. They accept my shark slides and rubber ducky shorts. And not just accept it, they *welcome* it. And this town also brought me to you, so I could never complain."

Well...that is...a lot.

I mean, he is a trauma surgeon? He was married? She cheated on him with Justin?

*Breathe in, breathe out Joy. He opened his heart up for you; now it's your turn.*

I shake his hand, finally. "Hi, my name is Joy Levine. I am thirty-one, as you know. I'm a pathologist, and I love my job. I went to KePah, finished early with distinction, and they offered me a job right off the bet. I have no social life; I spend it all in my lab. Ten years ago, I was cheated on by my high school boyfriend with my younger sister, Hope. Since then, I haven't spoken to her or Grace until we were all conned into coming here. Three years ago, I met a man who I thought would be my forever, but he ended up being a lying piece of shit, also known as Justin Hunt. I swore I would never get involved with another man until you sat next to me at LPs."

Jacob smiles a little. "I'd say that was some excellent talking, but we do have to work on that delivery. It was a bit dry." He tries to lighten the mood, and it's working based on a tiny smile tugging on my lips. "I guess it's a good thing we are getting married then. I'll show you how it's done."

A laugh bubbles out of me. "You are an idiot, and we are not getting married."

"Sure, we are, but can we go back to the fact that you dated my brother?" He's finally caught up with everything I said.

"It makes sense now why he was about to blow a gasket when he saw you in my arms."

"I'd rather not."

Jacob places his strong hand on my thigh, squeezing it lightly, lending me his strength.

"Come on, where is the harm in sharing with a stranger you won't ever see again? I might even help you figure it all out," he repeats the words he said to me on that first night we met, but this time, I don't shut him down. I look into his green eyes and find myself opening my mouth to spill it all out.

"First, I want you to know that I had no idea he was married. None at all. I found out a week before I arrived in Loverly. We had this awards dinner at KePah, and he showed up with her." I sigh, the memories of that scene flashing in front of my eyes. "Later that evening, he showed up at my place demanding we talk and go back to the way things were. Can you believe that shit?"

"Yeah, I can. It's Justin we are talking about, after all." He's right, and I should've seen what a bastard I was dating, but I didn't.

I bite my lip, not wanting to say the next words, but Jacob sees it, brings his thumb to my lips, and pulls the bruised one out. "Hey, I am here to listen, okay? But if you want to stop, we can."

"No," I shake my head. Jacob just shared his pain with me, and the least I can do is let him see mine. "Justin said things to me before he left." I swallow hard. "He brought up my weight and reminded me that I was never good enough to be his wife. That I'm cold and unfeeling. He was right, of course, but it still stung to hear it."

Jacob yanks my face to him, and I see two cloudy storms in place of his moss-green eyes. "Don't. Ever. Say. That." His lips crush mine in a searing kiss. It's as if he is trying to wash away my last words...and it's working.

Jacob makes me feel enough.

"You better get into my arms right this second and hold me real strong," he says, yanking my whole body this time until I'm in his lap.

"Why?" I ask in a small voice as I lay my head on his chest. Pressing it into his warmth and comfort.

"Go on, I want to hear the rest," he says, ignoring my question, and I go back to my story. This time, adding all the details about Zoe and the other girls who have filed the charges against him, and the whole time, he sits still, intently listening to my story and keeping his steady hand on me, twined in my hair. As soon as I'm done, the silence grows between us. Jacob wraps me in his arms tighter, his heartbeat greets me like my own lullaby, soothing all the rough edges I have lifted up with this retelling.

We end up sitting like that for what seems to be forever, but neither one of us have moved an inch.

"Sorry, I needed this," he eventually tells me. "I needed you to keep me here. Otherwise, I would be tracking that son of a bitch down and dragging him far into the ocean on my surfboard." My breath catches at his words. "You didn't deserve any of that. I wish I could take all that pain away from you, Wildflower. I wish it wouldn't have been caused by someone whom I share blood with. And for the first time in my life, I wish I would have gone to KePah and met you years ago. I could have protected you from all the heartache. I could have made you mine a long time ago."

No one has ever cared this much for me. My own sister betrayed me without ever looking back, while the other one knew about it the whole time and didn't tell me. Yet, this man whom I have known for only a little over two weeks is ready to kill for me, change the past, and make me his.

"Joy?"

"Hmm?" I can't talk. There is something stuck in my throat and eyes, and if I utter a word, something petrifying will happen, and I do not want to cry right now. I won't.

"You are mine now."

"Jacob..." I trail off because, once again, I am completely lost for words. I can't be his, I can't be anyone's, but I want to be very much. This, with Jacob, it feels nothing like before.

It never has. From the moment he sat on that barstool next to me, I knew he was different. But I am not what he needs in life. I won't be enough for him. I don't know how to live the way he lives. I don't know how to live, period.

For the past ten years, I've been putting on a strong front. Everyone knows me as the tough, cold, heartless body slayer when, in truth, my insecurities have been eating away at me my whole life. The same ones I am feeling now.

"Jacob, sex is one thing, but what you are talking about is something...something I can't give you. You don't want it with me. I'm not it for you."

He pulls me away from his chest and stares down into my eyes.

"What are you talking about?"

"I am not fit to live the way you do; I will hold you back, and eventually, you will resent me and leave me. I am not special or free or even happy."

"I thought I told you to never say that again."

"Jacob! The lust will pass just like it did for my other two boyfriends. Just let it go now, please, before it's too hard for me. I might have survived Brian and Justin, but I am not sure I could survive losing you."

I've never been this vulnerable. I've never been this open. I've said things I can't take back, but I needed him to know why this needs to stop.

"Wildflower." He cups my head in his strong hands, his eyes a few inches away from mine as the tips of our noses barely touch, and I feel his breath on my lips. "You might be the best, most amazing human out there, but you still won't be good enough for the wrong person. Yet you can be at your absolute worst, and you will be the most valuable, prized gift to the right one. I'm sorry to break it to you, but you just might be *it* for me. And I am afraid you are stuck with me because I may not be as book-smart as my half-brother is, but I am a damn genius when it comes to knowing you are pure gold, and I would be an idiot to let you go."

"Jacob," I breathe out. Damn it, I can't let go of my walls. I can't!

But do they even exist anymore?

"I don't know what you think it is I need, but I am very content with this grumpy woman who loves to bite my head off. Some believe relationships need to be fifty-fifty, but that is not true. At least not to me. I believe we are here to fill in the missing pieces. So, if today you are only feeling a twenty of yourself, I will be the eighty. Tomorrow, I might need you to be the seventy to my thirty. And some days, both of us can be at one, but guess what?"

"What?" I breathe out, looking at this man as if he is an angel sent from someplace higher than the heavens.

"We will still get through it all together. With a smile and some rubber duckies. And starting tomorrow, I will show you how to be free and happy, and I will definitely make sure you know how special you are. We have a few months before our wedding for you to unwind." He winks and kisses the tip of my nose.

"Jacob, we are not getting married."

"Our invitations say otherwise."

"What invitations?"

"The ones I sent out today through E-vite to everyone." He wiggles his phone out to me, and I reach out to snatch it, but the bastard is too fast.

"Jacob! Have you lost your damn mind? You actually sent those? I thought it was just for a show!" He shakes his head. "Invitations for a wedding that will not be happening? And to the whole town nonetheless?" I bulge my eyes at him, but he is unfazed. Not one bit. Jacob is just smiling and nodding away.

"That's it." Somehow, that comes out a lot calmer than how I am feeling right now. "You might have had me feeling all mushy and soapy just a second ago, but now I am back, and I will kill you."

"There she is," my *fiancé* who has a death wish says softly and tucks a loose strand of hair behind my ear. "If you want to be all mushy, go for it. But this, this is who I love. My feisty Wildflower."

Did I just hear what I think I heard?

Did Jacob just say the L word?

Did he?

My eyes are wide, and suddenly, the house feels too small, and he is sensing it as well.

Jacob gets up from the blanket, but not before he kisses me softly one more time. "I have to head to work, but I will see you later, okay?"

I'm stunned and frozen, my limbs and voice nonexistent as my little hussies take over my body. Walls, what? Those were never sturdy enough for his hammer.

He said it. He did. Love...

**Love Hive:**

Freeman1: Did we hear that right? Is operation Pink Mist officially a success?

CookieJ: WHAT??? What did you hear? Why haven't I heard anything yet? @rickyL, I swear if you pull me away from all the excitement like that again, I will switch out your arthritis cream with my own concoction of pepper and sand!

RickyL: You try that, and I will let our daughter in on all your schemes.

CookieJ: Ahhhh! (Clutches her fist to her heart) And to think I have spent my whole life with such a heartless man!

Fforall: It's true! I have seen it with my own eyes and heard it with my own ears!

CookieJ: Seen what? Heard what? I swear if you people don't tell me what is going on with *my* operation, I will disown you all, and I will not share my secret white chocolate chip cookie recipe at the next town meeting.

Ninasunshine: I second that. The only day I miss the morning workout is when something exciting happens. Someone kick me next time I agree to help my grumpy son in the morning.

Freeman1: I call the dibs on that kick. I am particularly partial to your cute butt, honey.

Ninasunshine: @freeman1, you naughty man of mine. You can kick my butt any time you want.

Youknowyouwantme: Ugh, mom, dad! Jesus. I am going to throw up right now.

Freeman1: Alec, love is love. We thought you better than that.

*Youknowyouwantme leaves the chat.*

CookieJ: @ninasunshine, let's keep sexting for our Wednesday sexting chat. Now, I need the details.

Willoflove: Pink Mist is officially a success. Check your inbox, woman. You might find an invitation to your daughter's wedding there.

# 28

# *50 Reasons*

Reason # 36
*Jacob: Less dirty dishes.*
*Joy: How does living with another person equals less dishes?*
*Jacob: I'll eat everything in the first go, so there will be no leftovers to pack.*

Reason #37:
*Jacob: You never get to hear another, "When is she finally getting married?"*
*Joy: Fine, I'll give you that one.*

Reason #39:
*Jacob: You are tired from work, your feet hurt…BAM, I'm right there with foot rubs and free massages.*
*Joy: Since when are your massages free?*
*Jacob: It's not my fault I get turned on while rubbing your sexy-as-hell body, and we end up having sex.*

# 29
# Jacob

*"In any perfect relationship, men should remember it's a matter of direction; she takes what's right, and you take what's left."* — Solitaire Parke.

"Alec!" I bellow as soon as my feet are stepping through the front door of our tattoo shop. His dark, slightly curly hair and blue eyes pop out from the hallway.

"What? What happened?" he asks, his voice is full of concern, but I'm just standing frozen, rooted in one spot. "Jackie, you gotta start talking actual words, buddy, because you are freaking me out."

"I nearly said it. My mouth started moving and making sounds I didn't allow it to make." I point to the said mouth, my eyes wide with fear.

"Said what?"

"That I loved her. Like, I think I might have actually said the word itself. But she just agreed to marry me, and now my father is in town, and I'm finally breaking through some of those walls of hers, and I had to go screw it up with that L word." I start pacing the length of our shop, my hands digging into my hair. I don't think I've ever word vomited like that before. I don't think I've ever felt panic before. Like ever! Even when I found my ex in bed with my half-brother. "Do you know what that means?"

"Um, no, I don't, and quite frankly, I will need you to go back and explain each one of those…I mean, what the fuck?" Alec whisper-shouts and bulges his eyes at me, but I am not seeing him right now. "Jacob, this isn't you. You don't freak out. Ever."

"I know, man! But it's not every day my worlds collide. And fucking Justin! Like, how does that happen?"

"Do you even need me here? Because you seem to be enjoying this conversation with yourself just fine."

"*Fine*! That word again. I don't like that word, but I think I dislike the word 'love' even more. No, I love love, but it's too soon! She's not there yet, and I didn't think I was either, but maybe I am. No, I am. I'm in love with her." My panicked gaze flicks over to Alec. "Alec," I say it like a plea. "What do I do now?"

"Take a deep breath, man, come on," my friend says, grabbing my shoulders and leading me to the chair behind our counter. I take in some fresh oxygen mixed with the scent of cleaning supplies and slowly recount the whole day to him. From the dance to my father's demands to my "meet my wife" line to Joy opening up to me about her history with Justin.

I don't tell him too many details about that particular part. It's her story to tell. I just paint the overall picture, but even that's enough to make his jaw drop.

"So, what you're trying to tell me is that I'm supposed to give you my favorite, lucky wave surfboard and tattoo your name on my ass now?"

"That's your takeaway from all this?" I spread my arms wide.

"No, you know what? This doesn't count! She didn't really agree to marry you." He crosses his arms in front, defiance written all over his face.

I squint my eyes at him. "Are you backing out of our deal? Is Alec Colson a chicken-shit now?"

"Dude! It's my lucky surfboard." Alec is on the verge of tears, and I would feel bad if I didn't want that surfboard almost as much as I want Joy. Ever since Alec spilled his Downer's Luck cocktail from LPs on it, he hasn't missed a single killer wave. Even when I took it out for a ride, it didn't fail.

Told you, those cocktails are magical. Maybe I should've gone over to Willow for another drink instead of here.

"Alec, when you came over crying for help with Hope, who gave you the best advice of your lifetime?"

He hums and crosses his arms again. "Running my hand through my hair slowly while pulling my smolder face on hardly qualifies as advice of a lifetime."

"Yeah, yeah, keep telling yourself that, nevertheless, it got you the girl. So, now shut up, give me my new surfboard, and help your best friend out!" I shout the last part.

"Jeez, fine, fine. The board is yours. Touchy." He does the whole sassy head shake.

"I am this close," I pinch my index and thumb very, very closely at his face. "This close to killing you."

"You, my friend, spend too much time with Joy. She is rubbing off on you."

"Alec!"

"Okay, relax! Firstly, did she freak out more when you called her your wife or when you slipped the L word?"

I pause to think it over.

"Not sure. I was too freaked out myself to watch her reaction when I said it."

"Okay, and the wife thing?"

"Not freaked out, stunned, then a bit pissed. Yeah, okay, a lot pissed. Especially after I told her that I did indeed send out the invites." I rub the side of my head. I should feel bad about invites, but I don't.

"Hmm..." he trails off cryptically, and I slowly turn my head towards him.

"What does 'hmm' mean?"

"It means hmm."

"You are aware I will be the one tattooing your ass, and I just might get creative. You know how much I love them rubber duckies."

"Hmm, can you make them in rainbow colors?" My idiot friend asks, and I slap my hand to my face.

"I am sorry to say we can't be friends anymore."

"That's right, because we are soul mates. You keep forgetting that part, Jackie. Now relax your balls and listen." He sits back smugly. "She didn't freak out! Miss I-will-kill-you-with-one-look didn't freak out about being married to you. Sure, it's a fake engagement, but it's an engagement, nonetheless. I think you, my brother,"—he slaps his hand on my knee— "have nothing to worry about, and simply need to keep pushing forward. If she is what—who—you want, then go for it, full steam ahead. Also, ignore that ridiculous family of yours, they can't make you do anything. And as for the L word. If it scares her...become the one who fights those monsters away. That's what I do with Hope." He shrugs. "It has worked for me so far."

"Push through?"

"Yeah," he says it as if it's the most obvious thing in the world.

"And if it doesn't work out?"

"Why wouldn't it? I think Joy just wants to be loved. Unconditionally. And if anyone can love a cactus and cuddle with it, it's you, Jackie." He bumps my shoulder playfully. "If she hasn't killed you already, chances are she won't ever."

I smile softly at him. "You know; I think she is the first woman I have actually loved. Truly loved." My voice is hushed and slightly trembling.

I am the fun guy, the heart of the party guy, the one who cracks jokes and doesn't take life seriously. Even with my ex-wife, I never looked back or got sad over our divorce because I didn't feel this much for her. She didn't make my heart squeeze at the mere sight of her body like Joy does. She was never the one I could sit and talk to for hours like I could with Joy. She was beautiful and smart but not mine.

Not in the way Joy Levine is with all her grumpy moods, penitentiary-style walls, and sharp edges. I love Joy Levine, and it's beautifully terrifying because if she freaks out and runs away from me, I just might follow her until the end of time.

"Then you show her that. Fill her life with so much love and Jacob that she won't be able to say no."

And I might do just that.

A few hours later, I'm walking into one loud, crazy, full of laughter and love dinner party at Levine's residence. I had a late appointment, and that tattoo was quite intricate, so I'm late getting here and step into pure chaos.

My favorite kinda setting.

Out in the backyard—which is a million shades of the rainbow—string lights are lit, a small fire pit warmed, and a couple of cloud-soft couches, Mr. Levine and Mr. Colson are having a naked dance-off with a couple of cocktails on top of their heads while their wives are trash-talking the other's husband and collect money for the bets they have made. Out in the corner by the house, Luke and Grace are having some sort of stare-down while the other two Levine sisters are sitting with their jaws on the grass, watching their crazy parents living it up. Alec has a protective hand thrown over Hope's shoulders as she nestles herself farther into his embrace.

But then my eyes travel to my girl next to them. My wildflower, sitting on the couch in her light summer dress and a chunky, knit cardigan draped over her shoulders. Her dark mane of hair, twisted into an elegant knot in the bottom, and her eyes tracking her father's movements while her head is propped on her hand in one of those "I can't believe I am watching this" position.

"Wifey?" I grin when she slowly turns her scowling face my way. Her eyes flash to the potted plant I am holding.

"Shut. It." she whispers through clenched teeth. "What are you even doing here? And you bought me another plant? I already can't take care of Bob." She grabs my hand and pulls me down to her.

"Baby Matilda." I extend my hands, holding the tiny cactus I got for her today. It's so cute with its little bubble of needles and a pink flower on top that I couldn't pass by. Not when it reminds me of my boo so much. It's sharp and hard to get to, but it's so utterly beautiful when it blooms.

"Ha, look at that," Hope snorts. "Jacob, I'd hide if I would be you." She barely contains her laugh, and Joy throws her signature glare.

"Sit. Do not draw attention to us!" she says, grabbing baby Matilda out of my hands, but it's too late.

"My new son-in-law is here," Mrs. Levine screeches and lunges herself toward us.

"Oh, fuck..." Joy muses as her mom attacks me.

"I knew you were the one for my Joy! I knew it from the very first time I laid my eyes on you." She pats my cheeks lovingly and smiles wide. "And here we are. You could have told me about your plan when we were arranging the music for you, you know. I could've helped more."

"Sorry, Mama, it was kind of spur-of-the-moment thing."

"Ahhh, it just hit you right there and then, didn't it? And you couldn't wait." Jenny swipes a loose tear from her eyes at the same time as Joy rolls her eyes and mutters, "Jesus..."

"Okay, lovebirds, we need to coordinate this properly with Alec and Hope's wedding."

"Mom, we are not getting married yet," Hope groans. "Please drop it."

"Shhh, Mama knows best."

"Of course you do," Joy mutters again. "Mom, look, Dad won!" She quickly redirects her mother's attention to Rick, who is currently jumping on his right foot, half-drenched in some red concoction.

"Woo-hoo, honey! You go! You show those Colsons how it's done! Suckers!" She fist-pumps the sky while Nina throws more trash-talk.

"Run, run, run," Joy whisper-shouts, grabs my hand and our plant, and the next thing I know, we are running as if the wolves are chasing us.

"But I'm hungry, and Mama was just getting to the good part about planning our wedding," I whine.

"We're not getting married, and I'm not leaving you alone with that woman. God only knows what the two of you will come up with next to torture me."

"But I am still hungry." I resort to pouting, and she sighs.

"Fine, I will take you out to eat. Happy now?"

"Very." I flash her a smile and both thumbs up.

"Ridiculous, insufferable, sexy man." I think she meant to say that to herself, but I caught it.

"I heard that. And you forgot, charming, amazing, handsome, biggest cock in the world, Superman in bed, master of orgasms, your hero—"

She interrupts me. "I am marrying an idiot." Slapping the palm of her hand to her face, sounding extremely exasperated with me. If this ain't love, I don't know what is.

"Ha! So, you agree we are getting married?"

"No. Get in the car before Mom comes looking for us."

"You are so bossy, Wildflower."

"If you don't like it, I can let you out on the next street." She starts the car and quickly drives off as Jenny comes running out of the back, and I laugh at the scene. Joy is biting her lower lip, watching the rearview mirror as Mrs. Levine undoubtedly lets out a string of cute curses. Cute because that woman cannot say the word "fuck" even if you pay her.

"Oh, no, boo, I love you bossy. It gets my dick so hard we might have to pull over right around that corner." I point to the end of the street as Joy's eyes track down to my shorts, and she spots the very defined tenting situation down there.

"Fuck..." she curses—not as cutely as her mom—and clenches her thighs together.

"What's got you so wound up, boo?" I slip my hand to her thighs, and she presses them together harder.

"Nothing." This time, her voice is squeaking.

"Nothing?" I drag my hand lower until I reach the hem of her dress and slip it underneath it, touching her bare skin, which immediately flashes with a whole lot of goosebumps. "Still nothing?" I tease her and myself as my fingers reach higher and higher.

"Jacob."

"If that was supposed to be a threat, you shouldn't have sounded so sexy." I lean over the console and press my lips to her neck, inhaling her rich Chanel No. 5 scent. It smells amazing, but I crave *her* scent. The way her skin smells fresh after a shower, after sex, in the early hours of the morning. I crave her.

She whimpers softly but then says, "If you don't stop this right now, we won't make it to Peace-Out to eat." Peace-Out is the only diner in town, and right now, it does not sound as delicious as something else.

"I am feeling more of a Wildflower all-you-can-eat buffet."

"Closed for business."

"Really now?"

"Yep, undergoing remodeling. There has been crazy hussies' infestation in the buffet."

"Hussies?" I raise an eyebrow at her.

"Mm-hmm." She nods and clicks her tongue.

"What a shame. I had plans. Meals I wanted to taste over there. Delicious, naughty, all-night-long kind of meals." I kiss her neck again, this time letting my tongue drag over the delicate flesh.

"We are here," Joy shouts and parks right in front of the packed diner. Loverly Cave townies love nothing more than to socialize all day, every day, and Joy must be oblivious to it. This is going to be good.

# MEET MY WIFE

"Okay, let's go." I open the door, and as soon as we meet in front of the car, I wrap my hand around her waist, hauling her toward me.

"What are you doing?"

"Holding my fiancée, now shhh, let's go eat." But as soon as we step through, we get assaulted by howlers, clapping, woos, and congratulatory chants from every corner. Joy freezes dead on the spot, her eyes wide saucers, and this time *she* grabs onto *me*. After two seconds straight, she turns around and leads us outside.

"Boo?"

"Nope, we can't eat here. Forget it. In another second, they were going to start clicking their glasses and shout kiss, kiss, kiss."

I stopped abruptly, halting our escape. "Wait, I like that. Let's go back." I start to drag her back to the front door, but she digs her heels in and won't move.

"I am not going back there."

"But I'm still hungry."

"We will find something else. That bagel place."

"It's closed already."

"Then LPs, they have food there too."

"They sure do. Yes, let's go there," I start moving towards the car once again, and this time, Joy is the one stopping us.

"Wait, why did you agree so fast?"

"No reason," I answer too fast, damn it, and she catches on.

"Oh, hell no. It's even worse in there, isn't it?"

"Wildflower, it's like that everywhere in this town. We love to spend time together, and when one of us is happy, the rest come together to celebrate. Today, they are celebrating us."

"I don't need to be celebrated. I am just fine on my own."

"That stupid word again," I mutter to myself. "Nope, that won't fly with me. Starting tomorrow, I am teaching you how to live Loverly Cave style."

"Oh, God, please no."

"Don't worry. It won't hurt. Much." I flash her a sly grin, and she groans. "But for now, we can grab some produce at Serendipity, and I'll cook for us."

"You can cook?" she asks, her mouth propped open as I steer her further down the street and into the only grocery mega-store we have.

"Yep, aren't you happy you are marrying me?" I wiggle my eyebrows at her. "I can cook and I have a huge co—"

"Ahhhh," she yells out, cringing and interrupting me mid-word. "I got it, I got it, no need to recount your gleaming characteristics.

"You are so cute, boo."

"Did you just call me cute?" she asks as we step into Serendipity, and there are people around here, too, so we get our set of congratulations, hugs, and kisses, much to Joy's dismay. But at least she manages a somewhat smile. Okay, it's more along the lines of a grimace, but it's progress.

We end up in the frozen section. I am looking for some frozen acai mix since Sue, the owner, makes the best one in town and stocks it up here, when Joy reaches for something in the freezer.

"Aha!" she exclaims in victory. "I love these." I look down at what she is holding, and it's a sad package of boneless barbeque wings. The generic kind.

I slapped it out of her hand. "Eww, put it right back."

"What do you mean, eww? These are the best wings ever." She narrows her eyes at me and takes the bag back.

"First of all, these are boneless. They are not wings; they are nuggets."

"Ahhh," she shrieks. "Take that back. Take that back right now."

"Nope." I snatch the bag from her grasp again, and she reaches over me, jumping and fighting me to give it back to her. "Second, there is no meat here. You are a doctor for crying out loud, and you eat this?"

"Give it back right now! That's my comfort food, and I'm feeling particularly stressed today. I need my wings, or I just might bite you instead."

"That's cute, boo, but I'm not giving it back to you. Come on." I swing the *nuggets* back in the fridge and haul her around the corner to the meat section.

"Stop calling me cute! I am not cute," she says as if that word physically assaults her, and I hide my grin, already knowing it will be my new go-to word for her. What can I say? I love to piss off my Wildflower.

Joy tries to get out of my grip on her hand the whole way to the poultry section. "Stop fighting me, woman."

"Stop pissing me off."

"Not gonna happen."

"I hate you."

"No, you don't."

"I want my wings." I wish she could hear herself right now. How could I not call her freaking cute?

"You will get your wings." I stop by the section where they sell the raw chicken wings and grab a few packs."

"What are those?" she points to them, scrunching up her nose.

"You've never seen raw meat?"

"I have. I can cook just fine myself. I just don't understand why you are holding it right now."

"I will make you the best wings in the world."

"With bones in?" She looks absolutely disgusted by the idea.

"Yep." I throw another grin her way.

"No. I need them boneless. Those are the best wings."

"Jesus, I am marrying a monster," I say but ignore her demands for nuggets.

"You are not marrying me," she protests as I fill our little basket with a few other ingredients.

"You keep saying that, yet our invitations say otherwise."

"If I were you, I wouldn't remind me of those." She throws one of her death glares my way. See? Cute.

"And speaking of, have you decided how to cancel our wedding? I am not planning on being assaulted by these crazies every time I step outside."

"If I cancel, they will assault you even worse, coming to your house with never-ending casseroles of comfort food to support you in your breakup."

"Oh, hell, no."

"Besides, I have no plans on canceling it. I plan on making you my wife."

Joy exhales loudly, tilts her head up, and looks up at the proverbial sky. "God, why me? What have I done to deserve this?"

"You were exceptionally good, and he rewarded you with the best hubby in the world."

Hope: **Jacob fucking Hunt, is that your name tattooed on my boyfriend's ass?**

Jacob: **What about the ducky? Did you not see the beautiful ducky on his right cheek?**

Hope: **I am going to kill you!**

# MEET MY WIFE

Jacob: **Woah, woah, woah, he lost the bet. It was all very fair.**

Hope: **What bet?**

Alec: **Shut it, you idiot!!!**

Hope: **JACOB? What. Bet?**

Hope: **I am giving you thirty seconds to tell me, and then I am setting the dogs loose on you.**

Hope: **You chose your side, and now you are gonna burn.**

*Hope adds Joy Levine to the group chat.*

Joy: **Jackie.**

Jacob: **Yes, my Wildflower.**

Joy: **What did we win?**

Jacob: **\*grinning emoji\* Oh, boo, we got Alec's magical surfboard. I am taking you on the water tomorrow!**

Joy: **Wow. Good job! I knew you were the best of the best.**

Joy: **Why did Alec lose?**

Jacob: **Psh, the idiot thought I couldn't get you to marry me before Hope agreed to marry him.**

Alec: **\*Groans\* You blithering idiot!!! She just sweet-talked that out of you!!! It was truly nice knowing you...**

Jacob: **Oh, fuck...**

Joy: **I hope you understand this is going to hurt. A lot!**

Hope: **Alec Colson, get back inside the house! We are not done yet!!!**

Alec: **Jackie, do you still have that cabin in the woods?**

Jacob: **I will pick you up in five.**

Joy: **Don't you dare.**

Jacob: **Scratch that. In two. I will be there in two.**

# 30

# Joy

*"The best and most beautiful things in the world cannot be seen or even touched — they must be felt with the heart."* — *Helen Keller.*

"Oh my God," I moan shamelessly as I bite into the chicken wings Jacob made for me. "This is heavenly good." I don't even care that his smug face is the size of Texas or that I was wrong. This is too good to worry about who is on top right now.

"Told you, boo. Stick with me, and I'll show you the world." He winks and digs into his own food.

An hour ago, we made it back to his tiny house since it is more equipped for life than my five times larger cottage is, and Jacob got to work right away, preparing the best meal of my life. I was skeptical at first, but man, this guy can cook. And he's not wrong, he is the best in everything, kitchen and bedroom included, moving fast and efficiently around the place. His strong hands were doing delicate work, and I had to wipe the drool off my chin a few times watching him.

I could totally imagine him in the operating room. Jacob is precise, thoughtful, brilliant, and so very skilled with his hands.

Those are amazing hands. So strong. So professional. His fingers were so thick, calloused, and long...

Ahh, it is too hot in this matchbox.

I finish my meal with more groans, moans, and licking of my fingers, and when I come back to Earth from this food cloud, I am greeted with Jacob sitting motionlessly in front of me, his mouth slightly open and his tongue peeking out to lick his lower lip and his throat bobs with a hard swallow.

I have my last dirty finger in my mouth, licking off the sauce, my lips wrapped around it because there is no way in hell I'm letting a single drop of it go to waste, but as soon as my eyes catch his, I stop. No, I freeze. With my finger still stuck in my mouth.

Jacob takes a deep, sharp breath, drops the wing he was eating to the plate, and looks at me with a whole other set of hunger. His hand reaches over the minuscule table and pops my finger out of my mouth. The tension is so high that the "pop" comes out with sounds particularly loud in this space.

My hand falls down, and I lick off the remnants of the sauce on my lips when he stops me, pulling my lip away from my tongue and pushing his thumb in instead.

Oh, fuck...

Somewhere in the far depth of my brain, I know I should stop this, especially since the waters around us got so muddled today with his family, the fake engagement, and his slip of the tiny L word.

But I am not willing to reach into those depths. Not when all the rest of my organs—with my vagina at their head—are chanting, "Give it to us," in unison. And give I do. I wrap my lips around his thumb and suck it clean, using my tongue to lick it perfectly clean. Jacob sucks in another sharp breath as my tongue roams over his finger, and when he deems it clean enough, he takes it away, replacing it with another.

"Fuck." His voice is hoarse and hard. And I might be putting in a bit more effort into cleaning his fingers than I did my own.

For once, I want to impress a man. I want to be enough—more than enough—for him.

Jacob yanks his finger out of my mouth, standing up abruptly, and scooping me up into his arms, walking us toward the couch where we shared our first night together.

Scratch that, where he fucked me senseless on our first night together. Only this time, the room is lit with warm lights and colorful lava lamps. The cold, dark night staying safely behind the walls of this warm, tiny house.

He sits down with me in his lap but positions me so I would straddle him, and as soon as I do, I feel how hard he is. Very, very hard.

The skirt of my dress rides up, and his hands slip beneath it, immediately cupping and squeezing my ass hard enough for me to let out a hiss. "I have never known a sexier woman in my life," he tells me along with another squeeze, and this time, he also uses his strength to grind my body on top of his. Somehow, he positions us so perfectly that my clit is right on top of his shorts-covered cock, pressing into me just right, and I am desperate for any friction.

He moves me again, and this time, I can't help the tiny moan coming out of my mouth. "Jacob." I have been craving him since he showed up at my parent's BBQ.

"Do you have any idea what watching you eat my food, moan, and then fucking lick your fingers clean did to me? Do you have any clue how much I want you?"

This time, I grind on top of him myself, and it's his turn to groan. "I think I have an idea."

"No, I don't think you do." Jacob grabs the back of my neck and yanks me to his lips, kissing me ferociously and bruising. Showing exactly how painful it was for him. The kiss is raw, deep, and uncensored. Our tongues move in a wild race, trying to get as much of each other as we possibly can. And meanwhile, my pussy grinds wildly over him, and he hooks his fingers through the straps of my dress, letting them fall down, and with them, my simple linen dress slips off my breasts.

Naked breasts.

"Agh...shit." Jacob sees my tits spring free, and a stream of curses falls out of his mouth as his head tips back. "How the fuck I haven't fucked your tits yet is a mystery to me."

His fingertips lightly graze over my sensitive nipples, causing me to shiver and buckle to his touch. My hands fly up to his head, digging into that wild, blonde mess I can't seem to stay away from. My fingers tangle themselves in his waves, and I relish in the softness of his hair against my skin.

He tweaks my pebbled nipples between his thumb and forefinger, humming in approval as I arch my back into him even more, presenting myself like the willing sacrifice I am, and then his bearded mouth descends upon them. His teeth scrape at the sensitive flesh while his tongue soothes all the pain right after, and he keeps torturing me like that for what feels like hours.

Hours of my whole body begging and aching for him, for his attention and love. My grip on his hair tightens, and the twisted weirdo groans in pleasure.

His mouth moves to my other breast to mark it as his as well. To leave the red scrapes from his beard on me everywhere while his hand cups the one he just played with, holding it in his protective palm and squeezing the still-wet nipple, causing it to pebble harder into sharp peaks.

While his mouth is busy at the top, his very stiff erection grinds into my sex from the bottom with dead precision, moving as if he can't help himself and hitting just the right spot even though we are somewhat clothed. But if he's moving mindlessly, then so am I because my hips shift, moving up and down to meet his thrusts, and we both moan loudly. Him into my breast, me into the dark night.

Just one more shift, one more bite to my breasts, and I am falling over the edge, my orgasm barreling through me like one of those waves down below.

"Yes, yes, yes..." I fist his hair harder.

"Wildflower," he whispers softly as if he is barely holding on to his last shred of control, and there must be something wrong with me because I do the one thing I know will make him break.

Because I want it. I want him. Us. Everything. I want it right now, and I will deal with the consequences tomorrow.

I will go back to the rational, pragmatic doctor I am tomorrow.

I will end this fake engagement tomorrow, and I will move back to Chicago this week.

But for now? For now, I let go and fall into my personal insanity. I can let go for one more night. I can be the woman I don't know just once again.

I go and say, "Please." The last letter leaves my lips, and in a flash, his mouth is off my breasts, and he lifts his head up to look into my eyes.

"Joy..."

"Please, Jacob. Please."

I hear a low hiss of more curses flowing out of his beautiful mouth, and then it's done.

The iron-clad control I've kept on my life is gone. And I'm falling apart at the feet of the man who has brought all my walls down and me back to life. Because all that crap I just said about *tomorrow*? It's just that, crap.

There is no tomorrow. There is only now.

And now I have to admit to myself that Jacob is here to stay. If not physically by my side, then in my head, forever.

Jacob shifts us effortlessly until I'm lying on the couch underneath him as he props himself on top of me. "I don't know what is going on in that beautiful head of yours, but if you think I will ever let you go, you are gravely mistaken." And with that, his mouth is right back to devouring my body.

He kisses my neck and my collarbone. He trails his kisses down my breasts as he tugs the dress the rest of the way down and groans when he discovers I didn't wear panties—again.

"Do you ever have any on?" he asks as he breathes me in down there, and I arch into his tickling breath, my pussy still sensitive from the explosive orgasm I just had. His mouth is still moving lower as he peppers my body with kisses. My thighs, calves, each and every one of my toes until he is done and moves back up.

"So?" he asks again, but my brain is a mush right now, and I have to concentrate to remember his question. Oh, right, panties.

"No," I breathe out and Jacob says, "Fuck, I should've never asked." He tosses my legs over his shoulders and buries his mouth into me. This man doesn't do anything half-assed, and eating me out isn't an exception. His sinful tongue knows all the tricks to my body as he licks, swipes, sucks, and teases me until I am trembling, and when those long, thick fingers enter into play, I am gone. Coming undone once again in the span of minutes.

"Yes. Good girl. Give it all to me. I want every drop in my mouth." Fuck...his words spur me on, and my release shatters through me on a whole new level.

"Please, please." I'm shaking and begging him to stop, but Jacob won't listen. He literally drinks every single drop of my cum, and when he finally lifts up, I see it glistening on his beard and mouth.

"I love it when you beg, Wildflower. You only beg me. You only let yourself go with me."

I nod mindlessly because fuck, he is right. Never in my life did I plead and beg for anything from anyone. Until my Viking.

With his eyes locked dead on mine, he one-handedly takes off his shirt like I've imagined it done in my every secret wet dream, only so much better. Jacob is the definition of perfection with his contoured, lean surfer body, scattered tattoos, sinful green eyes, and shoulder-length disheveled blonde hair. Disheveled by me.

In another flash, his shorts are gone, and I'm greeted by the most beautiful cock I've ever seen. And it's weeping for me. Literally.

A pearly bead of his cum is pooling at the top and my mouth waters. That desire from earlier resurfaces with a new edge. I need him in my mouth. I need to know how he tastes. I need to watch him fall apart for me like I do for him. Quickly, I scramble to get up and push him down until I'm towering over him. His hooded eyes watch me carefully.

"What are you doing, Joy?"

"I am going to suck your cock clean."

"Fuck," he breathes out, but whatever else he wants to say dies right there and then when I lower myself and take him in my mouth. That tiny salty bead spreads over my tongue, and salty deliciousness coats it.

I want more. I want him to come in my mouth and I want to drink it down my throat. I've never wanted something more. And I've definitely never wanted *this* before.

I have given a handful of blowjobs in my life, and seeing as he was the one fucking my mouth last time, I'm not sure what I am doing here, but instincts take over as I slide him farther into my mouth, hitting the back of my throat as my gag reflex comes to life.

"Ahhh, that's... that's so good, love. So, so good. Keep going. Show me how much you want my cock. Show me what a good girl you are for me and only me." His hands dig into my hair, pulling apart the elegant knot I spent an hour on, and I couldn't care any less.

He fists my hair hard, and I let out a guttural moan. He knows how much being dominated turns me on and uses it so very well. "Do you want me to fuck your mouth, Wildflower, hm? Do you like it when I treat your pretty lips as my toys?"

I can't speak with his thick dick filling my mouth fully, and I settle on nodding vigorously. I nod and nod until I hear him growl, take my head in both his hands, and fuck my mouth hard. It's so hard that the tears are streaming down my face, and I love it. I love every second of this.

"That's a good girl. Look at how you take me in that pretty, sassy mouth of yours. It was made for my cock, Joy. You hear me? Made for me and no one else."

I keep nodding because there is no one else who could ever take his place. No one who could break through my walls and make me kneel in front of him. We barely know each other, yet he knows me better than anyone else. He knows what I need even when I don't.

"This is all I could think of when you were licking your damn fingers, Joy. I wanted to shove my cock so deep into your mouth and have you lick my cum off the way you did that sauce. Fuck... I'm gonna come, love." He gives me a warning, but this is what I have been waiting for. Craving.

In a few more thrusts, Jacob grips my hair as hard as I did his when I was coming, and I feel his release shooting into my mouth, flowing down my throat, and I come right there and then simply from his pleasure.

"Fuuuuck, Wildflower, did you just come from having my cum in your mouth?" With one last lick, I slowly lift my head, biting my lower lip, and nod. My eyes glistened from fresh tears. "Jesus Christ." He gets up, snags me, and pulls me down to his bare chest. "Could you be any more perfect?" Jacob wraps his arms around me, kissing my hair and forehead, lifting my head up, and kissing my lips with his taste still lingering on them.

*Perfect. He called me perfect.*

"Please say something. I am getting nervous here, Wildflower." My head falls back to his chest, and I lay there in peace, listening to my favorite song. His heartbeat. It's a little faster right now as his heart comes down from the high we were on, but it is still soothing.

"I'm scared," my whisper is barely audible as I utter the words to him. The words I have never admitted to anyone before.

"What are you scared of?" His hands dig into my hair again, but this time is a gentle, loving caress.

"You."

"Why?"

"Because I think you are the first man capable of breaking me."

"No, Joy. I am not here to break *you*. I'm here to break the shackles strangling you. Will you let me?"

"I don't know how."

Once again, I am scraped raw by this man and find myself opening the doors to my heart wide open as well as laying down the red carpet for him to walk on.

"That part is easy. You just lean on me."

The long minutes pass as we lay just like that, with me on top of him, listening to his heartbeat and him caressing my hair with his fingers until I raise my gaze to meet his soft one and say, "Okay."

"Do you trust me?" Jacob flips us around, and his mouth is on mine again. His eyes are searching mine for the answer as my breathing picks up.

"I do."

"Good. Now, hold on."

The kiss starts out slow and sweet, but as his hand roams over my body, over my pointed nipples and wet pussy, it changes. With each second, the hunger grows stronger, and I feel his fingers dip into my wetness, coating himself in it.

"Trust me," he whispers into my mouth, withdrawing his hand from my pussy and trailing it lower until he is right at another entrance, and I momentarily tense up. "Trust me, Wildflower," Jacob repeats, and his words are enough to relax my overthinking brain.

He hooks my leg over his hand, and the finger he has pressed over my puckered entrance pushes in slowly as his hips start moving on top of me, slowly grinding his growing erection into me, and I whimper.

"More," my voice is barely audible because I do need more. I need it all.

No one has ever touched me there, and the thought of him being the first and only is enough to let go of any fears I had before.

"I'll give you more." Jacob lowers his mouth to my neck. "I'll give you anything you want, love. Anything." He pushes his finger in deeper, and I suck in a sharp breath. I already feel full, and it's only one finger, not his gigantic cock, but soon enough, Jacob pushes another finger into me, and I think it's too much.

My nails dig into his arms, trying to stop him, but he doesn't let up. "Relax, Joy. I will make it feel good. I promise." He pushes yet another—third—finger in, and this time, I'm confident it's too much.

"Jacob, baby, I can't. I can't. It's too much."

"You trust me, love. Remember that? Lean on me. You need me, and I need you." He kisses me. "So damn much."

His dick has been grinding into my pussy this whole time, and she is more than ready for him, but when the feeling of his fingers inside me is gone, it's not my vagina that gets the attention.

Jacob sits up, drags his other hand through my wetness, and coats his cock with it. He fists it until my juices are all over him.

"Fuck...that should not be that hot." I drop my head to the couch with a groan.

"You like that? You like me jerking myself off with you all over?"

"Yessss," I hiss.

"Good. Because that's the only lubricant I plan on ever using. Now be a good girl and put your legs on my shoulders," he says while still fisting his dick and I obey. Because when a powerful, hotter-than-life Viking with his long hair towers over you in all his naked glory, you do just that. You obey.

Jacob kisses my calves and then leans over me, folding my legs into my body as his cock presses to that puckered ass hole. "I will fuck your ass with your eyes on mine. Because I need to see you take my cock. Take me, Joy. Take me," he orders right before he breaks through me.

"Aghhhh," I groan, part in pain, part in pleasure. It's such a messed-up feeling.

"Fuck," he grinds out, his face in a mask of control and restraint. "You will make me come so much faster than I planned. Your ass is so fucking tight and perfect, Wildflower. Your ass is mine," he says through clenched teeth.

"Jacob. I'm so full." My breaths are shallow, and I feel the heavy pounding in my clit, begging for attention.

"That's right, you are. You are full of me, Joy. Now relax and let me in all the way. Let me in." He pushes in some more, and we both groan. "Ahh, good fucking girl." His head drops to my tits, and he sucks them in as his hips start slowly rolling over me. Letting my body adjust to his.

But it no longer feels painful. He grinds into me until I can't handle the sweet torment anymore.

"More, Jacob. Baby, I need more."

"Fuck yes, you do." He starts fucking my ass hard. His skin slaps against mine as he thrusts into me with punishing force. Fucking me like it's our last day on earth. I swear I feel him everywhere. I am full of him, from my toes to every last hair on my head. His hand wraps around my thighs and ass possessively, holding me in where he wants me.

"Touch yourself, Joy. Touch my pussy for me as I fuck my ass."

My hand immediately falls to my clit, rubbing the needy flesh as we both shamelessly moan and groan, filling this tiny house with our shouts and sex.

So much sex.

"Fuck, that's it, that's it!" he shouts as I scream, "Jacob!" And we both fall apart. I feel his cock pulsing deep inside me, branding yet another part of my body.

Dropping my legs, he falls over me but uses his arms to help support his weight as he groans and buries his face in my neck, breathing hard and ragged as his cock pulses for the last few beats deep inside of me. And suddenly, I'm not close enough. I need more. I need all of him on top of me. Using his weakened state, I pull down on his back until his arms give way and his whole weight is draped over me.

"Wildflower, I'm crushing you," He tries to lift himself up a bit, but I just pull him back.

"No. I need this. Stay." And I feel him relax, giving me exactly what I want.

Himself.

"You are all I will ever need. My Wildflower."

# 31

# *50 Reasons*

Reason #41:
*Jacob: I will fund your shopping.*
*Joy: With my own credit card?*
*Jacob: Hey, I've only used it once. The rubber duckies on those shorts had googly eyes!*

Reason #42:
*Jacob: You will always be adorable.*
*Joy: Why?*
*Jacob: Cause I will constantly ADORE you.*

# 32

# Jacob

*"By all means marry. If you get a good wife, you'll be happy. If you get a bad one, you'll become a philosopher."*
— *Socrates.*

If you ask me what that was just now between us, the only answer I have for you is love.

I love this woman. I know I'm crazy, but there is no other explanation. I won't push her. I won't say those words to pressure her into feeling the same. For now, I am content with what we have. I'm content with her letting me in, past all her thorns and poisoned spikes. And I am content with owning her body fully and irrevocably.

We are engaged, after all, so now I only need time to make her see the truth. And time is something I have.

"I need to go home," she mumbles into my chest. We climbed into the actual bed after we took a shower. Well, more like after I carried her into the shower because, according to Joy, I fucked her ability to walk out of her.

"You are home," I tell her, squeezing my arm around her shoulders.

"You know what I mean. I need to go to *my* home."

"Again, this *is* your home." The thought of having her here, in my space, and my bed, is intoxicating. I want it. I want to wake up with her head on my chest or wrapped in my arms. I want to make us breakfast as we get ready for our day. I want to rush home after work because she is here, waiting for me.

And I need to make it happen. Somehow. But I am nothing if not creative.

"Jacob." She sounds exasperated with me. "I need to go."

"Putting them walls back up already?" I ask her as she gets up, nearly hitting her head on the ceiling.

"Please don't make me regret ever cracking them open for you."

"Never." I push up, tugging her into my embrace. "You and I? We are a team."

"A team?" she asks skeptically. "And part of what team are we?"

"The marriage and family one, of course."

"Oh, Jesus, we are back to that." Joy rolls her eyes and climbs down the stairs, looking for her clothes. Makes it really easy when you only have a dress on. The little vixen was naked underneath there the whole time, and now that I know she never wears underwear, my dick will be in a permanent semi all the time.

"We never left. The wedding is set for September, and it is rubber ducky themed."

"Of course it is." She picks up the dress off the floor and slips it over her head, covering her curvy body away from my hungry eyes.

Down boy, we just got sucked half to death—a good death—and buried into her tight ass. That is enough excitement for one evening. I am euphoric over owning that one piece of her no one touched before. She trusted me enough to let go, and I won't ever break that trust.

Of course, my girl loved having her ass fucked, just like I knew she would, but that's beside the point right now.

Hastily, I get up, pulling on the first set of shorts I find, and they happen to be my favorite rubber ducky shorts. I have at least twenty different pairs of these. What? There can never be enough rubber duckies. Yellow, green, blue, pink, orange, glittery ones, and my personal favorite, the rainbow ones.

A soft, cute bark of laugh comes from Joy when she sees me wearing them. Oh, man, now these really are my favorite ones. If they make her smile—or laugh—I will wear them every day for the rest of my life.

"Love the shorts, hubby."

"They are awesome, right? I know they're awesome," I answer my own question, my mind already working out a new plan. Man, I'm on a roll today.

"Jacob, that was sarcasm."

"We should get you something like this too!" I announce my idea to her, but I'm greeted with an unimpressed set of dark eyes and one crooked eyebrow. "You know, the fun clothing stuff. But not shorts. You're not a shorts type of girl," I muse to myself, tapping my finger on my lips since she refuses to acknowledge my brilliant ideas. "How about shirts? I will get you some matching shirts. Yeah." I nod to myself. "That's a good idea."

"Oh Jesus, why did I open my mouth?" She drags her hands through her face. "No shirts, Jacob. None." She points her index finger threateningly at me, but I'm not listening to her anymore as I pull up my favorite Etsy shop.

"Oh, oh, look at this one." I flip the phone so she can see the shirt I found, barely containing my excitement.

Joy looks at the phone, back at me, back to the phone, and clicks her tongue. "If you get me that, I will stuff it up your ass."

"What? But it's sparkly! Look!" I point to the screen again because maybe she didn't get a good look the first time. "And the ducky even has a cute bow on."

"Do I give you an impression of a *sparkly* type of girl? Or a rubber duckies type, for that matter?" she deadpans me.

"I'm getting you this." I click the buy button before she slaps the phone out of my hand.

"I won't be caught dead wearing that thing."

"Sure, you will." I plant a kiss on her furrowed forehead.

"Delusional man...whatever." Joy turns around and opens the front door, letting fresh salty air inside, but with the gust of wind coming in, it also carries her scent toward me, and I sniff a lungful of it.

This. This is the scent I love. It's all her and none of that expensive perfume she likes to wear. The smell goes straight to my already-excited cock, and I have to calm him down before I catch up with her at her car, yanking the door open for her before she can. "I'll see you tomorrow, boo."

"Why? I've already had enough of you today to last me a week."

"No such thing. I am your fix, remember?"

"I foolishly hoped you forgot..." she mutters to herself and slips inside the car.

"Take care of baby Matilda until you move into my place, and I can take care of our babies." I point to the cute cactus sitting in her backseat.

"Bob and baby Matilda can make the move this second."

"They can't do that. They can't live without their mommy."

"I'm marrying an idiot," she mutters with a slight shake of her head and drives off into the dark night.

How did I live without this woman before? But I sure as heck don't plan on living alone now.

Plan *Make My Fiancée Fall in Love With Me* starts tomorrow.

James Hunt: **I just sent you an email with your ticket confirmation. The plane leaves in two days, as we have discussed.**

Jacob: **And Joy calls me the delusional one. She should hang out with you more.**

Jacob: **No, wait, scratch that. She should never hang out with you.**

Jacob: **Want me to pay you back for the ticket? Because I am not getting on that plane.**

James Hunt: **Don't piss me off, boy. You will do as you are told.**

Jacob: **You know, when I refused my inheritance when I left 5 years ago, I never could have imagined how sweet it would taste now. There is nothing you can do or say to make me come back.**

Jacob: **Go make more kids or claim your bastard ones to sit on the throne for all I care. I'm staying right here.**

James Hunt: **My dear son, you are so naive. The whole wedding scheme might be all for show, but I saw how you looked at Dr. Levine, so let me tell you, if you don't get on that plane, I will fire her.**

Jacob: **My dear old father, you are the naive one here if you think I will fall to your petty blackmail. You see, we have no secrets between us. So, I know she has more dirt on you than you on us.**

Jacob: **Now, kindly leave us alone. –Your weird son, Jacob.**

Jacob: **P.S. I can't wait to take my wife's name after the wedding.**

James Hunt: **Don't you dare!**

# 33

# *Joy*

*For beautiful eyes, look for the good in others; for beautiful lips, speak only words of kindness; and for poise, walk with the knowledge that you are never alone." — Audrey Hepburn.*

"Jesus, look at her. She is getting it so good from her *fiancé* she can't walk normally." This is what my little sister greets me with.

"I knew I should have stayed in bed and never showed up to this ridiculous breakfast," I grumble and drop into the booth opposite my sisters.

At least they picked Bagels and Love for this eight AM interrogation.

"Oh, yes, look at me. I'm poor, little Joy, I snatched one of the hottest men in town, but I forgot to take the stick out of my ass." Pretty sure Jacob did last night. I am still sore...

"Grace! You don't want to start with me right now. Not after you woke me up at six this morning and didn't even bring any coffee." I point to her, and she rolls her lips real quick. Yeah, that's right, it's only fun to talk about Joy's sex life but start discussing hers, and suddenly we are playing "whoever says the first word is a pile of poop."

"I was going to ask about that," Hope says. "Why were you there so early?" Both of my sisters surprised me with morning freak-out visits. Only Hope doesn't know about Grace's.

"That's irrelevant." Grace waves her off.

Sure, it is....

"We are here to talk about you two, not my sad dates with my vibrator."

"There is nothing to talk about."

"Oh, so our older sister getting engaged is nothing to talk about?"

"It's fake, relax your ovaries." Just as the words dry off my lips, the locals line up in front of our table, congratulating me...

And hugging...

They all *hug* me.

"It's fake, she said; I'm not getting married, she said," Grace continues her mocking while Hope quietly snickers behind her large cup of sewer—sorry, I mean mud—water. Bile comes up my throat just from watching her drink that crap.

"Okay, okay, ladies. I call this table of three idiots to order." She sits up straight, shaking her head as if her clowning face will simply fall off.

"Smooth, Gracie."

"Shush." She looks at me and places her hands palms down. "On today's agenda, we have JJ."

"Please, for the love of coffee, do not repeat and encourage his stupidity," I groan out because I am ninety percent positive that nickname will be stuck to us like the gum on my favorite pair of jeans. "And put it away; better yet, go dump it into the sink," I scrunch up my nose in disgust, gesturing at Hope's drink.

"What? This?" Hope extends the said poison toward me, and I gag. "Do you think she gags like that on Jacob's dick?" she asks Grace.

"Fucking hell." This time I choke on my smoothie, because that's my life now. Smoothies instead of delicious, aromatic coffees. "Can you not?"

"Is it as big as I have imagined?" Grace wiggles her eyebrows at me.

"And why in the world did you imagine my fiancé's dick?" Shit, that sounded bad.

"Did you hear that, Hope?" She grins like an idiot while vigorously elbowing our sister in her ribs.

"Oh, I heard it." Hope slaps Grace's elbow away. "Keep your bones away from mine."

"Sorry, I forgot you got fucked senseless last night, as well." Gracie lifts her hands up to the sky and, being our mother's dramatic doppelganger that she is, shouts to the skies with a groan, "God, when will I finally get a huge dick railing me for half the night?"

"If you mention Jacob's dick one more time, the railing will happen right here and now. And unlike your sisters, *you* won't be able to walk at all."

I don't know if the three of us have ever, ever moved our heads so slowly before while our jaws drop wide open, hanging on the floor.

A very pissed, very sexy Luke Colson is glaring at Grace, dressed in his LCFD get-up, arms crossed at his massive chest, feet apart in a defensive stance.

"Luke." Grace sits up ramrod straight, all jokes dying on her tongue as she swallows them in a thick lump.

"What, *sweetheart*?" She flinches at his nickname.

"I told you not to call me that!"

"But you love it when others call you that, don't you?"

Strangely, I like Luke, but no one gets to make my sister uncomfortable. "Why don't you leave my sister alone?"

"Why don't you mind your own business?"

"She is my business."

"No. She is mine," he growls through clenched teeth, and Grace sinks deeper into the booth seat.

"If you hurt her, I'll set Jacob off on you, and he will annoy you until the day you die. Jacob is very good at annoying people; you might find your deathbed a lot sooner than you have imagined."

"Cute." Again with the fucking cute bullshit. What is wrong with people? I am not cute!

"I warned you."

"I don't like you."

"Perfect. Because I am not a hundred-dollar bill for you to like. As long as Grace is happy, so am I. Got it?"

"Keep other dicks out of your mouth, got it, sweetheart?" he says, completely ignoring me, and struts away. Only once he is out of the cafe does my sister breathe out the breath she was holding.

"Fuck..."

"Now, how about we leave 'JJ' for later and focus on that." I point to the front door where Luke just disappeared from.

"How about we tackle that in our next meeting? I'm not ready to talk about it yet."

"Fine." I take pity on her.

"Please distract me from what just happened," Gracie pleads, and the big softy I am—I know that was a funny one—I tell them about my day yesterday in detail.

# MEET MY WIFE

And for the first time, I also tell them about Justin and our delinquent relationship.

"Oh. My. Harry. You banged two brothers?" Grace whisper-shouts, and I kick her foot under the table.

"Shut it. How was I supposed to know they were brothers? They literally could not be any more different."

My youngest sister is still smirking at me while Hope gets a deep, thoughtful look on her face.

"Joy." Hope lays her soft hand on top of mine, her eyes welling up with tears. "I am so sorry."

"Nothing to be sorry for." I wave her off, snatching my hand away from under hers. "It happened; now we move on."

"Did you ever cry or mourn that relationship? Did you ever let yourself get crazy mad about his betrayal? Eat your favorite birthday sprinkles ice cream and watch cartoons all day long?" Hope asks.

How does she remember all that? That used to be my MO for fixing my problems, and it always worked up until I turned eighteen, and my issues could not be fixed with ice cream anymore. Yet I still eat it.

"No."

"What do you mean no?" They both frown. "You need to let those emotions out, Joy. Or else they'll eat you from inside. Trust me, I know."

They won't understand that I have no emotions to let out. I thought I did, but when I saw Justin again yesterday, I felt nothing. Well, maybe a bit of disgust with myself, but that's it. And I won't admit to them that I have stayed with a man thinking he is it for me when, in reality, I never loved him. Shouldn't even have wasted all those plates I smashed, on him.

Heck, I don't think I have allowed anything—*anything*—to come close enough for me to bring out birthday sprinkles since Brian and Hope.

And I am now one hundred percent confident I never loved Justin. If I had loved him, my mind would be filled with thoughts of him all the time. My body would ache from being away from his. My sleep would be restless without his heartbeat lulling me into safety.

So, it's not thoughts about Justin that I need to let out. He's not the one plaguing my mind. He's not the one gifting me ridiculous plants and naming them.

It's a whole other Hunt brother.

"Oh, look, my assistant is calling me." I pick up my phone, silently noting down to give Zoe a raise for promptly saving my ass from my sisters and my own self. "Hey, Zo."

Silence.

"Zoe?" My tone takes on a concerned note, and then it goes straight down to terrified as I hear her sniffle. Zoe is crying. "Zoe? Please say something!"

"J-Joy," she says through tears. "Can I come to Loverly Cave? I need to get out of here."

"Yes. Of course, you can. Are you okay?"

"No. I am n-not."

The rest of the breakfast gets muddled by my worry for Zoe. She wouldn't tell me what was going on over the phone, but her plane lands tomorrow morning, and she had better be ready for an interrogation.

Please tell me I am not seeing what I am seeing as I walk up to my cottage after breakfast. Mrs. Nina Colson is standing on my porch, rocking back and forth as she chews on the corner of her mouth and watching the path in front and on the side of her.

Sucks for her, I use the back road to enter my home, and today is the day my rental vehicle decides to stop working and simply refused to start. So, I left it parked in front of Bagels and Love with a string of colorful curses and walked my ass all the way here since Hope doesn't drive her tin can anymore, as she works in the tattoo shop on Love Street with her boyfriend and Grace seems to live in the town gym, Tough Love these days.

Quietly, I sneak up closer and note my dad sitting behind the wheel of their car, patrolling the beach the same way Mrs. Colson is doing on my porch.

That only leaves me with one conclusion.

My mother is inside my home. Scheming away.

Oh, this is going to be good.

Nina's phone pings with a text message alert, and she glues herself to the screen, completely forgetting to keep watch. Equally, my dad is buried in his screen as well. Must be Love Hive news.

The stupid town gossip site deleted me from their chat, so I can't see what they are writing on there anymore. Apparently, my candor was not appreciated. Fine, it was more sarcasm than candor, but whatever.

I never thought watching my own parents, plus their bestie, sneaking around my place would be so entertaining. I'm standing on the side, just barely visible, and in the next minute or so, my mom quickly slips out of my front door, clutching something silver in her hands with a satisfied look on her face.

"Freeze. And drop whatever you are holding," I say calmly, but loud enough for Mom and Nina to yelp and jump in surprise. "Now, Mother," I add a warning note this time since she's making no attempt to show me what's in her hands.

I have a feeling I know exactly what she is holding there, but I'd like to have solid proof.

"Joy," my mom exclaims, overly happy. "How was your breakfast? We just came by to invite you to another dinner since you left last night's all too soon."

"Mom, I said drop whatever you are holding this instant." She purses her lips and scrunches up her nose, murmuring a quiet but irritated, "Poopie crap." That would be Jenny Levine's version of "damn it," in case you were wondering.

Without looking at me, she extends her hand and hands me my birth control pills. My tongue pokes through the inside of my cheek as amusement mixes with irritation. "Really, mom? Really? You are stooping that low now?"

"Sloppy Jenny, very, very sloppy!" Nina whisper-shouts to my mom. None of them are looking my way. "At this rate, the only grand babies we'll see will be in our dreams." She lightly slaps my mom's hand, the one still holding my pills.

"Excuse me? What happened to keeping a lookout, huh?" Mom bulges her eyes at her friend as she slaps her back.

"I got sidetracked."

"Well, that is just peachy. What do we do now?" She extends her hand in question toward me.

"Jesus, take the wheel," I muse to myself as the heels of my hands dig into my eyes. Mom and Nina keep bickering in whispering hushes as if I am not standing two feet away and can hear every word.

"There's still Grace!" Nina shouts out. "Look." She shoves her phone in my mom's face, showing her whatever it was that got her so enthralled she missed me showing up to my own place. Mom's gaze immediately widens, she straightens her shoulders and looks up to the yellow house next door.

Oh, no, no, no. "Don't even think about it," I tell her, snatching my pills from her grasp.

"We were never here." Mom starts waving her hands in front of my face like she is trying to hypnotize me. Fuck me standing, how are we related again?

"Mrs. L?" The very familiar, very sexy voice bellows from behind me, and when I turn around, I see Dad stepping out of his car, looking sheepishly my way—he knows he fucked up—and shakes Jacob's hand. "What are you doing here?"

"They," —I point to the three thieves— "were trying to steal my birth control pills."

"Pshh, steal?" Mom rolls her eyes. "What are we? Armatures? You would simply get a new pack."

"What were you doing with them then?"

"Switching them out with sugar candy, of course." Mom gives me her best "duh" face.

"Honey, I think you should stop digging that hole for yourself. You are already halfway to China as it is," Dad speaks up and motions for Mom to zip it.

"You," —she points her index finger at him— "I will deal with later! So, you zip it," she snarks at him.

"Mama," Jacob whispers in half accusatory, half-offended tone. "Why didn't you let me do it? She would have never found out."

"See?" Nina smacks her again. "Sloppy, Jennifer."

"Out!" I shout. My patience is all gone, and it's only ten AM. "All of you, out!"

At least my parents and Nina have enough common sense to trot away without further comments. "And in case you were planning to *tamper* with Grace's pills, I will be ordering her a new pack today."

"Maybe we can adopt a few grandkids?" Nina asks my mom as they get into the car and drive off, but my suicidal fiancé is still standing next to me, his grin wide and beaming.

"What are you smiling at? Go away." I push him out of the way and head inside, only to hear him follow right behind me.

"How is my girl this morning?"

"I am not talking to you." I push the button on my Keurig, in dire need of some caffeine.

"What have I done already?" I whip around sharply to look at him.

"Oh, I don't know?" I shake my head as my hands fly up, palms up. "Maybe you just suggested you would aid them in their insanity to get me *pregnant*," I put special emphasis on that last word.

"Well, I want to settle down." He thrusts his hand on his chest. "I'm ready to be a hubby and a daddy. So, what do you say, Joy?"

He cannot be serious right now...

"Please deflate a notch. I'm suffocating."

"JACOB!" I screech as the water hits me straight in the face with its violent outburst. I should have known better than to let his two left hands meddle in my bathroom plumbing.

"Go shut the water off," he yells out while trying to block the break with his hands, but the flow is too strong.

"I don't know where the switch for that is."

Jacob gets up from the floor, his poor excuse of shorts he always wears soaked through, and his bulge is overly exposed.

Damn it, I shouldn't be thinking about his cock when my house is literary flooded. *But what a cock that is...ahh.*

Calm the fuck down, woman, you just had it last night. *And?* My vagina muses. *We want more, we want more, we want more!*

Oh, hell, here we go with the fucking Jacob parade again. And yes, yes, I *am* thinking with my reproductive system these days. Please congratulate me.

A minute later, the water stops its assault on my half-demolished bathroom, and Jacob reappears in the doorway. "Well, that was not an empty wall," he says, rolling his lips together.

"You think?" This man is fine, so fine, but he's a freaking idiot, and I swear he will be the death of me. "When you offered me your expert hands in demolishing old bathrooms, you neglected to mention your exceptional aim. Out of the whole ass wall, you hammered into the one spot that had the pipe go through it." I lift up one finger to accentuate my point.

"Yep, I'm a professional like that."

"What am I supposed to do now?" I plant my hands on my hips, waiting for his smart ass to come up with a solution, but rational thoughts have left the Jacob house—aka his brain. His head is tilted to the side as his tongue licks over his lips, and then he bites them. All meanwhile, his eyes are roaming my body.

My wet body. I didn't bother with a bra this morning, and now that my white T-shirt is as "dry" as his shorts are, I am certain he is getting quite the show, and looking down at myself, it is confirmed.

My nipples are hard and pointed from the cold water, and are poking right through the shirt. Hell, it clings to me like a second skin, outlining every curve perfectly.

"Umph," a whimper leaves Jacob's throat, along with the best 'fuck me' eyes as he stares at me.

Sure, the boobs on display in the wet, see-through shirt are quite nice, but the rest? The mirror on the wall cringes from my beauty. I look like a plucked chicken. My mascara is smudged under my eyes, and my hair is in that awkward period when it's half-wet, half-dry, and not sexy at all, yet he is looking at me like I have hung the start and the moon.

I clear my throat, dragging his gaze away from my girls. "So, any suggestions?" I motion to my ruined bathroom.

"Oh, yeah, so, so many..." His tongue is back to playing a peeking game with his lips. Damn it, he will make me lose my—fine, his—shorts in one point two seconds if he doesn't stop.

"Jacob."

"I already wanted to fuck you senseless when you put on those shorts you stole from me after our first night, but then you had to go and look all wet and hot and so fucking sexy that my balls are about to burst." He takes a step towards me, and I step back.

"Jacob," I hiss. "We have a mess to clean up."

"Oh, we sure do." The sexy idiot lunges at me, and with nowhere else to go, I squeak as he throws me over his shoulder and marches out and into my bedroom. He drops me on my air mattress, drags my shirt, and shorts off, leaving me completely naked and at his mercy as he steps away and lets his eyes roam over me.

"What?" My voice is breathless and needy.

"Nothing, I'm just admiring the view. You are the most gorgeous woman I've ever met. Your nose is the perfect morning wave." He traces the shape of my nose with his finger in the air. "Tipping at just the right angle. Your dark hair, the road up the mountain after heavy rain, soft and velvety with its fresh scent still clinging onto the crisp air. Your soft pink lips." More tracing. "The magical sunset painted in all shades of pink and reds."

"You are making no sense," I tell him, but my voice is barely above a whisper. In fact, I am panting.

No one has ever said anything like that to me. No one has ever seen me so beautiful.

"I almost hate to wreck such a breathtaking sight, but your body was meant to be conquered by me like I do those perfect morning waves." And with that, he pounces on me, and the rest is a mix of groans, moans, whimpers, and so much cursing.

Needless to say, neither one of us went back into the messy bathroom to clean it up, and that night, I was moved into the tiny house.

Jacob: **If you don't call me a genius, I don't know what you are doing with your life.**

Alec: **Humble as usual...**

Alec: **What have you done this time?**

Jacob: **Apart from helping your sorry ass get the girl you drooled all over, you mean?**

Alec: **Yeah, yeah, you are the town magician. Now, quit the suspense and spill it.**

Jacob: **Joy is moving in with me into the tiny house!!!!**

Alec: **Well, I'll be placed out...how did you do it? Blackmail? Extortion? Pay off?**

Jacob: **Why do you think I had to stoop down to that to have her move in with me?**

Alec: **Um...because she is Joy-I-don't-live-in-tiny-houses-in-the-middle-of-nowhere Levine??? And you are not *that* good-looking.**

Jacob: **Oh, piss off. I am her dream.**

Alec: **I think you misheard her because I clearly remember the word "nightmare" leaving her mouth.**

Jacob: **I am never giving you that surfboard back.**

Alec: **NO! NO, wait, just kidding! You are the most handsome, ridiculously charming guy in all of LC.**

Jacob: **Suck up.**

Alec: **Can I have my board back?**

Jacob: **No.**

Alec: **Asshole.**

Alec: **Now, can you finally tell me how you got her to move in with you?**

Jacob: **Simple. I broke the water pipe in her bathroom.**

Alec: **Accidentally?**

Jacob: **I built my tiny house from the ground up; you really think I didn't know where those water pipes would be?**

Alec: **Oh, Jesus...It was nice knowing you.**

Jacob: **???**

Alec: **You do know you are a dead man walking, right?**

Jacob: **Pshh, what else is new?**

# 34

# *50 Reasons*

Reason #44:
*Jacob: Half the time spent in grocery stores.
Joy: With you? I think you meant to say double.*

Reason #46:
*Jacob: You won't ever be mad or angry.
Joy: Because you are delusional, and you can't get mad at sick people?
Jacob: No, because I'm the life of your party.*

Reason #48:
*Jacob: I will never get upset about little mundane things.
Joy: Is it a bad time to mention I lost your shark slides?
Jacob: WHAT???*

# 35

## *Joy*

*"I love being married. It's so great to find one special person you want to annoy for the rest of your life."* — *Rita Rudner.*

### *Week 1 in Tiny House*

"When you said you had an awesome new movie to watch, you didn't seriously mean this?" We are ten minutes into watching *The Proposal*, and my eye is starting to twitch. In another five, we will have a full-blown breakdown on our hands.

"What's wrong with this movie?" he asks, shoving a handful of popcorn into his mouth.

"If you don't turn that off right this second, I will flip this bowl of ice cream on your head, and then I'll rub it in for good measure."

"Sheesh, Wildflower. This is about loveeee, not violence."

"This is about me throwing up, and I have zero plans to do that, so turn it off."

"No."

"What do you mean, no?"

"I specifically chose this particular movie for you."

"To torture me?"

"Shhh, stuff your mouth with your happy ice cream, let it seep into your veins, and watch a story about us." He shoves a spoonful of my ice cream into his popcorn-filled mouth. "Only I'm much better looking than Ryan Reynolds, and you're a lot hotter than Sandra Bullock."

"Well, if you put it like that..." I roll my eyes and take my ice cream away from this monster.

"Tomorrow, you can pick a movie."

"Is this you compromising?"

"Yep, see? I told you, I'm awesome in it. Now watch, you are about to propose to me." He points to the TV and watches as if it's his first time, not what I assume is number sixty-three based on his lips moving to the script.

An hour later, I shout, "Noooooo, what kind of bullshit is this? Why would she leave him if she loves him?" I throw my hands up. "See, I knew it would be a horrible movie. What kind of psychopath writes all this romantic crap? Aren't we traumatized enough by reality?"

"Sit your cute ass down. It's not over yet."

A few minutes later, she gets down on her knees and proposes to him, and I'm glued to the screen, chewing on my ice cream spoon. "At the end, when you leave me because you end up falling in love with me, I expect nothing less than that." Jacob points to the screen and then to me.

"In your dreams, buddy."

The next day, it's my turn to pick, and of course, I choose cartoons.

"Seriously?" Jacob looks at me with a wide, beaming smile. "I knew you were the one for me, but this? This is soul mate level." He gestures at the TV, where I pulled up my favorite Disney princess movie, *The Beauty and The Beast*, and when the Beast lets Belle go, I feel some moisture pooling in the corners of my eyes like it always does in that moment.

Damn it, all these years later, it still gets me.

"Are you...crying? Oh my God, you're crying!!!" Jacob jumps off the couch.

"I'm not crying." I quickly swipe off the tiny salty bead off my cheek.

"You so are!" Jacob jumps up and down, fisting the air with a yelp, "OH MY RAINBOWS. SHE IS CRYING! How can you be this beautiful when you cry?"

"I hate you!"

Our conversation earlier...

Well, more like Jacob's monologue...

*You are the macaroni to my cheese, peanut butter to my jelly.*
*I am the eggs to your bacon, the ice cream to your pie.*
*You are the sand to my beach, the shade to my sun.*
*I am the water to your drought, the grass to your mud.*
*You are the sky to my stars, the shine to my moon.*
*I am the pages to your book, the wheels to your car.*

"Shall I continue, or do we have an agreement that I like you?"

"Jacob!"

"Yes, Wildflower?"

"Is that my blouse and pants from our first night here?" I am pretty sure I have smoke coming out of my ears at this point.

"Maybe," is all he says.

"And you wouldn't happen to know what they are doing under the mattress?"

"Nope."

"Nope?"

"Nope."

"That's it. I will really kill you this time!"

"Oh, yes, finally! I was waiting for you to sit on my face since day one!"

*Week 2 in the Tiny House*

"I'm not going up there," I protest and add a little stomp of my foot for extra effect, but Jacob is totally unfazed—as usual—and proceeds to zip up my black rain jacket.

"Yes, you are. You lost the bet last night, which means I won, and we are going hiking." Did I mention he is wearing a bright yellow rain jacket?

"You cheated," I bristle.

"Nope, my gorgeous girl."

The bet in question was totally falsified by him. We bet who could spell more medical terms correctly, and apparently, the guy who hasn't been practicing medicine for five years now won. "You totally had your phone open under the table. And don't butter me up."

"We were lying on the floor. No tables in sight."

"You still cheated. No one in their right mind could spell dimethylamidophenyldimethylpyrazolone correctly from the first try."

There is a game on my phone that reads the term for you, and you have to either spell it out like a spelling bee contest or write it down correctly. We did the writing down part, and Jacob wrote it out perfectly.

"Yet, I did. Lucky you, getting a genius for a husband. Now, suck it up, and let's go."

"I hate you," I tell him as he takes me by my shoulders, turns me around, and pushes through the front door.

"So, you've said last week, the week before, and this week, at least a dozen times; but that's okay. I know you secretly mean love, Wildflower."

"Delusional cheater."

"Agh, there's a spider!" Jacob shouts and jumps on the couch. His hand is clutched to his chest as his eyes are narrowed and tracking the said spider's movements.

I rush over from the kitchen to see what kind of tarantula we've got crawling over here when I see a spider smaller than half my pinky. I look up to the fear-crushing Jackie, then to the spider, then to my fiancé again, and I can't help the bark of laughter coming out of me.

I laugh so hard I'm doubled over, clutching my stomach and wiping my tears. "Please, please tell me you are not seriously afraid of that cutie?"

"Cutie?" Jacob's eyes jump to me as he bristles. "*Cutie?*" he whisper-shouts. "That's not a cutie! It's a spider."

"So kill it. Oh my goodness, this is priceless." I wipe some more tears off.

"I can't." Jacob scrunches up his forehead as if he's in pain.

"Why not?"

"I can't kill helpless crawling things, even if they are as evil as spiders."

"And you live in a forest?"

"Yeah, why?"

"Um, sorry to break it to you, baby, but the forest is full of them. It's kind of their home." I grin at him.

"Then why do they need mine? Joy, kill it, please. Or no, scoop it up and take it outside. Please!" He claps his hands together in a pleading manner.

"What will I get for it?" I click my tongue and cross my feet and arms, clearly enjoying this right now.

"What do you want?"

"Cancel the invites."

He snorts. "Yeah, no. I'll take death from the spider."

"You are ridiculous, you know that?"

"Will you please help your husband out?" He points to the spider, who is now climbing up the wall.

"You are not my husband."

"Joy, I will make your favorite wings, okay? I'll give you ten orgasms tonight. Just take it away." He shudders.

"Fine, fine." I start moving for the paper towel. "And make that twenty," I tease him as I scoop up the tiny creature and shake it off outside.

Jacob climbs off the couch and hauls me into a bone-crushing hug. "You are the best!"

"What did you do before I lived here?"

"I called Alec, but it's so much easier to negotiate with you." He winks at me.

"What? Why? What did he get out of you?" I follow him.

"Usually, at least a week of cleaning duty at the tattoo shop, a week of leading town workouts, a week of cooking for him, and a week of texting him each morning how amazing he is."

"Damn it, I low-balled."

"No, you just love me too much to be that cruel."

*Week 3 in the Tiny House*

"What's this?" I gesture to the new green thing he is holding in his hands.

"This is Gabby," he says with a proud grin, extending the plant over to me.

"I already have my hands full with Bob and baby Matilda. Now, you also want me to take care of Gabby?"

"Wildflower, our first two kids were easy. It's time to step it up." He kisses my cheek softly like he always does as soon as his feet come through the front door. "Gabby here, is a Ficus. She is gorgeous but needs lots of love and care to thrive."

"Now I know you hate me. You want me to kill off our child." I can't take care of such things. Baby Matilda is the perfect child.

"No such thing. That's why you have me. A team, remember?"

"Camping??? You want *me* to go camping??? Is taking hiking trips every day not enough for you now?" I might be shouting, but that's okay because Jacob just suggested we go *camping*.

"You lost again, boo," he says, stuffing a huge backpack with my clothes because I refuse to pack for a trip out of hell.

"Because you cheated again." I fold my arms.

"Please, do tell, how did I manage to cheat at crossword puzzles?"

"You looked at the back of the book where they had all the answers."

"Telepathically? Because as I remember clearly, you tore out those papers and stuffed them under the couch cushions, so I 'wouldn't cheat.'" The idiot air quotes me.

"Next time, I'm picking the game."

"You picked the last two."

"Fine, we're not playing any more games. Period."

"Come on, it'll be fun. I'll even cuddle with you in our sleeping bag." Jacob wiggles his eyebrows at me.

I lift my head up. "God, please, don't let it rain, but also don't make the sun shine too much. Oh, and the wind? Can it be light and breezy and not dead ass cold like it was yesterday on that hike?"

"Are you praying or reading the next week's forecast, Wildflower?"

"I hate you!" I glare at him.

"I hate you too." He winks back.

# 36

## *Joy*

*"You know you're in love when you can't fall asleep because reality is finally better than your dreams."* — Dr. Seuss

"**W**ildflower, I'm off." Jacob gives me a sweet kiss on my cheek as he leaves for the town workout.

I never in a million years could have imagined myself in a tiny house. Never. Yet here I am, lying in that little heaven of extra-soft bed and green sheets, but most importantly, my Viking's scent wrapped tightly around each corner.

It's been a month since I had to move in with Jacob.

Fine, I didn't *have to*. I could've gone to live with one of my sisters or, worst-case scenario, my parents, but unlimited access to orgasms and good food sounded much, much better. I didn't think I would be stuck out here for quite this long, though. Apparently, a plumber is very difficult to come by in Loverly.

What? You're not buying that load of crap either? Yep, me too, but for one more of those unreasonable reasons, I am not complaining.

In my thirty-one years of life, I've never lived with a man, and the thought of doing it with Jacob Hunt scared the shit out of me for more reasons than I care to voice.

But waking up and going to bed with him has been heavenly. Having his strong, hairy leg thrown over mine every night is a dream I never knew I had, and I won't ever admit to him that the only reason I wake up at this crack of dawn six AM is to get my dose of morning kisses.

I won't admit that the nights he stays out longer at You Know You Want It shop; I can't fall asleep until his warm body wraps around mine. I thought spending nights apart from your boyfriend was a normal, natural thing. It turns out I was dead wrong because I'm pretty sure I won't be able to fall asleep without Jacob.

Yeah, there isn't enough alcohol in this town for me to admit all that.

Sharing this matchbox with my man is easy and enjoyable. And don't get me started on the sex—agh—but it's not just that.

Somehow, the only way I feel complete, happy, and at peace is when he is around. My weirdo keeps pushing my walls down, and I'm all too happy to hand him the hammer at this point. Because how else do you explain me, me, willingly going hiking in the woods behind us nearly every day?

Or me submitting myself to cuddles and hugs? Or the fact that I love our three green babies so much I talk to them—when no one is around to witness my insanity. Not to mention camping, which I secretly loved but will never admit that to him either. How could I not when he made me scream loud enough for every squirrel to plug their babies' ears.

Jacob has quickly become the one stable in my life. Everything else about my current state is left desiring better.

I have been stuck in LC for over a month now, and despite my protests of not staying here, I've got no plans to leave either...

I almost feel suspended in air or time or some weird universe. My brain is telling me to go back home to Chicago. To return to the work I love so much. But my heart—also known as the organ I refuse to listen to—tells me that Chicago is no longer my home.

Both Grace and Hope make it seem so easy. They fit in Loverly Cave as if they have always lived here. Both are happy in their own ways.

And me?

I feel weird.

That is the best way I can describe it.

I know I should go back, especially now that Zoe needs me so much. She did end up coming here a month ago, and as much as my life sucks, I got nothing on my friend. What she has going on is nothing short of "fuck" and "this is not happening." I tried to have her stay here for a bit longer, but she decided to go back to handle our research, which *I* should be doing, but my skin literally crawls at the thought of driving up that hill and heading out to the airport.

Throwing the sheets off my body with a huff, I slowly crawl out of our bed. Slowly, because I have finally hit my head on the ceiling enough times to learn my lesson. I pull on Jacobs's huge sweatshirt and head out to the porch.

This has become my morning ritual, so to speak. Me barefoot in his clothes, sitting in my chair and looking out to the vast ocean. Just like I imagined doing while sneaking out that first morning.

The wind gently caresses my skin with its silky touch. The icy undertone shoots straight through me, raising up each hair on my arms, but I won't shudder, I won't wrap my arms around my waist and keep the chill away. I want it. I want the sting. I welcome it. It reminds me this is real.

The sight in front of me doesn't cease to amaze me all these weeks later. From the very first morning I walked out his door until now, I'm mesmerized. The sheer power and beauty of the dark waters are magnetic.

My peace gets disturbed by the buzzing sounds of my phone, and **Mom** flashes across the top.

I pick it up, only to roll my eyes as soon as she opens her mouth. "How are my grandkids doing today?"

"Mom, they are still just plants." I shake my head. Needless to say, Jenny Levine took it hard when both Hope and I told her we were not planning to procreate any time soon. And Grace?

Well, Grace has enough going on as it is.

"Well, it's not like I am getting any other kind of grandbabies, so I might as well make the best of it."

"Is that all you wanted to talk about this morning because it is way too early for your dramatics. I haven't had enough coffee yet."

"No, it is not. Why aren't you at the workout with your husband?"

"He's not my husband. He's a fiancé and a fake one at that."

"Lalalala, I did not hear that," she talks over me. "Anyway, meet me at your place after we are done here."

"Why?" I can't help the skepticism lacing my question. In the past month, we've all been reminded of what it means to be living near our parents again. The words *"I am thirty and can make my own decisions"* mean absolute fuck-shit to them. I've been forced to interact with my family and the locals far too much for my liking.

"Can't you just simply agree for once in your life? Do you have to question your mother on everything?"

"Um, yes? Your track record is not great, Mom."

She exhales loudly. "This is one of my good ideas, okay?"

"If you think that sounds reassuring, think again."

"Just come, okay?"

"Fine, fine. I'll see you there in an hour."

"My favorite eldest daughter, are you here?" Mom bellows as she lets herself into my home with her own key again. Life is not teaching me anything these days.

"I am your only eldest daughter, and yes, I clearly am here." I roll my eyes because she does this thing to each one of us.

"Oh, there you are." She finds me standing in my kitchen, which doesn't feel like my kitchen.

Actually, this whole house doesn't feel like my own, and truth be told, it never did. Maybe that is why I didn't bother with real furniture.

"I have the bestest news for you." Mom claps her hands together as she jumps in excitement.

"Great, let's hear how bad is it?" If Mom thinks it's good, that can only mean one thing for the rest of us.

"Dr. Loveland is retiring!" she screeches.

*Loveland*...only in Loverly Cave...

"Okaaaay? Good for Dr. Loveland?"

"No, Joy, catch up." She movs her hands fast and impatiently. "He is retiring, which means we need a new doctor to take over his practice."

"Okay, I still don't see how it pertains to me." I push off the counter. "Do you want me to look for someone?"

"Oh my God, Joy!" Mom groans, tipping her head back. "I am saying you should be the doctor that takes over his clinic."

"What? Why would I do that? I'm not staying here, and I already have a job. In Chicago." Why does that sound so bitter? I should be excited to go back, no?

"You mean you're still going to leave?" Mom sounds taken aback.

"Um…yes, no, I don't know, Mom." I sound like I am in pain. Dropping my head into my hands, I hide from Mom's assertive eyes.

"Honey? Talk to me." She lays down her warm hand on mine.

"There is nothing to talk about. I am fine."

"Joy Levine, don't you dare lie to your mother. I pushed you out for thirty-four hours out of a very small—"

"Please don't finish that. We all know this story." Because she's never failed to remind us every time we did something bad while growing up, and I still remember how traumatized I was when she explained it in detail the very first time. It was brutal then, and it hasn't gotten better with age.

"Then talk to me. Is it about Jacob? Justin? Work?"

"How did you know about Justin when I never told you? Hell, you knew about him being unavailable before I found out." This question has been bugging me ever since she mentioned it the first day we got here.

"I pay attention to my kids. That's all."

"Aha, sure."

"I'm serious." She sighs. "About three years ago, I noticed a shift in your behavior; you were different. You had days when you would be extra happy and others when your grumpiness took on a whole new level. That only happens when you are in an unhappy relationship. So, I started to dig deeper and looked up which professors joined your university around that time."

"Impressive, but that still wouldn't have told you who I was seeing."

Mom looks like she doesn't particularly want to share the next bit, but she blows a raspberry and says, "Oh, fine." She huffs. "I might've contacted a few students on campus who kept an eye on you." After a beat, she adds, "And him."

"Mom!" My eyes nearly pop out of their sockets. "You did what?"

"What I had to do. And I, unlike you, actually looked him up right away."

"Why didn't you say anything to me then? Huh?"

"Oh, yeah, because that would go over so well with you. You are as stubborn as me, and if I said he was bad news, you'd just cling onto him stronger."

"I can't believe this," I say, shaking my head at her.

"Poopie crap, all is well that ends well. Now you're on the right Hunt brother. The one that makes you happy, so do just that."

"Do what?"

"Be happy."

At that exact moment, I hear a knock on my door and Luke's deep, grumbling voice calling my name. "Joy?"

"Luke?" I ask at the same time as Mom runs up to him, wrapping the big brute in her small arms, and cries out, "Luke, my boy, what are you doing here?"

"Oh, um..." His cheeks grow faintly pink as he gives her an awkward hug back. Oh, this is priceless. The beast himself crumbles at my mother's touch. How adorable. "Grace mentioned that your water pipe still hasn't been fixed, so I came by to take a look at it." He scratches the back of his head sheepishly.

"Yeah, apparently, plumbing services are like a unicorn in here. Meaning there are none."

"What? Who told you that?" His dark eyebrows furrow. "I would have been here the day it happened if someone had told me."

"I wasn't aware that the fire department deals with broken pipes over here."

"The fire department, no. But me..." He points to his black t-shirt-covered chest. "Yes. I'm the part-time plumber in LC."

"What???" I shout. "You mean to tell me I could've had this fixed weeks ago and be on my merry way home a long time ago?"

"I guess if that's what you want." Luke shrugs, clearly not understanding my outrage.

"On that note, I will leave you to it." Mom smiles sweetly at us and quickly shuffles toward the door.

"Not so fast, Mother." I stop her. "We will talk about you lacking this information for a month later. For now, leave the key to my place on the counter, like I asked you to do weeks ago."

Either out of fear or guilt, she unhooks my key from her chain and hands it over.

"Thank you." I lift it up to her. "Now, if you'll excuse me, I have a certain Viking to kill."

# 37

## Jacob

*Love is a two-way street constantly under construction. — Carroll Bryant*

Today is one of those perfect days. You know the ones where you wake up with the woman you love sleeping soundlessly on your chest, her body slung over your torso, and you're sweating balls from the mutual heat, but God forbid you move. If you move, the said woman will wake up and pretend she wasn't just drooling all over you.

One of those days where you get to kiss her goodbye on your way to work and pray she doesn't kill you when the next silly shirt you ordered for her comes in the mail.

The day then flows into a perfect work morning and a trip to the beach because the waves are unreal, and you catch each one.

The day that keeps its perfect streak until a furious storm by the name of Wildflower comes marching your way. Her steps are so fast and urgent that she raises a whole wall of sand with each one.

"Jacob Hunt! You get out of that water right this second."

And just like that, my balls shiver from her voice and not the freezing West Coast water.

"Oof, I would not want to be you right now, brother." Alec grins stupidly at me and I contemplate how long I can stay in here before her fury gives her wings and carries her to me.

Crap, think Jackie, what have you done in the past few days?

Did she see the package with her new shirt in it already? I didn't get the notification it arrived yet. The one that says *Future MILF* on it. What? She is! All the shirts I got her so far are true.

*Queen of Blowjobs.*
*Not only am I funny... I have nice titties too!*
*I'm His.*
*Rubber Ducky for President.*
*Fun fact: Shut up.*
*Good girl.*

Anyway, you get the idea. They're awesome, right? The ducky one is all sparkly. So freaking cute, and she refuses to wear it.

Joy finally reaches the shore, and she must be really mad at me if she came this close to the cold water. *Okay, guys, Mommy just wants to talk, no need to shrivel up and hide, okay?*

Yeah, I wouldn't believe me either, and yes, my balls need some comfort from me right now because they are about to get it, and not in a good way.

"JACOB!"

"I'm coming, Wildflower. Just extra slowly. I'm giving you time to cool off so you don't kill me right away for whatever it is I have done. And if it's because of the shirt, I thought it was cute."

"You got me another stupid shirt?" she shouts some more, and I cringe. Great, it's not about the shirt, but now I might as well add it to the list.

"I think you should shut up," Alec murmurs to me. See, he is a smart man who uses hushed voices around my furious fiancée. Me, on the other hand? Well...I am engaged to the woman; I guess smart was never my thing, only ducking brilliant.

By the time I'm out of the water, her foot has tapped a whole two feet hole in the sand, her tongue that she keeps running over her teeth, pretty much brushed them clean for her, and her dark eyes are narrowed to itty-bitty slits, I wonder how she can see anything through them.

But God, she is so beautiful. She's always beautiful, and Joy in skin-tight leggings and a crop top—with no fucking bra underneath—is an instant boner giver.

"Whatever it is I've done, I'm sure I can explain." I lift both hands up in surrender.

"Really now? Okay, please explain how you failed to mention to Luke, who—surprise, surprise—is a plumber, and I need one. *Needed one* a month ago?"

"Ohhhhhh, thaaaaaat." I bite my lips and take a step back. "He's a plumber?" I meant it as a question or maybe to sound surprised by the news, but it comes out all high-pitched and squeaky, which makes Joy narrow her eyes even more.

She takes a step forward. "Get in the car, now! We will talk at home where there are no witnesses. I don't particularly want to go to jail because I happen to be engaged to an idiot."

"Yeah, I think I'll stay here," I say, slowly taking another step back until my feet are back in the water. Crap, I left my board over by Joy, and there is no escaping her now.

"Jacob, get in the car, or so help me God." Joy plants her hands on her hips and glares at me.

"Okay, I'm coming." But before I leave, I call out to my best friend. "If I die today, you can have your surfboard back."

To which he salutes me with a grin. The fucker now probably hopes for my painful death.

"If?" Joy asks me. "You are so cute thinking there is an 'if' here."

Thankfully, we drove in two cars today, so I have five extra minutes of bracing myself. I knew there was a possibility she would find out eventually, I just didn't think it'd be so fast.

"Explain," she simply says as soon as we step through the door, and I start peeling off my wet suit. Joy didn't let me do it back at the beach. She was probably afraid she would stop being mad with me once she saw my irresistible body.

"Okay, yes, I knew he was a plumber, and I didn't tell you or call him myself."

"Why?"

"What do you mean why?" My hands are out of the suit, and I see her eyes track my movements. I might survive this after all. "I wanted you to live with me."

"So, you lied to me?"

"No." I hold up one finger. "No. I didn't *lie* lie. I pretended to forget."

"Because that sounds so much better. Jacob. I've been stuck out here for a month, sharing two hundred square feet with you while my house could have been fixed and livable this whole time? Not only that, but I could have already rented it out and gone back home to Chicago? To my job."

I stop all attempts to take the wet suit off. "What do you mean, go back to Chicago? You are leaving?"

"Of course I am. That was always the plan."

"No."

"What do you mean, no?"

"It means you can't leave. You can't go back to the vipers' nest when I just got you out of it."

"I didn't know I ever asked for your opinion."

"But we are getting married!"

"We are not getting married."

"We have kids together!"

"Those are not kids; they are plants."

"Ahhh," I gasp and run up to Bob, Gabby, and baby Matilda. "Mommy didn't mean to say that. Shh." I pat everyone, even Matilda.

"You are ridiculous. Stop distracting me. I was angry with you. I was going to shove your balls up your ass."

"Oh, I know." I smirk.

"Then get back here and make me mad again."

"I'd rather not."

"I won't miss you when I leave." She throws at me, but there is absolutely no venom in her words.

"Of course, you won't." I look at my future wife and blind her with another smile. "Because I am coming with you."

"You're what???" Joy shrieks, her arms that were folded drop to her sides like limp noodles.

"I. Am. Coming. With. You," I state very slowly, letting each word sink in before I utter the next.

"W-what? W-why? H-how? But you hate Chicago." The voice that just a second ago was loud and boisterous is now small and quiet. Joy looks at me with her big, dark eyes as if I suddenly grew three heads.

I knew there was a possibility she would go back, and I've hoped she'd stay, but if she wants to go back to Chicago, then I'm going along. She might not fully understand this, but we are it. We have been in it since the very first night.

"You can hit me, scratch, and claw, but I'm not going to step aside. I won't back down or leave. So do your worst. Because you and me...we are forever, Joy. And what kind of a husband would I be if, at the first sign of trouble, I'd call seize fire?"

"You are not my husband," her voice is barely audible.

"Yet," I finish for her.

"I can't hate it if you love it because I will go where you go. And if it's Chicago, then it's Chicago. I go where you go, Wildflower."

Joy closes her half-opened mouth, opens it again, and closes it again. Then suddenly, she lunges herself at me, wrapping her cute little hands behind my neck as she jumps me like a monkey with her feet around my waist and kisses me like it's our last day on earth.

I peel away from her for long enough to say, "Make-up sex?"

She looks into my eyes, slightly breathless, as her tongue pokes out the side of her mouth, and she nods. "Yeah, make-up sex." And then her mouth is back on mine, and she digs her fingers into my hair the way she loves to. Hard and just on the verge of leaving me bald.

Never making it to the bed or even the couch, we tumble down to the hard ground in a frenzy of teeth, tongues, touches, and a lot of peeling off clothes—the rest of the wetsuit, in my case.

This is not like the other times we've had sex. This time, each of us is fighting for control. She pushes me down and straddles me on top, only long enough for me to toss her back down and pin her hands on top of her head and her body with mine. "You are not playing fair, hubby," Joy tells me with hooded eyes as she writhes beneath me.

Talk about unfair. My brain is operating with no blood at the moment, and her naked body rubs against mine.

"Never claimed I would, *wifey*," I say, pushing her legs apart and sinking inside deep and hard in one thrust.

"Aghhh," she groans as I fill her to the brink. But I only give her a few thrusts before I'm off her and flip her body until she is on her hands and knees, that fucking sexy ass up in the air, ripe for my taking. I drag my hand through the smooth globes for a second before my palm connects with it with a sharp sting for me and a burst of pain and pleasure for her because I know how much my girl loves this.

"That's right, my good girl loves it when I punish her ass, doesn't she?" My hand dips into her soaking wet pussy, and it's my turn to groan. "This fucking pussy of mine. Always so ready for me. So wet even when you are pissed and want to kill me. She loves me." Joy only whimpers in answer. "Yeah, of course she loves me."

Without giving her another warning, I withdraw my fingers and line up my cock with her entrance. Pummeling into her with ruthless power. This might be the most beautiful sight. Her back arched, her ass up, and that dark mane of hers laid over her shoulders like the finest silk.

I reach out to it and wrap my fist around the length of it, tugging on it, making her arch deeper. "That's it. That's how I like it," I tell her while fucking her like never before. Giving her all I've got.

"Oh God."

"Yeah."

"Jac—"

"I'm here."

"Fuck."

"I'll give you what you need, and you will forget whatever it was your smart mouth was saying before. Because we both know where you belong, and that's with me and on this cock." I withdraw, flipping us around until I'm the one on the ground. "Now, sit on it, take, and give exactly what you need and want. Because this marriage will never be one-sided. A team, remember?"

"There is no marriage."

"That fucking mouth of yours, I think I'll have to fuck it next until you are no longer able to talk back." She is just on top of me, but I'm not inside her yet, so I quickly fix it by slamming her down all the way until she screams my name.

Joy places her hands on my chest, and that sweet pussy of hers starts drawing slow, deep circles on top. Her movements are magnetic, driving me crazier than when I was fucking her like a maniac from behind.

My hands wrap around her hips, and I pull myself up until my face is pressed into her tits. Can't believe I still haven't fucked her full tits, but I give her another slap on her ass and cup her breasts in my hands, drawing those sweet nipples in my mouth one at a time and sucking them in, teasing them with my tongue until Joy is falling apart while her little clit rubs on me and my cock hits just the spot she needs inside.

"Do you feel me inside you? I'm deep, exactly where I'm meant to be." I give her hair another small tug. "You can say whatever you want, Wildflower, but your pussy wants my cock. It craves it and welcomes me every time with its slick, hot walls squeezing around me hard."

"Yes, yes, yes," she chants mindlessly, her head falling back as her climax takes over her, squeezing me until there is no more holding back for me.

"Oh, fuuuuuck," slips from my lips just before I lower my mouth back to her tits. I need them in my mouth as my cum shoots out of me, coating her slick walls. Joy's body goes slack against mine as we both come down from our highs.

But we were far from over; because just a minute later, Joy was on her back, and I was between her thighs, which was quickly followed by my once again hard cock in her mouth and my cum all over her tits as I marked them, really rubbing it into her skin so it would stay on like a permanent marker until I had to wash her off in the shower.

"Well, if this is what makeup sex is all about, let's fight twice a day." I kiss her shoulder. "Every day."

Alec: **Please, tell me I can have my surfboard back?**

Jacob: **I can't believe you. You wished me dead??? Me? I held your dick for you when you had to take a leak but were too drunk to not piss all over yourself. I literally saved you back then, and you wished me dead.**

Alec: **Drama queen *cough, cough* My dick is very nice. You enjoyed touching perfection.**

Jacob: **Pervert...**

Jacob: **You are never getting your surfboard back. Forget. It.**

Jacob: **Oh, and I might be moving away...**

Alec: **WHAT???**

Alec: **Where?**

Alec: **Answer me, Jackie!**

Alec: **You can't leave me!!! I promise I won't say anything anymore. I promise I will love you forever.**

Alec: **What am I supposed to do??? You just ripped my heart into pieces.**

# MEET MY WIFE

Alec: **Jacob, this is Hope. I need you to come over because currently Alec is washing our floors with his tears and beating them up with his fists...**

Alec: **Still Hope here. He is now packing our clothes, and I swear if you don't come here in the next three minutes, I am calling your fiancé.**

Alec: **Jacob! I mean that, as in NOW! Come now!**

## 38

# *50 Reasons*

Reason #50:
*Jacob: I—*
*Joy: Shhh...*

# 39

## *Joy*

*"To gain that which is worth having, it may be necessary to lose everything else."* — Bernadette Devlin.

My house has been all fixed up. Pipes in working condition. New tiles have been laid, floors refinished, kitchen cabinets repainted, and the bad ones changed out. I bought new, stainless-steel appliances for the whole house and even made the loft upstairs livable.

Just not for myself.

Because for the past month—well, technically two—I've still been living with Jacob in our tiny house.

Oh crap, and I definitely started calling it *our* tiny house. I haven't even noticed how that happened. I just never left after that fight we had over the plumbing—if you can even call it that—and have only gotten more and more comfortable. But now, as I am dusting up the last bits of the remodel mess, I have a choice to make.

A difficult choice. To stay or leave. To call Loverly Cave home or return to the one I had before. To allow Jacob to fully take over my heart or keep the last bits to myself, safely protected.

I'm lying right now. There was never a choice, never a dilemma I am pretending to have right now. I knew exactly what I would be doing from the very first step I made here.

Now, I just have to convince myself it's always the right one. And it would be much easier if my sister wasn't being an idiot, and I didn't have to spend my energy on making sure she doesn't lose the best guy in the world. Well, her best guy.

Mine is glued to me like that cinnamon gum, and there is nothing I can do to get him off me. Truth be told, I'm not even trying anymore. Ever since Jacob proclaimed he was moving with me to Chicago, the battle was officially lost.

I say I hate him, but that's not really true, is it...?

Jacob is the man who has slowly, piece by piece, shown me another way of life. The easy and carefree one. The life where a simple smile can make your day. Hell, he taught me *how* to smile. Period.

No matter how rude, sarcastic, or generally grumpy I have been to him, he's never taken a step back. He keeps showing up day after day, showing me that I'm enough, and I've started believing him.

Jacob's never done any of those crazy romantic gestures Alec keeps throwing at Hope, and I'm more than okay with it because my man is showing me reality. He's shown me what it means to be with him, to spend every day and night together. How to get past arguments we might have in the future and everything in between.

He's the man who gifts me potted plants and names them. The one who just bought me shirt number forty-one that says: *You better rubber ducky me...*

He's the one who makes me breakfast every morning and makes me my beloved coffee, even though the smell alone makes him gag.

He is the one I spend every evening with, sitting wrapped in a blanket and his arms around me on our patio. Sometimes, he talks my ear off, and other nights, we share the silence and the sounds of nature surrounding us.

He's one who knows which mood I'm in as soon as he walks through the door. The one who raised the roof at the tiny house so I would stop hitting my head on the ceiling. He takes the good with the bad and smiles through it all.

I should've been terrified of a new relationship after my last one just failed so epically—and with his half-brother, nonetheless—but Jacob's never allowed me to be afraid. He's never allowed me to take a step back, and no one, *no one*, has ever done that for me.

None of those things.

And if there is one person I could see myself doing life with, it would be Jacob Hunt.

My mind is sore from the onslaught of my realizations plus Hope's drama today, and all I want is to take a hot shower and climb into my bed naked and free from all this bullshit. But do I get to do that?

Of course not.

The last person I want to see is here, materializing from my nightmares.

Justin fucking Hunt, in his three-piece black suit, shiny shoes, and perfectly styled hair, is leaning against his car with a huge bouquet of red roses in his hands as I open the front door of my cottage to leave.

As soon as his eyes see me, he straightens up and walks over.

"What are you doing here?" I grind out and maybe shut the door behind me a bit too hard. The good, light mood I had a second ago vanishes.

How could two brothers make me feel so differently. Sure, Jacob pisses me off, but it's almost like foreplay for us, versus with Justin, we never had that easygoing vibe about us. It was always business-like, and I took those basic physical transactions for love. How mistaken I was...

"Joy," he says confidently. "Are you done yet?"

"Done?"

"Yeah, are you done playing games yet? Making me jealous?" My mouth parts at his audacity. "Come on, Joy, we all know that engagement show two months ago was for me. And I get it," —he raises one hand, palm up— "I went about our relationship a bit wrong. But I'm back, and I want you back." His eyes have a gleam in them, and he smiles a lopsided smile at me. The one I used to melt to.

Not anymore. He takes my stunned silence as his go-ahead to continue.

"You succeeded, by the way. I was very angry and jealous, and I wanted to kill that hippy brother of mine for touching you and you him, so I left before I could do something to jeopardize my career." Justin fixed the collar on his pristine white dress shirt. "How did you find him anyway? I don't think I ever told you I had a half-brother. But I forgive you, and am ready to move on."

Is he for real right now? I am trying to process everything he just said as my head lowers and my eyebrows rise.

Joy from two months ago would mask her true feelings; she would shut this whole conversation with one word and leave. But I'm not her anymore. Jacob has taught me so much more than just to smile. I used to hide it all, keep it bottled up and for my eyes only because I didn't want anyone to see my weaknesses or my failures. But Jacob has showed me that being vulnerable doesn't mean you are less.

It's a strength, and I'm now strong enough to unleash it all. He taught me to accept my emotions and feelings to not be afraid of sharing them with the world because who the fuck cares? It's my life, and I get to live it how I want.

If I weren't so exhausted, I would have masked my true emotions, but I'm whacked, burnt out, and worn out, so Justin is about to get the full treatment right here.

Also, this has been long overdue. When my sister told me I had to let my feelings out about this failed relationship, I didn't understand them until now.

Because it is not the sorrow I was feeling all this time.

It's anger. Anger for three wasted years. For fake hopes and words. For making me feel small and irrelevant. For using my brain for his career gain since I helped him with every stupid research he has ever done. No, scratch that, I did it *for* him.

So, with great pleasure, I put my hand in a fist in front of his face, and then with my free hand, I start making spinning motions on the side of it as if I am spinning a spinning wheel, and I keep doing it until my middle finger slowly starts raising.

Theatrical? Maybe. I am a Levine, after all.

I stop spinning when my 'fuck you' is loud and clear.

"This is how many fucks I give about what you're feeling, Justin. Get the hell away from me. I don't care about you or your desires. You can go rot in your anger and jealousy for all I care. And I'm not upset. Not even a little. I would have to feel something for you to be upset, and I don't. Not anymore, and truth be told, I never had."

"And what? You have *feelings* for Jacob?" He spits out that word like it's poison. "Do you hear how ridiculous that is?"

*Do I have feelings for Jacob?* I look at the man in front of me, the one who I always thought would be someone I ended up with. Someone who was perfect for me, yet all I want right now is my goofy, blonde Viking with his unruly hair, tattoos, shark slides, and rubber ducky obsession.

So, yes. I have feelings for Jacob. It's bigger than lust. Deeper than simple physical need.

"I do. He is a wonderful man. Kind, caring, gentle, and funny. He makes me smile, really smile. Smile like I have never smiled before. And he doesn't lie to me." My voice rises as I read off of the flashcards my heart wrote out for me. "You want to know the truth? Yes, the engagement is fake. But everything else is real. Jacob puts me first; he cares about me; he sees me. And every time I am in his arms, I feel cherished and loved. I. Love. Him. He is the love of my life, my rubber fucking ducky. So, take your sorry-ass flowers and leave us alone. They could never compete with Bob, Gabby, and my baby, Matilda."

"You are so naïve!" Justin's face is beet red as he shouts. "You think he can give you what you need? You think he will come back to Chicago to live there with you while you waste away at that lab of yours like a rat?" He lets out a humorless laugh and snaps his fingers at my face. I'm tempted to break each one of those. "Wake up, Joy! You just want the older brother, and you can't have me, so you're ready to settle for someone who is lesser, but somewhat close to the real deal."

"Lesser? Fucking lesser?" I return the snap of my finger at his face. "You wake up, Justin. Your brother is far more superior in everything. Especially IQ and sex!" That makes him shut up for a second. "Oh yeah, Jacob fucks me like you never could, and he easily manages to deliver multiple orgasms in one go. Multiple." Am I being petty? Maybe, but it is well deserved.

# MEET MY WIFE

"So, I didn't fuck you hard enough?"

"No, you weren't smart enough." In the blink of an eye, he drops the flowers and takes my shoulders in his hands. He's way too close, and I find myself recoiling at his touch. His scent makes me nauseous. How I ever found him appealing is beyond me.

I must have been getting poisoned by something in my lab.

"Let's go inside one more time, and I'll show you better sex." His grip is tight, and I can't move as his lips move closer and closer to mine. I'm trying to squirm away, but he is too strong.

"Let her go right-fucking-now." Jacob runs at us like a tornado, pushing Justin away as if he weighs nothing and landing a hard punch on his face. "Stay. Away. From my wife."

"She is not your wife," Justin says, spitting out blood.

"She will be soon enough, and if I ever see you near her again, I might not be as gentle next time."

"Fuck you, asshole! Joy was mine before you ever met her. She took pity on you and crawled into your bed to be close to a real Hunt, but soon enough, she will be back home with me, where she belongs, and you and this pathetic little town will be a distant memory."

"In your dreams, Justin! And please do keep dreaming, that's all you have left."

"Have your fun, Joy. We'll talk in Chicago."

And just like that, the choice that was never really a choice comes tumbling out.

"I quit." The words slips out of my mouth fast and without a second thought, because I was never going back to Chicago, to him, or even to my job.

The things I used to take for the center of my universe, stuff I thought made me whole and happy, were simply a mirage. A make-believe, sad little hole-plugger, and now that I know what it should feel like, I'm never going back to the half-life again.

"You what?" Justin bulges his eyes at me. "Do you understand what you're saying, or did his infected saliva already start eating away at your brain?"

I knew Jacob would come along with me if I decided to move, but that man keeps living to make me happy, and I want to do the same for him. *Wait until he sees what I got him today...*

"I understand everything, Justin. Everything. And the only one with diseases here would be you."

Justin is steaming mad; his nostrils are flaring like a wild bull, ready to pounce.

"Then rot in hell with your fiancé here." He spits out more blood. "You are done, Joy. No one will ever hire you again." With that, he finally shuts up and walks away.

Jacob quickly turns around from his protective stance and looks me up and down, gently touching my shoulders where Justin's hands were bruising my skin. "Wildflower, are you okay? Did he hurt you? I'm so sorry I left you here alone. I got held back at the tattoo shop."

"Stop, stop. I'm fine, everything is fine." And I find myself actually believing my words. I just let go of the one thing I ever truly loved—my job—yet I feel elated and free, and I smile. "I am very much fine."

"You know I really hate that word," he tells me with a small smile of his own as the back of his hand slowly caresses my cheek.

"Fine," I sass him. "I am not just fine; I am pretty damn good."

"There you go." His smile grows wider. "That's more like it." Jacob hauls me into his chest and lifts me up as he kisses me. "Well, I guess it's a good thing you are marrying me."

He takes my hand, and we walk back into the cottage together.

"I'm not marrying you, but just out of curiosity, why?"

"I have some savings, and I'll be a good hubby and support you." He thrusts his fist into his chest, and I start laughing.

"Let's get your hand iced, hubby."

"Did you mean it?" he suddenly asks. All humor is gone from his voice, and I turn my head to look at him and ask what he means, but he doesn't give me a chance. "Did you mean what you said about me back there to Justin?"

Oh. *That*. He must've heard our conversation.

"Um..." Well, that is not the way I wanted to tell the only man I have ever loved that he is the love of my life. The only one. But I guess nothing goes according to my plans anymore.

"Yes," I tell him truthfully. "Yes, I meant every word, Jacob, and it scares the shit out of me, but you have taught me that those feelings shouldn't be scary and that I can trust you. So, I trust you all the way. Besides apparently, my inside organs have all elected you to be their leader, and my heart and vagina decided to pledge their allegiance to you long ago."

The smile that graces his face is nothing I have ever seen before. We've laughed and smiled plenty together at this point, but this? It's absolutely breathtaking, and he runs up to me, scooping me up into his arms as his lips find mine and kiss every worry away.

"I love you. I love you so much; I never knew this kind of love existed. I have loved you for a while now, and it took so much effort to not let those words slip." He kisses me some more. "I didn't want to spook you away. I didn't want you to feel pressured."

I close my eyes, our noses rub together lightly, and I breathe in his foresty scent as he kisses every centimeter of my face.

"I think I have been in love with you for a while, too, I was just too afraid—or too stubborn—to admit it. You're the one I never knew I wanted; you are the one I never knew I couldn't live without. I love you, Jacob, with the shark slides, rubber ducky shorts, and your ostentatious personality. I love your weird and crazy. I love it all."

"I guess it's a good thing we are already getting married." He smirks into our kiss.

"We are not getting married," I tell him, but I might as well be talking to a wall. Jacob isn't listening as he carries me into the shower, strips me off all my clothes, and washes my body carefully and with so much love, and I end up in my bed, naked and free after all, only so much better than what I imagined originally because Jacob spends the whole night showing me exactly how much he loves me.

## Jacob:

"Wildflower? What's this?" I point to the box on our bed. It looks like a gift, except there are noises coming from the inside, it's wrapped in rubber ducky paper but has a ton of holes all around it.

We just got back from Joy's cottage after having all the orgasms our bodies could handle. We could have stayed the night there, I wouldn't have minded, but when my boo said,

"Let's go home, baby," I was out the door and buckling her in that second.

Now, I'm standing at our tiny table, staring at this masterpiece. I'm pretty sure it's from Joy, and she's never got me anything like this before. To say I'm curious is not to say anything.

"Go ahead, Jackie, open it." She smiles proudly, pointing at the box, and I carefully tear off the packaging—even though it already has holes in it. Because, come on, it's rubber duckies.

"Wildflower?" My mouth hangs open as I take out what—who—she placed inside. I look over at her, and my girl is bouncing on her heels, biting her lip sheepishly, watching my every move.

*Chirp, chirp.*

"So? What do you think?" she asks me, sticking her hands in her back pockets. My hands tremble. I'm speechless, and I trip over the chair in front of me and nearly break her—and my gift—in half as I run to her, pick her up into my hands, and twirl us around.

"You are the most amazing, the most caring wifey ever!" I give her a quick kiss and another and another. I keep going with these smooches until she is laughing too hard for me to keep going. "You got me a BABY DUCKY! A real, live baby duckling!!!"

"I thought maybe we could practice the whole parenting thing on something other than Bob, Gabby, and baby Matilda...you know, to prepare for the future, possible..." she trails off, biting her lower lip in such a cute, shy manner that I almost can't handle all of this right now.

"I love you so fucking much, boo!" I kiss her again while holding the tiny yellow ball of fur who is chirping happily in my hands. Our baby duckling. "What is her name?"

"Francesca," Joy says with a beaming smile, and my head falls back with laughter. She finally got to name something, and that is what she went with. For a duck.

"Daddy loves you so much, my little ducky." My voice breaks as I nuzzle my face into the soft, warm feathers.

"Baby, are you crying?" Joy comes up from behind, wrapping her hands around my torso.

"No one. No one has ever done anything like this for me, Joy!"

"Oh, Jacob," she says in a soft, sweetened voice. "I will do anything for you. I love you." She lays her head on my back.

"Anything?"

"Please don't ruin this moment."

And just like that, the world is right back on its track. My grumpy wife is back.

The rest of the evening, we spend watching Disney movies, cozied up with Francie until my girl starts getting too naughty, and I have to cover our baby's eyes as we defiled the couch once again. Because, what kind of movie night would it be if I didn't deliver an orgasm or two to my future wife?

**Love Hive:**

Peaceforall: Two operations are done. One more to go. Good work, friends.

LoveterM65: Maybe we should take a break for a bit.

CookieI: Breaks are for the weak!!! No breaks for anyone.

Ninasunshine: Hear, hear. We still don't have any grandbabies, so no relaxing yet.

RickyL: Honey, how about we get a dog? Or a cat?

CookieI: Honey, how about you make yourself comfortable in your shed tonight?

# MEET MY WIFE

Willoflove: We need to add one more operation!

Ninasunshine: What happened? Who are we adding? If you are talking about Julie, she is already on the list. The amber fire will take off next year for obvious reasons.

Jules444: I will pretend you didn't just say that I am part of your love operations. You all know very well it is not in the cards for me...Also, why next year? What don't I know?

CookieI: Don't worry, child. Let the professional deal with it.

Willoflove: No, it's not about Julie. Matteo is coming back home.

Freeman1: Your son? Our little Matteo is coming?

Willoflove: There is nothing little about that young man, anymore. Or gentlemanly!!! My son is a manwhore!!! I knew sending him off to college was a mistake. Look at what they have done!

Ninasunshine: Shhh, Willow, there is nothing we can't do. Now, relax, and let's make a new plan.

# 40

# Epilogue

*"I love you neither with my heart nor my mind. My heart might stop, my mind can forget. I love you with my soul because my soul never stops or forgets." –Rumi.*

### Joy

"Hey, boo? Where do you want this?" my crazy fiancé bellows from the front desk.

"Jacob," I hiss at him as I run out of my office. "It's Dr. Levine whenever we are at work."

"Oh, is it? Can I also call you that in bed later?" He wiggles his eyebrows, still holding the heavy box full of my medical books that I will probably never need but like to keep. They are perfect for dust collecting, you know?

"Doctor Hunt, I am your boss now. Behave."

"Aha, keep telling yourself that, Wildflower." He kisses my cheek, walking past me as our socks connect, completely ignoring everything I just said. No, you haven't misheard. Jacob got us socks that have little hands hanging off the sides and those that have magnets in them. So, now, every time we walk past each other, the sock hands reach out to each other, and we connect.

He is ridiculous. I know.

What else is new?

"It's Dr. Levine!" I shout after him, and yes, I might add a little foot stomp for added effect.

Zoe snickers at our antics from our break room. "You two are the cutest."

"I swear, my employees are in coalition to kill me this morning." I plant my hands on my hips and look up to the sky. "And don't call me cute. I'm not cute." Yes, there was another foot stomp.

Jacob comes out of my office box-less, smacks my ass, and kisses my cheek again.

"I'll tell you what's cute, your ass."

"PROFESSIONAL SETTING, people," I shout again, and it passes over their heads once again.

So much has changed in the past month that I don't even know where to start.

Yes, I officially took over Dr. Loveland's practice, and now I practice family medicine in a small hippy town. As soon as I called Zoe to let her know I'm not coming back, she packed her shit and moved into my beach cottage the next day, and now she is a fellow doctor in my practice.

Along with my dear fiancé.

Yep, Jacob pulled out his old, rusty MD degree from the box in the storage, got it renewed, and now works alongside us. Although he decided to take reception desk duties for now, saying he'd rather chat up with the patients than clean up their vomit, and who could blame him?

Pathology to family medicine is quite a change. One I am still processing.

"Also, please use my correct last name when you address your husband," Jacob calls out.

"You are not my husband yet!"

"In two days, I will be."

Yep, you heard that right. That crazy man has talked me into having our September wedding after all, and yes, my dress has rubber duckies on it. Because who needs a fancy-ass proposal when you had your own Viking striptease for you in front of the whole town. I mean, how much better can it get, right?

What can I say? I love him too much to deny him anything. Especially when Jacob is giving up his last name for me.

Yep, you heard me right again. He didn't want us, as a family, to have any ties to the Hunt name so in two days' time, Jacob will become a Levine. A fact that my father is still crying over since he was never blessed with sons.

Now he has two—Alec and Jacob, with the latter one taking our family name.

"Which shirt are you wearing today?" Zoe asks me with a grin. I prop open my coat and flash her the newest addition to my ever-growing collection of ridiculous T-shirts Jacob gets me. *This is what ducking perfection looks like.* Zoe laughs, and I join in. This has become sort of a daily tradition for us, and I might have started wearing them more often to make her and Jacob happy.

Oh, fine. I love these shirts, too. My future hubby is brilliant.

"I'm so happy for you," Zoe says, while leaning against the door with her head resting on the frame. My poor friend is living out a nightmare slash dream. Her situation is so fucked up, I don't even know how to help her.

"Me? Happy? Are you talking about that insufferable man over there?" I smile, hooking my thumb behind me.

"Your ass is getting spanked bright red for that one, Wildflower," the Viking that misses nothing calls out, and I have to clench my thighs from his devious promise.

Zoe smiles back, but it's a little forced, and I sigh. "You will be happy too, Zo!" I try to encourage her.

"Maybe. For now, it seems like I'm living in some alternate universe." She rubs her fast-growing belly.

Yep, another ding ding ding moment. Zoe is pregnant...

Pregnant and alone, and practically in hiding until we can figure out how to protect her baby from his/her father. Justin doesn't know, and Zoe has zero desire to tell him.

"No, you're in happy hippy-land now, honey. And no one is allowed to be sad here, isn't that right, hubby?"

"It sure is." Jacob grins, remembering our very first meeting, and kisses the side of my head. "Come on, Zo, your kiddo will have the best uncles and aunts in the world, and she already has a whole herd of grandparents lined up for babysitting duty."

Ain't that the truth. My mom, Mrs. Colson, Willow, Fifi, and pretty much all the ladies from LC are fawning over Zoe and have already bought her more baby clothes than she could possibly need.

"I don't know what I'd do without you guys," she says with tears in her eyes.

"Please! No crying. You know I can't handle that."

"I'll just go cry in my office." She turns and leaves us alone; my own tear ducks decide they'd like an in on this action, but I won't allow them.

Not yet.

I have a whole plan.

## Jacob

"Wildflower?" I exclaim happily as I spot a new box on the table wrapped in more ducky paper waiting for me.

This has become one of the best parts of each day because ever since she gave me our baby ducky, Francie, Joy has left a gift for me—or us, if you know what I mean—daily. And I'm here for it every single time.

A month ago, I came home to a shark blanket, and she told me, "It is not just a blanket. It's a full-body sleeping bag type of blanket. It has teeth on top of the hood and all. And there's room for two." To say we filled that blanket with naughty memories is not to say anything.

Last night's gift was particularly handy as she came harder than ever before.

Without waiting for her to go ahead, I rip into it and stop dead.

There is a shirt inside. One that says: *Daddy duck* with a papa ducky walking ahead of a baby ducky. I gulp, blink, and blink again as I take it out with shaky hands. Under the T-shirt, there is a pregnancy test and one tiny onesie that says: My daddy is my ducking hero.

"Joy..." my voice is a hushed whisper. My eyes are blurry as the tears roll down my cheeks. "Love? We're pregnant?" I slowly turn towards her, and she is smiling wide with her own tears falling down and nodding vigorously.

"Yeah, baby, you're going to be a daddy!"

Clutching both shirts in my hands, I rush to the woman who just made me the happiest man on this planet once again, and pick her up into my arms.

"I love you. I love you. I love you!!!!" I don't know where to kiss her first, so I settle on everywhere. "I love you so much, Wildflower!" Lowing her down, I slide to my knees, pull up her shirt, and kiss my baby. "Hey, tiny one. It's daddy here. I hope you know you are the most loved baby in the world! Daddy can't wait to meet you! I will take you surfing, hiking, and camping. We will catch bugs, but not spiders, and make s'mores outside. I will teach you all my funny jokes—"

"What funny jokes?" my Wildflower interrupts me with a sassy comment.

"Okay, we will get back to this conversation when mommy goes to sleep here." I kiss her belly one more time. "For now, Daddy needs to show Mommy all his jokes."

I lift her up with a squeal and carry her to the couch, showing her just how many jokes I've got but, most importantly, how much I love her.

Everyone in my family told me I was weird and didn't belong. Little did they know my perfect matching weirdo was walking around all this time, and now, we're on our way to having our own tiny ducky.

# 41

# *Bonus Scene*

"Zoe, if you don't stick that thing back in there and don't come up with a different answer, I will get off this table and shove it up you instead."

"Funny. And I can take it in and out as many times as your kinky-ass wishes, but that won't change the fact you are having twins."

I groan and let my head fall back to the exam table.

"Twins! Wildflower! We're having twins! I need to call Mama and all the other future grandmas of Loverly Cave."

I slide my gaze to my overly enthusiastic husband. An unimpressed gaze.

"Jacob, if you wish to see another day, you will shut up and stop bouncing around. This is not good news! This is horrible! I can't have twins! I can barely handle you, and I was adjusting to having two crazies, but now there are going to be THREE!" I groan some more.

"Wildflower." He looks at me with his Chihuahua puppy eyes, kneels by my exam table, and takes my hand in his, kissing it softly. "We are having twins."

"Yeah, Jacob, I heard Zoe the first time. No need to rub salt on the wound."

"Joy, you know why I'm so excited?"

"Because you will have an extra partner for your crazy?"

"No, because that's one more of you I get to love for life. Sure, they might get my crazy, but they will get their beautiful, smart, amazing mommy too."

Damn it, why does he always have to say something perfect and erase my anger. I'd like to stew in it a while longer, please. But now I can't.

Tears are falling down my cheeks, and Jacob picks each one up. "I love you so much, Wildflower. If anyone can have twins and handle them like a pro, it's you."

"I hate you."

He grins in response.

"WE ARE HAVING TWINS!!! Did you all hear that? That was my super ducky sperm's doing!" Jacob jumps up, his fists in the air, and then promptly runs out to call half the town with our news.

"Jesus..." I drag my hand through my face.

This is my life now.

And I wouldn't change it for a second.


THE END...
Just kidding...
It is only the beginning!

# Afterword

I don't think I have ever been this nervous about a book. Ever!

Joy and Jacob's story was so dear to my heart, and I wanted to make sure each of you really feel and live through every word, every emotion and scowl (cough, cough, Joy.) And I hope we all have a "Jacob" in our lives to teach us how to wipe those scowls off.

I hope you have enjoyed yet another wild ride in Loverly Cave and I assure you there is so much more coming your way this spring. Because next?

Next all your answers about Grace and our favorite grump, Luke will be answered. I promise. And I also promise that you do not see any of it coming!

And now, I would love to say a HUGE thank you to each and every one of you! All your support and encouragement mean the world to me, and there is absolutely no way I could have ever done this without you guys! Thank you for being here and reading my books. It is still surreal to me that you guys do!

Thank you to my husband who endured many many lonely nights because "I was on schedule!"

Thank you to my best friends: Snow and Y for brainstorming with me when I called you in panic and wanted to delete the whole book. You guys are life savers and Meet My Wife would not exist without you two.

Larger-than-life thank you to Marina for yet another spectacular cover! You know what I want even when I don't, and I am so grateful for you.

Thank you to the best beta readers for pointing out little details I missed and overall walking with me each step of the way.

Thank you, Caroline for your amazing job in editing my book! I appreciate your work and thank my lucky stars for finding you.

With Love & Always Yours,
Daisy Thorn

# The Romance is Dead

*Have you read Hope & Alec's story yet? No? Well, here is a glimpse for you.*

### Hope

Tonight is huge for my Brian. For the first time in ten years, the tickets to their concert were sold out within hours of going live, and now he is gifting everyone with his amazing talent. The crowd goes wild to his music, as they should.

I've always known and believed that we will get here. Ever since my Brian asked me to come with him to LA and Nashville and New York, and all other cities when I was a little seventeen-year-old girl.

We started dating when I was sixteen to his eighteen, living in the middle-of-nowhere-Ohio. We both went to the same school and hung around in the same circles. He was the prettiest boy in the whole town with his blue eyes and golden blonde hair, and every girl dreamt of sitting next to him with his arm wrapped around her, but I was the only lucky one to do so. *Or so I thought at that time, but that's beside the point right now.*

So, when he begged me to go with him, I didn't think twice about it. His sweet words still ring in my ears to this day.

"Hopie, I can't live without you. You are the love of my life. You are it. Come with me, I beg you, come with me. We will make it big together."

And when I see him grinning wide, covered with sweat because he was going wild on that stage, vibing with his favorite guitar, I know that all my sacrifices were made not made in vain. That the sleepless nights were worth it. Spending nights in the car——in the best-case scenario——and eating gas station snacks most of the days while he was trying to make a name for himself as a musician. That putting my life on pause for him was the right choice. That staying in the shadows so he could be fawned over was a smart, strategic move, and leaving my family behind was all for the greater good. Because what's better than seeing the one you love this ecstatic?

Brian and his band took off two years ago, topping the music charts with their albums, and they were gathering large crowds for a while but tonight? Tonight, it's a whole new level.

As our new manager, Suzanne, says, "This is it. This is the top of the freaking top."

Yes, after so many years of doing everything on our own——well, of me doing everything on my own——we finally have a good manager, and Brian works well with her, even though I am not a huge fan of that woman. She is giving me a weird vibe.

Am I jealous that he seems to be spending more time with Suzanne than me lately——the past six months——or that she *doesn't* have to stay in the shadows like I do? Well, maybe slightly, but I trust him. I know my Brian won't do anything to hurt me because he loves me. He values me and our relationship.

Am I a little frustrated that after all this time, I still don't have a ring on my finger?

Maybe a tiny bit of that too, but what does it matter, right? Marriage is just a piece of paper, and what we have is so much more.

Am I a little confused why Brian didn't find me right after the show?

Um, yes, I am. But I get it. My Brian is tired, and he needs his rest after such an adrenaline rush on that stage, singing to tens of thousands of people in the arena. So, I'll come to him. Like I always do, but quietly, so no one really sees me and won't find out our playboy singer has a girlfriend of ten years.

It's all for the image. It's all for his success.

I am giddy with excitement, bursting with pride after tonight, and I can't wait to shower the praises down on him.

Adjusting my jeans and a loose, button-up shirt, I strode up to his room behind the stage. I have a pass as his "assistant" to be back here, and I always have to dress modestly so no one suspects that we are a thing, but Brian says he likes me like this, so I don't see a problem. Even though what I wish I could wear was a tiny black dress I bought for this occasion but *didn't* end up wearing because Brian yelled at me for looking like a slut and his assistant can't look like that.

Sometimes, I hate being seen as only his assistant when in reality, I am so much more.

Maybe now that he made it big, I can come out of the gloomy shadows? Maybe we can finally showcase our love and step out of the closet?

I'll talk to him tonight about it.

With one last fix to my chestnut, waistline hair and a looming smile, I open the door.

Only to have that smile freeze on my blood-drained face. It's as if someone hit me up my head really hard, and the features on my face got stuck on the same expression without changing when in reality, there is absolutely nothing to smile about.

Maybe I am having a stroke? Or a hallucination?

Because no way in hell am I seeing my Brian's naked ass wrapped in another set of long, female legs with sexy, strappy, red-colored heels digging into it. The heel that I have seen before. The kind of heels that I was never allowed to wear in public.

There is no way I am seeing my Brian, my boring, I-love-good-old-missionary-sex-Brian, have hot, loud sex against the wall with another woman.

There is no way my Brian is making those grunting noises with his blonde head thrown back in pleasure when he is as mute as the button on the TV remote in our bed.

There is no way my Brian could do this to me! And the worst part? He is so into it that he hasn't even noticed me walking into the room, witnessing the live porn.

"Brian." His name is barely a whisper, a plea because that is all I could master while my heart was breaking as loud as the volcanic eruption on the Indonesian island Krakatoa at ten-oh-two AM on August twenty-seventh, eighteen-eighty-three. *Don't ask. Photographic memory.*

Somehow, though, he heard me through his grunting and skin-slapping and spun around to see who uttered his name. If I expected to see remorse, fear, or guilt, I was gravely mistaken. As soon as his blue eyes landed on my brown ones, they flared up in fury.

"What the fuck are you doing here? Get the hell out!" He yelled out, and instead of screaming back insults at him or at least planting a juicy slap on his pretty face he adores so much, I ran.

I ran away. Fast. Before the tears could pour down my face and wrap around my wounded heart. I ran away from everything I knew. From the only person, I've ever loved and lived for. I ran away, trying to shed the hurt he had just unleashed on me, but it wasn't helping.

The tears came in hotly, burning down my face. The chest tightened with pain, seizing all the air from them. My mind was fuzzy and drunk with the picture I saw and knew I'd keep seeing for the rest of my life.

My Brian, *my Brian*, wasn't mine.

And those red heels? They belonged to Suzanne, his new manager. But I didn't confront anyone, didn't cause a scene. I just ran.

I got home to our over-the-top, high-rise apartment here in Los Angeles. Packed all my stuff that easily fit into one suitcase——because most of our huge walk-in closet was for Brian's clothes——and threw it in the back of my car. I did all this in that same haze, without really thinking or wiping the streams flowing down my face.

But when I got into the car and started driving, I realized I had nowhere to go...

Absolutely nowhere, and the pain of betrayal twisted into raging anger.

Mostly at my own stupid self.

My whole life belonged to Brian.

I have no job to fall back on because, according to *Brian*, I didn't need one since we were a "team."

The bastard wanted me to be his personal assistant, cook, cleaner, cheerleader, and therapist in one for ten long years, and I did it all with those stupid hearts in my eyes, thinking I was supporting my boyfriend on the way to the top.

Of-freaking-course, he thought I shouldn't go to college and figured out that usually, people get paid for all the crap I kept on doing for free. But I guess that's not really the point here now. What is the point, though, that I am lost and without purpose.

In two seconds flat, my whole life plan collapsed, bringing me down to my knees. Because for ten years straight, the sole purpose of my existence was to serve Brian. And now? Who am I now?

I'll tell you who. I am a hopeless, lost cause of a woman with no ambitions or dreams. Because they all belonged to Brian.

I am a woman with no family or friends because Brian was it for me, and his friends were my friends since I lost my own when I ran away from home with him at seventeen.

I am a woman who loved a liar and got my heart broken in the process.

I am a woman who is driving her old beat-up Toyota car with fading red paint and over two hundred thousand miles on its odometer. It's the same car that I've been driving ever since I got my license at sixteen. And now I am the woman with her meager belongings and mascara-steamed face driving it into nowhere.

I'm sure you guessed it; Brian got himself a brand-new BMW from the dealer as soon as his first big check came through, and I was never allowed to drive it.

Funny how within a few seconds, you could go from love to hate. From pain to anger. From joy to misery. The line is very fine indeed. Because just an hour after I've witnessed his dick in someone else, the pink cloud lifted, and for the first time in a decade, I am seeing my life clearly.

I am finally realizing how stupid and gullible I was. What an idiot I was to run away with him and break the hearts of those I loved.

Brian used me....

He kept me out of convenience, not love, and I was just too naive to see through his lies.

What did I expect from a guy that dated two sisters at the same time?

Yeah, you heard that right...but I don't have the emotional capacity to get into that conversation right now. The only thing I can do is find someplace to lock myself away and cry for the whole night. Or ten.

I'm not sure which way I'm going or on what highway I am, but I see Motel 6 pop up at the next exit, and I swing right to take it.

Hope Levine, welcome to your new life...

# Also By

Race Me series:
*Fun, sexy Formula One romance with plenty heat and plot twists*
Race Me Never
Race Me New
Race Me Now
Race Me ...
Race Me ...


The Demons of New York series:
*Darker, more intense stories with morally gray characters.*
My Broken Demon
My Shameless Angel
My Heartless Soul (coming 2023)


Loverly Cave Town series:
*Romantic comedy, small beach town and dirty-mouthed guys.*
The Romance is Dead
Meet My Wife
Book 3 (coming 2024)
Book 4 (coming 2024)

Book 5 (coming 2024)

# About the Author

Her greatest passion in life is romance novels. So, one day, while reading a particularly spicy book, an idea hit her head. She wanted to write. So, there she was, writing her very first romance novel while rocking her seven-months-old baby to sleep in a closet during her grandparents fiftieth wedding anniversary. The need to put those words on the screen was too strong.

Daisy loves to create special characters with deeper stories and breathe the life into them. To write about love that changes lives.

And maybe believe that kind of magic really does exist.

Weird fact about Daisy: she doesn't drink coffee. Crazy author!

***For more fun facts visit, daisythorn.com and make sure to follow her on Instagram for updated and sneak peeks

With Love & Always Yours,
Daisy Thorn

Made in United States
Troutdale, OR
07/13/2024